THE TEES VALLEY KILLINGS

An absolutely heart-pounding crime thriller

C.J. GRAYSON

DI Max Byrd & DI Orion Tanzy Book 1

Originally published as *That Night*

Revised edition 2023
Joffe Books, London
www.joffebooks.com

First published in Great Britain in 2020 as *That Night*

This paperback edition was first published
in Great Britain in 2023

Cover art by Nebojša Zorić

ISBN: 978-1-80405-960-9

This novel is for my wife, Becky, and my three boys.
Without you, I wouldn't be writing.

Wednesday, early morning
Darlington

Ian Porter sighed into the phone and closed his eyes.

'Listen,' he said, 'I'm sorry. I should have reacted quicker. I . . .'

'What is it?' his wife, Julia, asked.

'I should have closed the gate. None of this would have happened.'

'It's done now. Don't worry about it. We just have to make sure it doesn't happen again.'

Ian smiled sadly. 'How's he doing?'

'He's . . . he's okay. The doctor said it's just a bump to his head, but he'll be fine.' Julia fell silent for a second. 'He's smiling at me, bless him.'

'Good. That's good.'

'I thought he'd be okay, but best to check.'

Ian nodded although his wife couldn't see him.

'How're the other two?' Julia asked.

'Fast asleep,' Ian said. 'I read them both a story. One of them is snoring upstairs. Where are you now?'

'We're just leaving. It was so busy. The waiting room was packed. One kid had a cut on his neck, he was there before us, and we were there for five hours. It's not the staff's fault, it's just too busy — they need more doctors there.'

Ian agreed.

'I'm starving,' Julia said. 'I didn't have any tea.'

'Go get a McDonald's on your way back. Just use my card.'

'Yeah . . . I'm passing there now. I might.'

Hours ago, their youngest son, Liam, who was almost one year old, had crawled halfway up the stairs and come cartwheeling back down. Their eldest, Adam, had watched it happen, saying he'd smacked his forehead on the wooden floor at the bottom. It was awful. So Julia had rushed off to the hospital to get him checked out.

'I'll see you soon, Julia.'

'Wait, stay on the phone. I'm going under the bridge soon.'

'Which bridge? Whessoe Road?'

'Yeah . . . it's dark. You know I don't like that bridge even during the day.'

'Of course it's dark. It's one in the morning.' Ian laughed.

'Very funny,' Julia said. 'We're just turning the corner now.'

'Okay.' Ian readjusted his position on the living room sofa. 'You through it yet?'

'No . . . there's a car going really slow in front of me. It's just around the corner.'

'What car? Who's driving around at one in the morning?'

'Ian . . .'

'What?'

Julia didn't answer.

'Julia, what is it?'

'The car's stopped in front of me.'

'Go around it, then.'

'I can't. It's too tight on the other side — there's a car parked opposite.'

2

Ian sat up on the sofa and felt his heartbeat starting to rise. 'What's happening?'

'It's just parked there.'

'Okay, okay,' Ian said, trying to remain calm. 'Just wait and see what happens. I'll stay on the phone.'

'Come on! All I want is a McDonald's,' Julia blurted out.

'Who's driving the car?'

'I can't . . . I can't see. I don't know — ahh, hold on. A woman is getting out of the passenger seat.'

'She's probably been out, got a lift home.' Ian's chest sank and his breathing eased.

'Yeah. Short skirt. Skimpy top. She's definitely been out. He's moving now — the driver. He put his hazards on as a thank-you for waiting.'

'Get me a cheeseburger, please . . .'

'I thought you were on a diet?' Julia said, with a smile in her voice. She was aware of his daily struggles with his calorie count.

'Just get me the burger . . . I'll start again tomorrow.'

'I'm going down the road to the bridge. Stay on the phone.'

'Not going anywhere.'

'It seems darker than normal,' Julia said. 'Some of the streetlights must be off.'

Ian made his way to the kitchen and flicked the kettle on. The smell of lavender hung in the air from a plug-in near the high table. He reached up and grabbed a mug from the cupboard above the worktop. Then through the phone, he heard the high-pitched sound of brakes squeaking.

'What's that?' he asked.

Julia didn't answer.

'Julia?' Ian stopped still, frozen. 'What's that sound?'

'There's . . .'

'There's what? What is it?'

'. . . a man standing in the middle of the road. He's looking at me.'

3

'A man? What man?'

'He's . . . I don't know. He's just stood there looking at me. He's just staring at the car.'

'What does he look like?' Ian's pulse quickened. 'What's he wearing?'

'Black. Black jeans and a black fleece.'

Ian heard Liam crying in the back of the car.

'Hey buddy, it's okay, we'll be home soon,' Julia said in a forced delicate tone, trying to soothe him.

'Go around him!' Ian shouted. He clamped his eyes shut, waiting.

'He's moved across the road. He isn't letting me pass.'

'Is there anyone else under the bridge? Are there any cars nearby?'

It took Julia a second to check her rear-view mirror. 'No, no one.'

'Shit, you need—'

Julia screamed.

'Julia, what?'

'There was a bang at the back of the car. Shit. What the—'

She screamed again.

'There's someone behind the car, I see him in the mirror,' she cried.

'Fuck,' Ian muttered. 'Right, listen, listen. You need to run him down, the man in front. Just fucking go for it.'

'I can't, Ian, I—'

'Just fucking do it — get around him, then, I don't care. Go!'

The Qashqai's engine revved, the wheels screeching a little before it was drowned out by the sound of Julia's screaming, which ripped through the car. The car door opened.

'He's in the back of the car — he's got Liam . . .'

Ian's breathing was rapid now.

'Get the fuck off him!' Julia screeched, her voice almost breaking. 'Leave him alone!'

The sound of another door opening came through the speaker, then the sound of a hard slap froze Ian to his core.

4

'Ian! Help me, please!' Julia gasped.

'Julia!'

Ian sprinted to put his trainers on, and within seconds he was in the Astra. He didn't think about his other children sleeping upstairs. He didn't have time to think. He put the phone on loudspeaker and threw it onto the passenger seat, started the engine, forced the gearshift into first and spun off the driveway onto the quiet, dark road.

'Julia?' he shouted towards the phone.

All he could hear was her screaming and Liam's crying.

'Hold on, I'm coming,' he shouted. He was shaking with anger and fear.

Ian reached the end of Brinkburn Drive, threw the car left onto Brinkburn Road, narrowly missing a parked car on the opposite side. He planted his foot and quickly reached sixty miles an hour. The Astra's engine echoed against the sleeping road, under the inconsistent flickering of the orange street lights on either side. No one was around. He reached the end of Brinkburn Road and took a sharp left, again, almost colliding with another car before he managed to straighten out.

'Julia?'

Julia didn't answer.

Ian saw the small road leading to the bridge. 'Come on, come on.'

Slowing the car, he angled left, guiding it down the narrow road under the bridge. It was dark. The only light came from a dim streetlamp halfway down on the right. He stopped the Astra behind the Qashqai, which was parked diagonally with two of its doors wide open.

Ian jumped out.

'Julia! Liam!' His voice echoed against the aging brickwork.

Wide-eyed, he checked inside the car, panting, desperate for air. Julia wasn't there. Liam wasn't in his baby seat in the back. 'Fuck!'

Then he heard Julia's scream.

It came from somewhere behind him. He turned quickly.

'Julia?' He galloped back through the tunnel, taking a sharp right onto a set of concrete steps, and climbed them two at a time. Reaching the top, he stepped onto the wide-open tarmac area in front of Hopetown Working Men's Club. He saw a white van quickly pulling away, the tyres screeching on the tarmac.

From inside the back of the van, he heard his wife's muffled scream and his baby's stifled cry.

The van turned the corner and raced up Brinkburn Road.

'Julia?' he whispered in desperation.

The sound of the van's engine faded into the quiet, cold night.

He doubled over, his lungs burning for air. His palms were pressed firmly on his knees. On the ground near his feet, he saw his son's blue dummy.

He picked it up, watched it shake in his trembling hand. His pocket buzzed — a text message. He lifted his phone out and unlocked it. His eyes widened.

It read:

Ian, this is all because of you. Because of what you did. Did you remember to lock your door? Doesn't matter — we've got keys now. We're about to surprise your other children.

2

Wednesday, early morning
Darlington

Ian held his breath and read the text message again. He was in so much shock he couldn't comprehend the words. Then it dawned on him — *we've got keys now. We're about to surprise your other children . . .*

The sound of the van had vanished, but the sound of his thumping chest remained.

'Fuck!' he shouted, his anger filling the quiet, cold air. He spun around and jumped down the stairs, two at a time, back to the narrow road under the bridge. He pulled his door open but, before he climbed in, heard quick footsteps behind him, then felt a sharp pain, followed by a short wave of white heat running across his neck and shoulders before he lost consciousness and collapsed to the ground.

Everything went black.

* * *

'Hey man, are you okay?' a distorted voice said. It sounded like a robot.

'He looks badly hurt.' The second voice was softer, a woman.

'We should ring an ambulance,' the man said.

He opened his eyes, blinked several times.

The woman was on her knees with her hand on Ian's shoulder. The man stood behind her, glaring down into the light of his phone. For a second, he vaguely thought the man looked familiar, but he couldn't place him. Darlington was a small town; everyone knew everyone. The throbbing pain made his head fuzzy.

Ian grunted.

The woman leaned in closer. 'What did you say?'

'Where are they?' Ian said, but it was barely a whisper.

'I'm sorry?'

'My family?' Ian said.

'Hey,' the man said calmly. 'You need to relax, you've been—'

'Lemme up!'

They helped him up. Despite their concern, Ian climbed into the Astra and slammed the door closed, the sound echoing under the bridge like an angry slap. With his head spinning, he did a three-point turn and raced back up the ramp, taking a right at the corner by the betting shop, then planted his foot down to the floor, working his way up through the gears until the Astra hit seventy.

As he passed the Brinkburn pub on the right his head pounded. Shooting waves of intense pain bombarded the back of his skull where something had hit him before he'd passed out.

He tried to ring Julia. No answer.

'Shit!' he shouted, banging his palm off the steering wheel. He breathed light and fast, his head swimming.

He'd never had a panic attack but thought it might be the start of one.

Ian slowed the car and turned right into Brinkburn Drive. The car barely stayed on four wheels as he rounded the sharp bend. He was lucky it wasn't wet because he'd taken it far too carelessly and was fortunate not to smash into the care home on the corner. He put the car into third gear and whizzed through the chicane-like bend, barely avoiding the front bumper of a brand-new Mercedes.

'Come on,' he growled through gritted teeth.

He must be less than a minute behind them.

He saw the front of his house on his approach.

The hallway light was on.

He slammed on the brakes, flung the door open and dashed inside.

'Julia?' he panted in the hallway.

The street behind him was silent. There was no sign of the white van in the street or on the road.

There was no reply.

'Julia?' he said again.

The sound of his plea filled every wall of the house. He looked up the stairs at the dim glare coming from the night light positioned on the small table on the landing. Absolute silence. Using the handrail on the banister he propelled himself upwards.

His body was on fire and the pounding inside his head worsened by the second, almost to the point of being too much to bear. At the top of the stairs, he took a right towards his children's bedrooms.

He went to Adam's room first.

Through the crack in the door, he could see it was in total darkness. He threw open the door with his shoulder and found the switch on the wall to his left. Cold, harsh light filled the room.

'Adam?' he cried.

Adam shuffled in bed, slowly opening his tired eyes, wiping away the sleep with the back of his small hand. He peered up at Ian, confused.

'Dad . . . turn the light off. I was asleep.'

Ian turned off the light and went to Cameron's room. He turned on the switch, the space erupting in bright light.

His heart skipped a beat.

9

Cameron wasn't there.

His bed covers were ruffled, and his teddy bear was upside down on the floor. Ian frantically searched for his son, his eyes darting around the room like a metal ball-bearing inside a pinball machine. He looked inside the double wardrobe where his four-year-old's clothes hung neatly.

'Cam? Cam? Where—'

'Dad, what's going on?' Adam said from his room.

Ian left the room and jumped across the dipped step onto the wide landing. He noticed the bathroom door was closed. He stopped and grabbed the handle.

'Cameron?'

The sound of the toilet flushed.

Ian opened the door fast.

Cameron was pulling his pants up wearily and frowned up at his dad. 'Daddy?'

'Oh, Cam!' Ian gasped, racing over to him. He picked him up and squeezed him so tightly he almost hurt him.

'Daddy, let me go!' He waved his helpless arms around.

'Sorry, sorry.' He put him down. 'Go back to bed now, okay?'

Cam yawned, nodded his sleepy head, then tiredly padded out of the bathroom. His little body moved across the landing and back into his own room. Ian sighed.

He checked all the rooms upstairs. Apart from Cameron and Adam, he found no one.

Back downstairs, the cold seeped in through the open front door so he closed it.

In the kitchen, the small digital clock on the oven told him it was 1.59 a.m.

'Eh? I don't understand,' he whispered. Then it dawned on him that the blow to the back of his head must have put him out for nearly forty minutes under the bridge. He didn't think about that. All he wanted to do was find Julia and Liam. He realised he should have called the police, should have done it when she'd first sounded worried about that car near the bridge.

He grabbed the kitchen phone and dialled 999.

Leaning against the worktop in the silence, trying to steady himself, the feeling of dizziness returned. The call connected. After two rings, the emergency operator picked up.

'Emergency services. What service do you require?'

He heard the question but zoned out. Something else grabbed his attention. The sound of—

'Emergency services, what service do you require?' repeated the operator.

—a baby's cry.

Liam's cry.

Every hair on his body stood on end. He peered into the hallway, where he figured the sound was coming from. Ignoring the operator for a third time, he lowered the handset and placed it on the windowsill above the sink.

The baby's cries grew louder.

It was coming from the dining room. Cautiously, he crept around the kitchen table, and out into the hallway. The door to the dining room was closed. Grabbing the handle, he pushed it down. The sound of crying spilled out into the hallway as he opened it further.

Inside, the room was almost pitch black.

But he could see something. An outline of someone sitting in the chair near the table.

On the wall next to him, he found the light switch and turned it on. The room quickly filled with light.

Sitting on the floor near the table was Liam. His little blue eyes flooded with tears and snot came from his nose as he sobbed, dampening his little grey sleepsuit. Liam looked up at Ian and cried harder.

Next to Liam, slouched in the chair at the table, was Julia.

Ian gasped, throwing both hands up to his mouth.

'Oh, God,' he panted. 'Jul—'

Tears formed in his eyes and spilled down his face as he dropped helplessly to his knees. Staring at Julia with wide terrified eyes, he couldn't help being sick on the laminate floor in front of him.

Liam continued to wail, desperate for his father's love, but Ian couldn't move, couldn't function. Instead of picking up his distraught crying son, he clamped his eyes shut and fell forward to the floor.

The sound of helpless cries filled the house as Ian started to wail.

What was in front of Ian was something he'd never forget — it was unlike anything he'd ever seen. It absolutely terrified him.

3

Wednesday, early morning
Low Coniscliffe, outskirts of Darlington

DI Max Byrd's phone rang on his bedside table, disturbing his sleep. Wearily, he slipped a hand from under the covers and grabbed the phone to see who was calling.

His colleague Tanzy.

'What does he want?' he muttered.

He accepted the call.

'Ori, what's going on?' He glanced at the bedside clock. A sudden panic enveloped him when he noticed it was 2.43 a.m. 'You know it's only—'

'Where have you been, Max?'

Byrd frowned. 'What? I—'

'Get dressed, Max,' DI Tanzy told him.

'Orion, it's not even three in the morning.'

'Max! Get your clothes on and come outside. I'm waiting in the car. The station has sent for urgent assistance.'

'What's going on?' Byrd asked, propping himself up, wiping his tired eyes. He'd only been asleep for two and a half hours. It wasn't unusual for Byrd to go to bed late. He'd always been the same. Whether it was being stressed or not being able to sleep, he'd always felt the effects of sleep deprivation.

'Come on, get dressed,' Tanzy said. 'I'll fill you in when you get down here. Bring your strong stomach with you, we're gonna need it today.'

* * *

Byrd climbed into Tanzy's Volkswagen Golf. He closed the door gently, mindful of sleeping neighbours. Inside, the car was hot, the blowers on full, throwing waves of heat in Byrd's face.

'Morning,' he said.

'Morning.' Tanzy turned down the heat a few notches.

Byrd pulled the seat belt down around his stomach. 'Ori, what on earth is going on?'

Tanzy put the car in gear and drove as he spoke. 'A body's been found. Have you not seen your messages?'

Byrd shook his head. 'I've not been sleeping well recently. I was probably flat out when we got it.' He checked his phone now, seeing all the unread messages. 'Shit.'

'It sounds bad, Max,' Tanzy said. 'Harrison phoned me. She's there now.'

'Where are we going?'

'Brinkburn Drive. Just near—'

'I know the place, one of my cousins lives near there', Byrd said. 'Who's the victim?'

'Woman, mid-thirties. There's a small team there now. Forensics are there too. It's an odd story: she and her baby son were kidnapped at around 1 a.m. from her car, under the bridge at the bottom of Whessoe Road. They were on their way back home from A & E; baby had bumped its head earlier in the day. One kidnapper blocked their path and then an accomplice came from behind, opened the car doors and took them.'

'That's very detailed. How do we know all this?'

'The husband was on the phone with her while it happened.' Tanzy paused for breath. 'He jumped in his car and raced there as quickly as he could, but he found the car empty, parked sideways under the bridge.'

'Where's her car now?'

'Still at the kidnapping scene — I've sent a team to block off the road and set up a perimeter.'

'Forensics?'

'Yeah. I spoke with McCabe. Said he'd get the new recruits and go down with them.'

'So they've found her body already? What about the baby?'

As Tanzy told him about Julia Porter's gruesome reappearance, Byrd looked out the window. The roads and paths were lined with a frost that sparkled under the streetlights. It was minus two outside, according to the temperature gauge on the dashboard of Tanzy's Golf.

'I bet your head is cold, Ori,' Byrd said.

'Joys of having no hair, Max.'

They both smiled. Tanzy pulled out onto the main road, leaving Low Coniscliffe to sit in the morning darkness.

DI Orion Tanzy was six foot two and slim. He'd shaved his hair off a year ago when it had started to thin. His wife, Phillipa, was so gobsmacked when she'd seen him that she dropped a pan of pasta in the kitchen. With his square jaw, nicely trimmed goatee beard and tanned skin, he could wear a tatty old rug on the top of his head and still be attractive.

Max Byrd was four years older and two inches shorter than Tanzy and didn't quite have the same washboard stomach as his colleague did. He liked to indulge in takeaways and junk food, and, because of that, he sported a slightly more rounded build than Tanzy. Although his diet wasn't the best, he burned many of the calories off playing five-a-side football, but he was — and always would be — a long way off from being athletic.

Byrd reached up, ran his hand through his thick head of black hair.

'I didn't realise how big some of these were,' Byrd said, staring out the window at the monstrous houses on Coniscliffe Road.

'Massive, some of them,' Tanzy said. 'We need to move. Our house is too small. We're under each other's feet all the time.'

Tanzy was referring to his wife, Phillipa, and his two children, Jasmine and Eric. They lived in a three-bedroomed house in Newton Aycliffe, in one of the new estates close to Tesco. It wasn't that it was too small right now, but they figured as the kids grew, it wouldn't cater to their needs.

'How's Pip doing?' Byrd asked.

Tanzy slowed the car down at the Elm Ridge roundabout, flicked the indicator on, took a left and planted his foot. The car surged forward to just over forty. The road was empty, the surface glistening under the staggered streetlights ahead.

'She's good. She's doing well.'

'Bet you're proud of her?' Byrd said.

'Yeah, she's done brill.'

It took a further five minutes for the Golf to arrive at Brinkburn Drive. They spoke more about Tanzy's wife and Tanzy asked about Claire, the woman Byrd had been seeing over the past eighteen months. After that, they fell silent, both mentally and physically preparing themselves for what they were about to see.

Tanzy brought the Golf to a halt behind a red Tiguan and switched off the engine. The car parked across the road was familiar.

'Your boy's here,' Byrd commented. 'Cornty.'

Tanzy followed Byrd's gaze, seeing the blue Peugeot parked up on the kerb. 'He didn't have to drive to the out-skirts of town and wake you up, sleepy head,' Tanzy replied.

Byrd pulled the handle of the passenger door and edged it open. Cold air rushed into the car and Byrd shivered suddenly, wishing he'd worn a thicker jacket.

They got out. The time was just after 3 a.m. An eerie silence filled the air.

There were two streetlights that didn't work, leaving certain areas of the path in almost complete darkness. Byrd made a mental note to report that to the council. Several lights were shining along the street, and no doubt people were curious about the arrival of the police car and ambulance. Some peeped out windows, others stood on their doorsteps in dressing gowns.

Down the street, one of the houses and much of the road around it had been cordoned off with police tape. Standing at the edge of this cordon, an elderly couple held each other, trying to battle off the night frost. They were dressed in thick coats, desperate to see what all the fuss was about. Next to them, a woman in her forties stood dressed in a bathrobe with a cigarette hanging from her mouth, the smoke spiralling into the air as she exhaled.

Several metres away from the temporary barrier, an ambulance was parked across the road, its rear doors open. PC Kim Harrison was talking with a man who was wrapped in a blanket. It was obvious from the man's body language how upset he was — that must be the victim's husband.

In front of the ambulance were two police cars, intentionally parked sideways to prevent any traffic access. Two officers were standing nearby. One of them spotted Byrd and waved in his direction then continued their discussion.

The slight shift in wind direction allowed the smell of cigarette smoke to hit Byrd's nose. A long time had passed since he'd made the decision to quit but, strangely enough, it smelled nice, the same way it does when you pass a beer garden on a summer's day.

They stepped up onto the path and made their way towards the barrier. Byrd tried to remember the name of the PC guarding the cordon, a new recruit, then he realised he'd never known it. The PC offered the detectives a smile and lifted up the tape, allowing them in.

'Forgive me, what was your name?' Byrd said, stopping and offering his hand.

'PC Leonard, sir.' He took his hand and shook it as Byrd introduced them both.

Byrd followed Tanzy under the cordon. Ahead of them, glaring down at his phone, was PC Phillip Cornty. He was thinner than a pencil and had the face of a mouse. His pointy little nose, for some reason, annoyed Byrd. Luckily for Byrd, he didn't have much to do with him because Cornty was on Tanzy's team.

PC Cornty, hearing the approaching detectives, looked their way.

'Hey, boss,' he said to Tanzy. He glanced past him and nodded at Byrd. 'Hey, Max.'

'Morning, Phil,' Byrd said.

'Why you here, Phil?' Tanzy asked him, stopping by his side. Tanzy was tall but Cornty had a few inches on him. He must have been six foot four. Maybe six foot five. His towering height didn't do anything for his very slim frame.

'I'm working.' Cornty frowned at Tanzy. 'I don't understand . . .'

'You're on days this week, aren't you?'

'I'm covering Mac's shift,' Cornty explained. 'He's on holiday.'

'Again?' Byrd chipped in, shaking his head.

An amused nod from Cornty.

'Who asked you to cover for him?'

'DCI Thornton.'

'When you finish, make sure you get enough rest. Won't do any of us any good if you burn out.'

'Yeah, okay,' Cornty said, but his attention was on the house. The bright light in the hallway spilled out onto the drive.

'What have we got?' Tanzy asked.

'It's bad,' Cornty said without hesitation.

'How bad?' Byrd asked.

Cornty sighed, briefly glancing down onto the concrete path below then meeting Byrd's gaze. 'I think you better go see for yourself.' He handed them each a pair of plastic disposable overshoes. 'I'll be just out here — there's no way I'm going back in there.'

Tanzy frowned.

18

Cornty looked past them into the bright hallway. 'Worst I've seen.'

At the front door, Tanzy stopped and turned to Byrd. 'After you.'

Without hesitation, Byrd stepped over the threshold.

4

Inside the house, they both picked up a slight odour seeping down the hall. At the end of the short space, under the bright light of a ceiling pendant, PC Anne Tiffin stood near the doorway, police radio in one hand and notepad in the other. Her head was down as she read her notes. Hearing the detectives' footsteps on the laminate floor she pulled her attention away and glanced toward them.

'Morning, Anne,' Byrd said quietly.

'Morning,' she replied. 'Have you been briefed?'

Tanzy and Byrd nodded.

'Cornty said he's not coming back in here,' Byrd commented.

'Cornty's weak,' Tiffin said, smiling.

Tiffin had been on Byrd's team for nearly two years. She was fresh, eager and beyond keen. Her diligence and attention to detail were second to none. No doubt she'd be climbing the ladder very soon. She was hard-working, straight-talking and motivated, and at the start of her career at the age of only twenty-three. Byrd would do his best to help and guide her the best he knew how. Her level of focus reminded him of a younger female version of himself.

Anne had been the first officer at the scene. When she'd arrived at 2.09 a.m., she'd cautiously opened the door and heard a man wailing and a baby crying somewhere down the hallway. Two terrified children were crying on the stairs. After seeing the body of Julia Porter sitting in the chair, Anne had made the call for emergency assistance immediately.

'Forensics are inside,' she continued.

'Who is it?' Tanzy asked. He had an idea it would be the senior forensics team, Jacob Tallow and Emily Hope, but forensics had recruited two new members who neither Byrd nor Tanzy had spoken with much.

'Hope and Tallow,' Tiffin confirmed.

'Pathologist finished yet?' Byrd asked.

'On his way. He says he'll want to transfer the body to the morgue as soon as he's seen it, so best look now if you want to see her in situ.'

He sighed, glancing towards the room for a moment. Today no doubt would be a long day. And, he knew by what he was about to see, that it would take a turn for the worse.

'Let's do it,' Tanzy said.

'Whenever you're ready.' She took a step back, allowing them enough room to pass.

Emily Hope and Jacob Tallow were in deep discussion over some marks on the floor. Tallow towered over Hope, as he did over anyone near him — a spare, unamused type. Hope seemed similar at first sight — short-cut hair framing neat glasses — but when she rolled up her sleeves her tattoos were suddenly on display, a surprising sight in that charmless little dining room. Not wanting to distract the forensics team, Byrd and Tanzy stopped a few feet inside the room and observed the scene in front of them.

'Jesus,' Byrd said just above a whisper.

Tanzy, staying silent, stared at the dead woman sitting motionless on the chair.

Byrd turned back to PC Tiffin in the doorway. 'So the husband says they were kidnapped at Whessoe Road Bridge around one?'

'That's right. When he got over there, he heard her screaming from inside a van at Hopetown Working Men's Club, but he couldn't get to it. And when he got back to his own car someone conked him on the head. He was out for about thirty minutes, he thinks.'

'Is that the bottom of Brinkburn Road?' Byrd asked, finding his bearings, trying to visualise exactly what had happened. Ever since he was young, he'd analysed everything. According to others, he was obsessive over details, but it was how his brain worked things out and processed new information. For example, with a tree, Byrd would think about the outer layer of bark, the way it had matured over the years, the inside of the tree, the structure and strength, the roots, how far they went under the ground, and how much moisture it held.

She nodded. 'Alliance Street, it's called.'

'Then he called the police?'

'No, he came home. He'd left his other two children asleep in bed and he panicked about them. Once he'd checked on them he phoned emergency services, then heard the baby crying in the dining room.' Her eyebrows raised a quarter of an inch. 'He . . . came in to this.' She opened her palms in the direction of Julia Porter.

'Where was the baby?'

'Right next to her.'

'God.' Byrd sighed sadly. 'Horrible.'

'He'll be too young to remember,' Tanzy reassured Byrd, having dealt with similar cases in the past.

Byrd looked away from his partner in the direction of the door. 'Why didn't the husband ring the police sooner? Can we get the recording of the emergency services call?'

'It won't be much help.' She glanced down at her notes for a second. 'The call was made at 1.59 a.m., but it was a silent call, from a landline. He says he heard the baby crying just as he was calling and went to find him.'

22

'Where are the children now?' Byrd enquired.

'With Ian's mother. The oldest kid knew her number, so I called her when I saw the state the dad was in.'

The two forensics officers, dressed in thin white overalls, were positioning yellow markers in various locations. The tall, thin guy, Jacob Tallow, snapped a couple more photographs and placed his camera slowly down by his side.

'I think we're about done for now, Detectives,' he said, knowing they were watching. 'Don't touch anything. We're taking a short break, but there's more to do.'

Byrd nodded. He knew the protocol.

The senior forensic officers left the room.

Tanzy turned to PC Tiffin. 'Where are her clothes — do you know?'

'No clothes have been found, sir.'

'Okay.'

'I'll be outside if you need anything. I need some air.'

She turned and headed for the door.

'I've never seen anything like this in my life,' Byrd said to Tanzy.

'Me neither, Max.'

5

Wednesday morning
Darlington

The dining room was square-shaped. It had a table against the centre of the back wall. Above the table was a wide rectangular mirror, making the room appear bigger than it was, as if there was a room beyond it. The wall opposite the table and mirror — the wall to their right — was lined with a huge shelving unit jammed with baby's toys, jigsaws, Transformers and battery-operated remote-controlled cars.

Julia Porter was tied to a black leather chair. The chair had been angled towards the door, so would be the first thing anyone walking in would see.

Byrd shivered.

On the floor, her bare feet rested in a pool of dark, congealed blood. Her legs were flaccid and awkwardly twisted open. Her stomach and breasts were misshaped by a tight, thin blue rope wrapped around her body and behind her, preventing her from falling forward. Her head was angled back with the nape of her neck resting on the top lip of the chair. Dark, red marks on her throat suggested she'd been strangled.

But one thing made both of them shudder: her eyes were missing. The deep empty sockets were the frightening focus of her pale face, pooled with deep, crimson clots. A thick trail of blood ran down her face like red slugs over her face, breasts, stomach, vulva, the inside of her thighs, then finally, onto the wooden floor.

Byrd, staying silent, absorbed the scene. After a minute of assessment, he scratched his stubbly chin. 'The question is . . . why?'

'Why what?'

'Why this, why this set-up?' Byrd turned to Tanzy. 'It's like a stage show.'

Switching their attention to the table next to her, they saw a message on the surface. It was written in what looked like a red crayon.

She didn't see it coming.

'See what coming?' Tanzy said, thinking out loud. He noticed Byrd edge a little closer to inspect the words carefully. 'Are you seeing anything?' he asked, angling his head toward Byrd.

'It's a message, Ori.'

'A message?'

'Yeah . . . and this message could mean absolutely anything.' Byrd sighed heavily and physically sank into himself for a second, taking a few steps back and letting his shoulders drop.

The room went quiet. Both detectives analysed the scene before them until Tanzy broke the silence. 'What does it mean?'

'I'm speculating here, Ori . . . so bear with me,' Byrd said.

Tanzy nodded. 'Go on.'

'This was meant for her husband, Ian.' Byrd indicated Julia and the scene before them. 'The body is angled towards the door — set up for maximum visual impact. Her nakedness signifies her vulnerability. The blood running from her eyes down to her vulva could signify a trail, maybe to

25

that particular place on her body — to somewhere personal. The missing eyes could tell Ian she had seen something that she shouldn't have, or maybe that she won't be able to see anymore.'

'You know I'm not one for riddles, Max. And it's too early in the morning for one of your complex intellectual explanations.'

Byrd half-smiled.

'Where are your eyes?' Tanzy asked Julia Porter. 'Where are your clothes?'

'Come on, let's go outside. If I stay in here any longer, I'll throw up and contaminate the room with last night's Amaretto and pizza.' Byrd stole one last look at Julia Porter and the table next to her, scanning the words in red crayon before turning and leaving the room.

In the hallway, he slowed. 'We'll speak to Ian Porter. If we ask the right questions, we'll hopefully get the right answers.'

They headed out into the darkness where the air was clean and fresh. Tanzy snatched a lungful. It felt good. They stepped off the driveway and headed over the road in the direction of Ian Porter, who was leaning on the back of the ambulance wrapped in a blanket. PC Kim Harrison was still with him.

Byrd took the lead. 'Mr Porter?'

He leaned forward and placed a gentle palm on Ian Porter's shoulder. 'I'm Detective Inspector Max Byrd of Durham Constabulary. This is my colleague, Detective Inspector Orion Tanzy. I'm very sorry for your loss. I can't imagine what you're going through.' He paused for a few seconds. 'Can we get you a drink?'

Ian Porter shook his head and didn't look up at Byrd.

'If it's okay,' Byrd went on, 'we'd like to ask a couple of questions down at the station?'

Porter jerked his head up quickly. 'I . . . I never did this!'

Byrd slowly raised his palm. 'Mr Porter, no one is saying or suggesting that you did. At the station, we can get you warmed up, get you a drink, get you comfortable. Maybe we—'

'Where are my children?'

'Your mother has them. One of my colleagues has spoken with her — your children are safe. Your children are fine, Mr Porter.'

'Are they?' Porter asked anxiously.

'They are,' Byrd reassured him confidently. 'We've got a car outside your mother's house. Don't worry about your children.'

Porter finally lifted his head, making eye contact with Byrd.

'Will you be willing to come to the station, and see if we can figure this out?'

Porter reluctantly agreed.

6

Once PC Kim Harrison had helped Ian Porter into the back of her police car, she closed the door and turned to Byrd and Tanzy.

'Are you coming back with us now?' she asked them.

'We need to see the kidnapping scene before we head back,' Tanzy said. 'See what's happening down there. You take Mr Porter back, get him a coffee. We won't be long.'

'Don't forget to get permission to take the usual exclusion samples,' Byrd reminded her. 'DNA and prints. And get his permission to take samples from the kids. Should help CSI narrow things down.'

Harrison nodded then made her way around the back of the car and lowered herself into the driver's seat. To their left, beyond the plastic barrier, the crowd started to thicken. The woman in her dressing gown was still smoking away.

Behind the small cluster of people, a man and a woman, perhaps a couple, watched the detectives. Byrd wondered why they were hanging back from the crowd — perhaps a neighbourly dispute. He saw Tiffin was making her way back to her post inside, her attention again on the notepad in her hand.

Byrd smiled at her commitment and dedication. 'She'll make it one day,' he muttered.

'Huh?' Tanzy said.

'Ah, never mind.'

* * *

At the bottom of Brinkburn Road, where it joined the corner of Alliance Street, Tanzy slowed and came to a stop. The police officer standing in the middle of the road held up her palm and squinted into the darkness to see who it was, ready to divert the driver of the car down one of the streets away from the scene. It didn't take long for her to recognise Tanzy behind the wheel. She lowered her arm, smiled and waved him through.

He followed the bend to the left, slowly veering around the Astra that the PC had parked intentionally preventing access to the bridge, and brought the Golf to a halt.

After he'd turned off the engine they both stepped out into the cold.

A long stretch of plastic tape had been tied halfway along the wall of Hopetown Working Men's Club, running diagonally to the metal railing that met the corner of the street just before the road dipped down under the bridge.

PC Josh Andrews was standing there.

'Morning, sir,' he said to Byrd.

He'd worked under the supervision of DI Max Byrd for nearly a year. His hair was neatly trimmed and tidy, and his posture was as stiff as a board.

'How are you doing, Josh?'

'Good, sir, thank you,' he replied.

One thing Byrd had always liked about Josh Andrews was his manners. He spoke correct English and carried himself like a gentleman. He'd told Byrd about his father and uncles being officers in the British Army and had taught him

29

how to stand, talk and conduct himself, so Byrd understood his almost unusual — but admirable — behaviour.

'What do we have?' Tanzy asked.

'The car is still down there, sir,' Andrews began. 'Forensics are here.'

'McCabe?'

'Yes. He's here.'

'He alone?'

'No. He brought the two trainees with him, Forrest and Beech. He thought he'd leave the scene at the house for Tallow and Hope — let the new guys check out the car to see what they can find.'

'They could do with the experience,' Byrd said in agreement. 'Come on, Ori, let's have a look.'

They crossed the open concrete area in front of the club. Tyre marks stretched across the ground, for about four metres in total. Byrd stopped for a moment and glanced down.

'That's where the van pulled away after they'd grabbed them,' Andrews said loudly, projecting his voice from the barrier.

Byrd and Tanzy continued towards the concrete steps and, once they descended them, they stepped onto the road under the bridge and found the diagonally parked Qashqai.

On the ground next to the Qashqai was an open brief-case, belonging to the forensics team. Byrd and Tanzy rounded the rear of the car. Standing on the kerb, with his hands tucked deep into his pockets, was the crime scene manager, Tony McCabe.

'Morning, Tony,' Byrd said. 'Trusting them already, I see?'

McCabe looked beyond Byrd to the trainee forensic officers. 'Got to learn somehow.'

McCabe was just over six feet tall and carried a broad set of shoulders. In his younger years, he was a great boxer, almost becoming a pro but never making the cut. His large, slightly crooked nose that had been broken on numerous occasions was a testament to that.

'How's it going at the house?' McCabe asked them.

'Pathologist's running late,' Byrd replied. 'But Tallow and Hope are doing a good job. How's it going here?'

'We've checked the car for prints. We found some on the door handles, but I have a feeling that whoever did this had the intelligence to wear gloves. Most of the prints were child-sized. The family has children, other than the baby?'

Tanzy nodded. 'Yeah, three kids.'

A sad frown appeared on McCabe's face at the thought of the children who would be left motherless. McCabe had been the crime scene manager for three years. In total, he had over seventeen years of experience in forensics. He'd done the majority of his time down in Birmingham, where he started as an assistant forensic. He did that for four years then spent another four years as a forensic officer. Then he joined the Durham division as a senior forensic and held that role for nearly eight years until, three years ago, there was an opening for the role of crime scene manager.

He had a passion for his work but it often upset him: he was only needed when someone had died or a serious crime had been committed. Any case involving children brought a lump to his throat. Some scenes he worked on were like something out of a nightmare.

Beech and Forrest were both leaning into the Qashqai, doing something with the baby's car seat under the light of a bright torch. It was still dark; the sun hadn't risen yet. Amanda Forrest was the shorter of the two, her straight blonde hair tied firmly back to avoid contaminating the crime scene. Paul Beech towered over her — he looked a little old to be so new to forensics.

'How are the new recruits doing?' Byrd asked. 'They getting up to speed?'

McCabe winced a little. 'These things take time. I've been doing the job for almost eighteen years and I still miss things. They're doing okay. Amanda joined us fresh out of university — she doesn't have much practical experience but her dissertation on blood spatter was *very* impressive. And

31

Paul's background's in IT, but it was all based in London and his wife wanted him a bit closer to home. He's just finished a degree in forensic science rather than forensic computing. With that mix of skills, he should be an asset to the team.'

'We need to head back, Tony,' Tanzy said. 'Keep us updated.'

'Of course,' he replied. 'We'll be in touch.'

Byrd and Tanzy crossed the quiet road. Before they climbed the steps, Byrd paused.

'What you looking for?' Tanzy asked.

'Cameras.' There were none.

They climbed the steps and headed back to the car.

7

Byrd and Tanzy used a small training room at the station to speak with Ian Porter. They both agreed that using an interrogation room could make him feel he was being accused of something, and it was necessary for him to be open and honest.

Painfully and slowly, Ian ran through the events, starting with the phone call to Julia, then returning to the house to find her and Liam.

'Someone hit you from behind?' Tanzy asked.

'Yeah.' He touched the back of his head.

'What happened when you woke up?'

'A couple was kneeling over me, asking me if I was okay.'

'Did you recognise them?'

Porter switched his focus to Byrd. 'I don't think so. I've never seen the woman. The man looked a little familiar. Darlington is a small town, I suppose.'

'Has your wife seen something recently, something she shouldn't have?'

'What do you mean?' Porter's tone turned a little sour.

'Anything in her life — or both of your lives — that has taken her by surprise recently. It could be anything. A person, an image, anything.'

Ian shook his head again.

'Are you sure?' pressed Byrd. 'Anything at all happened in your life where someone might want to cause harm to you or your family?'

This time Ian frowned silently, then slowly shook his head. Byrd noticed the hesitation.

'What does she do as a job?'

'She works at Lloyds Bank. As a cashier.'

'Okay . . . that's good. You're doing great, Ian.' He paused for a second. 'Would you like a coffee?'

Ian nodded.

He was tired. Dark semi-circles lined the bottom of his eyes.

Tanzy turned towards Byrd. 'Would you mind getting us a coffee, Max?'

Byrd bowed his head, slid his chair out and found his feet. 'Yeah, no problem.' He opened the door, stepped out into the well-lit hallway and walked towards the canteen.

'I sent Max because he really does make the best coffees. I'm hopeless,' Tanzy said.

Ian half-smiled.

'Ian, can you describe the van you saw near the bridge?'

'It was a big van.'

'What colour was it?'

'White, I think,' he said.

'Can you remember the registration plate?'

Ian thought hard for a moment. Then he seemed to lose his concentration.

'Ian?'

'Huh?' he said, snapping out of it.

'The reg plate of the van?'

He looked blank. 'No, I . . . I don't remember. It all happened so fast.'

'I understand.' Tanzy nodded and fell silent for a second. Then he said, 'So, when you—'

'Listen, I just want to go see my kids,' Ian said sharply. 'I don't want your coffee. I don't want to be sitting here talking to you. No offence, Detective. I know you're trying to help me, but I want to go.'

Tanzy understood his frustration. If it was his own wife that had been murdered only hours before, he'd feel the same.

'Any information you have,' Tanzy said. 'Even the smallest details could help us identify exactly what's happened and give us more hope of catching who did this. You want that, don't you?'

'Of course, I do!' he shouted, eyes wide. The sudden anger echoed around the room. As he looked away and focused back down on the table, Tanzy mentally noted the flash of frustration but didn't comment.

Silence filled the room.

Moments later, Byrd walked back in, carrying two plastic cups, steam twirling from them. He leaned over, placed one in front of Ian. 'There you go.'

'Thanks,' said Ian, but didn't reach for it or make eye contact with Byrd.

Byrd glanced down at his watch. Six thirty. 'You're probably tired. No doubt, you'll want to go back and see your kids. What are their names?'

Ian Porter frowned. 'What?'

'Your children. What are their names?' Byrd asked.

'Adam, Cameron and Liam,' he whispered. 'Listen, I need to see them. I need to go. They only have me.'

Porter's emotional words found their way to the hearts of the detectives. They'd seen relatives of victims crumble before their eyes, and it never got any easier. In fact, it got worse. Every time it happened, it reminded them how bad this world could be, how cruel life could turn on you in a second.

'Nice names,' Byrd commented.

A thin smile appeared on Porter's face.

'Before you go to see Adam, Cameron and Liam,' Tanzy said, 'can you try to think again if there's anything your wife may have seen — something you've maybe missed? I know we've touched on this briefly, but it's so important to help us. Had she seen you do something that she didn't expect? Something out of the ordinary? The message on the table may have been left for you?'

Porter pondered the question with furrowed eyebrows. Finally, he nodded. 'She caught me cheating four years ago — that's the only thing I can think of.'

Byrd and Tanzy didn't comment and waited for Porter to say more.

He didn't.

'What's her name?' Tanzy asked.

'Lisa Thorpe. Known her years. It was a silly mistake.' Porter looked down, slowly shaking his head as if disgusted with himself.

Tanzy made a note of the name.

Ported noticed Tanzy scribbling on the notepad. 'She's moved out of Darlington, so I don't think you'll be able to speak to her.'

'Won't stop us trying,' replied Tanzy.

Byrd this time. 'Did you get a good look at the van when it pulled away?'

'Detective Tanzy has already asked me that. The answer is the same, I—'

'A lot was going on. I can appreciate that,' Byrd noted.

'I wasn't really in the right mind for memorising letters and numbers, detective.'

'I understand, Mr Porter,' Byrd countered, with a soft palm, knowing Tanzy had asked the same questions while he was getting the coffees. A tactic they'd used over the years, to see if the person told the same story.

The silence grew until Tanzy said, 'Well, thank you for your time, Ian. You can go and see your children. One of our colleagues will drive you to your mother's house.'

'Thanks.'

'If there's anything that comes to mind or if you simply need to talk, don't hesitate to contact us, Ian.'

Without touching his cup of coffee, Ian stood up and headed for the door. Outside in the brightly lit corridor, he saw PC Kim Harrison waiting for him.

'Come on, I'll take you home,' she said, guiding him out of the building.

* * *

Back in the room, Tanzy looked at Byrd. He was slouching a fraction in his seat.

'You should stop sitting like that all the time, Max. That's doing your back no good.'

Byrd shuffled up a little. 'My back is fine, Orion.'

'It won't be when you're fifty.'

Ever since Byrd could remember, Tanzy had tried to guide him to a healthier lifestyle, whether it be eating right or doing more exercise. Byrd, however, claimed that playing football a few times a week kept his weight off.

Tanzy laughed every time he said it because he knew that Byrd was forty-one. Things would only get worse. Compared to Byrd, Tanzy was mega fit. He led a healthy lifestyle and had been doing judo since he was six years old. He'd mastered almost every throw and hold ever invented, a handy asset if you were backed into a corner. Byrd would never forget the time they went out for a drink four years ago. A careless drunk knocked into Byrd so hard it knocked Byrd's pint onto the floor. The smash of the glass echoed around the bar and everyone stopped to look.

As the situation developed, it turned out that it had been done on purpose. The man had recognised Byrd as one of the detectives linked to a trial where the man's brother had been sent down for drug dealing. The man and two of his associates had started on Byrd, backing him into the corner.

Tanzy, when he returned from the toilet, had seen Byrd on the floor, covering his head as the men kicked him. Tanzy lost it, went crazy. Within half a minute, he'd flattened all three of them. He'd helped Byrd up and told the manager of the bar that he would personally cover the cost of the damage to the toilet wall, through which he'd thrown one of the men.

They'd always kept that mishap between themselves.

As Ian Porter's footsteps disappeared down the corridor, Tanzy sniffed the air, thinking for a moment. 'Do you think he did it?'

Byrd shook his head. 'No. But forensics will hopefully come back with some prints and tell us what we need to know. We need to check for cameras in the nearby area — specifically Brinkburn Road. We know they drove that way back to Brinkburn Drive.'

Tanzy nodded.

'I do know one thing . . .' Byrd added.

Curiously, Tanzy raised his gaze. 'What's that?'

'Ian Porter knows more than he's letting on.'

'What's make you say that?'

'The way he paused when I asked him if there was potentially anyone that would want to cause him or his family any harm. He's lying about something, that's for sure.'

8

She heard footsteps enter the room outside and clamped her eyes shut. She had no idea what time it was, but her stomach was rumbling. Next to her was a pile of old clothes that smelled like they'd been there for ever. The musty smell reminded her of an attic, and feeling with her small fingers, she knew by reaching the four walls the area was tight.

She'd used a fleece of some sort, at least that's what it felt like in the darkness, to keep her as warm as possible when the temperatures dipped overnight. She had no idea where she was. All she knew was that she was confined to a small space surrounded by four walls.

There had been no sound for hours. They must have been sleeping. Near her was a box, about the size of a shoe box, maybe bigger, it was hard to tell, but she knew it was locked. She'd already tried opening it the day before and nearly broke one of her fingernails in the process.

She sighed, taking a long slow breath. The air inside the cramped space was still and stale. Rancid. Breathing had become a chore, but she'd taught herself to breathe slower. After three hours the need to urinate had overcome her, so she went in the corner of the room. Then two hours after that, she'd had to go again.

That was the first day.

How long had she been here? It felt like days. The smell of all that urine and faeces was bad enough to turn the strongest of stomachs, but somehow she'd gotten used to it.

She needed help. Badly.

She missed daylight, fresh air. She missed her home.

Near her feet, the empty plate rested on top of the pile of musty clothes. She couldn't see it, but she knew it was there because after she'd eaten the sandwich that had been made for her, that's where she'd put it. As she thought about the plate, she thought about the sandwich. It was ham. Just ham. But she was starving, her insides rumbled and contracted. A bottle of water stood near the plate too, and every few hours she took a sip. When it was empty, she knew it would be hours before someone came back to fill it up. Each day — or what she thought was a day — that's all she got: a ham sandwich with a fresh bottle of water.

She thought about her mother making her a ham sandwich while she was sitting down in the kitchen, watching cartoons on the television on the wall.

Oh God, she'd do anything to be there right now.

At home.

With her family.

Safe.

The footsteps came closer. She could hear someone breathing on the other side of the door. She shivered as she quickly pulled the fleece up close to her face, the musty smell temporarily masking the awful odour of her prison.

The footsteps stopped just outside.

Then the door slowly creaked open.

9

'So, what do we have?' asked DCI June Thornton. She was sitting on her chair behind her very large, tidy desk. Behind her, lining the walls, were several certificates, polished and proud. Byrd had never seen the glass-framed credentials with a speck of dust on them.

She knew the basics of what had happened earlier. It didn't take long for the news to get around the office. She leaned back, raising one leg over the other, and delicately placed her palms down on her thighs.

On the other side of the desk, sitting in the two chairs, was DI Byrd and DI Tanzy.

Byrd coughed before he spoke.

'Julia Porter was tied to a chair naked with a blue rope. Her eyes were missing. There was a note written in red crayon, "She didn't see it coming." She was taken while she was in her car with her youngest son, Liam, who's almost one. A man was standing in the middle of the road, so she had to stop. Then it sounded like — according to her husband,

41

Ian Porter — others came from behind and opened the back passenger door and grabbed them.'

DCI Thornton stared for a second, absorbing his words.

Just bordering on the age of sixty and divorced, Thornton was an attractive, petite woman, who kept herself in fantastic shape. Her short, chestnut-red hair was neatly cut and always pristine.

Another trait of the detective chief inspector was that she didn't take shit from anyone. She never had done. You didn't rise through the ranks by being soft and accepting rejections when someone told you no. You stood your ground. You spoke the truth, even if it meant ruffling a few feathers in the process. If something needed to be done, she'd get it done.

'I see,' she said, calmly. She turned to Tanzy. 'Orion, what are your thoughts?'

'Erm . . . I think it's a message. I think by removing her eyes, whoever did this doesn't want her to see anymore. And—'

'Have you located the eyes?' she asked.

'Forensics didn't come across them. They're carrying out a full investigation and will be getting back to us soon.'

When she spoke to Byrd and Tanzy, it was clear to her they had a good relationship. They'd been working side by side for nearly sixteen years. Byrd had joined the force when he'd turned eighteen. His father, Alan, was an army man in his earlier years, and when a young Max Byrd had told him he wanted to do the same, his father told him no. He said he should go into the police force instead, so he wouldn't have to travel the world and spend all that time away from his family. At Byrd's young age, many of his friends had joined the army, and his father figured that had been the reason for his interest. Byrd had agreed, although a little reluctantly, to give the police a shot. Twenty-three years later, not once had he looked back or regretted the decision he'd made.

Tanzy had been on the force for sixteen years. Now on the same level as Byrd, both being detective inspectors, Tanzy originally wanted to do forensics. At sixteen, he'd left school and went to university to study forensic science, after watching countless episodes of *Law and Order* and the early episodes of *Silent Witness*. His father, Andre, who lived with his mother, Claudia, down in York, still watched them relentlessly. After Tanzy had gained his degree, he joined the police at age twenty-one as a constable. He wanted to veer into forensics but, at the time, he enjoyed his team, enjoyed the relationships he was building. Now thirty-seven, having moved up the ranks, the dream of being a forensic tech had faded away, but he still occasionally watched *Silent Witness* and wondered how different his career could have been.

DCI Thornton nodded. 'What else?'

Byrd said, 'First impressions are that he never killed his wife. That story wouldn't add up with—'

'Add up?' interrupted Thornton.

'With the position of the Qashqai under the bridge. The tyre marks on the road where the car skidded. Also, one of the first things that PC Cornty checked on his arrival was the bonnet of the Astra. It was warm, meaning Ian Porter drove it a little while before.' DCI Thornton agreed and continued to listen. Byrd went on. 'Forensics have taken prints from the steering wheels of both cars. Chances are that both Julia and Ian drive both cars, so we can expect them on both, but if we can pick up another fingerprint from the Qashqai, maybe on the door handles, we may have something.'

'I read in the report that Ian was on the phone with Julia when she was attacked?' Thornton probed.

Tanzy and Byrd both nodded.

'Have the phone records been checked?'

'Yes,' Tanzy said. 'We have cross-referenced the phone call to the time that Ian said. It matches up.'

'Do we have Julia's phone? Bagged for evidence?'

Byrd shook his head. 'No. Her phone hasn't been found yet.' He paused for a moment. 'My gut tells me this isn't a random attack on Julia Porter. I think her killer — or killers — know her. I personally don't think Ian killed Julia. But I certainly think he knows more than he's letting on.'

'Why do you think that, Max?'

'Because I'm a very good judge of character,' he said, matter-of-factly.

'That's a fair comment.'

It was true. DI Max Byrd could judge the situation better than most, especially when it came to people and their behaviour. He observed their reactions and the way they moved. Even the slightest eye twitch spoke volumes and carried its own story.

'Thanks for your time. Keep me updated,' she said. She then diverted her attention to her computer screen. The detectives stood up and left her office, then headed towards the canteen in desperate need of coffee.

'She's hard work sometimes,' Tanzy whispered, taking a seat at his desk. Their desks were next to each other. Behind them, at the back of the room, was DCI Thornton's office, so they had to be mindful of what they said.

'Yeah, tell me about it.'

Byrd pulled his desk chair in until his padded stomach hit the edge of his desk. He placed his coffee down and wriggled the mouse to wake up the standby screen.

A central walkway ran from the double doors to DCI Thornton's office. On either side of the central walkway, pairs of desks ran parallel down the length of the room. There were six rows, four desks in total, two on either side. Eighteen of the twenty-four desks were being used but the other six were vacant, two of which contained piles of paperwork that Thornton had demanded be cleared by the end of the day.

'Gonna be a long day,' Byrd sighed. His eyes were tired. The lack of sleep was already taking its toll on him. He was looking forward to having a hot shower and climbing into bed later.

'You're not kidding,' Tanzy said, taking a sip of hot coffee.

Over the next hour, they caught up on emails and filed a personal report on the Julia Porter scene. DCI Thornton wanted everyone, whether you were a DI who'd been there twenty years or a PC who'd just stepped through the door, to file their own.

The morning ticked on with no news from forensics. The time approached twelve, and the level of activity started to dip as people made their way out for lunch. Some went to the canteen on the first floor, while others went to Greggs or McDonald's, or whichever convenient fast-food establishment tickled their fancy.

Tanzy focused on the report in front of him. It was about the missing seven-year-old, Evelyn Jones. She'd been missing for a week now, and they were no further forward. Tanzy had been in contact with her parents, who'd been ringing constantly. He couldn't blame them. As a father himself, he'd do the same. Bloody hell, he'd move heaven and earth for his kids. He'd promised the girl's parents that he, and his team, would do everything in their power to find her, but the trail was going cold.

Evelyn had last been seen eight days ago at three thirty in the afternoon. It was a Wednesday. A woman, after picking her children up at the local primary school, had seen Evelyn on the corner where Conyers Avenue joined Barnes Road. The woman said Evelyn had taken a left onto Barnes Road, but the woman and her children had taken a right, so after that, she couldn't assist the police concerning her next move.

After PCs knocked on nearly every door in the Mowden area, which took two full days, they were left with nothing. The corner near her school was her last known location. It was as if she had vanished like a ghost.

Tanzy hated it.

The only positive that came to Tanzy's mind was that Evelyn hadn't been found dead. And to him, that was hope. Every day, that hope decreased, but there was still a possibility she was alive.

10

Jacob Tallow and Emily Hope were in the lab. Byrd and Tanzy had popped in earlier, but they were in the middle of something and asked them to drop by later. After securing some evidence, they had returned to Brinkburn Drive. In the short time between the hours of 3.30 a.m. and 7 a.m. earlier that morning, they'd taken forty-nine pictures of the scene. All different angles, most of the shots focused on Julia Porter.

Tallow had also taken a video of the room before a tired-looking DI Byrd and DI Tanzy had arrived just after 4 a.m. It helped them look over things when they analysed them later. Once the detectives had left, Tallow and Hope went back inside the house to collect more evidence. They knew Byrd and Tanzy were experienced enough to keep a safe distance while they worked. They both knew the importance of what a forensic would look for, so contaminating the scene was something Tallow and Hope weren't too worried about. They also made sure the detectives, who knew the correct protocol, had been signed in on arrival and signed out as they left. An imperative process.

Back inside the house, they checked the room thoroughly. Sometimes leaving a scene to take a quick break allowed them to look at something with fresher eyes, enabling them to see things they may have first missed. They rarely made mistakes, but everyone did at some point.

The crime scene manager, Tony McCabe, entered the room just after 11 a.m. He'd been occupied under the bridge where Julia and her son, Liam, had been taken. Tallow confirmed they had things under control and would continue to work until the job was done.

'Hey, guys,' Hope said, looking at the doorway of the dining room where McCabe appeared, then behind him, to the trainee forensics, Forrest and Beech.

'Morning,' McCabe said. They were finished under the bridge and ordered the car to be taken back to the station for further analysis. Apart from the fingerprints on the door handles, they didn't expect to find much; however, a thorough search using more adequate equipment would have to be carried out.

Examining a scene outside was completely different compared to the inside. The conditions of a closed room would last longer in their original state. The air was still. The humidity was even. Often, the temperature remained the same. If a body was found outside, the weather conditions, such as wind and rain, could alter the scene, making it very challenging to collect accurate evidence. They'd need to make their analysis with that in mind.

The fresh-eyed forensic assistant, Beech, stepped forward a little. Although he'd been doing it a year, each crime scene still amazed him, how someone could have been so cruel in the first place. But more than anything he was excited about the process of carrying out the work, how they would look for things and collect the evidence.

'Ahh, wait,' McCabe said to him, holding out his palm.

Beech stopped, frowning at his superior.

'I know you're keen,' McCabe said, 'but let Tallow and Hope talk you through some things first. Okay?'

Beech nodded then apologised. McCabe looked towards Amanda Forrest, who stood next to Beech, so she knew this applied to her too.

'Have you found anything unusual here?' McCabe asked the senior forensics.

'You mean apart from a dead woman with no eyes?' Hope asked him with elevated eyebrows. She knew what he meant but he appreciated her humour.

McCabe smiled. 'Yes . . .'

'Hundreds of fingerprints. Everywhere.'

'Have you guys found anything near the bridge?' Tallow asked, looking up from his electronic tablet.

'Fingerprints,' Beech said.

'Nice.'

'Hey, I need to go,' McCabe said. 'You guys work together. I'll catch up with you later. There's someplace I need to be.'

'Don't forget to sign out, sir,' Tallow said, smiling at his superior.

'You got it, boss,' he said with a wink, and left.

They found several hairs around the room and bagged them for DNA analysis. Blood samples had been taken from the congealed pool on the floor directly under Julia's body. Countless fingerprints on the dining room table and the floor were found with the assistance of a powerful UV light. Some were smaller fingerprints, implying they probably belonged to their children, who were most likely sat at that same table when they had breakfast, dinner and tea the day before.

But then they found something strange.

There was only one set of footprints in the room.

Because of the nature of the crime, one would assume there were several people involved. That would be a fair assumption to make, generally thinking. Due to the moisture outside and the damp conditions on the ground, one would also think that while murdering someone then taking out their eyes and tying them to a chair, the last thing you would think of was cleaning the floor with bleach to get rid of footprints.

Sure, you might not see them with the human eye. You wouldn't normally unless they were wet or dirty. But under the UV light, you'd expect to see something.

There had been no smell of bleach lingering in the air or any sign of any cleaning products used anywhere in the house. Only one person had been in that room. That person wore size-ten footwear.

Chances are, judging by looking at her feet, it wasn't Julia Porter. The single set of footprints would be checked and cross-referenced with Ian Porter as he was the likely source. And most likely, the set of footprints was his.

It was clear to Hope and Tallow that they weren't dealing with clowns here. These people were smart. These people knew more than the average Joe. The scene was very clean from a forensic point of view.

When they finished examining the room under UV light, they switched the ceiling spots back on. Deciding they'd collected all they could, they moved out into the hallway and carried out the same process. It was a tedious task, but they loved their jobs and took pride in doing their best.

Out in the hallway, they found several fingerprints on the top surface of a radiator cover and dozens of footprints near the door. As an entry and exit point of the property, it was expected.

'Brilliant,' Tallow said sarcastically, staring down at the uncountable prints on the wooden floor.

They asked who lived at the property and were told there were two adults and three children. It was important to get samples of their DNA, so if any samples were analysed and didn't match, it could point them in the direction of something extremely important.

Back in the lab, on the computer screen in front of Hope, were several pictures of Julia Porter. Beech and Forrest had both gone to McCabe's office for a meeting. Every time they'd been to a crime scene, he wanted to speak to them, to see what they'd learned, to see how their training was going.

'It's very neat, isn't it?' Hope said, keeping her curious eyes on the screen.

Tallow, who was analysing the video from the Porters' dining room, pressed pause on the remote. The screen froze on a still shot of Julia Porter's bloody face.

To those in the know, it was obvious that a very sharp instrument had been used to remove the eyes. She'd seen this procedure carried out in the past, but she'd never seen this precision, not outside of a medical or pathology lab. It was almost mind-boggling, considering the time frame that the individual or individuals had to do it.

Ian Porter claimed he was unconscious for forty minutes under the bridge. He said when he'd woken, a couple was standing over him, asking if he was okay. He then left the bridge and raced home. Taking that into account would leave fifty to fifty-five minutes for Julia Porter to be brought back home.

During that time, she was tied to a chair, then someone removed her eyes. All traces of footprints, apart from one, which most likely belonged to her husband, had vanished.

'Yes, it is,' Tallow agreed, frowning. 'It's quite impressive, isn't it?'

'It's worrying,' she replied. 'That's what it is.'

Unless the footprints they found belonged to the single person who was responsible for the murder of Julia Porter. Unless it wasn't a stranger at all.

11

'You heard anything on Evelyn Jones yet?' Byrd asked Tanzy, who shook his head.

They were sitting at their desks eating lunch. Byrd had popped out to get them both a sandwich from somewhere in town, saying he needed to stretch his legs. Tanzy had told Byrd that while he was gone, he would check in on his team, see if they had anything more on the missing seven-year-old, Evelyn Jones.

There were no more updates.

Tanzy finished a mouthful of sandwich, then took a sip of Pepsi from the bottle next to his keyboard. It had been a week since her disappearance, but nothing had come back yet. A nationwide missing person's appeal had first been broadcasted four days ago, making it three days after she had last been seen. The article was written by a reporter, Steve Allan, who had a section on the *Northern Echo* website and a column in the paper. Each day he provided an update — a public appeal, begging people to stay vigilant and stating that Evelyn's parents needed their help. In today's paper, he said that Evelyn was 'one of our own and needed to be found ASAP. We are praying for her.'

There was a ping from Byrd's phone. He leaned forward and unlocked it. It was from Claire:

Looking forward to seeing you tonight. X x

Byrd smiled and replied straight away.

You too :) x x

'What you smiling at?'

'Nothing.'

'Maxi in love?' Tanzy teased.

Byrd leaned over and punched his arm, causing Tanzy to sway to the left, nearly falling off his chair. Byrd didn't have any children. He'd never really been inclined to start a family and never felt like he'd met the right person. Tanzy knew that Byrd had just pipped over the hill of forty, and becoming a parent at any age was hard work. Byrd had been with his partner, Claire, for nearly eighteen months. Tanzy liked her. She was educated and had her wits about her. She was good for Byrd, just what he needed, someone to take his mind off the job when he got home, otherwise he'd just stay in the office day and night.

Often, Tanzy, Phillipa, Byrd and Claire would go out for meals. A few weeks back, they went to Al Fornos on Skinnergate in town, then went for some drinks afterward. Nothing too heavy.

'What do you think they'll find?' Tanzy said, finishing his sandwich and sitting back to digest. 'Tallow and Hope, I mean, at Brinkburn Drive.'

Byrd cocked his head. 'They could find anything. They're the finest forensics I've ever worked with.'

Tanzy agreed.

DCI Thornton's office door opened.

'Hey, you two,' she said quickly.

Byrd and Tanzy both turned.

'What do we know?' DCI Thornton asked. 'He's just been on the phone.' By *he*, she meant Superintendent Barry Eckles. 'He's looking for an update. I said I'd ring him back ASAP.'

'Not much to add beyond what we told you earlier. We'll chase up with McCabe and his team shortly.'

'Okay.'

She returned to her office and closed her door. She seemed flustered, unsure about something, which was unusual because she was normally as cool as ice.

Eckles was on her back constantly, making sure she was doing things right. Not only right but fast. He wanted everything done yesterday.

Byrd and Tanzy turned, focusing on their screens.

Byrd's mobile rang. He stopped typing, picked it up and put it to his ear.

'Hello?'

'Max Byrd?'

'Speaking.'

'Hello, Max. I am a nurse from Darlington Memorial Hospital. My name is Amanda Horne. I'm sorry to tell you this, but we have some bad news. Your mother and father have been involved in a serious road traffic collision.'

The words ran over Byrd like a cold shiver.

'Are they — are they okay?'

'Please come to the hospital,' she said clearly. 'They're both in a very bad way.'

12

Wednesday afternoon
Darlington Memorial Hospital

It took Byrd just fourteen minutes from receiving the call to arrive at the reception of the Darlington Memorial Hospital.

'Good afternoon, how can I help you, sir?'

Byrd leaned forward, his stomach against the rounded edge of the high desk and looked down at the grey-haired female in her mid-fifties, dressed in white sitting on a swivel desk chair.

'My parents were in an RTC a short while ago. Name's Byrd. B. Y. R. D.'

'Hold on a second, sir,' she said, diverting her attention to the screen in front of her. The name Angela was sewn onto her right breast pocket. He watched her eyes reflect the screen's dim glare. 'Yeah, found them.'

'Which floor?'

'Ground floor, Intensive Care.' She glanced to the left and raised her arm down the corridor. 'If you go down there, then take a right, you'll—'

She fell quiet, realising Byrd had already left the desk, running down the corridor towards the Intensive Care Unit.

Everyone stared at him fearfully as he hurried, heavy footsteps echoed down the hall. He quickly passed an elderly woman hunched over in a wheelchair, almost taking her kneecaps out in the process. He muttered an apology under his breath but didn't wait for a response from her or the angry younger man who was pushing her.

Taking a left, he narrowly missed a pair of young doctors, who were forced to halt their strides to avoid the collision. This time, he didn't apologise. He needed to get there. His heart pounded through his chest as he slowed down in front of the double doors. Through the door, to the right, there was a wide, low desk with a sign indicating the ICU reception.

The handsome-looking man behind it lifted his head, looking up over the top of small, square glasses.

'Can I help you?'

Byrd rushed over. 'Yes, yes. My parents were in an RTC. I was told they were in here. Name's Byrd. B. Y. R. D.'

The time it took the man to search was merely seconds, but it felt like hours. Byrd anxiously glanced down at his wristwatch, breathing light and fast.

'Are they here?' Byrd pressed.

'Just a second . . .'

'I was told they—'

The man lifted his head. 'Yes, they're here. Take a seat, I'll get a doctor to come and speak with you.'

'But I—'

'Sir, if you can just take a seat and a doctor will come and see you as soon as possible — I'll tell him you're here.' The man behind the desk pointed to the two remaining seats behind Byrd. He sighed, went over and dropped into one of them.

He tipped his head forward, letting his face fall into his wet palms. Several long minutes passed before the double doors on the left opened.

Byrd craned his neck.

A slim man stepped through the threshold, wearing a tightly fitting pale blue shirt accompanied by a thin black tie. Byrd guessed he was close to sixty, although he couldn't be sure.

He appeared to be looking around, and it wasn't long before his stare found Byrd. Standing to his feet, Byrd met the doctor halfway between the doors and the small seating area.

'I'm Dr Ching,' he said, in a soft voice.

'Are they okay?' Byrd asked quickly, looking past him through the doors.

'Are you a family member?'

'Yes — their son. I'm their son, Max. Are they . . . are they okay?'

Dr Ching sighed lightly. 'Please follow me.'

The doctor turned and used his key card to gain access. After the beep, the doors opened automatically and Byrd followed the doctor down the dimly lit corridor.

13

Tanzy walked through the exit door of the station into the cold air outside. After the stressful day, he was glad it was finally over. He flashed a courteous smile to the colleague walking past him and she thanked him for holding the door open for her.

On the way to his car, his phone rang. He pulled it from his pocket and saw it was Byrd.

'Hey, Max.' Tanzy slowed his walk to the car so he could give Byrd his full attention. 'How are they doing?'

Byrd sighed through the phone. 'Not good, Ori. They're both in comas.'

Silence hung in the air. Tanzy stopped dead and raised a hand to his head. 'Max, I'm so sorry.'

Byrd coughed and Tanzy could hear the emotion climbing up his throat.

'Do you want me to bring you anything?' Tanzy asked.

Byrd fell quiet. This time, Tanzy gave him a few more seconds.

'Max, do you ne—'

'No, it's okay, mate. Thanks. I'll be all right. I'm seeing Claire tonight. She can bring me what I need.'

Tanzy started moving again, dawdling towards his car. 'I can if you want, Max. I'm not doing anything.'

'No, Ori, it's fine — don't worry about me. Honestly.'

'Ring me if you need anything, okay?'

'Will do,' Byrd said before he hung up.

Tanzy sighed, feeling the burden of his friend's pain, and put the phone back into his jacket pocket. Using the key he opened the door, climbed in and sat for a moment.

What a day.

He stared out the window, watched a car turn for the exit. The car park was thinning. The sun had long gone, the sky was now smothered by huddling grey clouds.

He scratched his goatee for a second and thought about his brother, Daniel, who lived down in York with their parents, Andre and Claudia. He renovated houses and did most of the work himself. Tanzy spoke with him on the phone — usually once or twice a week — but he was usually in the middle of something. Which was good. It kept him out of trouble and, at the same time, he was earning money.

Tanzy glanced at the dashboard. Almost six. His judo lesson started in fifteen minutes. A part of him couldn't be bothered today. He sometimes had those days. Finding the body of Julia Porter early this morning and finding out his best friend's parents were now in comas after a car crash had taken its toll. For a second, he thought about ringing Phillipa, and picked up his phone.

Staring at the screen, he decided not to. He placed it back down on the passenger seat. They'd argued last night and had gone to sleep on bad terms, which was something that hadn't happened in a while. Due to the early start this morning, he hadn't seen her or even spoken with her all day.

After his judo class, he showered, then put on his spare clothes and headed outside. It was dark. The air was filled with moisture, implying it was about to rain.

A group of teenagers were gathered around the bench along the path from the entrance door of the Dolphin Centre. On his approach, their mumbles fell silent. Noticing the sudden quiet, Tanzy looked up. Five of them. Three of them were on bikes, the other two were sitting on the bench, leaning forward with phones in their hands.

'Got a spare fag?' one of them, a skinhead, asked Tanzy. He was young. Sixteen maybe.

'No, sorry,' Tanzy replied, ambling past, his kit bag hanging over one shoulder, resting off his hip.

'Dickhead,' the lad replied.

Tanzy, after passing them, stopped and turned slowly.

'Problem, like?' The lad stood up and took a few steps towards him. 'Eh, dickhead, you got a problem?' He had thick chains around his neck.

Tanzy smiled and calmly asked, 'Excuse me?'

'Do. You. Have. A. Fucking. Problem?'

The lad was tall but not quite Tanzy's height. At six foot two, Tanzy was taller, but the lad stood taller than most boys his age. Tanzy guessed he was fifteen or sixteen. The brave young man was thickset too, with big arms and muscles protruding from his neck.

'I don't have a problem,' Tanzy said.

The lad wandered over and stopped a few inches from Tanzy's face, then glared deep into his eyes. He raised his hand to his mouth, smoking the last of his cigarette, then lowered his arm and quickly blew the smoke in Tanzy's face.

Tanzy didn't flinch or move an inch. 'That's bad for you, you know.'

'Piss off, eh.'

Tanzy understood the situation the young lad had found himself in. He'd challenged someone in front of his mates, someone much older. Someone he didn't know had done judo for twenty-two years. He'd have to follow through now because his reputation was on the line.

'Okay, sir. You have a pleasant evening.' As Tanzy attempted to move around him, the muscular lad reached

59

out quickly and grabbed Tanzy's forearm. As he did, he felt the solid muscle under the fabric.

Tanzy turned slightly, smiling at the boy.

'Your call, son,' he whispered, leaning closer.

The lad eyed him for a long moment and decided to let go of his arm. He backed away a few inches, giving him a stare that suggested he'd let Tanzy off this time. Tanzy smiled then turned and walked down the angled path back towards his car.

'Pussy,' one of the lad's friends said to him as he sat back down.

'I'd have knocked him out,' the lad claimed. 'I didn't want to, though.'

Tanzy climbed into his car. He put the bag on the passenger seat and plucked the phone from his pocket. He found his wife's number and called it.

'Ori . . .' she said when she answered. Her voice was weak.

Something was wrong.

'Hey, Pip, you . . . okay?'

'Ori . . . I'm so sorry,' she said.

'What's . . . what's happened?'

'I've done it again. I've ruined everything. You need to come home . . . now.'

Her words crept into his heavy heart as he dipped his head into his chest, knowingly. He ended the call and threw his phone into the passenger's footwell.

Then he tipped his head back and screamed.

14

Wednesday evening
Darlington

The man sat down next to his wife on the large sofa and glanced down nervously at his watch.

It was nearly time.

'It should be on any minute now,' he said. There was excitement in his voice. 'They're going to wish they never did what they did.'

Their eyes met for a second before she offered him a sad smile and squeezed his hand. 'They deserve all they get,' she replied, with determination in her voice.

On the television on the wall opposite, the ten o'clock news had started. He exhaled heavily. According to the reporter, who sported a dark blue suit and matching tie, a body had been found.

His hand tightened around hers.

'We have confirmation that the body of a woman has been found inside a property on Brinkburn Drive in Darlington. Let's go to Colin Chalmers, who was there in the early hours this morning.'

The screen suddenly changed from a studio setting to footage recorded of a man standing in a dark street, dressed in a padded black coat, a microphone clutched close to his chest. Below the clip, there was a headline: *Woman found dead in a house in Darlington*.

'Here we go,' he whispered, squeezing his wife's hand, who, for a brief moment, glanced at him before returning her focus back to the screen.

'I'm here outside a house in Brinkburn Drive in Darlington,' Colin Chalmers said, standing directly in front of the camera, 'where the body of a woman has been found. It's unclear what the cause of death is but we have information that indicates the victim's life was taken in a malicious, unlawful act. Her identity has been confirmed as Julia Porter, thirty-seven years old, the mother of three young children. It's believed that her husband found her body in the early hours of this morning. Police were informed and attended the scene to find the woman in a condition they described as "sickening" and "horrific". We'll update you as we find out more in the coming hours. If you look behind me —' Colin turned, the camera zooming in on the house in the distance — 'a team of forensics officers can be seen investigating the crime.'

A tall man dressed in white plastic overalls walked out of the house and down the drive, opened the boot of a car and returned into the house a moment later.

A shivering Colin turned back to the camera. 'Once we know more, we'll update the public. I have no doubt the police will do everything they can to determine the reason behind this horrific act. Until then, this is Colin Chalmers of *ITV News*.'

Once the screen switched back to the studio, the man on the sofa took hold of the remote and turned off the television. A deathly silence filled the living room.

The woman on the sofa stared at him. 'You okay?'

He slowly smiled, giving her a light nod. 'I am.' His smile widened. 'He'll send us a picture of Julia soon. I can't wait to see her blood.'

15

Byrd stopped his black BMW X5 on the driveway, applied the handbrake and dropped his head back into the headrest for a moment. Tears filled the base of his eyes before they trickled down his face. After stifling a short cry and feeling the salty taste in his mouth, he wiped them away with the back of his hand.

The time was just after 11 p.m.

He was starving. His stomach begged for food, but that was the last thing on his mind. He needed to get inside where he could find peace and quiet.

And a drink.

God, he needed a drink.

What a day it had been. He'd been at the hospital for hours, watching his mother and father lying on their beds, surrounded by the continual beeping equipment and the pitter-patter of the doctors and nurses moving around them, assessing what they could do to fix them.

Alan and Jackie Byrd had been driving northbound on the A1 at seventy miles an hour when a car had stupidly undertaken them on the inside lane. As Alan pulled across into the slower lane, he'd clipped the back end of the passing car, throwing their vehicle to the right, causing a collision into the central reservation before their Honda Civic flipped twice and landed on the roof. It took fourteen minutes for emergency services to attend the scene. The fire service had had to carefully pull them both out of the car before the paramedics could get them into the ambulance, where they were finally given an oxygen supply and taken straight to Darlington Memorial Hospital.

The first thing Byrd had asked was the whereabouts of the car that had undertaken them. Where was the person responsible for this? The report had said the car wasn't at the scene when emergency assistance arrived, and there was no way of asking his parents because they were unconscious. He'd speak to the highway patrol. See if it could be located and tracked down.

Dr Ching, who'd walked through the door when Byrd had been waiting at the reception of the Intensive Care Unit hours ago, had told Byrd what damage his parents had suffered. The severe head trauma from the impact had caused their brains to swell and the fluid had pushed against their skulls, creating pressure on their brain stems and damaging their reticular activating systems. Their injuries were almost identical, which was rare in situations such as this because the possibilities of what could have happened were almost endless.

The only thing Byrd needed to know was if they were going to make it.

Byrd was aware of their ages. He was also aware that his mother, Jackie, had COPD from years of heavy smoking.

When he'd asked Dr Ching the question, the doctor's eyes had narrowed. 'Due to their ages and considering your mother's condition, we don't know the severity of the damage until we can assess them in a conscious state. At the moment, we've assessed them using the coma scale. You should be aware the chances of recovery are deeply affected by their ages and their health — it's important that you understand that.'

'I do,' Byrd had told him.

'Your father is in good health,' the doctor continued, 'surprisingly good health. However, your mother is not so good. What I can tell you is that they could be like this for up to two weeks. If I was you, I'd go home and rest. Chances are, this won't be an overnight fix.' Dr Ching gave him a sad, sympathetic smile. 'We'll update you every step of the way, Mr Byrd.'

Byrd opened the door of his X5 and stepped out into the darkness of his driveway. The street was stone-dead quiet. Across the road, Mrs Lovell was standing at her bedroom window looking out at him. She noticed Byrd had seen her, and she closed the curtains quickly.

He could faintly smell fire in the air as he made his way to his door and knew it would be the kids at the river. They'd sit around a fire with their friends, telling ghost stories or smoking cannabis, often both. With the river only a few minutes away, Byrd and Claire often went for walks and had seen the leftover food wrappers and empty burnt bottles.

As he reached his front door, his phone rang. He glanced down at it.

Claire.

He'd texted her earlier, informing her what'd happened to his parents. She told him she'd drop by to see him when he was home. She didn't ask to visit the Intensive Care Unit because she hadn't known Alan and Jackie all that well, not well enough to warrant being there when they were fighting for their lives.

He answered the phone while fumbling with the key inside the front door. 'Hey.'

'Hey, Max.' Her voice was soft and caring. 'Are you home?'

'Just. I need to get this lock fixed,' he said, finally getting it to turn.

'You keep saying that.'

'I know,' Byrd said, stepping inside. 'Yeah, I'm home now.'

'You want me to come over?'

He closed the door, locked it and hung his long black coat on the wall hook to his left. 'If you like. I won't be the best company, mind, but it would be nice to see you.'

'Give me fifteen minutes,' she said.

Byrd put the phone back into his trouser pocket and walked into the long rectangular-shaped kitchen. At the far end, he flicked on the kettle and stood there as it boiled. Then he changed his mind and reached up, grabbing an empty glass and the bottle of whisky from the cupboard above. He poured himself a healthy measure and knocked it back. He filled it halfway up again. Knocked that back too.

He sat down at the square table, staring blankly at the surface of the wood, his mind briefly running over the day.

The body of Julia Porter.

His parents in comas.

Then he cried harder than he had done in years.

16

Tanzy pulled onto the bypass and floored the accelerator. The engine of the Mercedes CLS 350 roared as the torque pulled the vehicle into the night.

He could see, for the next mile, that the road was empty. No one around. Just him and his busy thoughts to deal with.

He did this when he needed to get out. When he needed to be alone. Fire up the Merc and waste some fuel. Normally, Phillipa drove it and he used the Golf for work.

He'd always liked his cars from a young age. He remembered — although he'd rather forget — when he was seventeen. He'd passed his test and bought a 1.1 litre Peugeot 106, and spent over a thousand pounds on modifications. He'd installed a new exhaust system and changed the air induction system. He'd bought some shiny new alloys, which, in hindsight, looked ridiculous. He had a photograph somewhere to prove it. He'd even talked about putting nitrous oxide in it, but after his friends had laughed at him, he'd changed his mind. Before the Merc, he'd gone through the whole gamut of young cars, ranging from his first Peugeot to a Clio to a

Civic Type R. The Honda was his favourite. He adored it. So did Pip. They used to go to Teesside park for meals and spend nights at the bowling alley.

They were the good times. The happy times.

Now it was different.

He couldn't believe it. All the hard work was wasted.

After speaking with Phillipa earlier in the car, he'd raced home and, walking through the door, heard her shouting at the kids. They were cowered in the corner of the living room holding each other, scared. Tanzy saw the vodka bottle in her hand, only a third remaining. Eric and Jasmine looked up and sighed with relief after seeing him.

They both got up from the corner, ran over and hugged him tightly.

'That's it, go and fuck off to Daddy, then!' she'd shouted. Her words were slurred as she waved the bottle around in mid-air. 'Same old fucking story, isn't it?'

'Listen, Eric, Jaz,' Tanzy had quietly told them, 'go to your rooms. I'll be up in a minute.' He held onto Jasmine's arm, but she winced a little. That's when he noticed the dark bruise. It broke his heart. He kissed their foreheads before gently pushing them towards the door away from their mother. When they'd gone upstairs, he stood up and faced her.

'What the fuck are you looking at?' she screamed at him. 'Don't you—' She stumbled a little, losing her balance, then pointed at him. 'Don't you fucking judge me, Orion fuck-ing Tanzy. You don't know what it's like. What I've been through.'

Tanzy breathed slowly, watching her sway side to side, taking another swig of the vodka. The upper half of her body swayed uncontrollably, threatening to topple at any second. Most of the vodka had missed her lips and fell down her chin, down onto the thin dressing gown that was hanging off her. She wasn't wearing a bra either.

'You're a disgrace, Pip. Speaking like that in front of our kids. Eric is ten and Jaz is *seven*, for God's sake.'

She stared blankly at him, as if she didn't understand what he'd said. She was in such a state. Tanzy turned and walked out of the living room and when he was in the kitchen, he phoned Phillipa's mother, Leanne, telling her what had happened. Leanne told Tanzy she'd come to collect the kids straight away. She lived on the other side of town, and she'd be there within ten minutes.

When she arrived, she didn't want to see her daughter. No good would come from it. Instead, she collected her grandkids and off they went.

Phillipa had been sober for nearly six months. She was so close to her six-month badge at AA. Tanzy had been so proud of her, until tonight anyway. He half expected it because it wasn't the first time she'd fallen back into her old ways. It was the seventh, but she hadn't been anywhere near the six months mark before. Tanzy knew what she'd been through, what she'd had to cope with, but it was the same for Pip's mother and she wasn't like that. They'd faced the same issues.

Pip's dad, Peter.

What a horrible man he was. He used to hit Leanne and Phillipa repeatedly. He also used to visit Phillipa's room after he'd been out on the drink and rape her. Leanne, of course, knew what her husband was doing to her daughter, but she was terrified of him. They both were. He used to lock them both in the airing cupboard and leave them in there for hours.

'I saw the bruise on Jasmine's arm, Pip,' Tanzy said, stabbing a finger in her direction. 'If you ever touch her like that again, it'll be the last thing that you do. I'll arrest you and send you away for a long time. Do you understand me?'

She continued to sway until she backed away, falling onto the sofa. He knew it wasn't the right time to have a civilised discussion with her. It was time he got out, away from her.

Tanzy drove aimlessly. The town was quiet. Not many places stayed open later than twelve during the week — all the fun was at the weekends in Darlington.

As he drove down Houndgate his phone beeped with a text message. He slowed the Merc and pulled over, stopping in the loading area behind the Dolphin Centre, and turned off the engine and his lights.

A text from Leanne:

Eric and Jaz are asleep. Safe and sound. We'll sort Pip out tomorrow. I know what she's been through, but we have to move on. We all have to move past it and get on with our lives. I'll speak with her tomorrow. Love, E x

He sat deep in thought for a moment. Then, through the gap in the window, he heard footsteps from across the road. He couldn't see anyone initially, but the sounds grew louder. Out of a dark alley, an elderly man stepped out and dashed across the road, passing the front of Tanzy's bonnet onto the pavement, then along the side of the car up towards Boyes. The man seemed to be in a hurry, as if something was bothering him.

Then Tanzy heard further sounds coming from the alley. Multiple footsteps. Three men, dressed in tracksuits, stepped out of the alley and looked around intently.

'There he is,' one of them said, pointing in the direction of the elderly gent. 'Come on. Let's see what he has.'

The men looked to be in their early to mid-twenties and walked with a youthful bounce of energy and attitude. Tanzy watched them pass the side of his car and heard one of them comment on his Merc. They obviously hadn't seen him sitting in the driver's seat.

'Hey, fuck the car,' one of them said. 'We'll come back for that later. Let's go. That old bloke has a few hundred quid on him. He's gone up the alley where Pizza Hut is.'

Tanzy waited ten seconds. He sighed heavily, slowly opened his car door and stepped out into the cold midnight air. Gently, he closed the driver's door and then, very quickly and quietly, followed the three men into the dark alley.

17

The alley was pitch black. Tanzy kept to the right, close to the wall, in case they turned and spotted his outline against the orange glare of the streetlights behind him.

'Where did he go?' one of the men said.

'Fuck knows,' muttered another. 'He was just here. We need that money. I need my fix.'

Tanzy's eyes started to adjust to the darkness. He could see the outline of the three men up ahead. One of them pulled a phone from his tracksuit bottoms and turned on the torch function.

Shit, thought Tanzy. If they turned, they'd see him creeping along the wall. He moved over and hid behind a large blue wheely bin for a moment.

'Hey, what's this?' one of them said. 'There's a wall on the right.' Their footsteps faded for a moment. 'Found him! He's hiding behind the wall.'

'Please,' begged the elderly man. 'I need to get home to my wife. She's waiting for me.'

'Give us your money, old man. Don't make us hurt you.'

Tanzy crept around the side of the bin and moved back close against the wall, slowly making his way up the alley.

'I can't, it's all we have. My wife, she . . . she needs medicine,' pleaded the man, his voice quavering in the darkness. Tanzy edged closer, seeing the three men surrounding the old man, who was cowered on the ground in the corner. He had no way out. 'Please, don't.'

Tanzy made his move.

'Hey!' Tanzy shouted, staggering towards them, purposefully appearing like he was drunk.

The three men whipped themselves around at the noise. The man with the phone light shone it on Tanzy, the dazzling light blinding him for a moment. He couldn't see anything.

'Fuck off, pisshead, stay out of this,' one of them said, before breaking out into laughter. Tanzy, because of the sound, guessed the space between him and them to be around three metres.

'Hey,' said Tanzy, 'I need some money.' Tanzy fell clumsily to his knees and put his hands together as if he was praying to them, then he started clapping slowly. His knees felt cold as they absorbed the moisture on the wet ground.

The man with the phone said, 'Hey, Craig. Deal with the pisshead, eh?'

'What should I do with him?'

'Whatever . . . knock him out if you have to. I don't really care,' he told him. 'We need this old bastard's money.'

The elderly man cowered further into the corner, raising his arms in front of his terrified face, losing hope that Tanzy would be of any help.

Little did he know.

'Right, pisshead,' said one of the men in a tracksuit walking confidently towards Tanzy. 'You're gonna wish you never came down here.' Tanzy, who was still on his knees, glanced up with wide eyes so they adjusted to the dim surroundings. He knew exactly where the man was and, as he approached, Tanzy slowly moved his left leg up, planting his foot down to steady his body.

He was ready.

The man kicked a high leg towards Tanzy's head. Tanzy waited till the man's calf was just above his left shoulder and threw his arms up to grab it, trapping his shin between his forearm and the side of his head. Tanzy then jumped up with the man's leg trapped on his shoulder, lifting him into the air, and threw him down onto the concrete with a sickening thump.

Wasting no time at all, Tanzy darted for the next man, who was in mid-turn after hearing bone hitting concrete, but by the time he realised what was going on, Tanzy grabbed the material of the man's hoody with his tight grip and swept the back of his legs from underneath him. The man made a 'whoop' sound as he collided with the hard ground with a yelp.

The man with the phone turned towards Tanzy. 'What the fuck?'

Tanzy didn't wait for the conversation to develop and quickly grabbed the outsides of the man's shoulders with both of his hands. He moved close to him, placing his right leg to the outside of the man's right foot, throwing him over his hip in one swift movement. The man landed upside down on the concrete and dropped the phone, which smashed onto the ground into a thousand pieces, causing the light to go out and leaving the alley in darkness.

Standing to his feet, Tanzy went to the corner and helped the old man up, telling him it was okay and that he was safe. The man thanked him and then left the alley quickly.

The men stayed on the ground groaning in agony as Tanzy casually strolled out of the alley, back to his Mercedes.

18

Ian Porter, too upset to be with his children, wanted to be alone. He stood in the small bathroom of the Travelodge and swallowed the remaining vodka from the glass in his hand. He went back into the room, grabbed the bottle on the desk, unscrewed the cap and filled it up again.

His eyes were sore from crying.

It had been nearly twenty-four hours since he had found his wife dead in the dining room of their home. DI Byrd and DI Tanzy had told Porter that to increase their chances of catching whoever did this, they needed him to stay away from the house so he wouldn't contaminate the crime scene.

The words written in red crayon on the table ran over in his mind in a constant loop.

She didn't see it coming.

'See what coming?' he said into the quiet room.

He didn't know what it meant. He couldn't help the detectives yesterday because he hadn't known himself. He wished he had.

Peeling himself away from the desk with the glass of vodka, he went to the window and looked out onto a dark, wet Yarm Road. Across from the hotel was Cummins. The place was huge and made up of several buildings.

He froze, narrowed his focus.

'What was that?' he whispered, turning around, glaring at the room.

It happened again. A sound, a vibration.

'Hello?'

He glanced at the door. It was locked. The latch was on. A lonely silence answered him until he shook his head and drained the remaining vodka, then he went back to the desk and placed the empty glass onto it.

The sound again.

It came from behind him. He swivelled and looked at the wide, low bed in front of him. Creeping out the bottom of the pillow near the headboard was his phone. He went over, pulled it out. The little blue light flashed at the top of the screen, telling him he had a notification. It could be from WhatsApp. Or Facebook. Or Twitter. Or an email.

It wasn't any of those.

Sliding the phone to unlock it, he tapped on his inbox and found two messages. The first was a text message from an unknown number. It read:

She didn't see it coming either.

His heart skipped a beat. He scrolled down to the next message, noticed the sender's number was the same but, for some reason, the message wouldn't open.

Something was wrong.

Seconds of confusion filled his head before a 'download' bar appeared on the screen. Ian frowned, anticipating its progress as it slowly crawled across the screen, then, after a few seconds, it was complete. The message had been downloaded.

It was a picture message. He tapped it open.

He stared at the image with wide eyes. It felt like time had stopped. Suddenly, he felt a nauseating white heat slowly filling his feet, making its way up the length of his frozen body, then it crawled up his back, across the top of his neck.

Dropping his phone onto the carpet, he threw his hands up to his mouth and gasped at the image.

'No, no, no . . .' he whispered.

He doubled over and vomited the contents of his stomach onto the floor.

It was now clear why his wife had been murdered.

19

Thursday, early hours
Darlington

In the world of medicine, the importance of taking proper care of surgical instruments was vital. On a professional level, each instrument that had been used for a medical procedure had to be cleaned properly. The man knew the cleaning process involved three stages. Cleaning. Disinfecting. Sterilising. He was an expert in this field.

He slid the chair back, stood up and had one final look at his tools, the ones he'd collected over the years, then rolled the pouch closed and placed it on a high shelf. He switched off the light and the garage fell into darkness.

Stepping into the kitchen, he closed the door, locked it and headed over to the kettle. His watch told him it was after 1 a.m. Another late one for him.

'Hey . . . have you seen this?'

He jumped when he heard the voice and frowned down the hallway. Normally, his wife would have been in bed hours ago, but tonight was anything but normal. She'd been busy doing designs for a new school project the council was building across town. An architect by trade, she designed the interior aspects of a building, too — it flaunted her inner creativity.

The kettle started to rumble. 'Seen what?' he shouted.

'Come here,' she said. 'It's the news. Come see.'

He sighed and padded across the tiled kitchen floor. 'Coming.'

'Here, come watch . . .' Her arm was extended in mid-air with the television remote fixed to the end of it. 'I can't believe it.' She tapped the seat next to her left, indicating for him to sit down. He did.

'What is it?'

'It's the ten o'clock news. I've recorded it.'

She pressed play. The people started moving on the screen. There was an ambulance, a police van and two police cars parked on the street. The house the camera was pointing at was cordoned off, with yellow tape in the shape of a square. A police officer was standing at the end of the driveway.

'What is it?' he asked impatiently, as if he had other things he wanted to do.

'Do you recognise it?' she said, pointing at the screen. 'The street?'

He narrowed his focus to the screen. 'I . . . I don't. Where is it?'

'Brinkburn Drive. About halfway down, on the left. I was there the other day, seeing a client who lived across the road. What are the odds?' Her tone was both sad and curious about what was about to follow.

'Now you mention it, I guess it looks familiar.' He eased back a little, letting himself fall into the soft back of the sofa, and joined in watching it. 'What happened?'

'A woman was found dead.'

'Jesus!' he said, giving her a concerned look.

They watched the report for the next four minutes. The reporter said he'd spoken to one of the detectives, a DI Max Byrd from Durham Constabulary, who claimed no leads had been found yet, and that it was an ongoing investigation. Forensics had taken everything they could, and everything that could be analysed would be, using the best resources available, over the next few days. The reporter claimed the detective said, 'No matter what, we'll find out who did this, it's only a matter of time . . .' before thanking the viewers for watching and that any updates will be aired as soon as they come in.

'That's awful,' he said, standing up.

'Where you going?'

'To bed. I'm up early.'

Her bottom lip curled outwards. It was tough being the wife of a man who worked long hours as he did.

'We're short-staffed,' he said. 'Especially this time of year.' He turned and walked away. Just as he reached the door, he said, 'The house is a mess.'

'I know. Lena's coming tomorrow.'

Lena was their cleaner, who'd just started working for them. She came twice a week, keeping the place clean and tidy. It was hard working all the hours they did and fitting in the time to keep the house nice too.

'Good.' He headed back to the kitchen, making a mental note about needing to give an update on Mrs Connor, and picked up his phone. Once he found the number he put the phone to his ear.

The phone was answered and they spoke for a minute.

'Yeah I heard about it,' he said, into the phone. 'We've just been watching it on the news, it's awful,' he explained.

'I hope they catch them,' the man replied.

'Yeah, me too. It's awful, especially being so local to us.'

'I need to go — Mrs Connor has pressed her assistance button.'

'Yeah, okay. Give her my best. I'll see you tomorrow.'

'See you then, Doctor.'

20

Thursday morning
Darlington

Ian Porter hadn't slept since seeing the picture message on his phone. His eyes were red and sore, his breathing still light and fast. Glaring at the image on the screen in front of him, he sat rigid on the hotel bed and managed to peel his eyes away from it.

The sound coming from the phone startled him, the ringing disturbing the silent room. It was his mother calling. He answered.

'Mam . . .'

'Hi, Ian. How are you holding up?'

Ian didn't answer.

'Love? Are you there?'

'I . . . I need to go.' He hung up. 'Shit, shit, shit!' he shouted.

He rubbed his face hard, sighing heavily, and thought for a moment. He bent down, picked up the phone and found the number he needed. After three rings, it was answered.

'Ian . . . this is unexpec—'

'Listen, James,' said Ian, straight to the point. 'Listen very carefully. I received a picture message a few hours ago.'

'Okay?' replied James.

'Do you remember that night?'

'Which night?'

'The night when . . . when she was killed?'

James didn't respond.

'Do you remember?'

'Of course, I remember, Ian. It was, what — fifteen years ago?'

'Yeah.'

'I was there. I remember. How could I forget that night? It was horrific. Wait — you said you received a picture message. What picture?'

'It's her . . . it's a picture of her.'

'She's dead, Ian . . .'

'I know she's dead, God dammit!' Ian sighed, hopelessly.

'What's she doing in the picture?'

'She's just how we left her in the garage that night.'

James didn't reply for a moment, then he said, 'Who sent the picture?'

'It's from an unknown number. I can't reply or phone it.'

'Hold on for a second, Ian. Just take it easy. Let's think for a moment here.'

'Who was there that night?' Ian asked. 'There was me, you, Greg, Stu . . .'

'I think so. What are you going to do?' James asked.

'I don't know. I'm a mess. I . . . found my wife dead yesterday.'

'I heard about that. I'm so sorry, Ian.'

'I think that night had something to do with my wife's murder.'

'Wait — what? Do you think he did it? He moved abroad, last I heard.'

'Maybe he's come back home.'

21

Tanzy hadn't got home till nearly 1 a.m. He'd turned off the engine and sat in silence for a moment before he headed for the house. Entering, he'd found Phillipa asleep on the sofa in the living room, dressing gown wide open, revealing her bare breasts and stomach.

He'd left her there.

She would have been in no fit state to carry a civilized conversation, and he didn't have the energy or patience to try. When he woke the next morning he didn't want to speak to her, so he'd left the silent house first thing without saying a word, assuming she was still asleep.

But when he got into the warm office and sat down at his desk, he found he couldn't stop thinking about his wife and the state she'd been in last night in front of the kids. Shameful. It had made it worse because she'd nearly gone six months without a drink.

The door behind him opened quietly.

'Morning, Ori,' DCI June Thornton said, stepping out of her office.

He turned one-eighty and looked up at her. 'Morning, boss. How are you doing?'

'Cold.' She stopped near him. There was a cup of coffee in her hand, steam twirling upwards from it. Today, she wore a white blouse, covered by a dark blue suit jacket and a knee-length pencil skirt. A scent of perfume enveloped her which was very sweet yet pleasing. 'You heard from Max this morning?'

He gave a sympathetic smile and shook his head. 'I haven't. I sent him a text before I left the house, but he hasn't replied yet. He'll no doubt have—'

'Good morning,' said a chirpy, upbeat voice.

Tanzy looked right.

Thornton looked left.

'What . . . what are you doing here, Max?' DCI Thornton asked, shocked to see him.

Byrd took off his long black coat, hung it over the back of his chair. 'I'm working,' he said, smiling. He sat down, turned towards his computer and dragged his chair in.

'Max, your . . . your parents are both in comas. You need to go home. I think it's—'

Byrd swivelled quickly, raising a sudden palm. 'I appreciate your concern. I do. And to be honest, if anyone else was in my situation, I would totally agree with you — I would advise it. But the truth is, I've already been to the hospital this morning. A doctor told me the likelihood of anything changing this morning is very low. If it's okay with you, I'd rather keep my mind active and be here. I'd only be sitting at home overthinking things. And I . . . I don't want to do that.'

Tanzy smiled sadly. He knew Byrd well and understood his point. Byrd was driven and needed to be focused on something. It kept him going. Tanzy, on the other hand, would happily sit on the sofa watching some Chinese martial arts film, if he had the chance.

'Okay, Max,' DCI Thornton said slowly. 'I understand. Just . . . take it easy. If things feel too much, go home.'

Byrd nodded. 'Okay.'

'Have we made any progress on Julia Porter?' she asked, pulling over a chair from the desk on the other side of the walkway and sipping her coffee expectantly.

Tanzy shuffled through the papers in his inbox and checked the email notifications on his phone. 'We haven't received anything back yet from forensics or the morgue. I'll chase them up today.'

She nodded and rose to her feet. 'Okay, good. I've got the superintendent on my case so let me know as soon as you have something.' Then she said to Byrd, 'I appreciate you coming in, Max. But, like I said, if at any time you need to go, don't hesitate.'

'Understood.'

Tanzy waited for Thornton to close her office door before focusing on Byrd. 'You all right?'

For a second, Byrd didn't reply.

'Max?'

'I have to be, don't I?' he said, without looking in his direction. Tanzy could see him fighting back the tears. 'The doctors said they'll get in touch if there's anything I need to know. There's no point sitting there, getting all upset over it. I can't physically do anything — it's up to them now.'

Tanzy leaned across and placed a palm on Byrd's shoulder. Byrd nodded. Tanzy could see he was holding back his emotions, so lowered his hand and returned his focus to his computer.

'I was up late last night,' Tanzy said.

'How come?'

'Pip — she . . . she nearly went six months, Max. Nearly fucking six months.' Tanzy dropped his head, stared at the floor for a moment. 'So disappointing.'

'How was she?'

'She was a state. She was out of it. Swaying around the living room. The kids were there. I thought she'd cracked it this time, Max, I really did.' Tanzy fell quiet for a moment, unsure whether to say the next part. Byrd knew there was something else and waited. 'There was a mark on Jasmine's arm . . .'

'A mark?'

Tanzy nodded and looked at Byrd. 'A bruise.'

'Pip?'

'Think so,' Tanzy whispered.

'It's awful what drink can do to good people. I hope she really digs deep and sorts—'

'I think I want a divorce,' Tanzy said. He surprised himself with his words.

It would break his heart ruining the family he had at home. His kids, Eric and Jasmine, would be devastated. But if he wasn't happy, his sadness would only rub off on them, and that's the last thing he wanted. He couldn't leave them with her. He didn't trust her anymore. She'd let them down time and time again.

'Big decision.' This time it was Byrd's turn to place a palm on Tanzy's back. After a few seconds, he pulled it back.

'Yup.'

'Where are the kids?'

'At her mam's. She doesn't want to talk to her either. She's had enough of her.'

Byrd digested his words. 'I hope you get things sorted, mate. It's certainly not a healthy environment for the kids.'

The office was warm and smelled of coffee. Tanzy stood up and made his way over to the office door after asking Byrd if he wanted one. Stopping near the doorway of the office, he had a short conversation with one of the civilian administrators, Charlotte, who was holding a pile of paperwork close to her chest. She looked nervous, but there was a confident sparkle in her eye.

Byrd tipped his head back, peering over the top of his computer screen, watching him. Did Tanzy know the effect he had on women, he wondered. Charlotte always seemed on cloud nine when she saw Tanzy.

There were only four years between him and Tanzy, but Tanzy dressed a decade younger. Byrd wasn't the biggest fan of fashion. He had nice clothes, but he'd choose comfort over fashion any day.

He looked back at his computer screen and clicked on the tab titled *Reports*. Once it opened, he read the report on Julia Porter.

Minutes later, Tanzy returned to the desk and sat down with his coffee. He rattled the mouse to awaken the computer screen, logged on and waited for the system to boot up.

'Anything with the missing girl yet?' Byrd asked. Eight days had passed since she had been seen.

'Not yet, Max.' Tanzy sighed and shook his head. 'Soon, I hope. I'm going to find her. I promised her parents.'

22

Thursday morning
Darlington Town Centre

High Row, in the centre of town, was busy. Small market stalls were being set up. Stallholders pinned up advertising banners and arranged their merchandise, telling passers-by about their daily offers. There were e-liquids, socks, rock band T-shirts, double glazing, you name it.

Their raucous calls — *three bottles for the price of two!* — fell on deaf ears when it came to Mary Richards. She held her phone to her ear, clutching her daughter's hand, as they weaved in and out of the early-morning crowds.

They passed Post House Wynd on their right and continued, heading towards Binns. In the window of Greggs, Mia saw a fairy cake covered with orange icing under a green-winged butterfly with big eyes. She slowed and tugged on her mother's hand.

'Mia, what?' Mary sighed.

'Mammy, I want the green butterfly!'

'Mia, come on,' her mother replied, her attention still on the phone call.

Mia stopped, causing Mary to come to a halt. 'I want it!'

'Let me call you back,' she said into the phone and placed it back in her bag. She lowered herself down to her daughter's height. 'Mia, I said no. We'll get something a little later, it's not even ten o'clock yet.'

Mia pushed out her bottom lip. It didn't take long for her expression to pull on Mary's heartstrings.

'Mia wants it,' her daughter said softly.

'Okay, baby,' said Mary, rising to her feet. 'You can't eat it now, though. You have to wait until after lunch. Deal?'

'Deal.'

Mary took her daughter's hand and they stepped up into Greggs. The heater above the door kept the place warm. The smell of freshly baked pastries spilled over the top of the counter.

'Which one do you want?' Mary asked.

'The one in the window!' Mia pleaded.

Turning away from Mia, Mary peeked over the glass counter and caught the attention of an aproned lady. The woman smiled at the order and walked away, then moments later, handed her the cake.

'Mammy, can I—'

'No, Mia,' Mary said firmly, 'I told you. After lunch.' The shop assistant smiled at Mary knowingly and watched them leave. As they turned right in the direction of Binns, they heard a coarse voice behind them.

'Excuse me, excuse me.'

Mary slowed, turning with Mia.

A man approached who looked to be in his forties, possibly older. He was dressed in a faded grey tracksuit, and carried an old shopping bag in one hand and a white Greggs packet in the other.

'Me?' Mary asked, pointing at herself.

'Yeah,' the man grunted. 'Are you Mary?'

Mary, subconsciously took a short step back, pulling her daughter a little behind her. 'Yes. I'm Mary?'

The man stopped before them. 'You left this.'

The man held out his arm, handing her a Greggs packet. She frowned. She'd only ordered the butterfly cake for Mia, hadn't she? Unless she—

'Here,' the man said, leaning forward, encouraging her to take it.

Mary took the packet and thanked him. The man smiled, gave them both a nod and turned. Within seconds, he was lost in the crowd.

'What is it, Mammy?' Mia asked. 'Cake for me?'

'I . . . I don't know.' Mary let go of Mia's hand for a moment and opened the packet. She tilted her head forward and peered inside.

Her eyes widened. She dropped the bag. The contents rolled out onto the pavement and she threw her hands to her mouth.

Everyone stared at her when she screamed.

23

Byrd headed back to his desk with a glass of water. He'd normally choose coffee but he felt a headache coming, and he knew from experience that coffee only made it worse.

Tanzy was at his desk, eyes on his screen. It was just before lunchtime, according to the clock near the door of DCI June Thornton's office.

As he sat down, Byrd noticed a box of salad in front of Tanzy. 'Ori, why are you eating salads?'

Tanzy looked at him.

'How much do you weigh?' Byrd asked. 'Thirteen stone?'

Tanzy raised his eyebrows. 'Good guess. How much do you weigh?'

'I apologise but Max Byrd isn't available right now. If you could leave a message and he'll get back to you on his return.'

Tanzy smirked, focused back on his screen and started typing.

'Thornton's been talking my ear off this past half hour,' he told Byrd.

'What about?'

'About you.'

'Me?' Byrd placed his glass of water on the desk. 'What about me?'

'She wanted to know how stable you are.'

'Are you serious?' Byrd said, frowning.

'Yeah,' Tanzy said. 'With what's happening with your parents, she asked if I thought you were in a stable enough condition to be at work.'

Silence grew between them for a long moment. 'What did you say?'

'I said absolutely not. I told her you're the worst DI I'd ever worked with. That you'd never been any good.'

They both smiled.

'I told her I'd never worked with anyone more capable and focused in my life,' Tanzy went on. 'I said, if anything, it would give you more focus because you know how to channel your concentration.'

Byrd nodded admiringly. 'Appreciate that.'

'Have you heard anything from the hospital?'

Byrd shook his head. 'I'll ring on my break to see if there's an update.' For the past hour, Byrd had been in a meeting with his team in room 102 along the hall, discussing ideas on how to crack down on shoplifting in and around Darlington.

Tanzy's mobile phone rang. He pulled it out and answered it.

'DI Orion Tanzy speaking . . . Oh hi . . . When? . . . Thanks for telling me. I'll be right there.' He put the phone on the desk.

'Who's that?' Byrd asked. 'You're frowning — it's something serious when you're frowning.'

'It was Cornty. He said he's in town on High Row. Apparently, it's important and I need to be there. Are you coming?'

'Yeah, why not? I wouldn't mind stretching my legs anyway.' Byrd stood and grabbed his long coat from the back of his chair.

'What's he found?' Byrd asked.

'He said a woman has found something in a Greggs packet.'

'Greggs packet? What is it?'

'Cornty said it could be just what we're looking for.'

* * *

They pulled up in front of Timpson's near the town clock. Byrd applied his handbrake, turned off the engine and climbed out. Up on the steps near Post House Wynd to their right, a small crowd had gathered at a police cordon. With the buzz of people around, it was perhaps the worst location for this to happen.

'Looks serious,' Byrd commented as they climbed the steps.

'Serious enough for people to stop their busy schedules and have a look, anyway.'

'If everybody could just keep back, please,' they heard a voice say up ahead. 'Thank you, thank you.'

They reached the back of the crowd and slowed. They scanned the small sea of people, trying to locate PC Cornty, which didn't take long. He was an easy find. He stood at the far side of the perimeter talking to a man.

In total, there were four officers and someone inside the perimeter. That someone was Jacob Tallow, the senior forensic officer. He was close to the ground, down on one knee, leaning over something. The perimeter was squared-shaped and covered the front of the Mountain Warehouse shop.

Byrd and Tanzy veered around the crowd and headed towards PC Cornty.

'What do we have here, Phil?'

'We need—'

'Hey,' someone said from behind them. 'Is this going to be much longer? I'm waiting on a phone call about a delivery.'

Byrd and Tanzy turned. A gentleman stood there, dressed in a dark blue jumper with a Mountain Warehouse logo sewn on.

'Listen, sir,' PC Cornty said, stepping forward with a raised palm. 'We're doing all we can. I can assure you of that. If you wouldn't mind being patient, we'll be able to finish more efficiently and be out of your way sooner.'

Byrd heard the frustration in Cornty's voice but admired his professionalism. He guessed it hadn't been the first time the man had asked.

'Come on, I'm losing customers. They can't get into my shop,' he pleaded, glaring past Tanzy directly at Cornty.

Byrd smiled and stepped forward. 'Mr . . . ?'

'Fortley.'

'I'm Detective Inspector Max Byrd of Durham Constabulary. This is my colleague, Detective Inspector Orion Tanzy. We can only apologise for the delay, and I can assure you, that we are doing everything we can.'

Mr Fortley gave a reluctant nod, then stepped backwards, now realising he was outnumbered. 'Fine!' He turned and stomped away from them to make a phone call.

'So, Phil, what do we have?' Byrd said, turning back to PC Cornty.

Cornty pointed to the other side of the tape, where PC Kim Harrison was speaking with a red-haired lady standing with a small blonde-haired girl. 'Go and see Kim over there. She's speaking with the witness.'

Tanzy and Byrd followed his finger and headed under the tape, crossing the front of Mountain Warehouse. To his right, he watched Tallow carefully place the evidence which had been found in the Greggs packet into a small clear plastic bag. Tallow glanced up at Byrd and gave him a courteous, professional nod.

On the other side of the perimeter, they ducked under the plastic barrier. 'This is Mary Richards,' Harrison said. 'And this —' she leaned down to the little girl standing next to her — 'is her daughter, Mia.'

'Hi, Mary.' Byrd smiled, then lowered to Mia's height and grinned. 'Hi, Mia. How are you?'

Mia nervously managed a shy smile and tucked herself into her mother. Byrd softly rubbed the side of her small shoulder, then rose, switching his focus to Mary. A small number of people stood nearby, so Byrd directed his attention away from the Richards and signalled to one of the PCs to move them backwards to prevent them from hearing what was being said. The PC nodded and, exuding authority, shifted the thinning crowd back a few paces.

'We came out of Greggs,' Mary Richards was saying to PC Harrison, 'and a man called my name — I don't know how he knew my name. I didn't recognise him. Then he handed me a Greggs bag and told me I'd left it. I was sure we'd only bought one item — the cake for Mia.' Mary squeezed her daughter's shoulder. 'But I took it, anyway, thinking I'd maybe made a mistake.'

'I opened the packet and that's when I saw . . . *them*.' She trailed off, her eyes on the little girl.

'Would you mind coming to the station to talk to one of our artists and help with a photofit image, give us a clearer idea of what this man looked like?'

Mary sighed impatiently and glanced down at her wrist-watch. 'Will it take long? I was meant to be dropping Mia off and going to work.'

'Not at all. Thirty minutes at the most. We need to find this man. Hopefully, with your help, we'll be able to do that. Considering the situation, I'm confident your employer would understand.'

'That's okay with you, honey, isn't it?' Mary said, leaning forward, directing the question at Mia, who bobbed her head three times in response.

Kim looked at Byrd. 'I'll take them to the station now, if that's okay, sir?' At his nod, she smiled at Mary and Mia. 'You two want to follow me?'

Tanzy watched them leave, then turned back to Byrd. 'Let's go see Tallow.'

Jacob Tallow stood near the entrance of Mountain Warehouse. A camera hung from his neck. He held an iPad in his right hand, and by his feet was a rucksack containing the evidence.

'Tallow,' Byrd said.

Tallow glanced up. 'Hey, Max. How are you on this fine morning?'

'Living the dream. Evidence all bagged up?'

'Yeah,' he said, pointing down to his rucksack.

'Would you mind if I had a look?'

'Be my guest.' He lowered to the bag and placed the iPad carefully on top of his folded jacket, then unzipped the bag and cautiously pulled out the small clear plastic bag. 'There you go.'

Byrd turned his body away from the crowds to hide what they were looking at. 'Jesus,' he gasped.

'Do you think they belong to Julia Porter?' Tanzy asked, leaning in.

Byrd sighed. 'It's likely under the circumstances. Eyeballs don't go missing very often. The question is why were they handed to Mary Richards in a Greggs packet?'

'Let's go find out.'

24

Ian Porter dropped his phone on the sofa. Thinking about the picture message he'd received, he threw himself forward and raised his trembling palms up to his face.

'God,' he cried, muffled through his cupped hands. He'd come straight home after checking out of the hotel. His mother was dropping the kids off soon. It would be their first time home since their mother was murdered. The last thing he wanted to do was tell his children what had happened to her, but he knew he'd have to.

The hurt would be unbearable.

Porter ambled to the kitchen and stared at nothing. He placed a hand on the worktop to steady himself. The thought of his kids walking through the door not knowing what had happened to their mother was destroying him.

After making a cup of coffee to distract himself from the horrible thoughts swimming around in his head, he drifted back into the living room and sat down. To his left, the door through to the dining room was closed. He had no intention of opening it any time soon. He placed the hot drink on the windowsill and picked up his phone to look at the image again. It made him feel sick to the pit of his stomach, and he bent over and retched.

There was a knock at the door.

'Shit.' He wiped his mouth quickly with the back of his hand and stared down at the sicky bile on the floor. The smell immediately filled the room. He padded down the hall and opened the door.

'Hey, kids.'

Adam, Cameron and his mother were standing on the front step. Liam was in his nana's arms. A cool breeze seeped into the house from outside. The sky was grey and the street was dim. Winter was truly on its way. His children — even baby Liam — all smiled at him with an excitement that crushed every part of his body. His eldest, Adam, stepped over the threshold and hugged him tightly.

'Hi, Daddy.'

'Hey, son,' Ian whispered, kissing the top of his head.

'Where's Mum?' he asked.

The question hung in the hallway for a long moment. Ian sighed and exchanged a brief look with his mother, Irene. This wasn't going to be easy.

Cameron stepped inside and hugged him. 'Where's Mammy? I want to see Mammy.'

'Come in . . .' he said, his voice almost breaking. 'I need to have a little word with you. In there.' He pointed towards the living room.

'Can I play *Fortnite*, Dad?' Adam asked, eagerly shuffling on the spot. He hadn't played on his Xbox since he was last there. Ian looked sadly at his son for a moment. Dressed in a blue Adidas tracksuit, his hair swept neatly over to one side, the innocent face staring up at him. He had no idea what he was about to be told.

'Where's Mammy?' Cameron repeated, clutching at his leg.

Ian winced, feeling the tears form in his eyes but fighting them back, and placed his hand softly on Cameron's head. 'Come on, in here. Daddy needs to tell you something.'

'What's that?' Cameron said, pointing to the sick on the floor in the living room. He brought his hand up to his mouth. 'Smelly.'

'Daddy, are you sick?' Adam asked, his little face adorably concerned.

'Don't worry. Daddy is better now. Please sit down.' He motioned them towards the sofa. Adam sat down. Cameron reached the sofa but remained standing with his back against it. Ian's mother took a seat on the single swivel chair to the left and placed Liam on her knee.

Taking a deep breath, Ian knelt in the middle of the room.

'I need to tell you something,' he began. 'I don't really know how to say this.' His eyes fell to the floor for a moment.

'Daddy, what's wrong?' Adam asked, seeing the concerned look on his father's face.

'It's about your mum.' He took a few slow breaths, then said, 'She . . . she's dead. She—' He expelled a sudden breath, stopping himself from bursting into tears. 'She isn't coming home.'

The silence that followed was deafening. It hung for a few seconds until Adam's face changed and he threw himself into the sofa and bawled his little eyes out. Cameron, turning to watch Adam, turned back to Ian, not fully understanding at the tender age of four, but cried too.

Irene wiped the streams of tears cascading down her face and kissed the top of Liam's head as he watched his brothers cry.

Porter had held everything back for the sake of the kids, but watching and hearing Adam wail on the sofa broke him. He rose to his feet, moved over to the sofa and sat down next to Adam. He put his arms around him and held him tightly. Cameron came over and hugged them.

Liam sat nicely in Irene's arms, oblivious to the news his father had just told his brothers. He didn't know, but now he'd grow up without a mother.

And it was all his father's fault.

25

Jennifer Lucas, the tall, thin well-dressed woman sitting at the desk in the control room of the Town Hall, heard the phone ring to her right. She picked it up.

'Hello, Jennifer speaking, DBC control room. How can I help?'

As usual, her voice carried the calm, confident warmth it usually did, making Tanzy smile on the other end. Born and raised somewhere between Durham and Newcastle, she had a unique accent.

'Good afternoon, Jennifer, it's—'

'Detective Inspector Orion Tanzy?' she said.

For a second he was lost for words.

'I can tell by your accent, if you're wondering,' she said.

Even though he'd left South Africa when he was four years old, he still carried a slight accent. Most people never noticed but others did when he pronounced certain words.

'I need your help, Jennifer.'

'What's up, Ori?'

'We had an incident today on High Row. I need to see the footage.'

'What time?'

'Between ten and half past ten this morning, please.'

'What part of High Row are you needing to see?'

'I need the camera closest to Greggs.'

'Okay. I'll send it over ASAP.'

'Thank you,' he said and hung up.

Tanzy put the phone down on the desk and focused on the computer in front of him.

'Have you heard back from forensics?' A voice said behind him. He turned to see DCI Thornton standing at her door, looking tired and impatient. 'Are there any updates?'

'Not yet.' He smiled. 'I'm just looking over the CCTV on High Row.'

'We need results, Orion.'

'I know . . . I'm on it.'

She nodded firmly then retreated back into the office and closed the door without saying any more. Tanzy understood the pressure she was under from the superintendent. If you looked in the dictionary for the word 'arsehole', you'd probably see the name 'Barry Eckles'. There was simply no way of dressing it up. Thornton, Byrd, Tanzy and the rest of the good folk sitting in this office were lucky he was stationed on a different floor. He usually only showed his face a couple of times a day, and even that seemed too much. Tanzy had seen him go into her office earlier. He'd raised his voice about something and, when he left, he'd slammed the door.

A 'ping' came from the computer. An incoming email. He opened it up. The footage from High Row was attached. Tanzy double-clicked it open. The time in the top corner informed him it was 10.00 a.m. The camera was positioned five shops along from Greggs, close to the House of Fraser, covering the width of the pavement all the way down to Barclay's bank.

Leaning forward, trying to block out the background hum of the office noise, Tanzy squinted in concentration.

Beyond Greggs he noticed a man sitting cross-legged on the ground, just past the cut of Post House Wynd. The camera picked up his light-grey tracksuit.

For the next fourteen minutes, Tanzy watched closely. People were moving in all directions. Then he saw Mia and Mary walking toward the camera. Although it was far away, he saw the man in the grey tracksuit glance up at them briefly as they walked by. Mia tugged on Mary's hand, and, after a short discussion, Mary led her daughter into the shop.

'Ahh, what's that?' Tanzy whispered.

Using the mouse, he scrolled back ninety-four seconds.

As Mary and Mia stepped into the shop, a man sitting on a bench to the right side of the screen, wearing a black fleece and dark blue jeans, stood up. He made his way over to the man in the grey tracksuit, bent down and said something to him. He then pointed in the direction of Greggs. The man on the ground asked a question, and the man in the black fleece nodded several times, reached into his pocket and handed him two objects.

One of them looked like a small white bag. The other Tanzy couldn't make out. He scrolled the timeline back and tried to zoom in but, whatever it was, it was too small to be seen.

Standing, the man in the black fleece turned and walked away from the camera.

As Mary and Mia stepped outside, the man in the grey tracksuit climbed to his feet and followed them. He said something. They turned, and the man handed her the small bag. The camera didn't show it very well, but it did match up with Mary Richards' description of the events.

'Who's the man in the black fleece?' he asked himself.

26

Thursday, late afternoon
Darlington Memorial Hospital

Byrd checked in with the Intensive Care receptionist, who instructed him to take a seat in the small waiting area. He turned slowly, ambled over and dropped into one of the empty chairs. A familiar clinical smell floated in the air, typical of hospitals.

The waiting room was empty, but the usual pitter-patter of feet filled the corridor to his right.

The door to his left opened and Dr Ching walked in.

'Good afternoon, Mr Byrd,' he said.

Byrd stood and extended his hand. 'Hey. How are they doing?'

'Follow me, please.'

Byrd went to say something, but Dr Ching turned before he had the chance. He led him down a short corridor and to an open door with 'Dr Ching' written on a white plate in thin black letters.

'In here,' the doctor said.

Byrd entered the small office and stood awkwardly, unsure if he should sit. There were three chairs, a high bed, a shelving unit, a window with blue curtains draped down either side and a desk to the left of the room in the corner. To the right, the shelving unit contained files and plastic boxes filled with medicinal equipment. A pleasant smell of deodorant lingered in the small space.

'Please, take a seat.' The doctor motioned towards one of the chairs, then lowered himself into his own chair at his desk.

Byrd sat down. 'How are they?'

For a moment, Dr Ching didn't reply. Instead, he sighed heavily and then half-smiled at Byrd, who leaned forward and waited patiently with his eyes locked on the doctor.

'Mr Byrd . . . things aren't going as well as we'd hoped, unfortunately.' He paused to let that sink in. 'Our first assessment of your parents,' the doctor went on, 'was that your father seemed in a healthier state than your mother. But, unfortunately, your father isn't recovering as well as we'd hoped. He—'

'What do you mean?'

'Your father's score is similar to when I first saw him.'

'You mean on the Glasgow Coma Scale?'

The doctor acknowledged the detective's awareness of the term. 'Yes. The good news is that your mother is showing signs of improvement. When she came in, her score was three, but now she's a seven.'

'What's my father's?'

'Four. He was three when he arrived.'

Silence grew. Byrd was starting to feel hot in his long coat and placed his fingers between his throat and collar to allow a little air in.

'Do you want to see them?'

Byrd nodded twice. 'Please.'

Dr Ching stood up. 'Follow me.'

Along the brightly lit corridor, they took a left. A nurse was sitting on a chair, writing something on the clipboard on her knee. Dr Ching stopped beside her, and she glanced up and smiled at him.

'This is Jan. She's the nurse who's monitoring your parents, Mr Byrd.'

She smiled, placed her pen on the clipboard and extended her hand towards Byrd. 'Hi, Mr Byrd.'

'Hi, Jan,' said Byrd, leaning down and taking it. 'Thank you for your care and everything you're doing for them.'

They walked further until they arrived at the door on the right. Dr Ching opened it and stepped inside. 'Take as long as you need,' he said, before turning and leaving the room.

Byrd entered the room and took it all in again. The two beds were in the same position as when he was last here, and the equipment beeped with flashing lights. He moved forward and stopped between them.

'Hi, Mam. Hi, Dad.'

For the next few minutes, he spoke to them individually, telling them how much he loved them and how important it was for them to wake up. He informed his father that Newcastle needed their number-one fan back and told his mother that *Silent Witness* was in desperate need of their number-one viewer.

After ten minutes, Byrd turned and left. He passed Janine in the corridor, who was sitting on the same chair.

'You going?' she asked.

'Yeah. Is Dr Ching around?'

'You just missed him. He took an urgent call and had to leave.'

'Okay, tell him I'll see him tomorrow.'

'I will,' she said. 'We'll keep you updated, Mr Byrd.' She smiled, showing perfect white teeth.

'Thank you. I'd appreciate that.'

In the wide corridor outside of the Intensive Care Unit, he turned right, joining the traffic of people heading towards the exit. In front, a man was hunched over, pushing an elderly lady in a wheelchair.

'It won't be long, Mam,' he said to her. 'They need to do more tests on you.'

'I'm sick of this. I need to get out,' she replied, her voice deflated.

'Soon, Mam. Come on, let's get some air.'

Byrd moved around them and walked down the centre of the corridor until he reached the end where he took a left. As he rounded the bend, something collided hard with his right shoulder and knocked him off balance, throwing him into the wall.

'Jesus!' he shouted.

'Shit, sorry,' someone said from his right.

Byrd touched his tender shoulder where it had come in contact with the wall and looked at the man. It was Dr Ching. He was holding a black case, which must be what had rammed into Byrd's shoulder.

'Are you in a hurry, Doctor?' Byrd asked.

'I am so, so sorry, Mr Byrd, I—'

'You need to watch where you're going, Dr Ching,' Byrd interrupted. 'If that was a little girl or boy instead of me, you'd have really—'

The doctor raised a palm. 'I'm truly sorry. Please accept my apologies.' He looked flustered as if he wasn't quite with it. His eyes darted left and right.

Passers-by came to a halt and watched the minor altercation. The man pushing the old lady behind them stopped too.

'Come on, we haven't got all day,' the lady in the wheelchair said in frustration.

Recovering himself, Byrd said, 'Hey, don't worry about it. No harm done.'

Dr Ching nodded and walked away with the small black case clutched under his arm.

'Show's over, folks,' Byrd said to the people around him, then continued towards the exit.

The fresh, cold air hit Byrd like a slap in the face. He thanked the driver of an ambulance that slowed, allowing him to cross the road and head for the car park.

'I'm coming, I'm coming,' he heard a voice say from his right.

Along the path near a small fenced grassy area, Byrd saw Dr Ching marching down the side of the car park. Through years of training in human behaviour, Byrd had acquired the talent of reading people's body language. He could recognise lying, truth, frustration, love — all by the way that someone moved their body. The doctor stepped off the curb down into the car park and hurried across towards a blue Skoda Octavia. He pressed the fob and got inside.

'There's definitely something on his mind,' Byrd whispered.

He picked out his phone and rang Tanzy to check on the latest cases.

It had been another tough day. Little did they know, tomorrow would be even worse.

27

'Hello, Mrs Ching,' said Lena, who'd just emptied the kitchen bin.

'Please, call me Tina,' Mrs Ching said, walking past her in the direction of the kettle. 'Would you like a coffee?'

Lena shook her head. 'Not while I work. I find it distracts me.'

'You've been working for over an hour already without a drink. Come on, five minutes won't do any harm.'

'If you insist. Just a sec while I do the bin.' Lena opened the back door and took the bin bag outside, then returned.

'You don't take sugar, do you?' Tina asked, standing by the kettle.

Lena shook her head. 'No, thank you, Tina.'

'Anything planned for the weekend?'

'Not really,' Lena said. 'I'll see what my husband fancies doing.'

'Have you got any other family?' Tina asked, then raised a quick palm. 'Tell me if I'm being too personal. You've only just started with us.'

It was only her second month cleaning at the Chings' house. She was there twice a week, without fail. It would normally last around two hours, sometimes three, depending on what they asked of her. Tina would have liked to have her there all the time, but Sion said a full-time cleaner was an unnecessary cost.

'Hey, don't worry,' Lena replied. 'If you mean children then no, we don't have children. My husband and I have been trying, but it hasn't happened for us yet. I'm not exactly a spring chicken anymore so I'm guessing it's too late now.'

'How old are you, if you don't mind me asking?' Tina shuffled across the tiled floor and handed Lena her coffee, who accepted it gratefully.

'Thank you. I'm thirty-six.'

'Plenty of time to have children. Your husband, does he—'

'Want children still?'

Tina Ching nodded then took a sip of coffee.

'I think so. He's only two years older, so we're not *old* old,' Lena said.

'Loads of time for you, don't worry. I'm sixty-three. And it's true what they say about the body changing. It does. But, trust me, you have time.'

Tina glanced towards the circular table near the wall. 'Hey, take a seat, we'll have a little chat while you drink your coffee.'

'I shouldn't, the bathroom upstairs needs—'

'The bathroom upstairs can wait,' Tina countered. 'Please, Lena, have a seat. Relax a little. It'll give me time to get to know you better.'

Tina Ching had hired her not only because she didn't like doing housework herself, but because both she and her husband had challenging jobs that took up much of their time. The last thing she wanted to do at six or seven in the evening was to come in and start cleaning. She wanted to get a bath and put her feet up, and her husband felt the same after his shifts. Life was too short for housework, so she'd decided two months ago that it was time for them to get a cleaner.

After Sion and Tina had discussed it, he'd walked in one evening with a recommendation from one of the pathologists at the hospital.

'So, Lena, have you lived in Darlington long?'

'Almost a year and a half. I was born in Durham and lived there until we decided to move to Darlington.'

'Durham is a nice place,' Tina commented.

'It's lovely. I might move back there one day.'

'What tempted you to move here?'

'It wasn't out of choice. My husband, Arthur, works in Aycliffe. We live near Cockerton and he said it's easy to get out on the A1. Plus, he's lived here all his life. I met him two years ago.' Embarrassment washed over her face. 'Online dating, as it happens.'

'Wow . . . so those sites do actually work?'

'Did for me . . .'

They both shared a smile.

Lena drained her coffee and stood up. 'Right, I'll clean the bathroom, then your en suite, and then I'll make a move.'

'Okay,' Tina said, also finding her feet. 'I need to get these plans done. If you need me, I'll be in the dining room on my laptop.' Tina carefully placed her empty cup in the sink and left the kitchen.

Lena gathered her box of cleaning sprays, gloves, wipe, and a selection of bleaches, and made her way along the hallway, then, taking a right, she climbed the stairs. At the top, she stopped and turned around to listen carefully.

After thirty seconds, she had ascertained that Tina really was getting on with her work report in the dining room. She smiled, then snuck past the bathroom and entered the large master bedroom.

It wasn't the first time she'd done this. It was the third. She got quicker each time, becoming familiar with the layout. Her eyes widened when she saw the object on the surface of Dr Ching's bedside drawer.

With the box of cleaning stuff, she padded around the bed and stopped at the bedside drawer. She smiled as she picked it up and placed it in her box, hiding it between the various bottles of cleaning sprays.

'What . . . what are you doing?' she heard a voice behind her.

Lena stiffened slightly and turned quickly. Feeling her face warming, she said, 'Hey, Tina . . . I was . . . seeing if the bedside drawers needed dusting,' she explained.

Tina's eyes narrowed. 'It's okay, Lena. Just do the en suite like normal. I'll ask if there's anything more.'

Lena smiled and nodded. 'No problem. Sorry.'

With the object hidden in the cleaning box, she made her way past Mrs Ching and entered the en suite.

In the confines of the bathroom, Lena sighed heavily.

That was a close call.

28

Thursday evening
Darlington

Mary Richards and her daughter, Mia, stepped through their front door into the dimly lit hallway just after seven. Mary closed the door, locked it and placed her keys on the table next to the base of the thin lamp. The heat coming from the radiator nearby felt nice.

'Stuart!' she called. 'We're home!'

'Mary, where have you been? I've been worried sick,' her husband called from the kitchen.

'We had to go to Sainsbury's. I did text you to let you know,' Mary replied.

She took off Mia's small purple coat and hung it on the post at the bottom of the stairs. After that, she did the same with hers, then made her way to the kitchen, following her daughter's little footsteps.

'My phone died,' she explained. 'I didn't have a charger.'

Mia ran up to her dad and threw her arms out towards him. He stopped and bent down to give her a hug. 'Hey, sweetie.'

'Hi, Daddy.'

Mia let go and turned to Mary. 'Mammy, can Daddy read me a story? Please, please?'

Mary leaned down and kissed her daughter on the head. 'Yes, but not a long one, Mia. You have nursery tomorrow. Go get your pyjamas on and I'll send Daddy up.'

Mia smiled and nodded, then trotted up the stairs towards her bedroom.

'She not want any tea?'

'We had something in the Sainsbury's café.'

He nodded. 'I can't believe what happened,' Stuart said. 'Are you okay?' He pulled her close and held her. 'You're freezing. I've just put the heating on.' He motioned towards the table. 'Sit down, tell me what happened.'

They took a seat at the small wooden table.

'I think I've told you everything over the phone already. I don't really want to think about it anymore.' She looked past him and sniffed the air. 'Sorry, have you made tea? Something smells nice.'

'I put some pasta bake in before, nothing fancy. No worries if you've already eaten.'

She rose, headed to the kettle and flicked it on. 'Nah . . . I need wine.'

She went over to the fridge, then paused a moment when they heard a hurried pitter-patter of feet coming down the stairs and then along the hall. Stuart turned, seeing his daughter walk in, her face a little worried.

'Mia?'

'Daddy, I heard something in my room.'

'What was it? It must be a monster,' he teased, raising both palms up in the air as if he was playing a role in an old Frankenstein film.

'Stop it, Stu!' said Mary. 'Don't wind her up.'

'Okay, okay. Let's go see your room. Daddy will go beat up the monster.' Stuart stood up and patted his daughter's head, then turned back to Mary. 'If you're having some pasta, put some on a plate for me too. I'm starving.'

Mary reached up, opened one of the top cupboards, pulled out two plates and placed them down onto the granite worktop.

'What were the sounds, Mia?' he asked, trailing his daughter slowly up the stairs.

She came to a halt halfway up. 'You go first, Daddy.'

'Okay, Mia, I'll go first.' He stepped past her and reached the landing. Inside her room, he turned on the switch near the door and watched the room flood with light. 'See Mia, there's no monster in here.'

Standing at her open doorway she peeped inside cautiously. 'I heard something in the corner.'

'Mia, there's nothing in here.' He dropped to his knees in front of her. 'Go to bed, it's getting late. I'll be up soon to read you a story.'

Reluctantly, she nodded, did as she was told and climbed into bed. She then leaned over, grabbed her pink dinosaur teddy off the floor and dragged her pink covers up to her small chin.

'Good girl. I'll be up soon.' He flicked the light off from the switch near the door and the room plummeted into darkness.

'She's a worrier, that one,' he said to Mary back in the kitchen, who was sitting at the table with a plate of pasta bake and a full glass of wine.

'Gets it from you, Stu,' she mused.

He sat down opposite Mary, watching her closely, imagining what kind of day she must have had. 'I was looking out for you guys before, standing at the window. And something weird happened.'

She frowned. 'What?'

'It may be nothing, but a man walked past the house four times within half an hour. I thought it was a bit strange.'

Mary's frown deepened. 'You think it has anything to do with today?'

'He looked through the window every time he passed. The last time I stood up to get a closer look. I haven't seen him since.'

'When was this?'

'An hour ago, maybe.'

'Well, we do have the house up for sale. Maybe it was a potential buyer.'

'It's possible, I suppose.' He paused a beat. 'But to wear a hood up in the darkness is a little strange.'

'Trust me, it's cold outside,' she countered. 'If I had a hood, I'd be wearing it up too. Anything else?'

'What do you mean?'

'You look like you were going to say something else?'

'You know me well.'

'I've been married to you for eight years. I *should* know you well.'

He made a 'fair enough' expression. 'When I was in the shower, I heard something out the back — rustling, that kind of thing. I turned off the shower and looked out into the garden. Next door were out in the garage, so I figured it was nothing. I don't know, I've got the creeps tonight. Especially you finding them eyeballs today. Some crazy cats out there.'

She inhaled another mouthful of pasta as if she hadn't eaten for days.

Stu rose to his feet. 'I'll go tell Mia a story. She's waiting for me.'

He took the stairs very slowly. His legs were tired from his day at work. He moved over the landing into Mia's room and turned on the bedroom switch. Mia sat up in her bed, looking down at something in her hand.

He frowned. 'Mia, what's that?'

It was a lollypop.

'He gave it to me.'

Stu lowered himself to the bed and sat next to her. 'Who? Who gave it to you?'

'The man . . .'

'Which man — someone at nursery? You shouldn't really be having lollies at your age. I've seen some nasty things where children choke on them. Give it to Daddy, please.' He held out his hand.

Unwillingly, she handed it over.

'Who gave this to you, Mia?'

'The man in the hood,' she whispered. 'He told me not to tell you.'

Downstairs in the kitchen, he heard Mary stand up, the sound of the chair scraping across the tiled floor, then a moment later, a plate was lowered into the sink. He craned his neck towards the door. 'Mary?' he shouted.

When she didn't reply, he returned his focus back to his daughter. 'When did the man give you this lolly, Mia?'

'When you went downstairs. He was standing in my room.'

A chill enveloped his whole body and icy fingers crawled up his spine. 'Mia, don't joke with things like this . . .'

Her little face filled with sadness at his harsh tone.

Stuart bolted up and checked the wardrobes and under the bed. 'Mia . . . there's no one here. You can't make things up like this. It scares Daddy.'

'He told me it was a secret. He said—'

'Stop it, Mia!' he shouted, pointing a finger at her.

She started to cry and looked down at the bed. Dropping to the bed, Stuart wrapped his arms around her and apologised for shouting.

'What is it, Stu?' Mary called from downstairs.

'Doesn't matter,' he shouted, angling his head towards the door. He turned back to Mia. 'Are you really scared?'

She nodded twice.

He bent down, scooped her up and took her into their bedroom, laying her gently on the bed. 'You can sleep in our room tonight, okay?'

She smiled, tucking herself into the thick covers and pulling them up to her small chin. He checked their bedroom, making sure the wardrobes were empty and there was no one under the bed.

'Daddy has checked this room. No monsters in here.'

She lowered her head onto the pillow and closed her eyes. 'You need to go to sleep now, baby. Go to sleep, get some rest. I need to speak with Mammy.'

At the door, he watched Mia get comfortable, holding the dinosaur close to her little chest. He smiled and turned out the light, then went to her bedroom again, checking for intruders, shaking as he did so. Again, it was empty, but her words had rattled him. From the landing, he leaned over the banister and shouted, 'Mary?'

There was no reply.

'Mary!' His voice echoed through the house.

Silence.

'Fuck,' he muttered as he darted down the stairs and checked the kitchen. 'Mary, where are you?' He turned then frantically checked the living room and dining room, but they too were empty.

Back in the kitchen, he noticed the bin had been pulled out away from the wall and was empty, the lid open. Was she out the back, emptying it? He went to the back door, peered out.

'Mary? You out here?'

He rounded the brickwork of the kitchen where the bin was.

He froze.

On the floor, near the open bin in the darkness, he saw something.

Using his phone's torch, he directed the brilliant beam towards the base of the bin.

It was Mary's shoe. Resting sideways on the floor. Next to the shoe, there was a small pool of blood.

'Jesus . . .' He leaned down and picked up the shoe. On the bottom of it was a message written in red marker pen:

She didn't see it coming.

A chill shot through him. 'What the fu . . .'

He angled the phone light along the path, following a trail of blood droplets until he reached the gate, which was wide open.

Then he heard his wife's scream rip through the air before there was a metallic bang and the screaming suddenly stopped. He raced through the open gate and galloped out

onto the driveway. The screech of spinning car tyres resonated down the road.

Frantically, he looked up and down the street, but he
saw nothing.

Mary had gone.

29

Byrd walked into the kitchen. Although he'd showered, he felt shattered. When he glanced in the mirror he saw dark semi-circles under his eyes, which made him look like he was knocking on the door of fifty.

'Morning, handsome,' said Claire chirpily. She sat at the table, sipping her coffee, leaning over her Kindle. 'You look good in that.'

He was wearing a light-blue shirt with a navy tie, and black trousers.

'Good morning.' He bent over and kissed her forehead. 'You smell nice.' He took a step back. 'How did you sleep?'

'Better than you,' she said. 'You tossed and turned all night long.'

'I did?'

She nodded. 'Yes.'

'Sorry if I disturbed you.'

She waved it away as if it was the norm. 'I made you a coffee,' she said, pointing to the mug on the opposite side of the table, then she pointed towards the worktop. 'There are also croissants in that packet over there. I've been out already.'

'Early bird catches the worm.'

She smiled. 'I didn't want to wake you.'

'Where did you go?'

'Mowden shops. Have you heard anything more about your mam and dad? I know we spoke last night but wasn't sure if they'd been in touch this morning.'

'No, nothing more.' A look of sadness swept across Byrd's face. Claire moved her chair back, stood up, ambled over to him and wrapped her arms around him.

He smiled into the side of her neck but didn't say anything in return. There was nothing to be said. Her familiar scent of Dolce and Gabbana perfume gave him comfort.

'I'll warm up your croissant for you,' she said, peeling herself away from him and making her way to the worktop.

Byrd grinned appreciatively, turned and took a seat at the table. On the table, next to her half-filled coffee, he laid his eyes on her Kindle. 'What are you reading on there?'

'One of Chris Carter's . . . erm . . . *Hunting Evil.*'

'Chris Carter. Never heard of him. Is he good?'

She closed the door of the microwave. The plated croissant inside started to turn under the dim light. 'Some of the crime scenes would make even you feel queasy.'

She opened the microwave door, grabbed the plate then placed it down in front of Byrd. The smell of the warmed pastry rose to his nose. 'You should read it after I've finished. It's really good.'

'I might just do that. I haven't read fiction in a long time. And don't worry, I have a strong stomach,' he countered.

'What was the last book you read?' she asked.

'*The Da Vinci Code*, maybe?'

'It's good — I've read that too. What time are you going to work?'

He glanced down at his watch. 'Not long, I'll have this and get a move on. What are your plans for today?'

'I need to see my mum. She's got some flat-pack furniture from Ikea and needs help with it.'

'Okay, have a good day. I'll ring you on my dinner,' Byrd said.

'If you get one?'

Byrd smiled and nodded. There were days, as a DI, when there wasn't even time to go to the toilet, but that was the nature of the job.

She leaned down and kissed him, grabbed her bag from the floor and her black fleece from the hook above the radiator, then walked out the front door.

Silence filled the house. Byrd remained sitting at the table, finishing his croissant until he received a text from Tanzy:

Get here, Max. The post-mortem is back from the pathologist. You need to see it.

30

Byrd parked his car in the third closest bay to the entrance. The third bay was usually occupied by DCI Thornton but, for some reason, she hadn't arrived yet. Byrd could probably count on one hand the times he'd beat Thornton into the office, and, because of that, he felt a small sense of victory.

As Byrd took his key out, it started to rain heavily. Byrd watched it bounce relentlessly off the windscreen and smiled. Typical. He made a dash for the entrance. Once inside, he gave himself a shake.

'Morning, Max,' said Charlotte, the admin girl who had the hots for Tanzy.

'Good morning.'

'Have you seen Orion?' she asked, clutching several thin A4 files close to her large chest.

'I haven't, not yet. When I do, I'll tell him you're looking for him.'

'Thanks,' she said, smiling. She pivoted and strutted off with the youthful energy Byrd remembered he used to possess at that age.

Before going to his desk, he went up to the canteen and made a coffee. He put two spoonfuls of granules in this time — he needed the extra boost. As he approached his desk, he saw Tanzy sitting at his computer.

'Morning, Ori. How are you today?'

Taking his eyes off the screen, he glanced up at Byrd. 'Hey, Max.'

Byrd placed the coffee on the desk, pulled out his chair and dropped into it. 'Charlotte is looking for you . . .'

'Is she?' he said, keeping his eyes on the screen. 'Did she say what it was about?'

'No.' Byrd logged into his computer. 'What was that about the post-mortem?'

'Check your emails. I'll let you read it for yourself.'

Byrd sipped his coffee, found the email titled 'PM — Julia Porter' sent from the Pathology department and opened it. For the next few minutes, he scanned the report.

'Interesting,' Byrd whispered.

'Yeah.'

'So the pathologists think what's been done to Julia Porter, in terms of her eyes being removed, was carried out by a medical professional?'

'That's what they're saying,' Tanzy replied. 'They haven't seen work so fine in a very, very long time. Especially outside of a lab.'

31

Friday morning
Cemetery Lane, Darlington

The morning traffic along Carmel Road was no different from what it had been like yesterday or what it would be like tomorrow.

Scott Anders turned left into Cemetery Lane with his dog, Milo, an eight-year-old Labrador, who, as usual, was trying to go faster than Scott allowed him to.

'Take it easy, boy,' Scott said, holding the lead with a solid grip.

Hearing footsteps in front of him, he glanced up. He noticed a woman around the age of sixty, also with a dog, walking toward him. They made eye contact and exchanged a brief smile.

'Morning,' she said.

The dimples on her cheeks were the cutest thing Scott had seen since his wife died last year. It had been a rough year for him, but he was managing, taking every day in his stride. Now retired, he spent a lot of his time walking Milo, often for miles a day. Around this time of day, he strolled down Cemetery Lane, something he had done for nearly four months.

Most mornings, he passed the woman with the dimples walking the opposite way. Sometimes, he missed her, but he tried his best to time it right, so he could see that attractive smile. As lonely as it sounded, it was often the highlight of his day.

In recent months, he'd played out the conversation with this woman in his head, trying to imagine how it would go, but he'd never been beyond 'Good morning'.

Today would be different, he decided.

'Good morning,' he replied, smiling.

Just as they crossed, she looked down at her dog. Some type of poodle, Scott guessed, but wasn't too sure.

'Erm,' he stuttered.

'I'm sorry?' she said, slowing and turning towards him. 'Sorry?'

'Did you say something?' she asked, awkwardly.

'You're beautiful,' he whispered.

She frowned, then smiled. 'I'm sorry?'

He couldn't help saying it — it just came out. She was even more beautiful than he had realised. He felt his face warming, knowing it wasn't going as well as he had visualised.

'What did you say?'

'I said good morning.'

'After that, you said something?'

'I did?' He frowned.

'You did,' she said quietly, smiling, knowing exactly what he'd said.

'You're right, I did. I wanted to talk to you.'

Her eyebrows furrowed.

'I was wondering,' he went on. 'Please don't think I'm a creep or anything here, but do you fancy a cup of coffee or something?'

A cold silence grew between them. Her smile faded very fast. 'I . . .' she said but fell quiet.

He raised a palm. 'Hey, it's okay, I didn't mean—'

'I'd love to,' she said quickly. 'When?'

Scott's eyes widened. A warmth he hadn't felt for nearly a year filled him. 'Whenever you like. I'm free this morning?'

She nodded. 'Sounds good to me. I'm free this morning too.'

An awkward silence hung in the air as he thought about what to say next. 'Good. Erm . . .'

'We could grab a coffee somewhere?' she suggested.

'That would be nice.'

'Okay, then.' She pulled back the small dog to her side. 'I'm Elaine. And this handsome little devil is Edgar.'

'I'm Scott.' He offered her his hand. She shook it. 'And this,' he said, pointing down, 'is Milo.'

They looked away from each other. A grin lined both of their faces and they started to amble down the lane. Moments later, Milo stretched the lead, tugging Scott towards a wide, low bush to their left. Then Edgar picked up on the same scent, dragging Elaine to the same place.

'Steady Milo,' grunted Scott. 'What have you found, boy?'

Milo pushed his face into the bush and immediately started to bark, the deep howls disturbing the quiet lane. Edgar joined in. Then both dogs backed away and growled, showing their sharp teeth at whatever they had seen.

'What is it?' Elaine said, concerned.

'Here, can you take him?' Scott handed Milo's lead over to Elaine. She held both dogs with a steady grip.

Leaning down, using his cold hands, Scott spread the leaves and branches apart, squinting down into the base of the bush. That's when he saw it.

He froze.

'What is it?' she asked.

'Jesus.'

'Scott, *what* is it?'

He didn't reply. He couldn't find the words.

'Scott?'

'It's a hand.' This time louder: 'It's someone's hand.'

He turned to her and watched the fear intensify in her face. She'd gone sheet white. Scott edged back a touch, glancing nervously up and down the lane.

They were alone.

The sound of the dogs' barking continued to pierce the icy air.

'It's . . . it's a what?' she mumbled, the words clogging in her throat.

Then he felt it.

Something on his face.

Raising his hand to the tip of his nose, he touched the cold liquid with a fingertip, then lowered his hand to have a look.

It was bright red.

'Blood?' he whispered.

He tilted his head back and peered up to the sky. A frosty shiver enveloped his body when he saw her. Elaine followed his gaze up.

Then she let out a blood-curdling scream that rattled the air.

The dogs barked even louder.

In the tree directly above them, hanging by a blue rope attached around her neck, the body of a woman hung silently. From the open cut where her hand once was, beads of blood dripped on the cold ground near Scott's feet.

32

Byrd carefully scanned Julia Porter's post-mortem report. Tanzy came over with another coffee for him and placed it to the left of his keyboard. Without taking his eyes off the report, Byrd said, 'Thanks, Ori.'

'No problem.'

Tanzy sat down and leaned back, closing his eyes for a moment, waiting for Byrd to finish it again. He knew Byrd was meticulous and had the finest attention to detail.

In their earlier years, it annoyed him how long it took Byrd to process information and come up with an answer or a solution. IQ-wise, Tanzy knew he had the edge. He was smarter. The thing with Byrd is that he worked harder and was more determined. And, usually, it was Byrd who came up with the answers.

Byrd picked up his mug and took a sip of coffee, then placed it back down and focused on the report on his screen. Byrd's focus was unparalleled by anyone at the station. Ever since Byrd's sister was murdered twelve years ago, he had changed. Once a month, he saw a therapist and had done for years. Neither Tanzy nor Thornton knew about it, nor anyone else on the force — no one apart from his best friend, Keith, who he saw now and again. He'd been meaning to tell Tanzy about his meetings, but as time passed, he'd left it and decided not to mention it at all. The therapy sessions lasted an hour, costing him seventy pounds. The therapist, Dr Alice Morgan, had noticed tremendous improvements in him over their time together. She'd told him he didn't need to see her anymore, but he'd insisted, telling her it was the only way he felt he could unwind and be completely honest. She'd asked him about his current partner, who she learned was called Claire. She'd suggested opening up to her, but he'd said he struggles to fully let his guard down with a partner, because of how badly it ended with a previous relationship.

'Okay,' Byrd said, peeling his eyes away from the screen and picking up the mug.

'So?'

Byrd scanned over the document on his screen again. 'Why the eyes?'

'Huh?'

'Why take her eyes? Why leave that message — I don't understand this, Ori.'

'You and me both, Max,' said Tanzy, scratching his goatee.

'If they were going to kill her, why not just strangle her? Done and dusted. Why go to the trouble of taking out her eyes and handing them to Mary Richards on High Row in the middle of town?'

Following his trail of thought, Tanzy said, 'It's as if someone is showing off their skills, wanting to be appreciated for their work.'

'Or to appear they know what they're doing, as the pathologist stated. As if they're trained in some form of medical or surgical procedures.'

Tanzy pondered his partner's words for a moment. 'So, apart from the missing eyes, which appear to have been taken out meticulously, and the strangulation, there isn't anything to go on.'

'Not yet. The footprints were Ian Porter's; the prints matched the trainers he was wearing that night.'

'So, the people who did this were wearing overshoes?'

'Likely.'

'Seems a thorough job,' said Tanzy.

'Very thorough. Someone who knows what they're doing.'

'I'm going to chase up with PC Cornty about the cameras on Brinkburn Road.'

'I'm surprised he hasn't come back with them yet,' Byrd commented. 'He's normally quick.'

'I know,' Tanzy replied. 'I'll go see him now.'

'I need to go see Ian Porter. I still feel like there's something he's not telling us.'

Tanzy stood and walked away from the desk. 'I'll be back soon.'

'You're not going anywhere,' someone said behind them. Tanzy stopped and turned. Byrd swivelled on his chair, seeing DCI June Thornton standing at her open door.

'You're both going to Cemetery Lane, just off Carmel Road.'

'Why? What's happened?' Tanzy asked.

'A dead woman is hanging in a tree.'

33

Friday morning
Cemetery Lane

Byrd and Tanzy stepped out into the cold and closed their doors. They waited for a gap in the traffic on Carmel Road, then crossed over when it was safe to do so. A crowd had gathered up ahead, at the metal gate at the start of Cemetery Lane. Tanzy squeezed through the people and showed his ID to the PCs manning the gate. They moved aside and allowed the detectives through.

Byrd glanced back at the growing crowds, then turned to Tanzy. 'The smallest thing in this town gets everyone out, doesn't it?'

'It's an area that's been cordoned off. Most don't care, but some people, they need to know why. It's the same anywhere. People are nosy. People have got nothing better to do with their time.'

They walked on towards the white-suited forensics team ahead. Byrd clocked Jacob Tallow standing next to PC Kim Harrison. He had a large clear plastic bag in his gloved hands. Emily Hope was crouching down near a bush.

'Morning, Kim,' Byrd said. 'What do we have?'

'A couple of dog walkers found her.' Kim pointed to the cut that led to Netherby Rise, where a man and a woman were standing awkwardly on the narrow path with dogs sitting beside them. Beyond them, a police car was parked purposefully, blocking pedestrian access to the lane.

At one of the houses behind, a woman stepped out of the green door of a semi-detached house dressed in a dark red dressing gown to see what all the commotion was about. She glanced in the direction of the lane. It didn't take her long to scream and throw her hands up to her mouth.

The detectives diverted their attention back to Harrison.

'They found her hanging,' Harrison said, turning and pointing upwards.

Byrd and Tanzy followed her finger.

Tanzy swallowed. 'Jesus. It's Mary Richards.'

'It certainly looks like her,' she agreed.

'God.' Byrd winced.

'You don't seem fazed?' Tanzy said to Harrison.

'I was told last night.'

'What do you mean?' Byrd asked.

'Her husband, Stuart, called saying she'd gone missing — disappeared from the house just after seven. He heard her scream on the street then heard screeching tyres. He didn't see the vehicle. He mentioned her daughter had told him there was a man in her room. He went downstairs and Mary was gone. He found one of her shoes and drops of blood on the decking near the bin.'

'Why on earth are we just hearing about this now?' Byrd said, with a heavy frown.

Harrison stared blankly at him.

'Was there a report filed for this?' Tanzy asked.

'I think so.'

'Who filed the report?'

'DS Stockdale. He went to the address and took pictures of the blood. He knew to file the report afterwards. I'm sure he did. I spoke with him last night and he mentioned he'd been over there. He said one of her shoes was left by the back door with the words "She didn't see it coming" written on it.'

Byrd frowned. 'The same message left for Ian Porter when he discovered his wife.'

Harrison nodded.

'And this was Stockdale?'

'Yeah.'

'How did he file it? Manually or through the new way?'

She offered a hopeless shrug. 'I don't know . . .'

'God's sake!' Tanzy glared up at the sky and clamped his eyes shut for a second. 'He'll have done it the old way. That's why we weren't notified.' He glanced at Byrd, then his eyes fell on Harrison. 'That's why the auto-filing system came in. So everyone knew what was going on.'

'DS Stockdale's just transferred over, though. Maybe he didn't know?'

'It's the basics, Kim,' Byrd replied, disappointed.

'Who attended the scene with Stockdale?' Tanzy asked.

PC Harrison narrowed her eyes, in deep thought. 'PC Cornty, I think DS Stockdale said.'

A look of disgust swept across Tanzy's face. 'Cornty? Why on earth hasn't he mentioned it to me?' Tanzy was raising his voice now. 'Where is he?'

'He's not here yet.'

Tanzy shook his head several times. Byrd scowled up into the tree. Mary Richards was wearing a black blouse with smart grey trousers. Her face was ghostly white, the colour of a porcelain doll. The blood would have settled in the lower half of her body when her heart stopped beating. The ambient frost wasn't helping her complexion either.

Byrd frowned. 'Where's her hand?'

'It's on the ground, in the bush where Hope is.'

'What the hell is going on in this town?' Byrd muttered to himself.

'Never a dull day in Darlington,' said Tanzy.

Both detectives drew closer, minding their footing on the muddy, slippery ground below. The smell of damp trees and mud hung in the air.

'Morning, Jacob,' said Byrd, rubbing his hands together. 'Cold one.'

'Morning, Max.' Tallow nodded towards Tanzy but said nothing, who returned the gesture in the same manner. Whenever there was a crime scene, and Jacob Tallow was involved, usually Byrd did the talking. Tanzy and Tallow had a falling out a few years back. Although both sides had apologised for their argument, tension still lingered between them.

'Where's McCabe?' Tanzy asked him.

'Said he's tied up somewhere. He'll be here soon with Paul and Amanda.'

'How long do you think she's been up there?' Byrd asked.

'My guess is as good as yours, Max.' He half turned, glaring up at the hanging dead woman. 'We'll know more when the coroner turns up.'

'Has Peter been contacted?' asked Byrd, grabbing Tallow's attention.

'He has. I made the call earlier. He said he also has a few ends to tie up, then he'll be heading straight over.'

Peter Gibbs was the lead coroner for the Durham and Darlington Coroner's office, which was based at Durham Miner's Hall. It would take thirty minutes to travel straight from the Durham office to Darlington on a good day with no traffic disruptions, so Byrd and Tanzy guessed it would be at least forty-five minutes before he turned up.

Peter had files on every death that had been recorded in the district of Darlington for the past one hundred years. For every crime scene which involved a death, Peter tried to attend and worked with forensic investigators to establish the cause of death. If the analysis suggested the death wasn't crime-related, then he would allow law enforcement to leave the scene. Obviously, in this case, a woman hanging from a tree with her hand missing would strongly suggest a crime had been committed.

'Has the fire department been contacted?' Tanzy said. Starting to feel the cold, he placed his hands deep into the pockets of his long grey coat.

'Yes, I've called them. They're on their way,' Tallow confirmed.

The fire department would have the necessary tools and equipment to access the body of Mary Richards, which, Tanzy judged, was at least fifteen feet in the air, or nine or ten feet above their heads.

'How on earth did she get up there?' Byrd whispered.

Tanzy shrugged. 'Beats me. Let's go see Hope, see how she's getting on.'

'Don't go too close,' Tallow said, 'there's blood on the ground near the bush. Don't want you contaminating it, Orion.'

Tanzy half-smiled and took a few steps before they came to a halt. They craned their necks and looked up at the woman hanging directly above them. Mary Richards was missing a shoe. Tallow moved away from them towards Hope, who stood up carefully from a crouching position, then backed away from the bush, holding the severed hand carefully in her right glove.

She placed it inside a clear plastic bag, which she sealed. The detectives stood about four metres from her and decided to give her some space.

'How did this happen, Max?' Tanzy said quietly in Byrd's ear.

In silence, Byrd digested the scene in front of him.

The tree.

The rope.

And Mary Richards.

A chill ran through him as he watched her motionless, white face. Her cold, still eyes stared off to the left. The rope wrapped around her neck went in a vertical direction up to a thick branch of what looked like an English oak tree, then around the branch, running down the opposite side at an angle, securely wrapped at the base of the next tree.

'It points to several people, surely,' Byrd commented. 'One person couldn't have done this by themselves.'

Tanzy nodded firmly. 'Yeah . . . to throw the rope over, tie her up and pull down on the other side. It's the work of three or four in my opinion.'

'Maybe more. To have the strength to pull her up is impressive.'

Somewhere in the distance, the approaching siren of a fire engine rippled in the air. Turning towards the noise, they watched a truck pull up behind them and slow down, the brakes hissing as the large red machine came to a halt. The doors opened and out stepped four cautious firefighters, who frowned as they looked over. Byrd noticed their gazes fall on the woman in the tree and was sure one of them said 'Jesus Christ' before turning and saying something to another fireman.

'Hey, Emily,' Tanzy said.

Byrd rolled his eyes, remembering Tanzy once mentioned he found her very attractive. He adored her tattoos. She had a sleeve on her right arm and a half-sleeve on her left.

'Hey, Ori. How are you doing?' Her blue eyes pierced through her stylish square, black-framed glasses.

'What are your first thoughts?'

'The cut to the hand is interesting.'

'Interesting how?' asked Byrd.

'A very sharp tool has been used here.'

'A surgical tool?'

She bobbed her head confidently, then glanced to her right when Tallow appeared. 'A surgical tool, similar to the one from Brinkburn Drive where Julia Porter's body was found.' She paused for a moment, then added, 'And a very, very steady hand. Pardon the pun.'

34

Tina Ching entered her bedroom and stopped in the doorway. She looked at her bed and remembered their new cleaner, Lena, standing there the day before.

She went to the same spot she'd seen Lena and stopped. For a few seconds, she felt silly, not really knowing what she was looking for, but there must have been a reason Lena was there. Something that she was interested in. Or had she really been going to clean the bedside drawers?

All that was on her husband's bedside unit was his electronic alarm clock, his hairbrush, a pack of mints and the thin charging point for his phone.

'Weird.'

Tina ran her finger along the surface, then lifted it to her face and noticed there was no dust whatsoever.

Or was it something inside the drawer Lena was interested in?

She felt bad doing it, but she bent down and opened it, then looked inside. There was more in there than she'd imagined. Money. Receipts. Chewing gum. Batteries. An old phone that she was sure he hadn't touched since 2016. God knows why he kept it, she thought. A diary from last year which looked brand new and unused. She lifted a few of the items out, so she could see the hidden objects underneath.

A notepad, a few pens.

Four bookmarks and a small paperback that she hadn't seen him read in months: *CSI: Real Stories*.

She plucked the phone from her jeans and called his number. Within five rings, he picked up.

'Hey,' she said. '. . . Yeah, I'm fine. Listen, something is playing on my mind. It's . . . well, you know the cleaner, Lena? Well, she's . . . Yes, I know she is but she . . . Okay, it doesn't matter . . . I know, I understand. I'll tell you later. Speak then.'

She dropped the phone on the bed, disheartened by his dismissal. He'd told her he was busy and that he didn't have time to speak with her.

Then she started thinking about Lena. Lena . . . what was her second name? She sat up, frowning.

'Keeton,' she whispered, remembering Lena had told her in the first week.

She grabbed her phone, unlocked it and opened up social media. She typed in the name Lena Keeton and pressed ENTER. A long list of profiles came up, all with various unique profile pictures. Some colourful, others dull. Some smiles, others miserable.

Meticulously, she scrolled down the list searching for the familiar face.

But she didn't see it.

After opening up another social app, she tried once more.

Again, nothing.

'Weird.'

Everyone and their dog was on social media nowadays, weren't they?

It was as if Lena Keeton didn't exist.

35

The man behind the desk looked up and smiled at Byrd. 'Can I help you?'

'Here to see my parents. Alan and Jackie Byrd, please.'

'Of course.' The man glanced down, focused on his computer screen and moved the mouse. 'Go straight through.'

Byrd was taken aback. 'Thank you.'

Byrd left reception and made his way into the dim corridor. It was unusually quiet in the department today. On previous visits, he'd heard murmurs coming from open office doors or idle chatter from the small canteen towards the left.

But today, there was nothing.

At the end of the corridor, on the wall in front of him, his eyes fell on a large poster. *Struggling with the loss of a loved one?*

Not yet, he hoped. Not yet.

Reaching his mother and father's room, he paused and courteously knocked twice before pushing down the handle and edging it open.

The room was fairly dark and cool. The blind to the left was halfway down, and he had a good view of the busy car

138

park. The window was open a few inches to allow air to circulate. The beeping of the machines quietly filled the room as he stopped at the foot of their beds.

Watching the wires and tubes linked to his parents, he couldn't help but feel sad. Seeing the people who'd brought him into this world and who'd looked after him in such a vulnerable state was truly a horrible experience.

He had a strange feeling. As if he wasn't alone. He glanced to his right.

Jan, the nurse, was watching him.

'Jesus,' he gasped, throwing his hand to his chest. 'You scared me.'

'Sorry,' she said, sitting on the chair in the near corner, one leg over the other. There was a pen in one hand and a clipboard in the other. 'How are you doing, Mr Byrd?'

When his heart rate lowered, he managed a nod. 'I'm okay.' He pointed towards the beds. 'How are they doing?'

'Sorry . . . no change yet, I'm afraid.'

Byrd nodded at her then focused back on his parents. 'From your experience, what do you think?'

Pondering his question, she sat in silence for a moment.

Byrd recognised her hesitation. 'Just your opinion, that's all. Nothing official.'

'I can't say, I've been told—'

'Please,' he begged in desperation. 'I need to know. I need to know what you think.'

She mulled over his anxious words, then nodded. 'Okay . . . in my opinion, and from my experience with older patients in comas, the chances of them waking up are slim. But time will tell.'

Her words crushed him internally. He felt tears well up in his eyes. He focused back on the beds, the sound of the beeping machine suddenly magnifying in his own mind.

'I'm sorry, I'm being—'

'It's okay,' he said, without looking at her. 'I asked for your honesty and that's what you gave me. I'd rather know the truth.' He took a step back towards the door. 'I'll pop back tomorrow. Let me know if there are any changes.'

She smiled sadly and nodded. 'Of course.'

* * *

After Byrd had left, Jan stood and placed the clipboard back in its holder on his father's bed, then waited for a few seconds. When she heard nothing but silence, she popped her head out into the corridor and saw that the coast was clear. She stepped out of the room and closed the door.

She felt sorry for Byrd. She could see the pain in his eyes when she spoke to him, as if he'd experienced a loss in the past and was readying himself, but hoping that he'd never have to go through it again.

It was lunchtime. She made for the canteen. As she passed Dr Ching's door, she knocked to see if he wanted anything from the canteen.

No answer.

She leaned into it and listened, but no sounds were coming from inside.

She knocked twice, then edged the door open.

Dr Ching was standing on the far side of his office, in front of the cupboard. He was leaning over a black case placed on the worktop. As the door opened, he slammed the lid of the small case closed, but there was enough time for Jan to see what was inside.

Surgical instruments.

'Jan! How . . . how can I help you?' he stuttered.

She frowned at him for a second and wondered why he was acting so strange. She asked, 'I'm heading out for dinner. Is there anything I can get for you?'

He shook his head quickly and dismissed her.

36

Byrd was sitting in his warm car with the heaters blowing. The sun had yet to come out and the afternoon was bleak and depressing. He pressed a few buttons on his phone, put it to his ear and listened to it ring as he stared out onto the dark street.

'Cornty,' he said when it was answered. 'I need to ask you a question.'

'Go on,' said Cornty.

'Did you check for cameras on Brinkburn Road when Julia Porter went missing? Tanzy told me he'd asked you?'

'Yeah,' he said. 'I had a look. I checked the council's CCTV and there were no matches in that area. I checked outside the perimeter as well. Near Cockerton, West Park and back into town. But there was no sign of the van. Sorry, I thought I'd told him.'

'Okay. Thanks for letting me know.'

'Speak soon,' the PC said before disconnecting.

Byrd sighed heavily and put the phone back into his coat pocket. He watched Ian Porter's house for a few moments.

The silver Astra was parked directly in front of it, reminding him the Qashqai was missing, still being analysed by the police.

Upstairs, a dim light shone through the open blinds of the large bay window, which Byrd assumed was Porter's bedroom. There was a light in the living room but it wasn't bright, probably coming from a lamp.

He pulled the key from the ignition and stepped out into the late afternoon chill.

He knocked at the front door and heard a muffled voice. Through the glass, he watched a figure approach. The lock clicked, the handle came down and the door slowly opened.

'Detective?' Ian Porter said. 'How . . . how can I help?'

'May I come in, Mr Porter?'

'Yeah, come in.' Porter moved back a little, allowing Byrd space to enter.

'Thanks.'

'Can I offer you a coffee? I've just boiled the kettle.'

'Yes, please.'

'Sugar?'

'I used to, but not anymore. Just milk, please.'

Byrd followed Ian Porter down the short hallway into the kitchen. On his left, he passed the room where Julia Porter's dead body was found two days ago. He remembered the scene so vividly: tied up naked to the chair, her eyes missing, the pool of blood beneath her.

He shuddered at the sickening thought.

'How've you been, Ian?'

Porter flicked on the kettle and turned to Byrd. 'It's been hard. The kids are struggling to come to terms with it.'

'I can imagine. It must be extremely difficult for you all. *Where* are the children?'

'Upstairs. I'm just about to make them something to eat.' He bent down and pulled some chips and chicken nuggets from the freezer and put them onto a metal tray. He looked sheepish. 'I never was a great cook.'

Byrd could hear the genuine sadness in his tone. 'Don't mind if I sit, do you?'

Porter turned. 'Not at all.'

Byrd dropped his weight onto one of the high chairs at the worktop.

'What is it I can help you with, Detective?'

'We have the post-mortem results back for Julia. I thought I'd speak to you in person about it.' Byrd noticed Porter freeze half a second after absorbing the news.

'I see.' He closed the oven door and faced Byrd with glassy eyes. 'What happened to her?'

'She was strangled. I'm sorry.'

'What . . . what about the eyes? How did that happen?'

'It appears they were removed using a sharp surgical tool.'

Porter digested his words in silence, then asked, 'Like a doctor's tool?'

Byrd nodded. 'We believe so, yes. We're trying to determine the registration plate of the van but, so far, have struggled to pick it up on the town's CCTV system.'

A thought came to Porter's mind.

'What is it, Ian?'

'Next door,' he said, frowning. 'The lady next door. She has a camera above her driveway. Maybe that picked it up?'

37

Tanzy passed through the automatic doors of Darlington Town Hall and stopped at the counter, where his eyes fell on the dark-haired receptionist sitting behind it. After she finished what she was eating, which looked to be a chicken sandwich, she glanced up over the top of her square-rimmed glasses.

'Can I help you?' she asked.

'You can,' Tanzy started. 'Could I please see Jennifer Lucas? She works in the—'

'Control room?'

Tanzy smiled and nodded.

'I'll see what I can do,' she said, picking up the phone quickly.

'Thanks.'

To the right, there was an open area in front of two lifts which took up the space of the back wall. In front of the right one, a woman stood with an impatient child, who was tapping the elevator call button. Tanzy grinned. His own son, Eric, used to do the same thing at that age.

'Go straight up, she's on the first floor,' the woman behind the desk said. 'Take the lift or the stairs. Follow the signs.'

'Thank you for your help,' Tanzy said, stepping away.

At the lift, Tanzy stopped next to the woman and the little boy. She was telling him to stop being silly as he hit the button for the umpteenth time. She turned to Tanzy and gave him a quick smile.

Tanzy returned the gesture, then glanced down at the kid, who looked up at him mischievously. Half of his small face hid behind his mother. It wasn't long before there was a 'ding' sound and the lift doors opened.

They stepped inside.

The little boy pressed the button for the first floor, then floor two and finally floor three.

'Stop it, Jackson.' She gently grabbed him and pulled him back, then looked at Tanzy. 'Sorry about that. What floor are you going to?'

'First floor,' he said. He could see her cheeks warming in embarrassment.

'Good job,' she sighed.

'Mine did the same at that age. Don't worry about it.' There was a pause. 'Nice name,' Tanzy added.

'I'm sorry?' the woman said, curling a few strands of her behind her ear.

'Your son's name? Jackson?'

'Right, yeah,' she said, now understanding.

'I don't know many Jacksons,' Tanzy said.

'Different, isn't it?'

'It is.'

The lift doors finally closed and the lift started to move upwards.

'I chose it. My husband is useless.' She laughed, then diverted her attention away from Tanzy back to Jackson, who had pressed another button. The lift stopped on the first floor and the metal doors pinged open. He held out his palm towards them, indicating for them to go first.

'Not only good-looking, but manners too?' she said, stepping out with Jackson.

Tanzy smiled at her and stepped out too. 'Have a good day. Be a good boy for your mummy, Jackson.'

'Bye, man,' replied Jackson, smiling mischievously.

Down the wide corridor, the dark grey carpet felt soft underfoot and a faint smell of fresh paint lingered on the high, white walls.

At the door marked 'Control Room', Tanzy knocked twice and opened it. The room was darker than the hallway. A haze of light came from the left side of the room. At the small desk in the centre of it, a woman sat facing the monitor. She'd heard Tanzy enter and turned her head towards him, then smiled widely.

His heart melted.

It was the first time he'd visited the control room and only the second time he'd ever seen her. All other contact had been done through emails or over the phone.

'Hi, Orion,' she said, softly.

In front of her were three rows of screens, eight screens on each row, each picture impressive in vivid colour. The light coming from the screens gave her face a gentle glow as she peered at him with the nicest eyes he'd ever seen.

'Hi, Jennifer. How are you doing?'

Tanzy stopped near the desk and smiled. He didn't know if it was the mild glare from the CCTV screens, but he couldn't stop staring at her face. She was beautiful.

'I'll be better in forty-five minutes when I finish,' she replied.

'Going out in town?'

'I am, actually,' she said. 'I have a date tonight.'

Although Tanzy was married, he felt a little stab in the heart. 'Oh?'

'See what happens, though. It's only a date. Some pizza, maybe a movie, a few drinks.' Her eyes drifted away, and she focused back on the screens. At the far side of the room, a lady entered through a door and asked her if she would like a coffee. Jennifer nodded at her then turned to Tanzy. 'You want one?'

'Please. Coffee. Just milk, no sugar,' Tanzy told the short, stumpy woman, who turned and disappeared back through the door.

'So, Mr Tanzy. How can I be of service?'

He had a hundred answers to that question but said, 'I need to see a few cameras, please. You remember the footage you sent over from the camera on High Row?'

'Yes?'

'Well, I found something. But I need to see more. I need to see other angles.'

'Sure.' She stood up and told Tanzy to come over to the large control panel directly in front of the twenty-four screens. He followed and dropped down into the seat next to her. 'So, if I remember correctly . . .' She typed in the date of when Mary Richards was handed the small Greggs bag. 'This should be it. What time was it again?'

'Around 10 a.m. If you could find the same camera angle that you sent me, and I'll check if I can see him first, then we can go from there.'

She clicked the mouse on the desk and tapped away on the keyboard. 'Here, watch that screen.'

They both looked up, watching the familiar scene in frowned concentration. It took Tanzy seconds to spot the man in the black fleece.

'You see this man?' Tanzy said, pointing at the screen.

'Yeah?'

'I need to know where he goes. Stay on this angle until he goes out of shot.'

For the next four minutes, the man remained on the bench, until he got up and walked north.

'Can you get the next camera?'

'Sure.'

The smell of her perfume pleasantly hit Tanzy's senses. He took a long, slow breath.

'What?' she said.

147

'Huh?'

'You sniffed?'

'Did I?' His cheeks started to warm.

'Do I smell?'

'No, not at all.'

She focused back on the screens.

The next camera that came up was near Barclays Bank. It clocked the man turning up a narrow alley, which Tanzy knew led to the car park behind High Row.

'He went down the alley. Have you got access to cameras in the car park?'

'Sure.'

The door to their right opened and the short woman came over with two coffees and placed them down on the desk where they were seated. 'There you go.'

'Thank you,' said Tanzy, smiling at her.

'No problem.' She turned and walked away, then stopped. 'Oh, Jennifer . . .'

Jennifer craned her neck in her direction.

'Leave on time today, please. There are no gold medals for stopping back.'

They both smiled at each other.

'What was that about?' Tanzy asked, picking up his coffee and taking a sip.

'I often work late,' she explained. 'I don't get paid any extra.' She paused for a moment, unsure about her words. 'I enjoy my job.'

'Isn't a bad thing, I suppose. Enjoying your job.'

She smiled at him and then focused on what she was doing. 'So . . . yes, here.'

On one of the screens, an image of the car park came up, showing a shot of the opening of the alleyway that the man had disappeared down.

Tanzy leaned forward an inch, squinting. 'There he is.'

On the screen, the man paced casually out of the alley into Abbott's Yard car park with his hands in his pockets. Passing a couple going the opposite direction, he angled

148

right towards the first row of cars and walked out of camera shot.

'Where'd he go?' Tanzy asked.

'I'll find the next one, hold on.' She moved the mouse and tapped away again. Next to her, Tanzy nervously rocked his right leg side to side as he waited impatiently.

'Shit,' she said.

'What is it?'

'The next feed is missing. I can't seem to—'

'Where's the one after?'

'Hold on,' she muttered. Tanzy fell silent and observed Jennifer working her magic. It wasn't long before she told him there were three exits to the car park, which he roughly knew anyway.

The camera on Skinnergate picked up the small road that vehicles used to leave the car park by the side of Tanner's pub. And the camera on Bondgate covered the two alleyway entrances, one where the vehicles went in, the other used by pedestrians.

'Right . . .' she said, changing the screens in front of them.

'You see him yet?'

'Not yet,' she replied.

The camera on Skinnergate picked up twenty-seven cars leaving the car park with a time frame of twenty minutes. The driver of each car could be seen clearly on the camera, but none of them matched the profile of the man they were looking for. Jennifer changed the angle and picked up the camera on Bondgate. After she scrolled along the time bar to the time they needed, she resumed it.

Another twenty minutes passed.

'I don't understand,' she said, sounding defeated.

'What? What is it?' he asked, frowning.

'It's weird.'

'What is?'

'I can't find him at all. It's as if he's just vanished into thin air.'

38

Friday, early evening
Brinkburn Drive

Through the obscured glass of the white front door belonging to the house next to Ian Porter's, Byrd saw a dim light at the end of the hallway. The light became brighter, and suddenly a small figure appeared then moved towards the door.

'She's coming,' Byrd said back to Ian Porter, who was standing on the block-paved driveway to his left.

There was the deadlock snapping open.

'Can . . . can I help you?' she asked, peering out nervously, chain still on the door.

Byrd, aware that Porter had used the word 'old' when describing his neighbour minutes before, would guess she was between seventy-five and eighty. Her frail, tiny figure was wrapped in a thick black bathrobe which looked far too big for her.

Byrd firstly apologised for interrupting her, then introduced himself. When she frowned in confusion, he reassured her there was nothing to worry about, then stepped back and pointed up to the camera positioned above the garage.

'Does that camera work?'

'The camera?'

'Yeah.'

'What is this about, Detective Burg?'

'It's Byrd,' he said, correcting her.

'Sorry, my hearing isn't what it used to be.'

He gave a sympathetic smile, briefly remembering what his own mother could be like at times.

'The camera works, I'm sure,' she went on. 'But I don't know how to use it. My son set it up for me a while ago. Six months maybe. Could have been a year. We had some not very nice people coming around and trying to rip people off.' Byrd could see her mechanical cogs turning, trying to think. 'There were a few break-ins too, and he said it needed to be a safe place for me, so if anything happened, then I'd have footage to send to the police. He did something with my computer, so it's able to record it. I don't know how to do it.' There was a lost look in her eyes.

'It's always a good idea,' Byrd agreed with a nod. 'Can never be too careful. Would it be possible to see the footage? Potentially it could help us with what happened to Ian's wife, Julia. Maybe the camera picked up something that could help us with our inquiry.'

'Oh, just awful, Ian,' she bellowed and switched her focus on him. 'I'm so sorry for your loss. If there's anything I can do . . .'

Porter half smiled at the common yet courteous line which was used when someone lost a loved one. Whether they meant it was a different matter. He glanced down at the floor as his eyes filled up.

'Come in, Detective Burg.' She moved aside, letting them both into the warmth of the house. Byrd stepped in, not bothering to correct her this time about his name, feeling the heat coming off the radiators. The heating had probably been on all day.

Byrd loosened the buttons on his coat and pulled the zip down to allow some air to enter. Further down the hallway, it smelled of lavender.

'Where's your computer?' Byrd asked, following her slow, measured steps.

'Follow me.'

They passed the living room and took a right into the dining room.

In the corner, beside a tall lamp, positioned on an old-fashioned brown desk, was a flat-screen computer. Byrd could tell it was dated and hadn't been used in a while. The lady pulled the desk chair out and slowly lowered into it, wincing as if in pain.

'Right, how do I do this?' she asked no one in particular, trying to find the ON button.

Byrd rolled his eyes. This could be a lost cause.

If she couldn't turn it on, what chance did they have of finding the footage from a specific time two nights ago? He stayed positive regardless and smiled patiently at her.

'How do I—'

Byrd leaned forward and pushed the ON button. 'There you go . . .'

'Oh, thank you. I've never been any good with these things,' she said. The sound of the computer starting up was like an ancient plane coming out of a rusty old air hanger after spending years collecting dust.

Byrd, standing directly behind her, looked to the left, noticing Porter had taken a seat on the small fabric sofa. He seemed to be staring at something in the other corner, which Byrd mentally noted could be the set of framed photographs he'd noticed when he first entered the room. He was continuously scanning and observing, taking note all the time of everything around him. He rarely missed much.

Against the wall next to him was a sofa facing the fireplace. In the left corner, a plant looked like it needed a hefty dose of water. A set of white French doors were positioned on the left wall, but Byrd saw very little through them because of the early sunset, leaving it dark outside.

Next to the computer, there was a small box with a wire dangling from the rear of it that draped behind the desk.

'If it's not turned on, can it record?' Porter asked, showing a similar level of doubt that Byrd had.

She sighed hopelessly. 'I think . . . you see this black box?'

Byrd and Porter focused on it. 'My son said that even if the computer is turned off, it still records and collects the pictures. Or something.' She frowned, unable to provide a solid explanation. Byrd nodded, knowing that was possible.

The computer screen turned blue for a moment before the desktop background image appeared. It was a stock image of a yellow flower on the bank of a shallow river.

A folder named 'Camera' was located at the top of the screen. She used the mouse to slowly navigate over to the folder and clicked more times than she needed to. 'I think this is it,' she said to Byrd.

Through the door, a pleasant smell seeped in from the oven in the kitchen.

'Ooo, excuse me you two,' she said, standing up. 'I'm baking cakes. I have family coming over tomorrow. Do you mind if I go and take them out? I don't want to burn them.'

'You do your thing,' Byrd replied, waving her off.

She shuffled across the soft carpet and left the room. The camera folder, after a lengthy wait, finally opened. Nearly seven months of files were saved inside the folder. Almost two hundred items. Luckily, each file name was dated, so Byrd right-clicked and sorted the files into date order to make things easier for himself. After the reshuffle, the file they were looking for was second from the top, and he assumed each day covered from midnight to midnight.

Byrd clicked. The media player opened and the time in the corner showed 00:00.

'Ian, what time did you go out?'

'Julia called me at quarter to one. I left around one,' Porter informed him. Byrd skipped an hour and let it play at 1.02 a.m. It wasn't long before he saw the Astra drive past two minutes later. By this time, the elderly lady had returned with three cups of coffee and a plate of biscuits and placed them on a low-level table near Porter's knee.

Byrd, trying to distract himself from the smell of much-needed coffee, recalled how long Porter had told him he had been unconscious under the bridge. He scrolled the time bar forward to 1.20 a.m.

Logically thinking, if the van came from the right, he'd see it immediately. However, if it came from the left, then it would take longer as they'd be at the Porters' house for a while with Julia before they left.

At 1.46 a.m., the white van slowly moved across the screen, so Byrd used the mouse to scroll the time bar back and then paused it. He leaned forward, squinting. Light from a nearby streetlight gave him a perfect view of the registration plate.

'Bingo!'

'What is it?' Porter asked, tensing.

'I have the plate,' Byrd told him. 'Can just see it from that angle.' Porter placed his coffee down on the table and leaned in, following Byrd's finger, then nodded. 'I'll run it through the system.'

Byrd plucked his phone from the inside pocket of his coat, tapped a few buttons and put it to his ear. It wasn't long before it was answered.

'I need a check on a plate.'

'Sure. Reg?'

Byrd told the operator.

'Okay, I'll check now. Bear with me.'

'No problem.' Byrd squeezed his tired eyes shut for a second. The past few days had taken their toll on him.

Moments later, the operator said, 'You there?'

'I'm here. Go ahead.'

'It's registered to a self-drive hire place on Whessoe Road in Darlington.'

39

DI Orion Tanzy sat at his desk facing his computer screen and jumped when his phone rang in his pocket. Earlier, he'd asked Jennifer Lucas at the Town Hall if she could email him the footage they'd analysed earlier so he could check it again. He knew she was very competent at her job, but maybe, if he double-checked, something might stand out that she'd missed.

He edged forward, pulled his ringing phone from his trousers, and answered it. 'Max?'

'Ori, I've got a plate from the van that took Julia Porter.'

'What? How?'

'Old dear next door to Ian Porter had a camera fixed above her garage,' Byrd said. 'Was just at her place. I got a plate.'

'You ran it?'

'Yeah. It turns out it's registered to a self-drive place on Whessoe Road.'

'I know it,' Tanzy replied. 'You checking it out?'

'I'm there now. It seems like it's just closing, so I'll catch them before it does. What's happening on your end, Ori?'

Tanzy sighed heavily. 'Two things, Max. One, I have the footage of the man in the black fleece on High Row. He goes into Abbott's Yard car park behind it, but there's no shot of him coming out on the other three cameras. He didn't drive out, nor did he walk out. We watched it for half an hour.'

'We?'

'Me and Jennifer, at the Town Hall.'

'How many exits are there?' Byrd asked quickly.

'There's four, Max. He came in through the alley-way into the car park and there are three others. One on Skinnergate and two on Bondgate.' Tanzy paused a beat. 'No sign of him.'

'Have you got the full half an hour for all four cameras?'

'Yeah . . . ?'

'You remember the surveillance training we did about seven years ago?' Byrd said.

'The one where there was that strange-looking tall fella sat in the back who kept taking his shoes off and itching his feet?'

Byrd smiled. 'Don't remind me.'

'I remember it. Why? Oh . . . I get you now. You mean check the first camera, right?'

'Yes, Ori, check the first camera. He's probably doubled back on himself. If he knows where the cameras were, he'd expect us to check the three exits and disregard that one.'

Tanzy didn't think it was likely, but indeed possible.

'It's worth a shot,' added Byrd. 'What's the second thing?'

'The second thing is about the missing person's report from last night. The one Stuart Richards made about his wife, Mary. He made a call, told the operator that he thought his wife had been taken. There were drops of blood on the path by the side of his house.'

'Okay?'

'I originally thought it hadn't been entered on the system correctly and entered the old manual way, so that's why we weren't informed about it.'

'Yes, we know this, Ori. What are you getting at?'

'Turns out it wasn't even reported, Max . . .'

'What? How is that possible? Who went to the house?' He sighed heavily, then said, 'You spoke to Stockdale or Cornty yet?'

'Tried calling them — they're not picking up. I need to find them.'

'I'll go in here and see who hired the van two nights ago. See what comes back. If we get a name, we could be on to something here, Ori.'

'Ring me soon,' Tanzy said, then hung up. He placed his phone back into his trousers and stood, then made his way down the walkway in between the rows of desks, scanning the people that still remained. It was getting late in the day.

Often on a Friday people left a bit earlier to get a jump on the weekend. At the desk near the door, he stopped and glanced down at PC Amy Weaver, a young woman, typing away on her keyboard.

She noticed him out of the corner of her eye and stopped typing. She looked up at him over the top of her thin, narrow glasses. Short blonde hair dyed with a touch of silver sat on the top of a tanned face.

'Detective Tanzy,' she said with a smile. 'You okay?'

'Hey, Amy. Have you seen PC Cornty or DS Stockdale?'

'DS Stockdale has gone home. Cornty is in the canteen, or he was five minutes ago.'

'Okay, thanks.'

Tanzy picked up his pace, climbed the stairs, made his way down the corridor and, in less than a minute, entered the canteen. At the large circular table in the middle of the canteen, under the hanging light, PC Phillip Cornty was reading a book. He hadn't noticed Tanzy enter behind him.

'Cornty?'

He rocked his head upwards and glanced over his shoulder. 'Hey, boss.'

Tanzy, with a stern face, made his way over to the table, pulled out a chair next to him and sat down. 'Listen, I need a word.'

'Sure.' Cornty placed a long, green bookmark on the page he was reading and closed the book. He placed it down on the table and gave the detective his full attention. 'What's up, boss?'

Tanzy noticed the front cover of the book he was reading: *How to Deal with a Crime Scene: Forensics 101*.

'Interesting read?' asked Tanzy.

'It's quite informative,' Cornty said, his eyes peering over his geeky glasses.

'Good.' Tanzy composed himself. It was part of the job he didn't like. He hated questioning people and implying they'd done something wrong, but it was a part of his role. 'Why was the missing report of Mary Richards not put into the system correctly?'

Cornty frowned. 'I don't understand.'

'It's pretty simple, Phillip. Stuart Richards made a call last night to one of the operators, saying his wife had been taken and that there were drops of blood on the path outside his home. He also said he'd found her shoe. As you know, when we found her this morning at the crime scene, she still had the other shoe on her foot. I did some checks on the system. Originally, I thought that one of you had entered the report wrong on the system — manually processed it instead of doing it the new way. That's why I thought it was Stockdale first. I know you know how to do it properly because I trained you on it.'

Tanzy paused for a second, seeing the frown across Cornty's brows deepen.

He continued. 'Then I checked the file. It turns out that the report hadn't been entered either way. It wasn't on the system. That's how we didn't know she was even missing.'

'Wait a second. I have no idea what you're talking about.'

'You and Stockdale went to the Richards' house last night and spoke to Stuart, her husband. Then you reported him finding the shoe and blood. The question is why you didn't process the report correctly.'

'I didn't go to the Richards' house last night,' he said, still confused. 'I went home at six. I had things on.'

'What things did you have on?' He didn't like to question his team usually but needed to know the truth.

Cornty's cheeks flash a colour of red for a moment. 'I had a date.'

'A date?'

He nodded shyly.

'With whom?' pressed Tanzy.

'I really shouldn't be—'

'With whom?'

Cornty could sense his serious tone and straightened his face. 'I . . . I don't think I should—'

'Tell me!'

'Okay.' Cornty broke eye contact for a second then focused back on Tanzy. 'PC Amy Weaver, sir. I promised her I wouldn't say anything.'

Tanzy absorbed his words and said nothing. He knew Cornty was a little on the odd side and he'd worked with him a while now. His instinct told him that Cornty had been honest from day one.

'Why was I told that you went to the Richards' house?'

He offered a hopeless shrug. 'I don't know. Who told you this?'

'It doesn't matter, my mistake. Sorry to bother you.' Tanzy stood and walked away. 'Have a good weekend, Phillip. Stay out of trouble.'

'You got it, boss.'

In the corridor, Tanzy stopped halfway down when a thought entered his head. Why had he been told that Cornty attended the scene when he hadn't?

Back in the office, he saw PC Amy Weaver still sitting at her desk, typing away.

'Hey,' Tanzy said, stopping beside her. 'What did you get up to last night?'

'I went on a date,' she said without hesitation.

Tanzy nodded. 'Who with?'

'Cornty.'

'When was the last time you saw PC Kim Harrison? I need a word with her immediately.'

40

Byrd opened the door and stepped into the warmth of the small van hire office. The man behind the desk was folding several pieces of A4 paper, and when he saw Byrd, he stopped and glanced up. Beyond him, in a room out the back, was a man standing behind a smaller desk, with a phone pressed against his ear. Byrd couldn't hear the conversation but could tell something was bothering the man, judging by his frown.

'Sorry, sir, we're closed now,' the nearest man behind the desk said.

'I'm hoping you can help me?' Byrd smiled. 'I'm Detective Inspector Max Byrd.'

'What can I do for you?' The man placed the paper down on the desk and gave the detective his full attention. Byrd had years upon years of experience speaking to people. He knew that his manner would determine which way a situation would go. If you were asking for help, being rude did absolutely nothing, regardless if you were the police or not.

Byrd plucked his phone from his jacket pocket and found the registration plate of the van that he'd found from

160

the camera belonging to the elderly lady next door to Ian Porter. 'I need to find out who rented a van on Wednesday night.'

After the man heard what Byrd had to say, he frowned in thought.

'What's the matter?' Byrd asked, not understanding the man's response.

'That's the van that was stolen on Tuesday night. Have you guys not found it yet?'

'Stolen?' Byrd said, frowning.

'I made the call on Wednesday morning. Spoke to a woman down at the station. That van — the one you've just told me the registration of — was stolen sometime between us closing on Tuesday night at five and opening up on Wednesday morning at seven. When I turned up, there were four vans. Not five. I checked with Ronny —' he pointed behind him towards the small room, indicating the man on the phone — 'and another lad, Karl. But they said it hadn't been rented out. Someone was meant to be picking it up at eight o'clock Wednesday morning. Luckily, we had another van, so they took that one. It could have been very embarrassing for us otherwise.'

'I'm sorry. I wasn't aware of this. Unfortunately, I don't have an update on that. Whom did you speak to?'

'It was a woman. She was sent over an hour after I made the call.'

'Who was it? Can you remember?'

'A woman. I forgot her name. Mid-thirties. She took some notes, and she told me she'd keep me updated.'

41

DI Orion Tanzy walked back to his desk, sat down in the seat and sighed. He'd checked Kim Harrison's desk, the canteen, the locker room and the gym. Finally, he'd bumped into one of their colleagues, who'd told him she'd already left and wouldn't be back for at least a week. She'd booked time off work last-minute for an emergency.

The clock on the wall told him it was nearly five thirty. The office was quiet. There were a few people dotted around at their desks, tapping away on their keyboards. A lot of them were new recruits, Tanzy assumed.

There'd been three new DCs taken on over the past three months, a strategic plan from higher up to balance the teams and improve the overall statistics of this station in comparison to the ones in the area. Tanzy hadn't met them yet, but they'd soon finish their initial training and be paired up with experienced detectives.

He plucked the phone from his trousers and found Kim's number. As he was about to press the CALL button, the phone rang.

Byrd.

'Max, how did it go?' Tanzy asked. He leaned back on his chair and stared at the ceiling, then frowned when he noticed one of the polystyrene tiles was out of place, not quite sitting in its ridged slot.

'Ori, the van that took Julia Porter had been stolen,' Byrd replied.

'Say again?'

'I checked with the rental place. One of their vans — that specific van — was stolen sometime between Tuesday teatime and Wednesday morning.'

'Shit,' sighed Tanzy.

'Yeah.'

'What about cameras?'

'At the rental place?' Byrd asked.

'Yeah. Did they see anyone take the van?'

'No. I checked with them after he'd said it had been stolen. There were five vans. The camera fixed to the side of the building was looking down on them from the side. Unfortunately for us, it was the wrong side. The van that was stolen was parked on the end furthest away from the camera. I didn't even see anyone on the video.'

'Nothing of the driver?'

'No, nothing.' Byrd sighed through the phone. 'The guy said one of our PCs took a statement. Described her in her mid-thirties with blonde hair. I'm assuming that was Kim. I need to speak with her about it. I don't see why she wouldn't have filed the report.'

'Maybe she already has.'

'Maybe. I'll check.'

'I've been looking for PC Kim Harrison too. You know the issue with the missing person's report?'

'Yeah.'

Tanzy lowered his voice. 'Do you trust Cornty?'

'He's your guy, you know him more than I do,' Byrd said. 'You know me, I barely trust you, Ori. And I've known you for years.'

163

'On a serious note, though, Max. Do you trust him?'

'He's a little weird. But I do think he has potential. And apart from this job, I don't think there's much else going on in his life. My gut tells me I'd trust him.'

'Okay . . .'

'Why are you asking?'

'I asked him about filing the missing person report. When we were at the Mary Richards scene, do you remember PC Harrison telling us that Cornty and DS Stockdale had been to their house, then filed the report?'

'Yeah.'

'Well, she said that Stockdale had told her that he'd personally filed the report and that it was on the system. Turns out the report was never there. And guess what?'

'What, Ori?'

'According to Cornty, he was on a date with PC Amy Weaver. He didn't even go to the Richards' house. My conclusion is that one of them is lying, Max . . . and I'm struggling to decide which one.'

'What does Weaver say?'

'She says she was with Cornty.'

Byrd didn't respond.

'Max, you there?'

'I'm here, I'm here. I've just remembered something the guy in the rental place said: an hour after he made the call about the van being stolen, an officer came and took a statement. Said it was a woman in her mid-thirties, blonde hair.'

'Sounds like Harrison. I don't like how this is looking, Max.'

'I'll check if the report is there, Ori. After all, it might be and we haven't seen it.'

'Either way, I need to phone Harrison and ask her what's going on. PC Leonard told me she'd left because of a family emergency. Said she'd be away for at least a week.'

'You didn't know about this?' Byrd asked, confused.

'I didn't know about it, no,' Tanzy admitted, shaking his head. 'I should have known, she's in my team. Every leave request from my team is run through me first. You know how these work. It's the same in your squad.'

Byrd agreed.

'Unless with it being an emergency holiday, it went straight to Thornton. I don't know — it doesn't happen very often. That might be a possibility.' Tanzy sighed through the phone. Byrd could hear his frustration. 'I need to speak to both Thornton and Harrison,' Tanzy went on. 'Either way, I should have known about this.'

42

Friday evening
Police station

In the large ground-floor meeting room in the corner of the police station, nine people were seated waiting for DI Max Byrd to come back. Tanzy was at the front, standing with his back against the table and the door.

Minutes earlier, he'd been on the phone speaking with his wife, Pip, who was at home. She'd told him she was missing the kids and wanted them to come home. She promised Tanzy she'd start again and that without a doubt, she'd beat the six-month mark to get her badge from AA.

DCI June Thornton was seated to Tanzy's right, just near the window. Her face was blank, which was a sign she was impatient and irritable. She'd just come back to the station and said the traffic had been a nightmare.

At the table, PC Cornty and PC Weaver were talking quietly between themselves. Next to them were DS Stockdale, PC Josh Andrews, PC Anne Tiffin and some other DCs. A couple of them Tanzy didn't recognise — more new recruits. They were discussing their weekend plans. One of them was going to Blackpool on a stag do and had shocking plans for the stag. It would be a weekend he'd never forget. Apparently.

'Where's Byrd?' DCI Thornton asked Tanzy.

Tanzy glanced down at his watch, then over to her. 'He won't be long, boss.'

She nodded, said nothing more and looked away.

They heard shoes smacking on the hard floor outside, then a moment later, Byrd stepped through the door.

'Sorry I'm late,' he said, taking off his jacket. 'Traffic. Bloody nightmare.'

Tanzy handed Byrd the remote. 'All ready for you.'

Byrd took the remote like a baton and stepped back, turning to the large screen behind them. All eyes focused on it as silence filled the room. Everyone was keen to hear the update, not only because they were interested, but to get things wrapped up and get a start on the weekend.

'This won't take long,' Byrd began. 'But it's important we all keep up with what's going on.' He did a quick sweep around the room. At first, he hadn't noticed DCI June Thornton sitting over to the right. When their eyes met, he held his gaze for a second.

'Most of you are aware that Julia Porter and her baby son were kidnapped by at least two people in a van in the early hours of Wednesday morning. Her husband, Ian, was knocked unconscious under the bridge at the bottom of Whessoe Road, then forty-five minutes later, he woke up and headed home. He found his wife naked and tied to a chair in the dining room with her eyeballs missing. Baby was next to her, physically unharmed.'

He paused, allowing that information to sink in with those who weren't as familiar as the others.

'At first, Orion and I were thinking that Ian Porter was involved. However, as time has gone on, it's become clearer he wasn't. But I do need to be honest and say I believe he's not being one hundred per cent honest with us. He's acting—'

'How would you act if you found your wife dead in the house?'

Byrd glared over at PC Cornty, who was staring at him over the tip of his glasses.

'I'd be very upset, PC Cornty. Why do you ask?'

Byrd did well to remain calm.

PC Cornty always had an unusual way of communicating with people. Byrd put it down to being keen and having his say in group meetings. A way of standing out to his peers. He wanted his voice to be heard. If you spent longer than five minutes with Cornty, you'd know he was aiming for the top. So whenever there was a senior member of the department in his presence, this time DCI Thornton, he was likely to speak up.

'Maybe that's why he's acting strange?' Cornty replied.

'Maybe,' Byrd countered. 'From a camera positioned outside Porter's neighbour's house, I managed to take note of the registration of the van that Julia Porter was transported in. After speaking to the rental place on Whessoe Road where the plate was registered to, I was told that the van that transported Julia Porter to her house was stolen sometime between Tuesday teatime and Wednesday morning.'

'Did they have CCTV?' asked PC Amy Weaver.

Her date with Cornty must be rubbing off, Byrd thought.

'The camera wasn't angled to show anyone getting into the van. It's either bad security planning or the person who took the van knew how not to be seen.'

'Hold on a second,' DS Stockdale said, holding up his hand. 'If the van was stolen, did they not report it?'

The question hung in the room for a while. Both Tanzy and Byrd had discussed this less than an hour ago between themselves. The last thing either of them wanted to do was blame a member of their own department, especially a member of their own team. You looked after your own.

'There was no report of any stolen vehicles recorded,' Tanzy said, with a shrug.

'Actually, there was,' Byrd chirped in. The eyes in the room focused on him. 'I've just checked. Kim *had* reported the missing van. It seems, for whatever reason, no one has acted on that yet.'

Thornton slowly shook her head, not believing what she was hearing. 'We need to communicate better than this.' Silence swept the room. 'Where are we on the Mary Richards case?' Thornton then asked, moving on.

'If you haven't seen the update, we found the body of Mary Richards this morning hanging from a tree by a rope,' Byrd said. 'Her right hand was missing, and her left shoe was also missing. We had forensics at the scene — Tallow and Hope. The body has been sent for examination, under the request of an emergency priority. We're waiting to hear back on that one. I'll update—'

'Was hanging the cause of death?' Cornty asked.

'We're waiting on the post-mortem results.' Byrd's focus fell onto DS Stockdale. 'You want to enlighten the group about the situation regarding Mary Richards?'

'I went to the Richards' house last night,' Stockdale started. 'Her husband, Stuart, phoned, saying his wife went out to empty the bins and never came back inside. He heard her screaming and the sound of a vehicle driving away. There was a small pool of blood and a shoe by the side of the house. We took pictures and returned to the station.'

'Thank you, DS Stockdale, but—'

'Well something's gone wrong here,' DCI Thornton interrupted. 'I didn't see the report — where was it?'

'You didn't?'

'No. Where is it?'

Stockdale frowned, feeling the heat. 'I entered the report as usual.'

'Did you use our new system?' Tanzy asked.

Stockdale appeared more confused. 'New system?'

'Come on!' Thornton pleaded. 'We need to be better than this.' She turned to Tanzy. 'Orion, can you please educate your team on how we do things here.' She focused on Stockdale. 'I know you haven't been here long but you should know how we file the reports.'

'Apologies, Ma'am,' he said, looking away from her.

Byrd jumped in. 'Yesterday, if you have read the earlier update, you will know that Mary Richards and her daughter, Mia, were on High Row in town. They came out of Greggs and a man stopped them. He handed her a small Greggs packet and when they opened it, a pair of eyes fell out onto the ground. After DNA analysis, they were matched with Julia Porter. It seems there's an obvious link here.'

'Seems that way,' DCI Thornton commented. 'Let's get to the bottom of this. What's the latest on Evelyn Jones?'

'Evelyn's parents are doing another press conference tonight,' Tanzy said. 'I'm going to meet them later. I'm in touch with them daily. We decided it was time to release another one, raise the profile again. We haven't had much luck so far.'

Tanzy's watch told him it was approaching six. 'Right, that's the end of the meeting. I'll stay back and hand over to the other shift, let them know what I've just told you and see if we can make progress here. For the ones who've been kind enough to stick their hands up for overtime over the weekend, I'll see you in the morning. For those of you with a life outside of this place, have a good weekend.'

Most of them stood up and made their way to the door. Remaining in the room were Byrd, Tanzy and DCI Thornton.

'Before you two go,' Thornton said, 'let's have that update.'

43

'So explain to me,' said Thornton, 'how a kidnapping report didn't raise alarms with any of us. I checked myself: that report isn't on the system.'

Tanzy sighed lightly then glanced at Byrd.

'Don't look at Max,' she said. 'Go on, spill the beans. Don't be shy.'

'He must have entered it manually, and it hadn't come through. That's all I can think of.'

'Like I've said, we need to be better than this. Please educate Stockdale on how to do it properly.'

'Yes, Ma'am,' said Tanzy with a nod. 'When we saw Harrison this morning, I asked her specifically why Max and I weren't made aware of Mary Richards' disappearance. She'd said that Stockdale had returned to the station and filed the report. At first, I wondered if it was done manually and it hadn't been updated yet. I checked, like you, and found out that the report was never created, so he can't have completed it. So Harrison says Stockdale told her that he'd processed it. And he says she did it. One of them is lying.'

171

'Plus there's one other thing that we didn't share,' Byrd told her. 'That stolen van. There was no report filed, but the owner did report it. The attending officer was a blonde woman, short, glasses — he doesn't remember her name. Sounds a lot like Harrison. And now she's nowhere to be found.'

'Hmmm,' she said.

'What is it?' Byrd asked, leaning forward.

'She came to me earlier,' Thornton said. 'Told me she needed to take a week off — family emergency. You weren't on shift and it had come up suddenly, which is why she came to me. But I thought she'd sent you a message to let you know.'

Tanzy shook his head. 'No. At least she mentioned it to you. I'll give her a ring. It's obvious we need to speak to her about this.'

Tanzy found Harrison's number. 'Straight to voicemail,' he sighed.

'You need to get hold of her, Ori,' Thornton told him harshly.

'I'll go to her house. See if she's there.'

44

In the small room at the back of the house on the first floor, the man was slouched at his desk, staring down at the document in front of him.

He wiped away the last of his tears and breathed.

His wife, Grace, entered through the open door behind him.

'Hey,' she said quietly, fully aware of what he was looking at.

He sniffed and wiped his face with both palms, then propped himself up in the seat. 'Hey. You okay?'

She came up behind him, placed her arms loosely around his neck and gently kissed his cheek. He smiled, but his focus remained on the A4 document on the desk. For the next minute, they both concentrated on the words in front of them. His sadness was replaced by a burning desire for revenge.

'That's two down, Grace,' he said. 'Two to go.'

'How do you feel?' she asked, staring up at the items on the wall.

173

He followed her gaze. 'I'm feeling better. A little better each time. There's more work to do, though.'

'There is. I'm here till the very end.'

'They look good up there, don't they?'

Grace kissed him on the cheek and let go, slowly unwrapping herself from him. After her footsteps faded down the stairs, he picked up his phone.

He sat still for a moment, envisioning what would happen next with his eyes closed. Then he opened them and searched for a number, and once he'd found it, pressed CALL.

It was answered after four rings.

'Hey.'

'Hey,' said the man. 'How did it go with Mary Richards? I haven't seen the report yet.' Excitement filled his voice.

'Easy stuff,' the man on the phone said. 'Your pals were a big help and did everything I asked. We couldn't have done it without them. What's happening next?'

'I'll tell you tomorrow. I'm coming up with a plan. There's another two on the list.'

'It's unforgiveable what they did to her. They deserve all they fucking get.'

'I couldn't agree more.'

'Give me a call tomorrow and let me know what you want us to do.'

'Okay, speak soon.'

The man hung up the phone and placed it down next to the paper on his large, brown desk. He leaned back in his chair and glared at the wall behind his computer screen.

On the wall, there were two pictures. A4 sized. Full colour.

One was of Julia Porter. Tied to a chair, naked, blood running down her stomach. Her eyes were missing.

The other was of Mary Richards hanging from a tree. A rope wrapped tightly around her neck. Her right hand missing.

'Perfect,' he whispered.

He'd positioned them to the left side of the wall, leaving space for two more. Now he stood up and pushed the chair under the desk. He hit the switch on the wall and the room fell into darkness, then he plucked a key from his pocket and locked the door.

45

Tanzy sighed heavily at his desk, deep in thought. He knew he'd soon be doing the press conference with Evelyn Jones's parents and thought about what his answer would be when the reporters asked if the police had made any progress.

The answer was no.

But they didn't want to hear that — nobody ever did.

Most of the people who waited for the meeting had now gone home. DCI Thornton was finishing up some paper-work in her office behind him. Byrd had left.

He took a deep breath and logged off his computer. As the screen went black, he pushed himself out, stood up and put his long coat on. The office was warm. Heat blasted from the fans positioned high up on the wall behind him.

He pushed his chair in and left his desk.

Then he remembered something and stopped suddenly. He looked up at the ceiling directly above his desk. One of the ceiling tiles was slightly out of place, which was strange. He padded back a few steps until he was underneath it and glared up at it. It was too high to reach from floor level.

Deciding he couldn't leave it, he glanced around him and noticed a stool tucked under one of the vacant desks across the other side of the office. He remembered the maintenance man was in earlier, changing light bulbs, upgrading them. He recalled seeing something about energy-saving methods in one of the newsletters, not that he took the time to sit and actually read it. Usually, he'd tell the man not to leave his shit around, but in this case it had aided him, so he placed the stool directly under the dislodged tile and carefully stepped up.

Reaching up he pushed the tile upwards and placed it nicely back where it should be, so it sat flush with the rest of the ceiling.

Then he started to think. Why had it been like that?

He looked across the ceiling, and noticed the nearest light was three metres away. Could it have been something to do with the electrical wires that fed the lighting system?

Maybe.

But he hadn't seen any electricians in, only the maintenance man, Barry. Electrical work was carried out by qualified electricians. Not Barry.

He slowly pushed the tile upwards, moving it out of the way. He pulled his phone from his pocket, opened the camera app and made sure the flash function was switched on. He then reached up, placed his arm through the open space and took a picture. The flash lit the space in the ceiling for half a second, then he lowered the phone and had a look at the shot.

An empty void. At the back end, he saw the flat wall.

He tried again, but this time, turning ninety degrees. He pressed the button, then lowered to check it again. Nothing. He swivelled slightly on the stool, careful not to unbalance it, and was now one hundred degrees from where he took the first snap. He pressed the button and checked the screen again. On the picture in front of him, if he hadn't looked as carefully as he did, he would have missed it.

Something small. Black.

'What is that?' he whispered.

He reached up, pushing his hand through the gap, and felt around. There. Plastic. He pinched it deftly between his thumb and fingers then slowly lowered his hand back down.

Straight away, he knew what it was. He'd seen dozens of them.

It was a listening device with a built-in high-spec microphone, the type you'd hide somewhere so you could hear people talking if you didn't want them to know.

Somebody had been listening to them.

46

Tanzy jumped into his Golf and closed the door, then pulled the phone from his trousers and rang Byrd. The sky was full of rain and the car park was dark and nearly empty. The lack of cars gave Tanzy a clear view of a small group of teenagers hanging around the front entrance of the flats opposite, looking like they were up to no good.

'Hey, Ori,' answered Byrd.

'Listen,' Tanzy said quickly, 'I found something at the office.'

'What is it?'

'I found a bug, Max. In the ceiling above our desks.'

Tanzy turned the engine on and let it idle. The lights, which were set to automatic, flicked on and cut across the cold, shadowy car park with brilliant xenon-white beams.

'How on earth did you find that?'

'One of the tiles was dislodged above my desk. I stood on a chair and had a look. A little black bug, standard device.'

'God,' Byrd said. 'What have you done with it?'

'I've left it there,' he told him. 'I don't want whoever did it to know that we know. We need to watch what we do and say from now on.'

Byrd sighed heavily and said nothing.

'I've just left the office. I'm meeting Evelyn Jones's parents for the media appeal very soon. On my way, I'm going to Kim Harrison's house to see if she's there. I've tried ringing but she isn't answering.'

'Where on earth is she?' Byrd said, frustration clearly filling his voice.

'God knows. I'll get hold of her.'

'What time will you be on tonight?' Byrd asked, referring to the media appeal.

'It's the ten o'clock news, Max.'

'I'll stay up for it,' Byrd replied. He hadn't gone to bed earlier than 10 p.m. for at least a decade. 'Let me know what's happening with Harrison.'

'I'll keep you updated. Have a good night.'

'Speak soon.'

Tanzy slipped the phone back into his pocket. Across the road, he noticed the dodgy-looking youths had disappeared, so he put the car in first gear and rolled across the tarmac until he hit the exit, then pulled out, took a left and headed towards Yarm Road.

It took him less than four minutes to reach PC Kim Harrison's house. It was a semi-detached house on Neasham Road, set back from the road, giving the property the attribute of a little privacy and a long driveway. The front garden was big and square. Along the fence that separated the house from its neighbour, a plethora of flowers and plants stood tall and colourful in the streetlights.

Only one car sat on the drive. It wasn't Harrison's, which made Tanzy wonder if she was at home. Assuming the other car belonged to her husband, he thought it wouldn't cause any harm to ask him where she was. If Tanzy was being honest, he'd started to worry. She'd never gone so long without responding to phone calls or messages.

Tanzy switched off the engine and stepped out. The whistling wind chilled him as he rounded the bonnet of the Golf and made his way down the driveway until he reached the door. He knocked three times.

Through the glass, a figure came into view and gradually got bigger as it drew closer. The lock clicked and the door opened.

'Can I help you?' said the man, with a frown on his face. There was a tea towel wrapped over his right forearm and the smell of cooked chicken seeped down the hall.

'Jack?' Tanzy asked.

'Yes?' The neutral expression on his face was replaced by worry.

'Hi,' Tanzy said, extending his hand. 'I don't think I've had the pleasure of meeting you before. I'm Detective Inspector Orion Tanzy. I work with your wife, Kim. I don't see her car here but I'm wondering if she's at home. I need to speak with her. I've tried calling but she isn't picking up.'

'She isn't here, I'm afraid. Not yet, anyway,' Jack said.

'Not yet?'

'No. She hasn't come in from work yet. I figured she was staying back to work overtime.'

Confusion enveloped Tanzy. He narrowed his eyes. 'Are you sure? She left a little while ago.' It must have been about three hours since Harrison had left the station.

'I'd know if she was here, Detective.'

'I see.' Tanzy thought for a moment. 'When was the last time you spoke to Kim, or had any contact with her?'

'She rang me around four, I think.' He tipped his head, squinting. 'Yeah, it was around four. She told me there was an issue at work. She wasn't sure how to handle it.'

'What was the issue?'

'She didn't get into it. She just said that it could get complicated. That she didn't fully trust one of her colleagues. At the time, I had the TV on watching a football game I'd recorded earlier in the week, so I wasn't really listening to her.'

'Could you do me a favour, please?' Tanzy asked. The man gave a slight nod. 'Could you phone her? I need to ask her something regarding work. I've tried but she isn't answering my calls.'

'Sure. Come in for a second, keep the heat in.' He allowed Tanzy to enter, then found her number and pressed CALL. 'Straight to voicemail. Her battery must have died. She shouldn't be long if you want to wait?'

'Is her family okay?' Tanzy asked.

'I'm sorry?'

'I was told that Kim had left work and had put a week's holiday in for a last-minute family emergency.'

He shook his head slowly. 'You must be mistaken . . . unless she hasn't told me about it. As far as I'm aware, there's no family emergency.'

'Okay. When you see her, can you tell her to call me? It's important.'

'Sure thing, Detective.'

Once Tanzy had stepped down onto the driveway, the man closed the door. Back inside the car, he tried calling her again.

Same result. Voicemail.

He found Byrd's number and pressed CALL. Tanzy told Byrd about what Harrison's husband had said, that there was no family emergency, according to him.

'Well, where is she, then?' Byrd said.

'At this moment, we have no idea.'

'What the hell is going on?'

'I'm sure there's a logical explanation, Max.'

Tanzy started the car and turned the blowers on full. It was freezing outside. The rain, which was light before, had suddenly got heavier, now pelting against the windows of the car.

'Shit, I need to go, Max. I'm seeing the Joneses soon.'

'Keep me updated,' Byrd said. 'I'll call around, see if anyone has seen Harrison. If I hear anything, I'll let you know, Ori.'

'Thanks.'

'Hey . . .' Byrd said quickly.

'Yeah?'

'Good luck with the media,' said Byrd. 'I know how much you love them.'

47

Friday evening
Darlington

Tanzy placed the phone down on the passenger seat and edged out onto the road. It wasn't long before he arrived at Business Central Darlington and found one of the remaining spots near the entrance. The car park was half full; most of the cars had piled towards the spaces near the entrance so people spent less time walking in the cold. Tanzy knew most of them would be media reps and local reporters.

As he walked across the tarmac, he glanced around and noticed the Joneses' car over to the left. There was a colourful sticker on the rear windscreen that made him feel sad about Evelyn. For over a week now, he'd stared at her photograph on his desk, promising her little face on the picture that he'd find her.

Through the double doors of the building, Tanzy felt the warmth of the heating system instantly. The reception area was bright, well-lit, white and modern. Every surface was new and had been designed to stand out.

A man standing near the desk raised his palm towards Tanzy on his approach.

'ID, sir?'

Tanzy showed him. The man nodded and let him pass. A small crowd of people stood on the other side of the reception, behind the desk. He recognised Evelyn's parents, who were standing with Neil McMahon, Evelyn's teacher, offering them some emotional support. He was tall and slim, considerably taller than Ray Jones. Next to Ray was Evelyn's mother, Tricia. She used a tissue to wipe her tears away and nodded several times at the man. Maybe he was advising her on what they should say in the upcoming media interview.

'Hi,' said Tanzy, extending a hand to Ray first, then Tricia. Tricia didn't smile as Ray had done, and it was hard to miss the pain in her teary eyes.

'Have you heard anything yet?' Ray asked quickly. 'How's the investigation going?'

It was another question that Tanzy would have to answer in a negative light. There hadn't been any updates or progress yet. If there had been, Tanzy would have already notified them. He understood their desperation; he'd be the same if either Jasmine or Eric had been taken. Usually, after the forty-eight hours had passed, the parents of missing children started losing hope. After that time, the chances of finding a missing child alive hugely decreased.

'Nothing yet, Mr Jones,' Tanzy said. 'But this is why we're here. We need to ask the good people of this town to help us, to keep an eye out for her.'

'It's been nine days!' Tricia gasped. 'Nine days. Why is this taking so long?'

Ray Jones digested his wife's anger and sighed in her direction. Neil McMahon gave a thin smile and put his hand on her back.

'We'll find her, Tricia,' he said softly.

Ray Jones gave Neil a thankful smile and looked back at Tanzy with tired, lost eyes.

'We're absolutely devastated about Evelyn's disappearance. Her class friends are very upset.' McMahon spoke with an educated, warmly northern accent. His face was kind, giving the impression he had the patience and aura to educate younger children.

'Good of you to support them, Mr McMahon,' Tanzy said.

'Absolutely, Detective. It's a dark cloud hanging over the classroom — and the school — every day,' the teacher said. 'The children have been doing some colourful drawings for Evelyn.' He faced Tricia and Ray. 'We've put them up on the drawing board for everyone to see. We're all praying for her.'

Tricia raised a finger to her eye and wiped away a tear. Ray stood still, fighting back obvious rising emotions.

'We're nearly ready,' said a small, thin woman, dressed in a dark blue suit with a clipboard. 'If you'd like to follow me, please.'

Tricia used a soggy tissue to dab her eyes one last time then shoved it back into her pocket. She and her husband were both in their mid-thirties, but after nine days of worrying they were both looking older. Her long, dark hair sat straight down to her shoulders. She turned and, side by side, she and Ray followed the petite woman. Neil, Evelyn's teacher, trailed them, while Tanzy hung back a few feet and entered the conference room last.

The room was rectangular and, to the right wall, closest to them, was a long table with chairs behind it, which was the focus of the room. Tanzy made his way to one of the chairs, dropped down into it and peered out onto the sea of reporters, media representatives and photographers watching him. When he noticed the microphone on the table, his heart started beating quicker, knowing soon enough he'd have to speak publicity. He didn't like it one little bit. All those eyes watching him, judging him. To his relief, there was a jug of water and five stacked plastic cups, so he leaned over and poured himself half a cup to dampen his throat.

The table where Tanzy was seated was lit up with two large lamps supported by flimsy-looking metal tripods that were positioned two metres back, separating the first few rows of people.

Tanzy took a deep breath as they stepped into the spot-light and found their seating positions. Ray and Tricia were in the centre, Tanzy on their left nearest to the door, and Evelyn's teacher, Neil, took a seat to their right, near the wall.

The well-presented woman in the dark blue suit with the clipboard introduced herself to the camera, then introduced Evelyn's parents. She then explained the reason for this, although most of the people who were there knew, and finished by mentioning that Ray and Tricia had something to say.

The room fell silent. All eyes fell on Ray as he slowly rose to his feet. His cheeks blushed under the attention.

'Thank you everyone for coming here tonight,' he started. 'It's been . . . It's been an emotional time for my wife, Tricia, and me. As you know, our daughter, Evelyn Jones, has been missing for nine days now.' He stopped, fighting back his emotions.

Behind the bright spotlights, the cameras clicked constantly. 'I beg you for your help,' Ray went on. 'I beg for all of you to help us find our beautiful little baby girl. She . . . she needs to come home. Please help us.'

When Ray had stopped talking, a reporter seated over to the right asked, 'Are things okay at home? Was Evelyn troubled at all?'

Ray and Tricia looked shocked. Typical reporters. All they wanted to do was to get a reaction and a good story. Everything said would be recorded and documented, so for them to persuade the public and get them on their side, they needed to keep calm and be liked.

Tanzy was about to stand up and take the pressure off the grieving parents, but before he could another reporter fired off a question.

'Is it true that Evelyn ran away?'

Where on earth were these reporters getting this information from?

'Do you think you will see your daughter again?' another reporter asked.

'My wife and I sincerely hope so,' replied Ray, to the second question. 'We know with every day that passes . . .' He paused a beat, choosing his next words carefully, changing what he was going to say. 'I believe in the police.' He glanced unexpectedly over to Tanzy, who met his gaze. 'I believe they'll do everything they can to find our daughter. We are distraught. We're broken. We can't cope without her. But I believe in them.'

Ray looked away from Tanzy and straight into the light of the cameras and the eyes of the eager reporters.

'As I mentioned in our last appeal a few days ago, Evelyn was wearing her school uniform and a red coat. She had a bright green bag with her schoolbooks, pencil case and a pink teddy inside. If anyone has seen anything that could help, please, please get in touch with the police.'

The woman in the suit with the clipboard, who was standing to the right, raised an assertive palm. 'That's enough questions for now. Evelyn's teacher, Neil McMahon, has a few words to say.'

Ray sat down, looking shellshocked.

Neil McMahon found his feet and began with a nod. The cameras continued to click. Flashes hit the back wall like stabs of lightning.

'Hi, everyone. I'm Neil McMahon,' he started. 'I'm Evelyn's teacher at school.' Everyone focused on him. 'All I really want is to add to what Evelyn's father, Ray, has said and firstly thank everyone for coming. Evelyn Jones is such a beautiful little person. I've had the chance to teach her for a few years now. She's an absolute joy to be around and the other children love her. Today, we spent the afternoon drawing pictures for Evelyn. And we are all going to show them to her when she is found.' He fell silent and wiped a tear from his eye.

Tricia wiped away a tear and Ray watched him with admiration of what the man was trying to do: send this heartfelt message across to people, hoping someone somewhere knew where she was. After he said his bit, he sat down. Ray patted his back as a thank you for his words.

It was Tanzy's turn to stand up. His heart beat faster when he realised everyone was focusing on him. Although he was a confident guy, public speaking wasn't one of his specialities. He'd often let Byrd step in if they needed a DI to do any press talks.

The first question: 'Why hasn't Evelyn Jones been found?'

Tanzy swallowed the query and took a breath. He knew this was the question on everyone's lips. He explained what the police had done so far: how his team had knocked on doors, relentlessly searched the local area in which she was last seen and devoted a small team to find her. He said they would not stop until she was found.

'I promise you that,' he said lastly.

Once the conference was over, Tanzy walked outside.

The cold hit his face and immediately calmed him. The rain had stopped and it had noticeably dropped a couple of degrees compared to when he went in.

Ray and Tricia finally walked through the sliding doors, followed by Neil.

Neil said something to them then glanced towards Tanzy and gave him a wave, then made his way towards his car.

Tricia and Ray padded sluggishly towards Tanzy. The life was being drained from them before his eyes. Ray looked up at Tanzy and half smiled, while Tricia stared vacantly at the ground, visibly empty.

'I think it went okay,' Tanzy said, encouragingly.

Ray nodded. 'Yeah. Hopefully, someone comes forward now.' He wrapped his arm around his wife and squeezed her close.

'I just need to see her,' she whispered, curling up into Ray's chest. 'I need to see my baby.'

Tanzy sighed hopelessly, wishing he could tell them it was going to be all right. The truth was it had been nine days since their daughter was last seen and not a single piece of information had been put forward, leaving the police with nothing to go on. He'd almost lost hope, but he had to believe that somewhere out there, Evelyn Jones was alive.

To their right, they heard the sound of an engine.

They looked over to see Neil McMahon in his dark blue Ford Mondeo, crawling along the layer of frost on the tarmac. He gave the Joneses a soft wave as he passed.

'He gave a good speech about Evelyn,' Tanzy noted.

'He did. He's lovely,' Tricia said, looking up. 'He knows how we feel. He's seen her five days a week for over three years. And obviously, because of what happened to him.'

Tanzy frowned at her, unsure what she meant.

'His own daughter went missing many years ago. She was playing football with him in the local park. She kicked the ball. Neil went to get it and went out of sight only for a moment. When he came back, she was gone. He hasn't seen her since.'

Tanzy digested the story with a twisted stomach. Why hadn't that come up in their investigation? Was it an oversight or something more sinister? He tried to remember who had been doing the background checks on family and friends.

'He wants to find Evelyn just as much as we do.'

'I understand,' Tanzy replied.

'Come on, Tricia. Let's get you home. It's freezing.' Ray squeezed her closer and looked at Tanzy. 'Please find our daughter, Detective Tanzy. We can't go on without her.' They moved away from him and shuffled over to their car.

Tanzy, mindful of the ice, slowly walked across the glistening tarmac to his Golf and climbed in. He turned it on and put the heating on full blast to clear the misty windows. The Joneses' car edged out from the right and slowly crawled past him.

In the back window of the car, something was resting on the parcel shelf — a teddy. It was too dark to see properly, but Tanzy was sure it was pink. The same colour as the teddy that Ray had told the media Evelyn had when she went missing.

48

Ian Porter closed the door to his son's bedroom, making sure to leave it open an inch, so the lamp on the nearby table would prevent his room from falling into complete darkness.

'Good night, Daddy,' said the little voice inside.

'Good night, Cameron. Sweet dreams, little man.'

Adam and Liam were already asleep in their own rooms. Adam had been very emotional today, getting used to life without his mother. He'd crashed out about 6.30 p.m. Porter hadn't heard a peep since then. Liam had been given his bottle of milk and put to bed just after.

When he was downstairs in the kitchen, he cracked open the bottle of whisky and placed it down on the worktop. He reached up, grabbed a glass from the cupboard and positioned it next to the bottle. He picked up a handful of ice cubes from the freezer and threw them into the empty glass then poured the drink into it, watching the thick amber liquid crack the ice cubes and fill the glass. He was going to wait a little while until the drink was cold. It tasted better that way.

He made his way to the silent living room, placed his glass down on the small table and closed the curtains. He then padded over to the lamp near the window and switched it on, letting the warm light illuminate one side of the room, before dropping down onto the sofa.

The past two days had been the worst of his life.

Losing his wife.

Losing his will to live.

The television came on. Channel three. The ITV news was just starting. It wasn't something Porter spent much time watching, but he couldn't be bothered looking through the assortment of boring channels to find something which was probably halfway through by the time he'd found it. All he wanted to do was sit and do nothing. He dropped further into the sofa and sipped whisky.

The man sitting behind the desk in the studio told the viewers that a body had been found hanging from a tree on Cemetery Lane in Darlington. The woman had been identified as Mary Richards and had been found earlier that morning by dog walkers. The television switched to a photograph of Mary Richards for a short time before switching to footage that was taken earlier, showing the scene after the body had been removed.

It switched to a screen where a local reporter was standing with DI Orion Tanzy, a local police detective, at the end of Cemetery Lane. The detective explained briefly what they had found and asked anyone with any relevant information to come forward and contact the number that rolled along the bottom of the screen.

'Jesus!' Porter gasped.

The name, Mary Richards, sounded very familiar to him. He'd heard the name before.

He plucked his phone from his jeans and opened social media. He wasn't sure if he was connected to Stuart Richards as a 'friend', but he searched his name. Without typing his full name, a profile for Stuart came up. After recognising the man in the profile picture, he clicked on it and confirmed it was him.

He scrolled down his profile.

'Shit,' he whispered after seeing it.

There was a post on his page wall: *Omg Stu! I'm so sorry for your loss.* Along with the picture, there was an image of Stuart and Mary at some kind of fancy dinner party, both of them dressed in black, with smiles on their faces.

The next post was something similar, letting Stuart know to call if there was anything his family needed of him.

'Shit, it *was* her,' Porter muttered in the silence of his living room. Porter sat back, thinking about Julia, then about Mary.

Why had this happened?

He didn't have Stuart's number but that wasn't the end of the world. Because he was connected with him, he could message him. He started typing. After he'd finished, he re-read it a few times to make sure it made sense. Then he clicked SEND.

In the corner of the message, he watched Stuart's picture icon appear, indicating to Porter that the message had been read.

Three dots appeared, hovering at the bottom of the screen, telling him that Stuart was replying. Porter waited nervously. He hadn't spoken to Stuart since he was nineteen.

Stuart wrote: *What the FUCK do you want?*

Porter replied: *Please ring me, Stuart, it's important.*

He pressed SEND.

It wasn't long before the ringtone disrupted the serenity of the living room. He sighed and answered it, raising his arm to the side of his head.

'Stuart.'

'What the fuck do you want, Ian?'

'I need to talk.'

'Be quick about it. I'm in the middle of something,' Richards said, 'I don't know if you know, but I've just watched the ITV news report about my wife. She was found dead this morning hanging from a fucking tree and—'

'I know, I know,' Porter admitted, 'that's why I'm ringing. I've just watched it too.'

Richards didn't reply but managed a beaten sigh.

'Listen,' Porter went on, 'I don't know if you know, but my wife is dead too.'

'Julia?'

'Yeah.'

Silence grew between them for a moment, until Richards said, 'Jesus. When?'

'Wednesday night.'

'Two days ago?'

'Yeah.'

'What happened?'

'She was murdered,' he told him. 'I found her naked. She was tied to a chair. Her eyes were missing. In our dining room next to our baby son, with a pool of blood at her feet.'

'God . . .' Stuart said. 'I'm . . . sorry, Ian.'

Porter didn't reply for a short while, then he said, 'I think they're connected, Stuart.'

'You think what?' His voice sharpened.

'I think there's a connection,' Porter explained. 'Because of that night.'

Silence.

'Stu, you know—'

'I know what night!' he barked.

'I think he's found out what happened. Found out what really happened to his sister.'

49

Darlington
Fifteen years ago

The house was filling quickly, most of the downstairs now occupied with people ready for a good time, chatting in their little groups with drinks in their hands. Music blared from the CD player inside the house, spilling through the open back door that led to the decking area. Short steps led to the rest of the garden, where there was a pond on the right and a patio to the left, which included a wide rectangular table with six chairs around it.

Sarah, leaving a small group of her friends, walked from the bottom of the garden towards the house, stepping up onto the decking. She glanced to her left and half smiled at Stuart Richards and Ian Porter, who sat on two plastic chairs, each holding a cigarette and a can of the cheap lager they'd brought with them. They watched her fade into the noise inside to refill her wine.

It was nearly 9 p.m.

Sherina Barker, or Shez as her friends called her, was one of Sarah's best friends. Shez's parents owned the house, but they were away. What better way to spend a birthday than to host a party while your parents were away? All of the people who she'd invited, plus more, had turned up. It was looking like it would be one of the best parties of the summer.

Alison Thorne's birthday party had been spoken about for weeks. Sherina never liked Alison. She thought she was up her own arse. That was a few months ago. This was now. Shez would make sure this would be a night to remember.

Sarah, after filling her plastic cup, came back outside and sauntered across the decking wearing a short skirt, a low-cut top and black high heels. Her legs were tanned and muscular, and her bum was something that every man at the party would have a peek at at some point during the evening.

She was beautiful.

Long dark straight hair fell onto her shoulders and her face carried the kindness of someone so innocent it almost contradicted her physique.

Ian and Stuart watched her closely as she moved down to the garden.

'Would you?' Stuart whispered.

'I wouldn't hesitate for a second,' Ian replied, smiling.

Ian Porter, as well most of the men there, fancied the arse off Sarah. Most of them had gone to school with her and, at some point, had fantasised about her in the five years they'd known her. The party was pretty much a school reunion. It had only been three years since they'd left, but everyone kept in touch in some way or another.

When Shez knew her nineteenth birthday was coming up, what better way to spend it than to get all her old classmates together and get drunk, play loud music and dance like they hadn't a care in the world?

At nineteen, you didn't.

You thought you were old enough to know everything about life, but the simple truth was that you didn't. People tended to be naive at that age.

Sarah returned to the bottom of the garden and stood with her friends. Shez noticed another drink in Sarah's hand.

'You might want to slow down, Sarah,' Shez commented.

Not that Shez was counting, but she knew Sarah was on her fourth glass of wine. The night was still young. She didn't want to spend her birthday holding Sarah's hair back while she was sick in the toilet.

'Don't worry about me. I'm in control,' Sarah said. Her tone was playful but a hint of annoyance was there, Shez could tell. It hadn't been the first time Shez had told her to slow down a little. And she knew it wouldn't be the last.

'I know, Sarah, I'm just saying you don't—'

'Don't worry about it,' she said again, this time more sternly. She took a big gulp and laughed.

Shez glared into her glassy eyes and said nothing more about it. 'Where's your brother?'

'He told me he isn't coming.'

'Why?' Shez's pet lip came out. Everyone knew Shez had a thing for her brother.

'I don't know, to be honest. He never said.'

Shez nodded, raised her hand and had a sip of wine. 'It's strong stuff this.'

'It's only thirteen per cent, no harm can be done . . .'

They both broke into laughter and drank some more, then turned to the small group of friends, joining a conversation about what had happened to a singer who'd been found dead in a hotel room over in America.

Back up on the decking, Stuart and Ian were watching them.

'I'm going to fuck her,' Ian Porter said quietly.

'What?' Stuart frowned and jerked his head towards him. 'You can't be serious?'

Porter nodded confidently. 'I am.'

'You tried that in Year Eight and she was having none of it.'

'Stu, we were thirteen back then. We're nineteen now, it's different.' Porter took another long gulp of cheap lager, swallowed it with a smack of his wet lips.

'It makes no difference, Ian. She's stunning and . . . well, you're not. I bet it doesn't happen.'

'Would you put money on it?'

Stuart Richards laughed out loud. The people closest to them turned and stared for a moment. 'How much, Ian?'

'Twenty quid?'

They shook hands quickly and smiled at each other. Porter turned away, glancing back down at the garden, and watched Sarah laughing with Shez. Stuart knew Ian had no chance.

But watching him, he saw something different. Something dark in his eyes.

Determination.

Power.

A desire to get anything that he wanted.

Maybe tonight would be different.

50

Neil McMahon turned on the television and took a seat on the large sofa. He leaned to his right and picked up his mug of coffee from the low table then leaned back and took a sip.

To his left, his wife, Judith, was sitting comfortably in the corner, with her legs tucked under her bum and her eyes focused on the screen. She'd been there most of the night, catching up on the programs she'd missed over the past few weeks.

'How are they?' she asked him.

'They're a wreck,' he said, sadly.

'Bless them. It doesn't get any easier, does it?'

'No. It doesn't.'

The ITV news had started moments ago but Judith had paused it while Neil was tidying the kitchen. The first story was about the discovery of Mary Richards' body which had been found in Cemetery Lane just off Carmel Road. They had heard about it from colleagues and friends, but the details of the scene were harrowing. The shot went to an interview where a local member of the police, a DI Orion Tanzy, spoke into the camera, appealing to the public for information.

'That's the detective helping Ray and Tricia,' Neil said. 'He's a nice chap.'

Once the report about the body had finished it switched back to the studio, where the smartly dressed reporter told the camera about the update on the missing seven-year-old, Evelyn Jones.

'We go to Business Central Darlington, where the parents of Evelyn spilled their hearts out to the public, asking for their help to find their missing daughter,' he said.

The screen changed to a shot of the wide table in the conference room. Ray and Tricia were seated behind it in the centre chairs. The lights on them were so bright it almost made their skin appear hollow.

'There you are,' Judith said, seeing him seated next to Ray.

Ray Jones spoke into the camera for a short while, as his wife wiped away her tears. Then Neil stood up and said his part. When he sat down, DI Orion Tanzy stood up and filled the reporters in on how the investigation was going from a police perspective.

'I'm proud of you,' Judith said to Neil. 'Takes balls to stand up there and speak in front of all those cameras.' She leaned over and squeezed his hand.

He waved it away modestly. 'I just hope they find her soon. I know what Ray is feeling, I know how he—'

She squeezed his hand again, this time tighter. 'I know, Neil. I know. It's a pain that never goes away. I think about Casey every single day. She's left a hole in our hearts that will never be filled.'

When their daughter, Casey, went missing all those years ago, after a month went by, they'd lost all hope. At the time, they were told that if she wasn't found within three days, chances were that she'd never be found. Not alive, anyway. When they finally accepted that they wouldn't see their daughter again, they tried for another child. Months went by, but Judith didn't fall pregnant. They even tried IVF, which proved a pointless, costly effort.

'I still miss her now,' he said. 'I think about what she would look like. What she'd be doing. What she'd have chosen to study at university. What job she'd end up having.'

Judith smiled at him.

He went on. 'You remember she used to dress up in a little white nurse's outfit and walk around with a plastic stethoscope?'

She nodded, absorbing his heartfelt words with tears in her eyes.

'I wish I never went to get that football . . .' He trailed off and leaned back, resting his head on the back of the sofa. 'She'd still be here.'

Judith squeezed his hand.

'If Evelyn's not found, at least they'll have the money.'

'What money?' she asked, frowning.

'The life insurance money,' he said. 'Ray told me they took out life insurance for her in case anything bad happened. He said if anything ever did happen to her, they'd be too heartbroken to work anymore.'

'How much money will they get?'

'I'm not sure exactly,' he said. 'But I'm sure he said it was over half a million.'

51

Saturday morning
North Road, Darlington

James Whittaker had popped into work to get a holiday form on his day off. He'd grovelled to get the dates off he needed. The supermarket stated that their holiday request policy was fair, but depending on staffing levels, it was up to the line manager. Colin Tapper was an arsehole, but he'd given him the time off after making him wait about a bit.

He'd left his wife, Karen, and his five-year-old daughter, Layla, waiting in the car, which was parked towards the back of the car park. Karen was deeply engaged on her phone, checking her social media updates — which recently had started to get on James's nerves — and Layla was playing with her talking doll. Even with Colin's pratting about, he hadn't kept them long.

He stepped down off the kerb, minding the slow-moving traffic coming towards him. The road was too narrow, and the spaces were difficult to park in due to their slight width. It didn't help that the car park was beyond busy.

He crept down between the side of his car and a Range Rover. The driver of it was obviously the type who thought they were above everyone else and didn't need to keep within the lines.

'Prick,' he muttered, reaching for his car door. He edged it open and carefully slid in, mindful not to scratch any paintwork.

Once he got in, he realised his wife wasn't sitting in the passenger seat. Frowning, he turned to the rear of the car to see his daughter was also missing.

The passenger door opened and a strange man wearing a stocking mask climbed in and stared at him.

'Who . . . who the fuck are you?' James said, frowning at the stranger sitting beside him.

'It doesn't matter who I am. What matters is where your wife and daughter are.'

'Where *are* they?' James whispered, his words clogging his throat.

The back door opened, and another man wearing a similar mask lowered himself in.

He repeated the question.

The men said nothing. James switched his focus between them. 'Listen, if you hurt them, I'll—'

'Do nothing,' the man in the front passenger seat calmly said. 'You'll do absolutely nothing.'

'If you fucking touch them, I'll kill you.' He glared into the back of the car. 'You as well, I'll fucking kill you too!'

'You have a choice to make, Mr Whittaker,' the man in the front seat said. Again, his voice was even and composed.

'How . . . how do you know my name?'

'That isn't important, James. What's important is that you have a choice to make.'

'A choice?' Whittaker shook his head wildly. 'What choice? Where are they?' He stared out the windows, all around the car, trying to locate them somewhere in the car park.

The men stayed silent, both fixated on James Whittaker, watching the sweat run down his forehead and his body tremble in terrified confusion.

'What? What choice do I have?' he finally asked, returning his focus to the strangers.

'Many years ago,' the man in the front seat said. 'When you were nineteen, you made a terrible decision.'

James frowned. 'What?'

'A decision that caused a lot of hurt to others. A decision that took someone away from me. A decision you're now going to really, really regret.'

'I don't understand,' he pleaded. His eyes started to well up.

'If you had to choose either your wife or your daughter to survive, who would you pick?'

'I don't understand what you're saying!'

'Let me simplify this for you: if one of them was going to die, which one would you save?'

He absorbed the question, staring into the man's black eyes. It was an impossible question. He didn't have an answer.

'Well?'

'I can't answer that, I—'

'Who!' the man in the front shouted.

Whittaker felt his blood boiling, exchanging frantic looks between the front and back of the car.

'Hopefully when you wake up, you'll have an answer.'

Whittaker frowned, unsure what they meant, and didn't see the cosh come from the back of the car, colliding with the side of his head, knocking him out cold.

52

Saturday morning
Low Coniscliffe

Byrd was sitting at the table in the kitchen, eyes on his laptop. Next to it was an empty plate containing the crumbs from the bacon sandwich that he'd demolished moments earlier. He gulped some coffee to wash the remnants away and placed his mug down on the table.

Outside the window, a thin layer of frost covered the grass and a chill hung silently in the air. Several birds occupied the bare branches of the tree, but they didn't hang around for long, coming and going continuously, as if playing a game with one another.

Claire was on the opposite side of the table, reading her Kindle, cosy in her dressing gown. The kitchen was peaceful and warm.

'What are we doing today?' Claire asked, peering over her Kindle.

Byrd glanced up. 'What do *you* want to do?'

She shrugged.

'We'll do that, then,' he said, smiling. 'Give me half an hour on here then we can go out if you like?'

His eyes fell back to the screen.

'Where?'

He sighed, focused back on her. 'Wherever you like. We can have a drive into town, get some coffee. You can show me that dress you keep mentioning.'

She grinned, joyfully lifting her shoulders for a moment. 'Sounds good. I need to finish this chapter anyway . . . Oh, have you heard from the hospital?' she asked.

'No updates yet. I'll pop in later this afternoon after we've been into town. If you don't mind?'

'Of course I don't mind, Max. Don't be silly. Did you think I would?'

He smiled. 'No, I didn't. But I did say that today would be our day. And here I am —' he pointed down at his laptop — 'doing work again. Sorry.'

'Don't be sorry. This is your career. It's important. And seeing your parents at hospital is certainly nothing to apologise for.'

He half smiled, appreciating her understanding on both matters.

His phone rang in his pocket. He picked it out, looked at the caller. It was Jacob Tallow.

'Jacob?'

'Hi, Max,' he started. 'I didn't tell you the other day, but when we examined Julia Porter's Qashqai, we found a hair on the passenger seat. We've run the DNA. It doesn't match any of the Porters.'

'Whose is it?' Byrd asked.

Claire looked up from her Kindle.

'Don't know. It doesn't match anyone on the database.'

Byrd digested his answer, then said, 'Is there any update on Mary Richards?'

'Funny you should say that. We found a very short strand of hair stuck in her fingernails. It was a different colour from her natural hair. Just hold on a sec.' His voice became quieter as if he'd leaned away from the phone, speaking with someone else. 'Yeah, I've told him. Okay, no . . . no sugar. Thanks.' He brought the phone closer. 'Sorry, Max, I have Amanda and Paul here. We're going through the analysis on the hair.'

'When will you know more?' Byrd asked.

'Sometime today.'

'Good. Let me know when you know.'

'No problem,' Tallow said. 'Thought I'd mention, we're going out for a few drinks tonight in town. Amanda, me and Paul. Tony said he'd try and get down, but he might have other things on.'

Byrd considered the response and looked towards Claire, who was watching him over the top of her Kindle. He had told Claire that he would devote his day to her. Would it be rude to go out tonight with work colleagues for a couple of drinks? Only one way to find out, he guessed.

'Yeah, okay. I'll bring Tanzy along too.'

Claire lowered the Kindle to the table and frowned at him.

'Yeah if . . . you like,' Tallow said, his tone a little dull.

'I thought you two had sorted things out?' Byrd asked.

'He's okay. We'll never be best friends, put it that way.'

'I'll drag him out, Jacob. You two can have a chin wag. What time are you going out?'

'I'll text you.'

He ended the call and placed his phone down on the table, feeling Claire's stare.

'What was that about?'

'Couple of the guys are going out tonight for a few drinks. Asked me to pop along.' He left that hanging in the kitchen, then finally they made eye contact. It was obvious she wasn't impressed. He leaned forward and grabbed his phone. 'Sorry, I did say this was going to be our day. I'll message him and say I can't—'

'Just go, Max. We'll spend the day together. You can go out tonight.'

Byrd smiled and said nothing more.

53

James Whittaker woke up with a pounding head from the blow of the weapon. He brought a trembling hand up and touched where his temple was bleeding.

'Shit.'

He looked around the car, remembered the men who were sitting there, and the absence of his wife and daughter. He got out of the car and frantically glared around the busy car park in search of them.

What if this was all a wind-up and they were safe?

Shaking his head, he knew that wasn't likely judging by the aggression of the men inside his car moments earlier.

He leaned over, grabbed his phone and dialled his wife's number. It rang until it went to voicemail.

'Shit,' he said, sighing heavily. 'Where the hell are you?' He ended the call and tried again. Same result.

He leaned to the side of his door and grabbed his pack of cigarettes, opened the flap and took one. Once lit, he took a heavy draw and knew the next step was to phone the police. He dialled the number and put the phone to his ear.

He explained the situation and dispatch informed him to sit tight and a car would be there within a few minutes.

'Fuck this,' he said in reply, and put his phone in his pocket, deciding to check the car park for them. He had to do something. It took him almost two minutes to check the whole of the car park, collecting odd stares from the public as he ran along the paths and dodged through moving cars, frantically looking for his family.

In the distance, he heard the police siren and sighed a little, knowing help was on its way.

Back at his car, he clicked on his mother-in-law's number. Karen had mentioned wanting to go to her mother's house after James had got the holiday form signed, so it could be possible she had gotten sick of waiting and started walking there with Layla.

After three rings, her mother answered.

'Hello?'

'Is Karen and Layla there with you?'

'Here?'

'Yeah. Are they at your house?'

'Not yet. You're coming soon though, aren't you?' she said. 'James, are you there?'

'I'll call you back,' he said abruptly, then hung up.

Standing next to him was his daughter, Layla. There was a look of fear in her eyes that he'd never seen before.

'Where's . . . where's Mammy?' he asked her.

A tear fell from her eye down her cheek. 'They've taken her. She's gone, Daddy.'

54

Saturday afternoon
Darlington Memorial Hospital

Byrd and Claire walked into the Intensive Care Unit. They'd been to town for a coffee at Costa and then to Next, where Claire had bought a dress. They'd arranged to go out the following weekend. Nothing flash, just into town, which they hadn't really done in a while. She'd suggested it after Byrd had told her he was going out for a few drinks later. He couldn't really say no.

They entered the room where his mother and father were. The white walls, the beeping of the machines, the lights, the wires, the cleanliness, the medicinal smell lingering in the air — he wished it wasn't so familiar.

Dr Ching was standing between the beds, his attention focused mainly on Byrd's father. He turned when he heard the door open.

'Mr Byrd,' he said quietly. 'Nice to see you.'

'Hey, how are they doing?' he asked. Byrd stepped forward slowly, Claire trailing a step behind.

'Your mother is improving, Mr Byrd. I think she'll wake up in the next few days naturally.' The doctor stopped there.

'My father?'

The doctor's face changed to something emotional, but he remained professional. A sign he'd done this many times before.

'He's showing no improvements yet, unfortunately.' He paused for a second, thinking carefully about how to say his next words. 'If we don't see any changes in the next day or two, you might need to prepare yourself.'

Byrd stayed silent and watched his father closely. A mouthpiece was lodged between his lips, a wire trailing down over the bed across to a machine. There were drips placed in his arms. Beeping. Lights. Were these things really the only thing keeping his father alive? It was heart-breaking.

Suddenly, it got too much for him; he turned quickly and dashed out of the room, out of the building.

The door opened and closed quickly. He was gone. The sounds of his shoes clapping on the hard floor faded down the corridor. Claire gave the doctor a sad smile and rushed after him. Outside, he stopped at a metal railing and placed his hands firmly on it. He took several deep breaths of cold air and closed his eyes.

'Max,' Claire said, catching him up.

She placed a palm on his back, and he looked at her with tears in his eyes. It was something she'd never seen before. She looked unsure of what to do. 'I'm sorry,' he said quietly, fighting the emotion that filled his voice. 'I'm sorry for walking out like that.'

'It's okay, Max,' she said softly.

A smell of smoke hovered in the air. Byrd looked up and noticed a man standing on the other side of the zebra crossing at the edge of the car park, smoking.

'Wait here,' he told her.

'Max . . . what—'

He left the railing abruptly and marched over the road towards the man, who'd spotted him, but turned away, assuming the anger on Byrd's face had nothing to do with him.

'Hey, you!' Byrd shouted.

The man took a short step back. Byrd was tall and broad. If a man like Byrd charged at anyone with a face like thunder, they'd likely do the same.

'Me?'

'Yes. You.'

'What?' The man took another drag of his cigarette, which Byrd noticed was nearly finished.

Byrd stepped forward, grabbed it from the man's hand and threw it down onto the ground, then stamped on it. The sound of his boot scraping the cold concrete echoed around them.

'What the f—'

'You fucking listen to me,' Byrd said sternly, getting closer, his finger pointing in the man's face. 'There's no smoking in these grounds. Do you understand that? There are signs everywhere.'

After seeing the wrath in Byrd's eyes and reading his body language, the man knew he meant business. Instead of retaliating, he thought better of it and nodded.

'Good. If you want to smoke, go over there, behind that wall. Where you're bloody meant to. Other people don't need to breathe in that shit.'

Byrd turned abruptly and made his way back over to Claire, who was still at the railing, her mouth slightly open, wondering what the hell had just happened. In the eighteen months they'd been seeing each other, he'd never let her see this side of him.

'I'm sorry about that,' he apologised. 'Come on, this way.' He headed in the direction of the car.

'Max . . . are you okay?'

He nodded. 'I need to get out of here. I'll come back and see them again tomorrow.'

* * *

Back in the car Byrd turned on the engine and turned up the radio volume. Claire leaned over and turned it down. Byrd

212

sighed, knowing she'd want an explanation for his random outburst moments earlier.

'What?'

'Are you okay? Really?'

'Listen, Claire . . . I'm sorry about that. It's all . . . it's all getting a lot for me. I just need them to get better. I need them to wake up.' He paused. 'They're all I have in this world.'

'You have me,' she told him, sounding a little hurt. 'You know that, right?'

He realised what he'd said. 'I do, I know. I'm sorry, I shouldn't have said that. I *do* have you.' Their eyes met for a long moment.

She reached for his hand, interlocked her fingers with his and squeezed. She opened her mouth, ready to say something, but Byrd's phone rang in his pocket, disturbing the moment. She let go of his grip, dipped her head and looked out the window.

He put it to his ear. 'Hello.'

'Max, there's been a call through from a man who claims his wife has been taken on North Road. I'm heading over there now.'

Byrd considered Tanzy's words carefully, thinking about the woman sitting next to him. She'd faintly heard what Tanzy had said.

'Just go, Max,' she said quietly, still staring vacantly out the window.

Byrd nodded at her, although she wasn't giving him her attention, then said to Tanzy, 'When are you going?'

'Right now. Want me to pick you up?'

'No, I'll meet you there. What's the address?'

Tanzy told him.

'I'm not far from there. Be there soon.' Byrd hung up and shoved the phone back into his pocket.

He turned sheepishly to Claire. 'I'm sorry.'

She didn't reply.

'Do you want dropping off or do you want to go to mine? When I'm finished, I could come home, and then maybe we could—'

'Take me home, please.'

And that's what he did.

On the way over they never spoke. He wanted to apologise and tell her that he thought that the abduction of this woman Tanzy had mentioned might have something to do with the previous two murders. That was important. But he felt like it was something he'd already said repeatedly. She understood his job, understood that he would prioritise that over everything else.

Maybe she was getting sick of it.

When she got out, she didn't kiss him, nor did she say anything to him. Byrd watched her walk up her path, open the door and step into her house without looking back.

He shifted into first and edged out into the road, then headed in the direction of the address that Tanzy had provided.

55

Saturday afternoon
Zetland Street, Darlington

It took him six minutes to arrive at Zetland Street. It was a narrow, terraced road, lined with cars and vans on either side. Children were playing football halfway up, so Byrd drove carefully, tinkering along at fifteen miles an hour while keeping a close eye on them. After he passed them, he noticed Tanzy's Golf parked up on the right and found a space across the road to pull in.

The day had warmed up. The early frost had dissipated, leaving the ground dry from the sun that shone brightly down on the street.

At the house, Tanzy answered Byrd's knock.

'Hey.' He stepped out of the way, allowing Byrd room to enter. 'Come have a look at this, Max.'

Byrd followed Tanzy through the small living room into the back of the house where the kitchen was. Halfway down the kitchen, a man standing with a photograph glanced up at him.

Byrd shook his hand firmly. 'I'm Detective Inspector Max Byrd.'

'James Whittaker.'

'What do we have?' Byrd asked, turning to Tanzy. Tanzy told him. Occasionally, Whittaker nodded, confirming Tanzy's version of the story.

'But look at this,' Tanzy added, holding his hand out towards Whittaker, who leaned forward and handed him the photograph. Byrd glanced down.

There were four men on it.

James Whittaker was one of them. Byrd, although they were young, recognised two others.

Stuart Richards.

Ian Porter.

He didn't know the fourth.

The background was dark with a bright green light coming from the right-hand side of the shot. Ian Porter held a can of lager and Stuart Richards had a cigarette hanging from his mouth. Behind them, there were people in small groups partying.

'How do you know these men?' Byrd asked, still focusing on the photo.

'We went to school together,' Whittaker began. 'We were friends until we were around twenty, but then lost touch after that.'

Byrd absorbed the information with a nod. He looked at Tanzy then back to Whittaker. 'So, what exactly happened?'

'I had to go in to get something signed. When I came out, they were gone. I phoned her mother because we were going there after, wondering if she'd just walked with our daughter, Layla, but she said she wasn't there. That's when Layla came back and told me she'd been taken.'

'Is your daughter in?'

'Would you like to speak to her? She's upstairs.'

'Yes, please,' Byrd said.

'I'll go get her.' Whittaker left the detectives in the kitchen.

They both stared at the photograph of the four individuals. On the reverse, it was dated, 14 July 2004.

Fifteen years ago.

'Interesting, isn't it?' Tanzy said quietly.

Byrd nodded. 'Very. When did you get here?'

'Only minutes before you did,' Tanzy said. 'I noticed a pile of photos on top of the microwave. I recognised Porter and Richards, so I asked him about it. He said he'd been sorting things out and needed to put them away.'

Byrd nodded.

'Strange though, isn't it? Ian Porter's wife. Then Stuart Richards' wife. Both within three days. Now Whittaker's wife goes missing. There's a pattern here.'

Footsteps pounded across the thin ceiling overhead and then down the wall to their left. Moments later, Whittaker appeared with his daughter, who looked about five years old.

'This is Layla. Layla, say hi to the detectives.'

Despite the situation, she smiled and displayed a youthful bounce, oblivious to the reality of the situation.

'Hello, Layla,' Tanzy said softly, lowering to his knees. 'How are you doing?'

'Good.'

'I like your dress. It's very pretty.'

She nervously shrugged, contracting her small, square shoulders, then glanced up at Whittaker, who smiled down at her. Tanzy asked his permission to ask her a few questions. He agreed.

'You say your mummy got into a van?' Tanzy asked.

She nodded several times. 'Yeah.'

'How many men were there, Layla?' Byrd this time.

'Three, I think . . .' She frowned, trying hard to remember.

'Good, that's good. You're doing great.'

Byrd and Tanzy were both down on their knees listening to the story. It was important when talking to young children not to tower over them and talk down to them. When an adult came down to their level it made them feel equal, and they tended to be more open.

She went on: 'They got into our car and my mammy screamed. I was playing with my doll, but I looked up. Two

217

of them got into the back. One on this side and one on that side.' She pointed left and right.

'What did they look like? Can you remember?' asked Tanzy.

'They had white masks on . . .' She winced at the thought.

'Were they a little bit scary?'

Exaggerated nods. 'Yeah.' She paused for a moment, screwed her face up. The detectives assumed she was thinking. 'The man in the front showed Mammy something but I couldn't see it. He said, "Do you understand?" Mammy nodded. She looked scared. Then we got out of the car.'

'Where did you go?'

'To a big van. They put Mammy in and then told me to come back to the car and wait for Daddy.'

'Where was the van?'

'On the big road outside.'

'What colour was the van? Can you remember?'

'White. A big white van.'

The detectives nodded several times, then stood up. 'Thank you, Layla, that was very helpful. You can go play now. We need to speak with your daddy.'

'Go on, sweetheart,' Whittaker said. 'Go back upstairs to your room and play with your toys.' He placed a palm on her back, guiding her back towards the stairs. Once she had disappeared, Tanzy stared back at the photograph.

'Mr Whittaker, did anything happen to you four?'

Whittaker glanced down at the photograph. 'I don't follow.'

'Not sure if you're aware, but there have been two murders over the past three days in this town. The women were married to two of these men. Ian Porter and Stuart Richards. I find that a very strange coincidence.'

Whittaker frowned, then shrugged. 'As I said, we were friends at school. We hung around a bit after but lost contact when we were twenty.'

'Why?'

He shrugged again. 'Work, I suppose. I went away down south. At the time, I was doing joinery. That's where the work was. I think the others maybe stayed in contact for a bit, but I went away for nearly three years and kind of lost touch with them.'

'Have you spoken since?'

Whittaker narrowed his eyes and shook his head. 'I've seen them in passing, but nothing more. Darlington's a small town, people tend to see each other every now and again.'

'You haven't spoken to them any time in the last week? Has Ian or Stuart attempted to contact you?'

'No.'

'Okay. Who's the other guy in the picture?' Byrd asked.

Whittaker followed his finger and looked at the man. 'That's Gregory Timms.'

'Does he still live in Darlington?'

He shrugged. 'No idea. I haven't seen him in years.'

'Have you got Gregory's number, by any chance?'

Whittaker shook his head. 'I don't. As I said, I haven't actually spoken to Gregory in fifteen years.'

'That's a long time,' Byrd commented.

'Yes.'

'We need to speak to Gregory Timms as soon as possible,' Tanzy chipped in. 'It might help us find Karen.'

Whittaker nodded. 'Have you got a picture of her?'

'Yes.'

'We'll need that if that's okay, so we can inform the media. Get her picture out to the public, get them looking for her too.'

He bobbed his head in understanding. 'I've got a good one on my phone. I'll go get it — hold on.' He left the kitchen, went upstairs, his footsteps creaking directly above them.

Tanzy turned to Byrd. 'This is beyond a coincidence. It has to be.'

Byrd agreed with narrowed eyes. 'Did you notice how shifty he looked when I asked if he'd spoken to Ian Porter or

Stuart Richards? I think he's lying. I think one of them has noticed the connection and been in touch.'

Whittaker returned downstairs with his phone in his hand.

'I can message this to you?'

'Thanks.' Tanzy gave him his number and waited for the picture to arrive. 'If you hear anything, let me know. I'll be in touch soon.'

Whittaker gave a thankful nod and walked the detectives out.

At Tanzy's Golf, Byrd said, 'Have you heard from Harrison yet?'

'No. I've tried and tried but she's not picking up. Her husband hasn't seen her yet either.'

'Fuck sake.' Byrd sighed and sniffed the air; the smell of cannabis caused him to turn and have a look around. All he saw were the children still playing football on the road. 'You don't see that very often, do you?'

Tanzy angled his stare towards the kids. 'See what?'

'Kids playing outside. It's normally iPads and Nintendos. Normally glued to them, most kids.'

Tanzy's kids weren't. 'I'll go back to the station with this, put it on the system. Then I'll go to Aldi, see if I can have a look at the cameras. Might be able to spot something.'

'I'll come with you.'

'You not spending time with Claire today?'

'I was. We went to town and got a coffee. I'm all yours.'

'How romantic. Jump in,' Tanzy said. 'We'll come back later to get your car.'

They both got into the Golf and closed the doors. Once Tanzy turned on the engine, Byrd leaned forward and put the blowers on full.

'How's your mam and dad?'

Byrd turned his head. 'My dad isn't getting any better, but my mam is improving a little.'

Tanzy didn't know whether to say that was good because his mother was improving or bad because his father wasn't, so decided to say nothing. They took a left at the end of the road onto Haig Street then took another left onto Lansdowne Street. Half a minute later, they hit North Road.

'Traffic's a nightmare.' Tanzy counted fourteen cars that refused to let him out, but finally an elderly gent in a red Micra slowed and flashed. Tanzy waved thanks and joined the rush, heading towards Aldi.

Byrd plucked his phone from his coat, found a number and put it to his ear.

'Who you ringing?' Tanzy asked.

'Thornton.'

Tanzy slowed the car at the traffic lights.

Thornton answered.

'We've just been to James Whittaker's house, the hus-band of—'

'Karen Whittaker, taken from the car park near Aldi a few hours ago?'

'No flies on you, are there?'

'That's why I'm the boss,' she said. 'I'm at the office now reading up on the dispatch logs. What's the story?'

'Whittaker says his wife and daughter went missing briefly, then only his daughter returned. His daughter said three men got into the car. She said they showed her mother something and then she went with them and got into a van. They told the kid to go back to the car.'

'Could have been a knife or a gun,' Thornton replied. 'If they were serious enough, Karen will have gone with them to save her daughter. Where are you now? You with Orion?'

'Yeah, he's driving. We're heading to Aldi to see if we can have a look at the CCTV of the car park. Might need to try the other shops there, depending on what we find at Aldi.'

'Okay,' she said.

'We found something else at his house,' Byrd added. 'He had a photo. Four of them were on it. Ian Porter, Stuart Richards, James Whittaker himself, and a guy called Gregory Timms.'

'The four of them?' she asked.

'Yeah. He said they went to school together but haven't spoken in years. Lost touch around the age of nineteen or twenty, he claims.'

'How old were they in the photo?'

'They looked about that age,' Byrd said.

'Strange coincidence,' she said. 'Two wives of the men on there have been murdered, now another has been taken.'

'Maybe not a coincidence at all.'

'Talk to Gregory Timms, then,' she suggested. 'I'll do some digging.' She thanked him and hung up the phone. Byrd put the phone in his pocket as Tanzy took a right into Aldi car park.

'Here we go.'

56

Saturday, late afternoon
Aldi car park

After explaining to the manager of Aldi that a wife of an employee had been kidnapped, they watched the CCTV footage from earlier and found absolutely nothing.

One camera picked up the entrance of Aldi, while the other showed down the side of the shop. The one they needed, unfortunately, was down for maintenance. A guy was coming to fix it tomorrow, according to the manager, who apologised profusely and made an urgent call to get it fixed sooner.

The detectives stepped outside, ignoring the *Big Issue* seller next to the sliding exit door. The car park was fairly quiet for half five on a Saturday. Although it was mild, rain was starting to spot down.

'Gonna pour down.' Byrd sighed. 'I can feel it.'

'How can you feel it?'

'Just before it's about to rain heavily, the temperature dips a few degrees. You can feel the moisture in the air.'

'We'll try over there, Mr Weatherman,' Tanzy said, pointing in the direction of Iceland.

Fifteen minutes later they left Iceland feeling deflated. The store's cameras only covered directly outside the shop and didn't even reach the second row of parking spaces.

Then they checked Poundland. They didn't even have cameras.

'God's sake,' Byrd said, getting back into Tanzy's Golf. 'Why isn't anything ever easy?'

They both closed their doors, happy to be out of the rain. Their hair was damp, their skin cold and prickly.

'What are you doing later, Ori?'

'Nothing,' Tanzy said, starting the car. 'Why?'

'Tallow is going for a few drinks with Forrest and Beech. McCabe said he might pop out later.'

'Are you going?'

Byrd nodded, putting on his own seat belt. 'Yeah, I'm going. You up for it?'

Tanzy mulled it over for a few moments. 'I've got nothing planned. The kids are at Pip's mother's anyway. What time?'

'They said seven at William Stead's, then take it from there. I won't be staying out too late. At my tender age, I can't handle the hangover anymore.'

'That makes two of us, then.'

57

Saturday evening
William Stead's, Town Centre

Standing at the bar, over the drone of idle chatter and careless laughter, Tanzy told Byrd he wanted a Coors Light. Byrd nodded and faced the cheery barman, telling him the order. Next to them were Tallow, Beech and Forrest.

Tallow was dressed in a white long-sleeved Oxford shirt, dark jeans and brown shoes. Beech was wearing a black T-shirt under a leather jacket and light-blue, almost skin-tight jeans and white plimsols. Next to him, Amanda Forrest wore a black jumpsuit and black heels. Dangling by her side was a gold-plated bag hanging from a gold chain looped around her shoulder. Around her neck was a gold necklace that looked expensive and classy.

'Rule number one tonight,' Tanzy said to the others while Byrd was ordering the drinks.

'What's that?' Tallow asked, smiling, obviously already feeling the buzz of a couple of drinks.

'No talking about work. I need a break from my life and my life is mainly work, so no talking about work.'

Tallow nodded, held up his palms. 'That's fine with me. I was wondering, where did you get that shirt from?'

Tanzy wore a black, tight-fitting long-sleeved T-shirt which hugged his athletic figure well.

'Next. Nothing flash,' he said modestly.

Tallow nodded. 'Nice.'

Byrd turned away from the bar with the drinks and handed Tanzy his lager. 'So, have you had a good day at work?' he asked the forensics. Tanzy turned abruptly, about to cause a fuss, then realised Byrd was grinning at him, overhearing what he'd said about not mentioning work.

'Dickhead,' Tanzy mused, then took a long sip. It felt good.

'You coming for a smoke?' Tallow asked the group.

'I don't smoke,' Byrd said, 'but I'll come outside with you for a little second-hand smoke.'

Tallow laughed and led the way through the crowds until they climbed the few steps, pulled the door open and stepped outside. The smell of cheap perfume and cigarette smoke hit them. Tallow stopped at one of the free tables, leaned over, pressed the button for the patio heater, then pulled a cigarette out of a packet and lit up. 'Anyone want one?'

Paul Beech nodded. 'Go on, just the one. I don't normally.'

'Anyone else?'

Byrd, Tanzy and Forrest all shook their heads. Byrd had once tried smoking when he was sixteen and was sick. He hadn't touched one since. At the time, he'd wanted to be like his dad, who religiously smoked forty a day. Then his dad had a health scare and packed them in. His mother still smoked twenty a day, and there was nothing Byrd could do to stop her.

As the heat from the wall-mounted lamp started to warm them they talked about places they liked to go drinking, although Byrd and Tanzy never really got out much. They mentioned the names of the places they used to go to when they were in their teens. Amanda Forrest hadn't heard of most of them. Then they talked about football. Then rugby. Apparently, Beech used to play rugby in his younger years, for the Newcastle Falcons development team, but broke his ankle, so his once ambitious idea of playing at a professional level was now a distant memory.

'Is Tony coming out later?' Byrd asked.

'He said he was, but he's not answering his phone.' Tallow pulled his phone from his pocket. 'I'll try him again.'

Tanzy, Forrest and Beech headed back inside to the bar. It was a nice, easy-going atmosphere. The heat lamps kept them comfortable and the buzz of the alcohol warmed their cheeks. Friendly, drunken conversations surrounded them as people came and went.

'How are they doing?' Byrd asked Tallow.

'Beech and Forrest?' Tallow asked.

Byrd nodded.

'They're doing well,' he said. 'Beech is a good guy, committed, hard-working. He sees things how I used to see them when I first started. He thinks outside the box and asks the right questions, which, as you know, is what you need in this game. Forrest is, well . . .' His face changed, as if he was about to say something less positive. 'She's—'

The door opened to their left. Tanzy appeared with four Jagerbombs cupped in his hands and a cheeky smile on his face. The others trailed with an array of drinks.

'Here you go.'

'Just a quiet few tonight, eh?' Byrd laughed.

'Only live once.'

They shared a smile.

They grabbed a shot each, clinked glasses and downed it. Forrest gagged but kept it from resurfacing, causing Tallow to laugh and Beech to spill some down his chin, which he dabbed with the back of his hand. Tanzy then washed the horrendous taste down with some lager; it had been years since he'd done shots.

'Who's up for Sambucas, then?'

'No way,' Beech said. 'Not yet anyway . . .'

'Did Tony reply?' Tanzy asked Tallow.

'No, not yet, he . . .' He trailed off, feeling something in his jeans. 'Hold on.' On the phone screen, there was an incoming call. It was McCabe. 'Here he is.' He put the phone to his ear. 'Hello?'

Tanzy turned away to face Byrd. 'Going straight to my head, this.'

'Mine too, mate.'

McCabe told them he'd join them later, and the group left William Stead's for the Green Dragon. It had loud music, flashing lights, a sticky dance floor and the drinks were cheap. They got another round of shots in.

* * *

A few hours after, they were all worse for wear, standing in the Speedy Pepper takeaway shop holding themselves up on the shelf positioned on the left under the wide menu on the wall. McCabe had met them in Hoskins and started as he meant to go on, ordering three shots of vodka in his first round. By the time they'd entered the Gate, he'd caught them up. In the Grange, they'd bumped into one of Beech's cousins, Jason, who was out with his wife. They'd shared a few jokes before Jason and his wife left and got a taxi from the closest rank.

They'd had a great night together. It was something they hadn't really done as a group before. Usually, they'd socialise with their own teams, but it was Tallow's idea and had been enjoyed by all. He and Tanzy had had a laugh, finally settling their differences. Both were intelligent men but sometimes let their egos take over.

Amanda Forrest leaned on the shelf, her forearm holding her unbalanced weight, her drunken gaze down on the floor, her eyes half closed. She was completely out of it.

'Are you okay?' Byrd asked her, concerned.

'She'll be okay,' McCabe said, rubbing her back softly. 'Some sleep and she'll be sorted.'

She let out an inaudible grunt in response.

'Number forty-seven,' the server said from the counter.

Byrd moved aside to let Tanzy get to the counter, where the server handed him his food with a smile.

The takeaway shop was filling now, groups piling in, loud conversations and sullen name-calling. Byrd glanced around, absorbing the people around him. The world had changed. It wasn't until now he realised how old he'd got. Not that forty-one was particularly old, but when surrounded by barely twenty-year-olds, it put things into perspective.

'The fuck's your problem?'

Byrd heard the voice to his right. He spun around and frowned, trying to concentrate on where it came from. A few feet along the shelf, Paul Beech was holding himself up and staring warily at the young man who'd challenged him.

'The fuck you up to?' the young lad said. He wore a tight-fitting top, almost skin-tight, his muscles protruding through the material.

'Go on, then, Trev. Hit him,' said a friend standing behind him.

Byrd turned fully and stepped forward, moving around McCabe and Forrest. 'Whoa, whoa, just hold on, what's the problem?' From what he saw, Beech was barely able to stand up, and whatever the lad's problem was, surely he'd made a mistake. Beech wasn't doing anything wrong.

'Fuck off, old man,' the lad snarled at Byrd. 'Go home and eat your pizza, fatty.' He glared back at Beech. 'Come on then, fucker.'

'Go on — hit him!' shouted one of the lad's friends again.

The pizza shop had become quiet now, the people inside realising a fight was about to break out.

All eyes fell on them.

Byrd noticed Tanzy, who had just picked up his pizza, turn at the sudden silence and digest the scene. The boisterous young lad shoved Beech hard into the shelf, his back colliding with the edge of it. Beech yelled in pain and fell to the floor, clutching at his side. The lad moved closer and kicked him in the back. Again, another shout from Beech.

'Hit him again!' a voice shouted from the front of the shop.

Byrd observed Tanzy place his pizza on the side and dash over to the front of the shop.

'Fuck do you want? You want some as well?' The lad screamed at Tanzy with eyes full of alcohol-fuelled rage.

'You need to calm down, young man,' Byrd heard Tanzy say firmly, holding his palms out in front of him. He stopped a few feet from him, glanced down to his right, noticing Beech crunched up in pain. 'What was that about?'

Without answering, the lad swung a right hand towards Tanzy's face. Tanzy had expected it and ducked, quickly leaning forward, tucking his head under the lad's armpit and wrapping his right arm around the lad's neck, grabbing his hip with his left hand. Byrd readied himself, watching the others in case they intervened. Then in a sudden movement, Tanzy swung his own right foot forward and used it to sweep the back of the lad's legs away, causing him to go down with a thud onto the white-tiled floor.

'Calm the fuck down!' Tanzy shouted, his steady voice filling the shop. He turned suddenly, glaring up at the lad's friends. 'Who's next?'

Byrd counted only two of them, eyeing Tanzy warily, calculating their chances. After a few seconds, they backed off, deciding they didn't fancy a go.

Minutes later, the lad got up and left the shop with his friends. Byrd and Tanzy helped Beech up. From the pain he was in, they guessed his ribs and back were both bruised.

'You should go to the hospital,' Byrd said.

'They're just bruises, Max, I'll be fine,' Beech said.

A group of women, who had watched what Tanzy had done, trailed past, staring at him. 'Call me,' one of them said, blowing him a kiss. Byrd smiled at the comments and focused on Beech.

'You okay, man?'

'I'll be fine, thanks. I don't even know what their problem was.'

230

'Some idiots around this town,' Byrd replied.

'No kidding.'

Once they were outside, they noticed the taxi rank to the right was at least twenty people deep. They wobbled down Skinnergate towards the other taxi rank outside of the Turk's Head pub, which was usually a lot quieter.

'I'll take you home,' Byrd heard Tanzy say to Beech, who nodded appreciatively, holding his ribs. A taxi pulled up. They opened the doors and got in.

McCabe was holding Forrest up, who was hanging from him with her loose grip around his neck. 'I'll take her home, Max. She won't make it on her own.'

'Okay.'

A taxi pulled up and McCabe helped Forrest in.

'Mind your head,' he told her.

He opened the front passenger door, resting his hand on top of it. He turned to Byrd and nodded. 'Apart from the pizza shop, it's been a good night, Max. Speak tomorrow.'

'Will do,' Byrd replied. After the taxi pulled away, he whispered, 'There's never a dull day in this town.'

58

Darlington
Fifteen years ago

It was almost ten o'clock. Sarah was still at the bottom of the garden, talking with Shez, laughing about something that had happened at school a couple of years earlier.

The music was still loud, and the party had become noticeably busier. People had sent texts out to invite more people. The garden, as well as the downstairs inside the house, was almost full now.

'I'll just go check inside,' Shez said to Sarah, leaving her with two of their friends.

'Okay, don't be long.'

Shez wandered up the garden, feeling herself wobble a little under the influence of the alcohol she'd already consumed. God, those drinks had gone to her head faster than she'd have thought. After all, it was her party but it was important she kept some level of control. She'd told people to text anyone they liked, as long as they could vouch for them being decent and wouldn't wreck the place; the last thing she wanted was for her mother and father to return from their weekend away to find the house turned upside down.

She passed Stuart and Ian on the decking and smiled briefly at them.

'Hey, you all right?' Porter said.

She nodded, then disappeared into the house. Two people were sitting on the sofa in the conservatory, arms wrapped around each other, leaning back, indulging in a passionate kiss.

'Get a room,' Shez said, laughing as she passed them.

Inside the kitchen, the CD player was blaring. It filled the space with nineties dance songs that were practically already classics. She weaved through little groups, smiling and saying hi to people she knew. There were a few unfamiliar faces; she was fine with that because she wanted this party to be the best ever. She wanted people to talk about it for ages. They'd say, remember that night at Shez's house . . .

After checking the house and chucking a couple out of her parents' bedroom, she went back downstairs, topped up her wine, then went back outside.

The sun had almost vanished now. The temporary lighting she'd hung across the side of the garage and along the side and rear fence lit the garden up well. It gave the space a warm glow, reflecting the happy buzz on people's smiling faces.

It was noticeably colder too, the temperature dipping slightly compared to when she went in.

On her right, she noticed Ian Porter and Stuart Richards still sitting on the bench, smoking and drinking, staring down into the garden. She suspected they were watching Sarah. It wasn't a secret that Sarah was hot. With that figure, she could have her pick.

* * *

On the bench next to Stuart and Ian sat James Whittaker and Gregory Timms. They arrived a few minutes ago and had already been in the kitchen and grabbed a few drinks off the worktop.

Stuart informed them both that he had a twenty-pound bet going with Ian that he could sleep with Sarah. James and

Gregory laughed hysterically. They reminded him that he'd tried before and failed miserably, so what made him think this would be different?

'I'm going to fuck her,' he told them, despite their doubt.

The others smiled at him.

'Watch me.' He stood up and confidently made his way across the decking. Dressed in a crisp white shirt and dark jeans, he stepped down onto the path and strutted down to the bottom of the garden.

'He does know he has no chance, right?' Ian heard Gregory laugh as he left.

On his approach, Sarah and Shez stopped talking and glanced his way. He kept solid eye contact until he stopped a few feet from them.

'Hi, Sarah,' he said.

'Hey.'

Her smile was magnificent; her perfect white teeth reflected the glare from the hanging lights around them. The music had shifted into eighties hits. Everyone loved it, some moving slowly while others moved faster.

'Can I get you a drink?' he said, leaning forward, trying to get closer. He could smell sweet perfume. It excited him. The thought of being on top of her, his face buried deep into her neck, the smell and touch of her skin, sent a rush down his body.

'If you like?'

He nodded like an eager dog. 'More wine?'

'How did you know I was drinking wine?'

'I can see in your cup . . .'

She mulled over his words for a moment, then finally nodded. 'Yeah, okay, not too much though, I've had a lot already.'

'Okay, I won't be long.'

Ian Porter left Sarah and Shez at the bottom of the garden and almost skipped back up. As he passed the boys, who were still on the bench, he gave them a wink.

'Where are you going?' Stuart asked.

'Getting her a drink.'

'You have no chance, Ian!'

'We'll see,' Ian laughed, but there was a feeling of determination inside. He'd failed in the past; it couldn't happen again. So far, so good; she'd agreed to a drink. Even if he wasn't buying, he was willing to go and get her one. Maybe that counted for something.

In the kitchen, where the collection of drinks was slowly disappearing, he found an empty cup and poured wine into it until it was half full. He placed the bottle back next to the other bottles — wine, vodka, sambuca, apple sours, cans of cider, lager and brown ale. Most of the food was gone, although a few cold pizza slices sat with crumbs on plates.

Without making it obvious, he glanced around the kitchen to see who was there. A couple was arguing nearby. They were occupied with each other and wouldn't notice what Ian was about to do. The other people were too engrossed in their worlds to care.

Ian put his hand deep into his pocket and pulled out a tablet. He used one of the wine bottles to crush the tablet into powder and scraped it into the plastic cup, mixing it with a spoon he'd found in a drawer to his right.

When it had fully dissolved, he left the kitchen, headed back outside.

'Go on, lad!' James teased him as he walked by them.

Stuart added, 'Twenty quid, mate, you giving it to me now or later?'

'Fuck off, Stu!' he joked, then concentrated on not stepping on the empty beer bottles that people had carelessly dropped on the floor. Down at the bottom, he held out the plastic cup towards Sarah. 'There you go.'

'Thanks, Ian,' she said, taking it from him, then she abruptly turned her back on him and faced Shez, who then laughed at what she'd done.

'Awkward,' joked one of her friends. He stood there for a moment, his face growing warm and cheeks on fire with humiliation, watching the back of her head as she continued to ignore him and talk to her friends. After a few embarrassing seconds, he slowly turned, feeling the world was watching him, dying to break out into laughter.

He stepped up onto the decking and sheepishly angled back over to Stuart, James and Gregory, who could barely contain their laughs. He felt so stupid.

He'd never felt so embarrassed in all his life, even more than the time when Rupert Marllons pulled his trousers down in Year Seven chemistry and at least five girls saw his penis.

'Don't worry about it, mate, it's only twenty pounds,' laughed Gregory hysterically, sliding along the bench making space for him to sit. 'Here, there's your drink.'

Ian took it quickly, his cheeks still warm, his blood boiling. 'The silly cow,' he said. 'The fucking bitch!' he muttered a little louder, then stared down at the floor, still feeling everyone watching him. The reality was that only the three of them were watching, and now, seeing him staring at the floor so upset, they must have realised how humiliated he felt.

'Hey, don't be daft mate,' Stuart said, 'we can't get them all.'

'Just means you owe him twenty quid, pal,' added James, smiling widely.

Ian half smiled at them. 'The night is still young.'

'You still have time,' Stuart replied, encouragingly, looking her way. 'To be fair, she does look unreal tonight, doesn't she? I might try it on if you fail.'

'Hey, I might try have a crack too,' added James. 'She looks unbelievable.'

Ian glanced their way. 'Pick your jaw up from the floor, she's mine.' The bright hanging lights illuminated Sarah's gorgeous figure, which turned him on as nothing else had ever turned him on.

He'd keep an eye on her because soon the tablet he'd mixed into her drink would start to take effect.

Then he would make his move.

59

Sunday afternoon
Police station

Emily Hope was sitting at her computer in her lab coat. Underneath, she was wearing a dark red turtleneck jumper, blue jeans and high black boots with zips at the sides. Often when they worked overtime at weekends, the dress code didn't matter as much.

She leaned forward, reading the analysis of the hair sample they'd found under Mary Richards' fingernail. The lab door opened, and in walked Paul Beech and Jacob Tallow.

'Ahh, here they come,' she said. 'Finally.'

'Give me a break. My head is pounding,' Tallow replied, squinting as his eyes adjusted to the lab's bright lighting. He went over to his desk and pulled a chair out, then dropped in it, as if his body weighed more than it did.

'Good night?' she asked.

Beech pulled out a chair and took the seat next to him.

'Yeah . . . good laugh. But these hangovers are getting harder.'

'I have no sympathy,' she told him, turning away and focusing back on the screen.

'Why didn't you come out?' Beech asked.

'I had plans.'

'What you got there?' he said, pointing at her computer screen.

'Results from the hair found on the body of Mary Richards.' She slowly faced them both, their faces all puffy and red-eyed. 'Jesus, have you two even slept?'

'It doesn't feel like it,' Tallow joked, clamping his eyes shut.

'Barely,' Beech added. 'What does it say?' he nodded towards the screen.

'Well . . . turns out the hair we found in Julia's Qashqai and the hair found under Mary's fingernail are a match. It's the same person.'

The news filled the room quickly and suddenly there was an energy around them. Tallow sat up straight, rubbed his eyes and leaned forward. 'Really?'

'That's what the DNA suggests. If this is true, then the same person was involved in both of the murders.'

Beech stared wide-eyed at her, as if not absorbing the information fully.

Tallow nodded slowly. 'I need a coffee. Who wants one?'

Beech raised his arm. 'Please. Put two spoonfuls in. I need it.'

'Yes, please,' Hope added.

Tallow padded away gingerly, the effects of the alcohol consumed hours earlier clearly weighing on his balance as he made his way to the door of the lab.

Beech leaned forward . 'A double killer?' he asked quietly, sounding as if he didn't quite believe what he'd heard.

'It seems so, Paul.'

'Jesus.'

'Is Amanda coming in today?' Hope asked, tapping away on her keyboard. 'Did she have a good night?'

'She had a lot to drink — *a lot*. She was worse for wear when we were getting a pizza. McCabe took her home in a taxi, last I heard. Tanzy texted me when he got home to let us know. Don't think she'll turn up today.'

'No?'

He shook his head. 'I sent her a text an hour ago — no reply. I don't expect her to be awake just yet.' He winced.

'What's the matter?'

'Some little shit in the pizza shop last night. Pushed me into the shelf and kicked me when I fell on the floor.'

'What? Why?' She angled her body towards him.

'You know what this town is like. I didn't even know him. Full of idiots! But Tanzy came over and flipped the lad onto his back. Jesus, you should have heard the sound. They backed off after that.'

'I can imagine.' She turned away, focused back on the screen, confirming the details of the DNA report. She reached for her phone on the desk, unlocked it and found the number he needed, then put it to her ear.

'Who you ringing?' Beech asked.

'McCabe. Let him know about this.'

Tallow came back in, opening the door with his hip, still looking rough, dark semi-circles sitting under his eyes. In his hands, he was carrying three cups of strong coffee, and it didn't take long for the smell to fill the lab as he placed them down on the wide desk where Beech was sitting. He walked around him and handed Hope her cup.

'Thanks,' she said, taking it with her free hand.

'Who's she on the phone to?' Tallow asked, taking a seat.

'She's trying to get hold of McCabe.'

After she tried three times, each time going to his answerphone, she hung up. 'He must be asleep.' She glanced down at her watch. It was nearly half ten. Through the window of the lab, the skies were dark and grey. The rain was imminent. Hope hadn't had the chance to eat yet, and her stomach now grumbling. 'I need food now.'

'I'll get something delivered,' Tallow said, pulling out his phone. 'What do you want?'

Hope and Beech gave him their orders and he phoned the nearest café, which told him it would be ready in twenty minutes. He changed his mind and said he'd go pick it up. The place was only two minutes away, and he needed some air.

* * *

Byrd jogged into the station, hair all over the place and hands firmly in his pockets against the late-morning chill.

Tallow was just in front of him. When he saw Byrd, he said, 'We've just got sarnies in. I'd have got you one if I knew you were coming in.'

He opened the door for him.

'Don't worry, I've had something already,' Byrd replied.

They made their way through reception and down the corridor. In the lab, they found Hope and Beech finishing their coffee.

'Look who showed up,' Tallow said.

Tallow placed the bag of food down on the desk and the smell of bacon filled the air.

'Morning, Max,' Beech said. 'How's the head?'

'Sore,' he replied. 'I've felt better.' Byrd dropped down into a spare chair and sighed heavily. 'How's your back?'

'It hurts bad.' Beech winced, leaning forward, touching the area on his right side, a spot between his hip and lat muscle. 'If I wasn't drunk, I wouldn't have slept at all with the pain.'

'Is Tanzy here yet?' Byrd asked them.

'Haven't seen him yet,' Hope said. 'Is he coming in?'

'He said he might, I'll ring him soon.' Byrd stood up. 'Who wants coffee?'

They shook their heads and watched him go in the direction of the canteen. 'Oh, Max . . .' Hope said quickly. He stopped before the door and turned. 'The results came back from the DNA of the hair found under Mary Richards' fingernail. It's a match to the hair found in Julia Porter's car. The same person was involved in both murders.'

240

For a second, he stood in silence, absorbing what she'd said. Then he nodded, turned and made his way to the canteen, mulling over what had been discovered, thinking about the photograph that he'd seen at James Whittaker's house.

The same person.

A double killer.

If things went the same way for Karen Whittaker as they had for the other kidnapped women, it might well be a serial killer.

He had to tell Tanzy. At the canteen, he pulled out his phone, found his number and pressed CALL.

'Max,' he said.

'Ori, are you coming in?'

Tanzy moaned something inaudible.

'Orion?'

'Sorry?' Tanzy said.

'Are you coming in?' Byrd asked again.

'My head is pounding, Max. I'll grab a shower. I might come in later. I need to . . .' He trailed off.

'Need to what?'

'Ignore me, Max. I've just woken up. I'll get sorted. Be in later.'

'Before you go . . . We've got the results back from the DNA. Both hairs at the separate crime scenes match up. We have a double killer on our hands.' He paused a beat, flicking on the kettle in the canteen. 'Have you heard from Harrison?'

'She hasn't got back to me yet. Her husband hasn't been in touch either. There's something seriously wrong here — I think she's in trouble.'

Byrd didn't reply.

'What are you thinking, Max?' Tanzy asked in response to his silence.

'What if she's in trouble, but a different kind of trouble?' Byrd asked.

'What are you talking about?' Tanzy's tone turned sour, knowing what he was insinuating.

'What if she's done something seriously wrong and has disappeared because of it? We've been dancing around it without saying anything, but perhaps this is more than a case of incorrectly misfiled reports.'

'I don't know, Max, I—'

'Did she lie to us about that report?'

Tanzy didn't like the sound of it, but it was hard to ignore the possibility.

60

Darlington
Fifteen years ago

At the bottom of the garden, Sarah wobbled a little on her feet.

'Easy, Sarah, easy,' said Shez, holding her up. 'The drink's gone to your head. Do you need to sit down?'

Sarah recklessly shook her head, then removed Shez's grip. 'No!' She moved away and started dancing to the sound of the music coming from the kitchen back inside the house.

'Okay, fine,' Shez said. There was no telling her. They'd often drink together at weekends, but she'd never seen her get so drunk so quickly.

'Come on, let's go inside, Sarah,' Shez said to her.

Sarah was almost out of it, her state deteriorating rapidly. She gave in and nodded, leaning on Shez's shoulder.

'I'm going to take her inside,' Shez told the other girls, 'I don't know what's wrong with her.' The atmosphere around them changed and suddenly they started to grow concerned as they watched Shez lead her across the decking and into the kitchen.

'Why is she like that?' asked one of the girls. 'She hasn't had that much . . .'

Sarah took a step forward and stumbled, and would have hit her face on the floor if not for Shez holding her weight up.

'Jesus, Sarah, hold on . . .' Shez begged, struggling to keep her upright. 'Hey, Jessica, give me a hand over here.'

'How many's she fucking had?' one of the lads nearby shouted, then laughed.

'Where are we taking her?' Jessica asked, quickly helping Shez.

'We'll take her up to my room, lay her on the bed.'

They helped Sarah into the house and slowly up the stairs.

In Shez's bedroom, she turned on the light. On the floor next to the bed there was a boy on top of a girl, his pants down around his ankles. It seemed they hadn't started what they had intended to do.

'Get out now!' Shez demanded.

'Shit!' gasped the girl. 'Sorry!'

'Just get out.'

Once they had left, Shez and Jessica lowered Sarah onto Shez's double bed and placed her head carefully on her pillow.

'Why's she like this, Shez?'

'God knows. She hasn't drunk any more than we have,' she replied. 'Must be . . .'

They stopped. 'What?'

'Has she taken anything?' Shez's eyes hardened at Jessica.

'You mean drugs?' Jessica raised her eyebrows.

'Yes! Have you given her any drugs?'

Jessica edged back. 'What! No, of course I haven't . . . why would I?'

'Because I've never seen her like this before. She's never done this. And everyone knows you take drugs!'

'Don't blame me!' Jessica snapped. 'Whatever this is, it isn't my fucking doing!'

Jessica stormed off through the open door. The sound of the music downstairs came through — it sounded like someone had turned the CD player up. Shez would deal with

244

that after she'd sorted Sarah out. The best thing for her was to close her eyes and sleep it off. She went over, closed the door and returned to the bed.

'Aww Sarah, what's happened to you?'

Sarah didn't reply. She was out of it, somewhere between being semi-conscious and sleeping. Shez, doing the best she could, lifted her and pulled the duvet covers back, then slowly lowered her back down on the bed again and pulled the covers up over her.

Using the back of her hand, Shez felt her friend's forehead. She was hot. She pulled the covers back down to her stomach to keep her cool.

'I'll get you some water.'

Shez rose and left the room, padded along the landing to the bathroom and filled up an empty cup from the tap, then returned to her room. When she got there, a man was standing in the middle of the room, staring down at Sarah.

Shez froze behind him. 'Hello?'

The man turned slowly towards Shez.

'What you doing in my room, Ian?'

Ian Porter shrugged. 'Is . . . is she okay?'

'No, she isn't. I think she's been drugged or something. She's out of it. I'm going to let her rest on her own for a while. So please, if you could go.'

'Do you need any—'

'Ian — go, please!'

Shez watched Ian quickly leave the bedroom, then turned to check on her friend one last time.

61

Monday morning
Police station

It was Tanzy's unwritten rule that the manager of a team should arrive first, so when the team turned up, the manager had an update and a plan for the day ahead. He or she needed to make the right decisions, which took preparation, patience and time. At least thirty minutes of it, in Tanzy's opinion.

So, at half seven, when he pulled up and turned off his engine, the only car there belonged to DCI Thornton. A brand-new black Range Rover.

Tanzy, sitting at his desk with a coffee, turned on his computer. He waited, watching the morning traffic out of the window.

He heard DCI Thornton on the phone in her office. He turned slightly and noticed her door open half an inch. It sounded like she was on the phone with one of her friends, judging by the nature of the conversation, discussing possible plans for the weekend, he assumed.

He picked up his phone from the desk and tried the number for PC Harrison again. He hadn't heard from her in three days now. Byrd told Tanzy he'd tried and, yet again, he'd had no joy.

The phone call went straight to answerphone. The phone battery was dead, Tanzy assumed. He found the number he had saved for her husband and dialled that. That, too, rang out, but he received a text straight after saying:

Can't speak. Still no sign of Kim yet. Thanks.

Deciding it was time, he pushed his chair back and stood up, took a few steps to DCI Thornton's office and rapped on the door.

'Come in,' she said.

'Morning,' he said.

'Hey, Ori. Good weekend?'

'It was okay. Was in here so wasn't the most exciting.'

'I saw the news,' she said. 'The press conference with the Joneses. You did well.'

'Thanks. Still, nothing come in yet, though.'

She smiled. 'Give it time. How can I help?'

Tanzy took a seat and composed himself. 'I'm worried about PC Harrison.'

'Have you not heard from her yet?'

He shook his head. 'No. I—'

'When did you last see her?'

'Friday afternoon. Her husband has no idea where she is either — he was expecting her home on Friday. I'm not sure why he hasn't filed a missing person's report yet, but if he doesn't, I will. Did she say anything specific about this family emergency?'

'No, she didn't say much. But she seemed distracted as if something was on her mind. Let me try her.' Thornton picked up her phone from the desk and called her. She frowned after it went straight to voicemail and placed the phone back down on the desk.

'Voicemail?' Tanzy asked.

She nodded. Thornton thought in silence for a moment. 'I must say, knowing Kim, that is unusual. But what if — now hear me out, Orion, this isn't what I think, it's just a theory — what if she went away with someone, someone who wasn't her husband?'

Tanzy mulled over her words. 'Unlikely.'

'Why?'

'Because I know her. I know she wouldn't do that. She's happily married.'

'How do you know that?'

'Because she told me.'

'Ori, just because she told you, it doesn't mean it's the truth.'

'Fair enough.' Tanzy paused a beat. 'Regardless, it's time to report her missing.'

'Yes, maybe you're right, Ori. Leave it with me. I'll sort it.'

'Thanks,' he said. He stood up and left her office. Back at his desk, he noticed Byrd was sitting on his chair, a mug of steaming coffee in his right hand.

'Cosy talk with the boss?' Byrd joked, a grin lining his face. 'Always knew you wanted fast promotions . . .'

Tanzy smiled and took a seat. 'Expressing my concerns about Kim — I think there's something seriously, seriously wrong. Where on earth is she?'

They said nothing for the best part of two minutes while Byrd's computer booted up. The system, like it often did, was playing up today.

Tanzy clicked his fingers to get Tanzy's attention, then leaned back and pointed upwards to the ceiling, reminding Byrd of the hidden microphone that he'd found.

Byrd bobbed his head in understanding. 'You want a coffee?'

'Yeah. I'll come with you.'

They both stood up and made their way through the office in the direction of the canteen.

'Morning, boss,' said PC Amy Weaver, who was sitting at her desk.

Byrd nodded. 'Good morning, Amy. Have a good weekend?'

She smiled. 'Yes, thanks. It was very good.'

'Morning, Orion,' said a voice from their right. It was PC Cornty, who sat bolt upright in his chair, his beady eyes peering over his glasses, which rested on the end of his nose.

The canteen was quiet. DS Stockdale walked in as the kettle was boiling and kept his side of the conversation to a minimum. He seemed to be more interested in what was happening on his phone, which the detectives didn't mind because they needed to speak in a place they knew wasn't bugged: a place nobody was listening. He gave them a professional nod before leaving.

'Did Jennifer Lucas find the man in the black fleece on the CCTV?'

'We couldn't find him. Not on the cameras we were looking at anyway. She said she would get in touch if she saw him.'

'A needle in a haystack in a town like this.'

'Tell me about it,' Tanzy replied, deflated.

They made their way back to their desks. The office was filling up now. Back at their desks, they noticed DCI Thornton's door was closed.

'You tried Harrison again?' Byrd asked, taking a seat.

'Yeah. Not answering. Even Thornton tried.' Tanzy slumped down, rubbing his palm over his tired face, and sighed, then glanced up for a second at the ceiling, imagining the exact location of the listening device above the ceiling tile.

'Did you get a chance to file the report on Karen Whittaker?'

Byrd nodded. 'Yeah. It's in the system. I've forwarded it to local services too. Also updated Thornton on it.'

'Good.' He leaned forward, took a sip, then picked up his phone. 'I need to find a number and make a phone call.'

62

Ten days ago
Junior school, Darlington

Evelyn Jones, after she packed her bag, stood still in the cloakroom just outside the classroom.

'Is everything okay, Evelyn?' Mr McMahon had seen her through the open door.

She tried hard not to cry, but tears were already forming in her eyes. The teacher noticed, stood up and dashed over.

'Evelyn, dear. What's wrong?' He lowered to his knee. 'What's with the long face?'

'I don't understand.'

'You don't understand what?' he asked, frowning with concern.

'Bye, Evelyn!' a voice shouted from the open door of the classroom. Evelyn faked a smile and waved at Sophie. She wanted to say, 'I'm coming, wait for me,' but she wasn't sure she'd be able to speak without crying.

'What don't you understand, Evelyn?' he asked again.

'The question.'

'The maths question?'

She nodded. A tear fell down her cheek.

'Aww, Evelyn.' He patted her small arm. 'Don't worry about it. We'll go over it tomorrow, okay? You're not alone, you know. Some of the others don't fully understand it either, so we'll go over it again to make sure everyone knows what to do. How does that sound?'

Her eyes still glassy, she sniffed and nodded. 'Yeah, okay.'

'Right, go on, get your coat on and catch up with your friends. You'll be the last out. It'll be getting dark soon.'

She slowly zipped up her coat and left the classroom. Usually she walked with Sophie and her mum to their house, then Evelyn would walk the extra thirty seconds to her own home. They walked down the street, crossed the road, went down the bank of grass, through the woods and out on the other side. It was the same route they took every day.

But when Evelyn got outside this time, Sophie and her mother were gone. She was alone in the playground, the last of the parents shuffling out of the gates in the distance.

'Wait for me,' she shouted towards the gate that seemed a million miles away. She recognised the coat that Sophie's mother usually wore and ran along the path, heading towards the gate, her school bag bouncing side to side across her back. 'Wait!'

When she reached the gate, she took a left and looked down the street. Sophie and her mummy were gone. She froze, unsure of what to do. She glanced the other way, hoping to see a familiar face.

There wasn't one.

Her mother always said if a parent wasn't there for whatever reason, to go back into school and ask a teacher what to do. So she turned around and ran back along the path to the school door she'd just left through.

The door was locked.

She knocked a few times and, after waiting for nearly a minute, she gave up.

'Are you okay?' she heard a voice say behind her.

She turned quickly. 'Huh?'

'Sorry I scared you, honey,' said the man. She'd seen him before. It was the caretaker. 'Are you okay?'

251

She nodded, then shrunk into herself, as if she'd done something wrong by standing there after school had finished. 'I'm . . . fine.'

'Do you need to be back inside — have you forgotten something?'

She shook her head, avoiding his eyes. 'I was looking for my friend.'

'I think everyone's gone home, little one.'

She looked up at him. He was tall and thin, almost gangly. His dark, almost black eyes watched her closely, and a thin smile reached the corners of his mouth.

'Sorry.' She moved forward to go around him but stopped when he held up a palm. 'Will you be okay, walking home by yourself?'

She nodded several times. 'I can walk home.'

'You sure?'

'Yeah.'

'Which way do you walk?'

'It isn't far.'

The caretaker looked up to the sky, noticed darkness was creeping in. 'Are you sure? You're not very old.'

'I have to go down the street and through the woods. It doesn't take long.'

'Okay.' The man stepped to the side, allowing her to pass.

Evelyn knew where she was going. Would it matter that she wasn't walking with Sophie and her mummy? As long as she walked the same way, she'd get home like she did any other night. After she turned the corner into Barnes Road, she crossed over, then took a right and walked around the bend until she reached the grass.

She walked down the grass bank, stepped into the woods and hurried along the dirt path in the direction of her house. The sun was falling quickly in the distance.

It was different on her own. She felt vulnerable. Alone.

She wasn't alone, but Evelyn didn't know that. Somebody was walking behind her, watching her closely, closing the gap with each stride they took.

63

Monday afternoon
Darlington

The pleasant smell of freshly cut wood hung in the air as Tanzy stepped into Jewson Builders Merchants. He passed an array of shelving and stopped at the counter, where a thin man was looking intently at the computer screen.

'Is Gregory Timms in?' he asked. Tanzy noticed a name tag fixed to his chest with the name Harry on as well as the word 'manager' printed underneath it.

Harry peered up at Tanzy over stylish thin-framed glasses. 'He is. Who's asking?'

'Tell him it's the police,' Tanzy informed him. 'I spoke with him earlier.'

'You did? What's this about?'

'Would you mind getting him, please?'

The man with the glasses held his gaze on Tanzy before he took out his phone, pressed some buttons and put it to his ear.

'Come to reception. Police are here for you.' He lowered the phone, put it back into his pocket. 'He's coming right out.'

A minute later, a small man that Tanzy recognised from the group photo to be Gregory Timms, walked through the open door, wearing a black fleece with a yellow Jewson logo sewn on his chest.

'Did I speak to you earlier?' he asked Tanzy.

'Detective Inspector Orion Tanzy.' He reached into his inside pocket and pulled out the photograph to show Timms.

When Timms recognised the four teenagers, his eyebrows furrowed. 'Where is this from?'

'I got it from your friend, James Whittaker. Two days ago.'

'I don't understand,' Timms said, confusion enveloping his whole face.

'Well,' Tanzy began, 'this man's wife —' he pointed at Ian Porter — 'was brutally murdered five days ago. You may have heard it on the news?'

Timms shook his head.

'She was found at their home, tied to a chair. Her eyes were missing.'

'Jesus.' Timms raised a hand to his open mouth.

'And this guy —' he pointed to Stuart Richards — 'this guy's wife was found hanging from a tree with only one hand.'

Timms tried to say something, but whatever it was got stuck in his throat.

'And this man —' his finger now on James Whittaker — 'his wife was kidnapped on Saturday morning by three men in a van. We haven't found her yet.'

Timms found his voice, but it came out weak. 'God . . .'

'Two murders and a kidnapping. You knew these men when they were last in contact with each other. What's the connection?'

For a long moment, Timms stared at the photo, then said, 'We were friends back in school. All in the same class. We kept in touch for a while, but we kind of lost touch.'

'Why did you lose touch? Something happened, didn't it?' Tanzy asked.

'I worked more hours.' He shrugged. 'I found a girlfriend, settled down.'

'Is that right?'

He nodded confidently. 'We're married now.'

'True love, eh?' Tanzy said.

'Guess so.'

'When was this photograph taken?' Tanzy enquired.

'Erm . . .' Timms focused on the background behind them in the photo. 'At a party. It was at a party. Someone's birthday, I think.'

'Can you remember who?'

He expelled a sudden pocket of air from his mouth. 'I have no idea. We went to all sorts of parties back then, I think — hang on . . . Shez someone, maybe?' He frowned, tilted his head back, thinking hard, then nodded. 'Her name was Shez. Yeah.'

'Has Shez got a second name?'

'She's a girl from school. We weren't in her class, but she was in our year. I only knew her as Shez.' Timms wouldn't look Tanzy in the eye.

Tanzy nodded, knowing he was lying.

'The main reason for my visit here today is to offer your wife some police protection.'

Timms frowned, clearly not keen on the idea.

Tanzy stabbed his finger at the photo. 'If this is anything to go by, with what's been happening, then there's a real possibility she could be in danger, Mr Timms.'

'Okay.'

'Can you think of a reason why anyone would want to cause harm to these men's wives? Or your own wife?'

'As I said, I haven't spoken to them in years. I don't even know their wives. I . . . I . . .' He trailed off.

'What?' Tanzy asked, tilting his head.

'I can't think of anything at all.'

* * *

Once Tanzy was back in his car, the heavens opened. Stone-sized droplets pounded the windscreen in a fast rhythmic beat, which made him feel relieved he was under shelter.

He made a phone call to DCI Thornton, telling her about his conversation with Timms and suggesting they send an officer to watch his wife, Samantha. Thornton said she'll sort it and thanked him for his diligence. He ended the call, plucked the photograph of the four from his pocket and stared at it for a long moment, knowing this was more than just a photograph of four friends.

64

Tuesday morning
Neil and Judith McMahon's house

Judith flicked on the kettle and asked Neil if he wanted a cuppa.

'No, thank you,' Neil McMahon said to his wife. It was just after seven, and they'd both been awake for nearly an hour. It was their routine. Even at weekends, they'd get up early and make the most of the day.

McMahon was sitting at the table, looking at the local news.

'Have they heard anything yet?' she asked him.

'No, not yet. I spoke with Evelyn's parents last night, but we're no further forward. The kids in the class almost see her as a distant memory now. It's awful. Upsetting. A couple of them, the ones who sit with her at her table, look almost lost next to the empty chair. Whenever the door opens, I pray I'll look up and see her walk back in.'

She padded over in her fluffy slippers and placed a hand on his back but didn't say anything.

Then they heard something.

McMahon frowned and glanced up. As did his wife. The sound was coming from upstairs. It was like a cry — or a wail.

'What on earth is that?' McMahon said.

Judith frowned.

He stood up, looked up at the ceiling. 'What is it?'

The more they concentrated, the more it sounded like a cry. A child's cry. He left the kitchen and stepped into the hallway.

'Where are you going, Neil?'

'It's coming from upstairs, I think.' He ascended the stairs slowly, carefully listening for the sound he didn't understand. At the top of the stairs, he heard it again.

His wife was right behind him. 'Neil?'

'Shhhh.' He turned his head to listen. 'It's coming from in there . . .' He stepped up onto the landing and crept into the back bedroom. His wife followed, then stopped behind him when he came to a halt.

The cry broke out again. A helpless cry.

'It's coming from the cupboard I think?' McMahon said, moving towards the sound. He reached for the handle and pulled it open. The crying suddenly came to a halt. Inside the cupboard was an array of shelves to the right and clothes hanging from a rail on the left.

He stared intently, confused. 'I don't understand.'

'What's there?' she asked.

'Nothing. Just our wardrobe,' he said. 'I need to knock next door, it'll be their daughter. She sounds upset.'

'Yeah, she does.'

McMahon moved past her, padded down the stairs and put his shoes on. If next door's daughter was that upset, the question was: why? He loved children. It was his job to look out for them, to guide them to better futures. It took him less than half a minute to knock on her door. Through the small piece of glass in the window, he saw Alex, the girl's father, appearing closer until the door opened.

'Hi, Neil?' he said, appearing flushed, his cheeks red. Sweat dripped from his brow.

'Hi, Alex . . .' he started. 'Strange question, but is your daughter okay?'

Alex glowered at McMahon. 'Yeah . . . why?'

'We heard crying upstairs in our house. It seems like it's coming from maybe your daughter's room?'

'So?'

'And . . . I'm just checking that she's okay, if you hadn't heard her crying?'

'I heard her. She was getting told off for something bad she did . . .'

McMahon stared at the man, wondering if any physical abuse had been used. 'Okay.'

'Is there anything else?' he said sternly.

'No,' Neil said. 'Sorry to have bothered you.'

The man closed the door quickly, almost slamming it. McMahon stepped down then walked along the short driveway until he hit the path.

Outside the house, he noticed the white van that Alex had been driving around in wasn't there anymore.

65

Tuesday morning
River Tees

Derek Pratt, as he did every day, parked in the car park of Broken Scar. He got out and opened the boot, allowing his dog, Hugo, to bounce out, leaping about with excitement about his walk. A chill hung in the air.

'Come on, boy,' Derek said.

Hugo kept still long enough for Derek to attach the lead to the red collar around his neck. They strolled along the man-made path, heading along the side of the river.

This morning it was almost deserted, as if the path had somehow been forgotten.

In the distance, fifteen metres up in the sky, a flock of birds circled furiously, one of them occasionally swooping down for something. No doubt picking off the fish in the river, he assumed, waiting for the perfect time to catch their prey.

After stepping over the metal hop-up by the side of the closed gate — designed for keeping the sheep and cows inside — they continued, following the footpath by the wide area of grass. The ground was soggy and damp, the mud stuck to the bottom of his shoes like glue from the rain that had hammered down the night before.

Suddenly, Hugo darted right, yanking on the lead, which extended to its full length. Derek struggled to keep a hold of it, slipping on the mud. 'Easy boy, easy!'

He angled in the direction the dog wanted to go. Hugo was desperate, as if he had picked up the scent of another canine nearby. But there was no sound, no barking, no noise — apart from the gushing flowing river beside them.

Hugo pulled Derek closer to the river. An angled bank of grass led to a small area of stones, almost hidden by a small cluster of trees.

'Easy boy,' he said again, feeling the power of the dog's desperation as he dragged him down onto the stones. The dog slowed and started sniffing, his wet nose close to the ground, his head moving frantically.

Out of nowhere, a bird flew up into the air and darted off into the sky. Hugo barked at it until it disappeared from their sight.

Hugo edged forward again, pulling on the lead. Then Derek heard the sound of buzzing. The closer he got, the continual buzzing sound overpowered the sound of the river. It sounded like a beehive.

And then he saw it. It wasn't a beehive.

At first, he wasn't sure if it was real. Somehow, it seemed . . . not right.

It was unlike anything he'd ever seen.

'Jesus Christ.'

66

Tuesday afternoon
Broken Scar, River Tees

Tanzy slowed the Golf and took a left into Broken Scar. Standing in front of the temporary tape was PC Cornty. After he realised it was Tanzy and Byrd, he moved aside and let them through.

As Tanzy stopped his car down in the bottom car park, Byrd released his seat belt and opened the door. Tanzy did the same. The air outside the car was freezing. They headed up the ramp and could smell dampness in the air, the way the trees and plants had soaked up the rain from the night before.

'Whittaker?' Byrd asked.

'There's a good chance it's her.'

Along the muddy path, not a word was spoken between them, until they reached a metal hop-up at the fence, where Amy Weaver was standing, stopping any members of the public from accessing the area. 'Afternoon,' she said.

'Hi, Amy,' Tanzy said. 'Are forensics here yet?'

She nodded. 'They're all here.'

'Tallow, Hope, Forrest, Beech?' Byrd asked.

'Even McCabe,' she said.

262

'Full show today. Must be important for the Hollywood stars to show up too.'

PC Weaver smiled at him.

The detectives made their way around the bend and came into view of another officer standing in the middle of the grass. It was DS Stockdale. He pointed behind him, just off to the right. 'You wanna be down there.'

'Thanks. You been down?' Tanzy said, carefully stepping over the overgrown grass in his not-so-perfect footwear.

Stockdale nodded. 'Yeah . . .' A look of sadness swept across his face.

'What is it?' Byrd asked.

'You should see for yourselves.'

Byrd and Tanzy passed him, carefully making their way down the wet, grassy decline, then stepped down onto the small area of stones. There, in front of them, was the forensics team. Hope was kneeling in front of the body. Tallow was standing beyond her on the other side of it, taking photos, and Forrest and Beech each had a pen in their hands, scribbling down notes on their separate notepads towards the right. To the left stood McCabe, staring at the river. He seemed to be in a trance.

Hope spotted the approaching detectives and stood up, allowing them room to step forward and have a look. The body in front of them was female, they could tell by the matted, soaked blonde hair. There was a clump of entwined blood stuck to the back of the victim's head, telling them she'd been hit by something hard, hard enough to damage the skull. Most likely, at a glance, the kind of damage that a baseball bat would do, but it was difficult to tell. Her face had swelled with water, her skin seeming transparent. Her body looked overweight due to the water it had absorbed in the time it had been there. It was evident that areas of her face had been eaten by birds and fish, parts of flesh hanging loosely off her.

'Jesus.' Byrd edged forward some more then came to a halt, feeling a lump rising in his throat.

Tanzy hung back a few steps to absorb the scene and the lifeless woman in front of them. The smell that surrounded them changed from the damp plant life smell to something else, something—

'Oh, God.'

He recognised her now, despite the bloating. It wasn't Karen Whittaker.

Tanzy's stomach flipped then twisted inside out, forcing him to turn away, lean over and be sick on the grass to their right. Hope winced in his direction but understood why.

'Why?' he said, quietly at first, then: 'Why!' His voice echoed through the air, then he turned back to her. 'Why her?'

'How long has she been in the water?' Byrd asked Hope.

Tallow answered. 'Hard to say. Judging by the skin, the way it's swelled, could be three to four days, in my opinion.'

McCabe, who was now standing next to Tallow, the height of Tallow making McCabe look like a child, nodded, confirming Tallow's theory. Testing would be done to find out exactly what had happened to her.

One of the things running through Tanzy's mind was ringing her husband to tell him that she was dead. *He* had to do it. Not Byrd but him. It was his duty.

'I'll find whoever did this to you,' Tanzy whispered to her lifeless, swelled body. 'I promise you that, Kim.'

67

Darlington
Fifteen years ago

Shez stepped out of her bedroom and closed the door, her shadow dancing on the ceiling above her as she descended into the flashing lights of the party. Ian Porter stepped out his hiding place in the bathroom and stopped at the closed bedroom door, then glanced left. There was no one on the stairs. No one coming up. Quickly, he opened the door and slid inside. The room would have been in total darkness if not for the dim lamp on the bedside table.

Even in the state of unconsciousness, she was beautiful.

Ian padded over the white carpet carefully, finding his bearings in the room. Sarah was on her back, her head tipped to one side, her body slightly turned, her face angling towards the window.

It was a shame the way she'd been put to bed, Ian thought. The covers were up over her stomach, keeping her warm. That was no good.

'You don't need these on, dear. We don't want you getting too hot, do we?' he whispered, then prudently pulled them off, dropped them to the carpet by his feet. He was getting hard in his jeans just looking at her.

'Wow,' he whispered.

Conscious of the time he had remaining, he unclipped his belt, let his jeans drop to the floor, then pulled down his red boxers and kicked them to one side. He dropped down onto the bed, leaned forward and yanked at her underwear.

Then he climbed on top and forced himself into her.

68

Byrd could see the grief in Tanzy's face as they walked back to their desks. He knew his friend felt the weight of responsibility on his shoulders, that he felt accountable for what had happened to PC Harrison. Byrd knew the sight of her dead body wouldn't leave his own head. He tried his best to block out the mental imprint and clamped his eyes shut, but nothing seemed to work. The way her skin had lost its colour and appeared thinner, the way her body had swelled, making her appear like someone else entirely, but at the same time, obviously her.

Tanzy headed for the canteen. Byrd took off his coat and sat down slowly, letting his weight fall into the chair. He felt numb. One of their own had died.

Did she drown? Did she accidentally slip? Why was she there in the first place?

Judging by what he saw on the stones, it looked like she'd been struck over the head with something hard. Hard enough to draw blood. But could it have been accidental — a strike from a rock in the river, perhaps even after death? He wasn't sure which was worse. He'd speak with Hope and Tallow later to get a better idea of exactly what had happened.

Byrd turned on the computer and waited impatiently for the screen to come on, thinking about his mother and father, how helpless they both were, lying there in comas at the hospital. It was horrible. He wanted to see them; that's what he did when he felt down. They picked him up, especially his father. A very positive guy, always seeing the best in people and the situations he found himself in.

Once, Byrd recalled, they were driving back from Scarborough and got a flat tyre. They'd just set off, and Byrd, a boy of nine, really wanted to get home for a party at his friend's house. He'd been looking forward to it for ages, but the recovery company couldn't come and fix the car in time, so they had to go back to Scarborough and stay overnight. The only room they could find was in a seafront pub, the Lord Nelson.

His father had told him that, although he would miss the party, he had to change the way he looked at things. He told him that every cloud had a silver lining if he looked close enough. And when Byrd had woken the next morning, snuggled up to his parents in probably one of the smallest rooms he'd ever slept in, the sunrise through the seafront window was the most beautiful thing he'd ever seen. That same morning, they got candy floss and went to the fairground again. Then they had the chance to go on the speedboat that was docked the day before due to bad weather. So in a way, he was grateful for the car having a flat tyre because that morning was so good, he'd never forgotten it.

It was, however, a difficult task searching for a silver lining regarding the current condition of his parents. There simply wasn't one.

Tanzy returned with two cups of coffee, handed one to Byrd and took a seat on his chair, then sat back and sighed heavily. The office was quiet. Eerily quiet.

'Gonna be a long day,' Tanzy muttered.

'Yeah, I know.'

For a long moment, they both just sat, still and quiet, as if on standby mode, reserving their energy for what was coming next. A lot had happened over the past couple of weeks. Darlington hadn't witnessed the disappearance of a seven-year-old, three murders and a kidnapping inquiry within the time frame of ten days before.

It was all happening too fast.

It was tiring.

* * *

Tanzy had almost closed his eyes, when he heard the door open behind them.

'Orion . . .'

He blinked a few times and turned to the voice.

'Yeah?' said Tanzy.

'My office, please?'

He nodded, found his feet and went into DCI Thornton's office.

'Close the door, Orion.'

He did.

'Sit down.'

He did.

'How are you doing? I heard the news about Kim . . .' she said.

'It's awful,' he began. 'She was a lovely girl with a brilliant future ahead of her. Always so pleasant to people. Hard-working. Why would anyone do this to her? It's . . . it's . . .' He trailed off, dropping his face into his hands for a moment.

She gave a sad smile, observing and sympathising with his emotions. 'I know . . . but listen, Orion. We'll do everything we can to find out what happened to her.' She leaned forward and squeezed his hand. 'We'll find whoever did this, I promise you that. It's hard enough when it's a member of the force, but when it's your own, it's . . .'

He glanced up and sighed, 'Yeah.'

'You can take a day off, or a few days if you need it. We can handle things here.'

'I'll be fine . . . but thank you.'

'Okay. Well, let me know if there's anything I can do for you.'

'Thanks,' he said, then he stood up and made his way back into the main office.

'Orion.'

Before he stepped through the door, he turned.

'We'll get them, you know. Don't worry about it,' she said with determination in her eyes.

'I know we will,' he said. 'We always do, boss.'

69

Tuesday afternoon
Emergency control room

Matilda Ellis had been at the forefront of emergency dispatch for the best part of twenty-two years. Over that time, countless employees had come and gone, some moving on to better things, some leaving the police force entirely.

On seven occasions, she had been offered a promotion. She'd declined every time. She loved her job as a call handler, answering emergency calls and allocating services to various locations, and the calls were certainly diverse. They varied hugely, from a girl trapped inside a lift to an elderly man who'd had a plant pot stolen.

There were some weird and wonderful people out there, that was for sure.

It had just gone three in the afternoon. She finished her coffee and placed the empty cup next to the keyboard. A call hadn't come in for twenty-four minutes, which was unusual. On average, there were 170 calls daily, all of them handled by Matilda, Jackie, Alan and Peter. This number doubled on a bank holiday, and the average usually increased during the summer months.

She sat back, waiting for the next call, then right on cue, the phone rang.

Raising her hand to her headset, she accepted the call.

'Emergency, what service?' Matilda said into the headset.

'Erm . . . I . . . I . . .' The caller's voice trailed away.

'Emergency, what service?'

'It's dead. I haven't seen anything like it . . .'

'This is emergency response,' Matilda said loud and clear. 'What service do you require?'

'Police — I need the police.' A few seconds of silence followed. 'Or maybe an ambulance.'

She guessed it sounded like a male, most likely between the age of fifty to sixty, an ability she'd picked up over the years.

'You require the police?'

'Yes. It's not . . . it's just on its own . . .'

'Sir, where are you?'

'In a back alley. Back of Greenbank Road . . . near the hospital,' replied the flustered man. 'I'm in front of the bin.'

Immediately, she put the address into the system and waited for further information from him.

'What's inside the bin?'

'It's a . . . oh, God . . .'

'Sir, can you please tell me what's in the bin?' she said calmly.

'A woman's head.'

For a second, Matilda was stuck for words, wondering if she'd heard him correctly. 'Can you confirm you have found a woman's head in the bin?'

'Yeah . . . it's a head.'

'Emergency response is being sent to your location right now, sir.'

'Okay.'

'Can you please stay on the line until they get there? Is that okay, sir?' she asked.

'Erm . . . yeah. Okay.'

'What is your name?'

'Patrick.'

'What's your second name?'

'Walton. My full name is Patrick Matthew Walton.'

'Okay, Mr Walton, thank you for calling me today. Is it okay to call you Patrick?'

'Yes,' he said. 'That's fine.'

'Okay, Patrick. Are you alone?'

'Yes.'

'And who did you see?'

'A man. He . . . he was acting weird and looking inside the bin, then he ran into the house through the back gate next to the bin.'

'What did the man look like?'

'Scared. He panicked.'

'What was he wearing?' Matilda asked.

'I only got a glimpse of him. A red jumper, I think. He had black hair. Or maybe brown. That's all I saw before he went inside the gate.'

'Okay, that's great. How old is the man?'

'I . . . I don't know. Maybe forty? Could be fifty . . . it was hard to tell. Maybe older.'

'Emergency services should be there very soon, Patrick.'

While holding the phone to his head, Patrick heard sirens somewhere in the air, growing louder by the second.

'I can hear them,' he told her.

'They're arriving right now. I can see their location on my screen. Thank you for your call, Patrick.'

* * *

A marked Astra flew around the corner of the alley and came to a sudden halt in front of Patrick. The brakes pinged, and the tyres squeaked on the damp cobbles. The lights on the top of the car spun in synchronicity with the near-deafening siren. The driver leaned forward and pressed something on the dash. As the blasting noise abruptly stopped, he threw the driver's door open and jumped out. The officer sitting in the passenger seat did the same and closed her door.

273

'Mr Walton?' asked the man, dashing towards him.

'Yes, yes,' Patrick replied.

'I'm PC Cornty. This is PC Weaver.'

'Hi,' he said.

The two PCs observed the bin to the man's right. Cornty took a step forward. 'Could you just take a step back from the bin please, sir?'

'Sure.' Patrick moved back several paces as PC Cornty carefully placed a fingertip on the corner of the bin lid and lifted it, then tipped his head forward to have a look.

The buzz of blowflies rushed out and inside. There must have been dozens and dozens of them around the woman's head, which was inches below the top of the bin, facing upwards. Her eyes were wide open looking up to the sky. The head was severed three inches below her chin by what looked like a very clean cut, although multiple strings of veins, arteries and God knows what else hung out the bottom of it, pooling the household black bin bags with thick blood. The skin of the head appeared white and pasty, several areas of the face blotchy from the way the blood had settled.

'Jesus,' he whispered, edging back. He faced Patrick. 'What happened?'

Patrick turned, pointing. 'I walked from down there.' He turned back and lowered his arm. 'Then I saw a man standing where you are looking inside the bin. He must have heard me or something because he looked right at me. Then he panicked and ran.'

'Ran where?'

'Through that gate.' The man stepped forward, stabbing the air towards the dark blue gate just left of the bin. 'In there. In there.'

Cornty turned to Weaver. 'Get backup now. Forensics too.'

With urgency she grabbed the radio from her belt and called for backup, telling dispatch the situation and confirming they'd found a woman's head. She also said that the suspect had gone through the gate next to the bin and that they were going in.

Cornty told the man to take a step back, then turned towards the gate. On the step, he saw drops of blood. He pulled out his baton and, using his left hand, unlocked the catch of the gate and pushed it open. The concrete path on the other side of the gate was smeared with blood. Bright and red. It looked like a trail.

He followed the path with wide eyes, following the direction of the trail. It veered around to the right out of sight.

'Amy, I'm going in.'

'Right behind you,' she replied.

He stepped up onto the path, carefully placing his feet, and went through the doorway. The backyard was rectangular. Roughly ten metres long and four metres wide. On the left side of the yard, plant pots and bright flowers lined the wall.

The right side of the yard was a different story. He gulped hard, seeing the thick trail of blood.

'Hello!' he shouted. 'Hello, police here . . .'

Weaver stepped up behind him with wide eyes. 'Can you see anything?'

'No.' Cornty scanned the window ahead of him, then along the windows of what seemed like a kitchen extension to the right.

On the ground, the trail veered off to the right down a thin narrow alley by a brick-built shed.

'What the hell?' Weaver muttered behind him, staying close.

'Shhhh . . .'

Level with the alley, to the right, Cornty noticed the shed door was half open. Down on the ground, the blood trail went inside.

'Stay back,' he told her, edging around, following the trail.

Close by, sirens wailed in the air, indicating that backup was very close. Cornty thought for a second about waiting, but he needed to see what was inside, needed to see where the blood was coming from.

Using his left hand, he pushed the door open and peered into the darkness.

70

At the back of the concrete shed, a naked body sat upright against the brick wall. The legs were straight out, resting on the floor in the shape of a thin V. Between the legs was a blood-soaked sheet of paper with the words *She didn't see it coming* written in a thick black marker pen.

Blood ran from where the head used to be down the body, smothering the stomach with thick, chunky trails. There was enough blood to fill a small pond.

He pulled back suddenly.

'What? What is it?' Weaver asked.

'The rest of Karen Whittaker, looks like. He's not in there. Come on. We need to find him now.'

He dashed around to the back door and tried the handle. Locked. Taking a step back, he lunged hard with his right boot. The shudder shot up his leg, causing an uncomfortable throbbing pain, but the door never budged.

'Fuck,' he screamed, lowering his leg. He tried again, ignoring the pain and giving it everything he had. This time, the door gave way, the wood and lock mechanism sheered and the door swung open, pieces of wood flying off in all directions.

He hobbled into the kitchen. It was empty. He darted out of the kitchen into a dining room. The smell of lavender hung in the air from a candle on the wooden table in the middle of the room.

'Police. Come out right now!' he screamed, standing at the table, scanning the room frantically.

'Police, police!' Weaver said, overtaking him, heading toward the hallway.

'Wait, Amy! Wait!'

Down the corridor ahead of them, the front door smashed through; Byrd and Tanzy charged in.

'Police! Police!' They slowed when they spotted Weaver and Cornty.

'Where is he?' Tanzy asked.

* * *

Tanzy charged up the stairs. Byrd was a few steps behind him. Both of them gripped their batons, ready for whatever they might come up against. Weaver followed them up and, at the top of the stairs, the two detectives took a right and reached the landing, whereas Weaver went left into a small room with her baton raised.

Tanzy went left off the landing towards the bathroom. Byrd went straight ahead, pushing open a door into one of the rear bedrooms. Apart from a bed, bedside drawers and a basic-looking wardrobe, the bedroom was empty.

'Hey, here, come here,' shouted Tanzy, standing outside the bathroom door. 'This is locked — it won't open. He's in here.' He banged five times on the door. 'Open the door, it's the police.'

There was no response from inside the bathroom.

He banged again with a clenched fist. 'Police. Open the door!'

No response.

He moved back a few spaces, took a breath, then threw himself into the door, his foot colliding hard into the wood. The door flung open with a loud crack and swung back against the wall.

In the corner of the bathroom, curled up on the floor, was a man Byrd recognised.

'Dr Ching?'

Byrd stepped into the large bathroom. Weaver, after hearing the commotion, appeared behind him.

'This is a mistake,' Dr Ching blurted out. 'A mistake!'

Byrd's eyes widened. 'Dr Ching, what's going on here?'

Tanzy moved past Byrd and lowered himself to the doctor, who cowered.

'It's a mistake, it wasn't me.'

'We'll see about that down at the station, won't we?' replied Tanzy, grabbing his wrists and hauling him up like he weighed less than a bag of sugar. He turned him around and cuffed him.

'My arm!' pleaded the doctor. 'Watch my arm.'

Tanzy lifted his wrists an inch. 'Is that any better?'

'Ahhhhh,' he cried out, wincing in pain.

'Ori, that's enough . . .' Byrd told him. 'Take him downstairs.'

Weaver stepped forward, grabbing Dr Ching's arm, and guided him to the landing.

He followed Tanzy, Weaver and Dr Ching downstairs, then outside to the police van. Cornty was waiting for them at the rear of the van, the door open. Tanzy handed him over and Cornty took his arm, guiding him up into the back of it. The doctor, with tears in his eyes, took a seat on the white, flat plastic seat.

'I didn't do this — this is a mistake,' he whispered to himself.

Cornty stepped up into the cramped space, leaned forward, and with his mouth close to his ear, he whispered, 'Fucking sicko.'

Once the van doors were closed, Cornty banged twice on the back door, the metallic sound pinging down the street. Byrd and Tanzy watched the van pull out onto the road and disappear in the direction of the station.

'I don't fucking believe this.'

'What?' Tanzy said, seeing the surprise on Byrd's face.

'That's the doctor who's looking after my parents.'

'Really?' Tanzy was surprised.

'Yes. Dr Ching.'

Tanzy was speechless. PC Cornty approached them. 'Good work,' Tanzy said. 'Were you the first here?'

Cornty nodded. 'Yeah. Weaver and me were close when dispatch got the call from the man with the dog.'

'Where is he?' Byrd queried.

Cornty pointed across the street to a man sitting on a low brick wall.

'Okay, thanks — we'll speak to him.'

'Have you been inside?' Cornty asked. 'Have you seen what's in the shed and the bin?'

'Not yet,' Tanzy said.

'It's Karen Whittaker — her head's in the bin, and the rest of her is in the shed. The scene in the shed looks a lot like the way Julia Porter was laid out. There's the same note. "She didn't see it coming."'

Byrd sighed. 'What on earth does it mean?'

'You'll need your strong stomachs,' he added.

'Forensics are here,' Byrd said, seeing the familiar van down the street. 'We'll give them space to work.'

'Well, if what I think is true and this has something to do with Julia Porter and Mary Richards, then I think it's safe to say we've found our serial killer.'

Byrd and Tanzy both absorbed his eager words, but Byrd didn't want to believe it; he didn't want to think the person who'd been caring for his unconscious parents could do something like this.

It just didn't add up.

'Maybe,' he said. 'We'll see what he has to say down at the station.'

71

Darlington
Fifteen years ago

He'd done it. He'd finally done it. He could now go down-stairs with a half-smile on his face and claim his twenty pounds off Stuart Richards — not that he'd achieved any-thing apart from raping a girl he'd fancied for longer than he could remember.

He slowly lifted himself off and stared at her. With sweaty, trembling hands, he pulled up his jeans.

'I enjoyed that,' he whispered coldly.

The beat of the music still drummed through the house, and although mostly blocked by the closed door, the energy resonated through the walls into the darkened room. He did up his belt and took a few steps back, taking in her naked body once more. He'd even managed to pull her top off with-out much of a struggle to feel her breasts. Oh, they were so perfect.

As he turned towards the door, it suddenly opened, and a rush of dance music and flashing lights flooded in.

He froze.

'Ian . . . what the fuck?'

Stuart, James and Gregory all staggered in, absorbing the scene before them.

'Ian,' said Stuart. 'What's happened?'

'What's happened is you owe me twenty pounds . . .'

Gregory took a few steps forward, glaring wide-eyed at him, then down at Sarah. 'You fucking raped her?'

Ian carelessly shrugged, looking back at her. Gregory raced to the door and closed it, making the room private.

'Ian! For fucks sake! You can't go around fucking raping people!' Gregory shouted, shaking his head in disgust, appalled by Ian's actions.

'I said I'd fuck her. That's what I did,' he explained, shrugging without a care in the world.

'Are you actually mental? You're going to jail, mate!' James lunged forward, knocking Gregory out of the way, throwing his arms towards Ian's chest, causing him to tumble back until he finally tripped and collided with the back wall. 'Fucking idiot!'

Ian landed hard and fast, rubbing the back of his head. 'What the fuck?' He jumped up quickly, dashed over to James with his fist cocked high.

'Calm the fuck down!' Stuart bawled, grabbing him. 'Chill out!'

Ian tried to shake him off but Stuart had pinned his arm around his back. 'Calm the fuck down.' Ian eased off a little, shooting daggers at James, who was in the middle of the bedroom, ready for him, fists clenched.

Stuart turned to Ian, raising a finger. 'Wait, did you use a condom?'

He shook his head. 'No, why?'

'You didn't come in her, did you?'

'Don't be stupid, of course not.'

'Right, listen,' Gregory said calmly. 'Everyone take a second. We need to figure this shit out!' He pointed at Sarah, who was shuffling slightly. 'What are we gonna do?'

Without answering, they all stared at each other. They didn't know. They had never been in a situation like this before. Gregory noticed Ian had calmed down a little and had taken a few steps back to be alone.

'I've raped her . . .' he muttered to himself, just loud enough for them to hear.

'Yeah, you fucking have,' James yelled. 'Fucking disgusting little man you are!'

Ian tensed up and darted towards him again. Stuart stepped across and pointed a firm finger in his face. 'Sit the fuck down or I'll put you on your arse, Porter!' He pushed hard on his chest, knocking him back a few steps.

Ian retreated to the corner of the room, muttering some inaudible drunken shit to himself. Stuart turned, looked at the other two. 'The fuck we gonna do, boys?'

'We'll just leave,' James said. 'That's all we can do.'

The three of them stared down at Sarah, who lay on her back with her legs open, her arms on either side. Completely out of it.

'Unless . . .' Stuart whispered.

'What?' James asked, frowning. 'Unless what?'

Stuart's eyes widened. 'Unless we fuck her too?'

James's mouth opened. 'Are you out of your mind?'

'Yeah, go on . . . fuck her!' Ian shouted from the corner. 'Do it! She won't remember anyway. You're never gonna have this chance again. Not with her.' He paused a beat. 'Or . . . or are you all too scared . . . ? Fucking virgins!'

'I'm no virgin!' James retorted. 'But I'm not—'

'I'm not scared,' Stuart replied, unbuckling his belt quickly. 'I'll do it!'

'Stu, come on man, don't do this,' James begged. 'It isn't right, man.'

'If you're too chicken shit, then leave!' he teased him, stepping forward with his penis hanging down. James and Gregory exchanged worried glances, then looked back at Stuart, who climbed on top of Sarah and inserted himself into her, holding her wrists down on the bed.

Over the next ten minutes, the four of them raped Sarah, to the beat of the dance music seeping through the closed door. The stuffy air inside the room smelled of sweat, perfume and a sense of false masculinity. After they'd had enough, they got dressed, high-fived each other and snuck out of the room. They closed the door and casually descended the stairs as if nothing had ever happened.

72

Dr Ching sat in the interrogation room alone. Through the window to his right, although he wasn't aware, Byrd and Tanzy watched him closely.

'What you thinking, Max?'

'I don't know, Ori,' he said, keeping his focus on the doctor through the one-way glass. 'It doesn't add up.'

'If he's involved in the other murders, he's one serious nut job — they're running his DNA now to see if there's a match with the hair found at the other scenes.'

Byrd glanced at Tanzy. 'When will we know?'

'ASAP. They're doing it right now.'

Byrd nodded, looking back through the glass.

'He's an oddball though, Max, you have to admit.'

'You should never judge a book by its cover.'

Minutes later, they headed inside, leaving DCI June Thornton, PC Cornty and PC Weaver on the viewing side of the glass.

The door opened. Tanzy went in first, then Byrd. They pulled their chairs out and sat down, not saying a word. The air inside the small room was warm. Since the detectives had arrived, the doctor hadn't looked up from the table.

'Can I get you a coffee?' Byrd asked softly.

The doctor seemed surprised at the generous offer but shook his head.

'Then we'll make a start . . .' Tanzy said, leaning forward, turning on the recording equipment. 'It's 18.43,' he began. 'I'm Detective Inspector Orion Tanzy with Detective Inspector Max Byrd of Durham Constabulary. We are interviewing Dr Sion Ching, who's been arrested for first-degree murder. Dr Ching has rejected representation from a lawyer or anyone associated with the criminal justice department. Can you confirm this is true, Dr Ching?'

'I can.' His voice was flat, quiet.

'Can you tell us why we found a headless woman inside your shed at the bottom of your yard, and why her head was inside a bin at the rear of your property, outside in the alleyway?' Tanzy asked.

For a moment, the doctor stayed silent, as if forgetting why he was there. As if what he'd been told didn't resonate with him.

'Doctor?' Byrd said.

He coughed. 'It's a mistake. I had nothing to do with this.'

Tanzy looked at Byrd, then back to the suspect. 'Interesting. What makes you believe that?'

'Believe . . . what?' he replied.

'That you had nothing to do with it? It's your property, it's your bin. Please explain. Detective Byrd and I are very keen to hear.'

'I . . . I received a phone call.'

'From whom?' Byrd asked.

'I don't know.' He gave a small shrug. 'It was a man. He asked me if I was Dr Ching. I said yes. Then he told me to look in the shed outside and then in the bin in the alley. I asked who was calling, but he wouldn't tell me. He said it didn't matter who he was.'

Ching was very convincing — his body language told Byrd he was telling the truth. He knew this because he knew Dr Ching to a certain degree. Once you knew someone when they told the truth, you could distinguish when they weren't. Their facial expressions differed. Their tone of voice changed. Their body language altered. Byrd was confident the doctor wasn't displaying anything different to what he'd seen before, and was therefore sure his story rang true.

However, deep down, Byrd knew people were capable of things beyond their imagination. He'd been in this game as long as anyone, but he didn't, however, want to believe the doctor was guilty.

'Then what happened?' Tanzy said, leaning forward, a frown lining his forehead.

'I was confused. I went outside, saw the blood in the yard near the shed. I looked inside and . . . oh God!' He fell silent for a moment and threw his hand to his mouth as if reliving the moment earlier in his mind. 'It was horrible. I remembered what he said about the bin and looked outside and saw the . . .'

'The head?' Tanzy said.

He gave several short nods. 'Then a man walked by and saw me. I panicked, went inside quickly. Someone was hammering at the door. I didn't know what to do. I ran upstairs and hid in the bathroom.' His body sank into the chair a little, embarrassed by his words.

'Dr Ching, why didn't you ring the police?' Byrd asked, curiously.

'I—'

The door to the interrogation room opened. In came PC Weaver, with a sheet of A4 paper in her hand. Her face was flat, emotionless. She didn't smile, nor frown. After she placed the paper in front of the detectives, she nodded and left the room, closing the door behind her.

Byrd reached forward, picked up the paper.

Tanzy leaned in, so they could both read it. On the other side of the desk, the doctor stared, wondering what was so important.

It was the DNA results.

After flicking through three pages over the next minute, the room remained silent. Even their breathing had slowed down.

'Please, go on,' Byrd said finally, glancing up from the paper, back to Ching.

'I didn't ring the police because, like I said, I panicked. It would look like I'd done it, for crying out loud!'

His voice slapped off the back wall and came back. He sighed heavily, stared back down at the table.

'No,' Tanzy said. 'You didn't ring the police because you murdered her. Using a sharp instrument to cut her head off.'

'I . . . I . . . please listen to me, I—'

Tanzy raised a quick palm. 'What I don't understand is why you went to so much trouble covering your tracks with Julia Porter and Mary Richards.' Tanzy angled his head towards Byrd. 'It doesn't make any sense, does it?'

Byrd shook his head. 'It doesn't . . .'

'Who are they? Mary Richards and Julia Palmer. I've never heard of them?'

'Julia *Porter*, her name was. I see you're playing that card?' Tanzy muttered, smiling.

'What card?' the doctor asked, confused.

'Making it appear like you never did it, that you—'

'Because I didn't do it!' he shouted. His cheeks glowed red.

Tanzy didn't react to the outburst. 'We've matched your DNA to two other crime scenes. A strand of your hair was found in the passenger seat of Julia Porter's Nissan Qashqai, and then under the fingernails of Mary Richards when we found her body hanging from the tree you hung her from.'

The doctor edged back suddenly. 'Listen, you've me mixed up with someone else here. I can one hundred per cent guarantee you that I don't know these women. I never did these awful things.'

'Why is your hair at both crime scenes?' Tanzy asked.

'I don't know. It wasn't me.'

'We have the proof here, Doctor,' Byrd added, who'd been sitting in silence for a while.

'Mr Byrd, please listen to me. I've done nothing wrong here. You know me. You know I'm a doctor. A good doctor. That's all I've ever known. Do you think I'd be capable of doing these awful things?'

The doctor aimed the question at Byrd and Byrd only.

'I think people are capable of anything,' he replied.

Ching sighed.

'Dr Ching,' Tanzy said, 'you're going to prison for a very, very long time.'

'I need a lawyer,' he demanded.

'Interview terminated at 18.56. The suspect in custody now requests legal representation.'

73

Darlington
Fifteen years ago

It was approaching midnight. The music had been turned down, a sign of respect to the neighbours, although still loud enough to wake the dead in the nearest cemetery. Shez Barker said bye to a couple of friends at the door and waved them off as they walked down the drive, then closed it. Roughly half the people had left, jumping in the dozens of taxis that had pulled up over the last thirty minutes. Some party-goers had work in the morning, others headed into town, while others had vomited their drink in the back garden or down the toilet and were put into a taxi and sent home.

Back inside the hallway, she looked around, feeling a warm buzz about how the party had turned out. There were more people than she'd ever imagined. This would be news for a long time.

Before she went through the kitchen, she popped her head into the living room. People lay on sofas, watching music videos on the television. So far, nothing had been broken — nothing that she was aware of, anyway. No doubt she'd find out in the morning when it was empty and quiet.

It would give her a full day to clean up and sort the house out before her parents returned.

Turning, she moved merrily into the kitchen. She noticed most of the drinks on the worktop had been consumed, bar an inch left in a selection of the not-so-desirable drinks, including port. She had taken that from the drinks cabinet in the dining room, then locked it, hiding the key, knowing the whole lot would have gone within the hour if she hadn't.

'Hey, gorgeous!' she heard a slurred voice say behind her.

She turned to see a boy called Ernie — it wasn't his real name, only a nickname — who glared at her through glassy eyes.

'Ernie.' She nodded politely. 'Hope you've had a good night.' She attempted to walk around him, but he gripped her forearm, pulling her back a little. 'Hey, that hurts!' she told him.

'Calm down, Shez . . .' He glanced up to the ceiling and hiccupped so hard he winced at the pain. 'How about you and I go upstairs . . .'

Using her free hand, she loosened his grip and placed his hand back by his side. 'How about you go outside and go home?'

He smiled and swayed for a second, then leaned to the left, leaning on the breakfast bar that Shez hoped was solid enough to hold his weight. Moving past him, she stepped into the conservatory, then onto the decking. The temperature had dipped. Only a handful of people were there, smoking and chatting more quietly than before, a sign of the night whittling down.

To the left of the decking, she noticed a ray of light seeping under the side gate. Just a sliver, but it was enough to catch her eye.

'Fuck's that?' she whispered to herself.

She opened the gate and stepped out onto the long driveway. The garage light was on. Through the small window of the garage beside the door, she saw four people. She leaned closer to the glass, peering through it with her hands cupped at the side of the head to help her focus. She'd had a lot to drink and used the window to steady her balance.

Inside she saw Stuart, Ian, James and Gregory.

'What the fuck are they doing in there?' she muttered. They were huddled close together, their arms wrapped around each other, speaking quietly among themselves. Shez could hear the mumble of voices but couldn't make out what was said.

'Shit,' she whispered, suddenly remembering Sarah, who she'd left upstairs a while ago. She wondered what they were doing in her garage, but there wasn't anything worth stealing, so she'd check on Sarah first then come back to them.

After making her way through the house, she took a right at the base of the stairs and climbed them as quickly as she could while maintaining her balance. She opened her bedroom door and stepped into the dark room.

The bed was empty.

'Sarah?' Her eyes flitted around the room. 'Sarah, where are you?' In the corner, on the other side of the bed, was Sarah, crouched down low to the carpet, sobbing quietly to herself, dressed in only a bra.

She dashed over to her.

'Sarah?'

Lowering to her knees, she gasped again, not understanding why her best friend was only wearing a bra and nothing else.

'Sarah, what's — what's happened?'

'They did it to me . . . I heard them,' she said. 'I felt them inside of me, one at a time . . .'

'Who did?' Shez demanded, now understanding the severity of the situation. 'What happened to you?'

'They raped me, Shez. They fucking raped me.'

Shez was down on her knees, holding Sarah in her arms, when Sarah broke into proper tears and clung to Shez tightly.

'Who raped you?'

'I . . . I think they were four of them . . . four different voices.'

Shez blinked hard and sighed. Four of them.

She'd just seen Stuart Richards, Ian Porter, James Whittaker and Gregory Timms in the garage together discussing something that seemed very important.

'I think I know who it was,' Shez told her.

74

Wednesday morning
Darlington Memorial Hospital

James Whittaker had been contacted yesterday about the suspicions that the body and the missing head found at the rear of the property in Greenbank road could be his wife, Karen.

Butterflies circled and bounced inside his stomach as he walked through the hospital doors into the busy corridor. Was there ever a quiet day in these places? He hadn't slept a wink. He was sure he looked terrible. Felt even worse. He had tried to sleep, but ever since he was asked to come, he'd imagined over and over in his head if it was Karen.

He reached the reception desk. 'Hi . . . I received a call yesterday. My wife went missing, and they think it could be her . . .'

The woman smiled sadly in a practised way, but James felt it was genuine. 'Just a second.' Her green eyes flitted across her computer screen for a long moment. 'Are you James Whittaker?'

'I am.'

'Okay.' She leaned forward an inch and raised her arm into the air, pointing to the double doors to her right. 'Go through there, then take a left. There's a room straight ahead. Someone is waiting for you, Mr Whittaker.' He went past a series of reception desks where people directed him further and further into the hospital, until he found the pathology department. Through another set of the double doors, he found a man in a suit who seemed to be expecting him.

'Mr Whittaker?' the man said. He nodded. 'I'm Dr Jason Lannark, the pathologist. Can you please follow me into this room?'

As both men sat down in the small office, James observed an envelope in the pathologist's hand. Dr Lannark leaned forward, placed the envelope onto the small, low circular table that split the two chairs they were sitting on, and clamped his hands together, interlocking his long fingers. He moved smoothly, almost methodically.

'What I'm about to show you are three photographs. One of them is of a woman's face close up. I'm sure you have been told the nature of the body when it was discovered — our photographer has ensured that the image doesn't show below the chin. The second photo is of the woman's hand, showing her wedding ring. The third image is of a tattoo located on her right forearm.' The pathologist allowed that to sink in. 'That okay, Mr Whittaker?'

'Yeah,' he replied, breathing heavily.

Dr Lannark grabbed the envelope and pulled the images out. 'All I need you to do is confirm if this is your wife, Karen Whittaker.'

Whittaker nodded.

The first photo was of the tattoo. James knew straight away it belonged to his wife; she'd got it when they went away to Amsterdam nearly ten years ago. The pathologist showed him the next two images, but it wasn't really necessary.

'Yes, that's my wife,' Whittaker said after seeing the next photographs. He hung his head, his lost stare finding the dull linoleum floor below them.

'I'm so very sorry, Mr Whittaker.'

James nodded solemnly, lost for words.

'There will be a full autopsy carried out by myself. I will work alongside the police forensics team, who've been to the property on Greenbank Road. Then, we'll determine exactly how this happened.'

James nodded again. His focus was still down by his feet. 'Okay.'

'As you've just received some devastating news and I know the effects it has on loved ones, can I order you a taxi to get home? I need to advise you, on a professional level, that you shouldn't drive. You may think you're fine, but something this devastating can affect people.'

He fell silent for a second, thinking. 'I'll be fine. I can drive.'

'You're sure?'

Whittaker's body went rigid. 'I'll be fine.'

'Can I call anyone on your behalf? Any family members that you need to inform?'

'My mother is looking after my daughter, so I need to tell her, but it isn't important to tell her right now — it makes no difference. There's no bringing her back.'

The doctor offered a thin, heartfelt smile, then leaned to his right where there was a shelving unit located against the wall. On the middle shelf, he grabbed a thin pile of paper-work and placed it down on the table.

'If possible, could I ask you to sign this document to confirm you have identified this woman as Karen Whittaker.'

James Whittaker signed the document, stood up and left the hospital, feeling drained. The sky above the car park was clear and blue, the sun low but bright, its light glistening off the car windscreens. Once he was back in his car, he dropped his head into his hands and cried harder than he ever had.

75

Wednesday morning
Darlington

Byrd made the coffees this time. While he was away, Tanzy was on the phone to Ray Jones, who'd rung to ask if there had been any developments on his daughter's whereabouts.

Today made it the twelfth day Evelyn Jones had been missing. So far, there'd be nothing to go on, no clues or evidence that had given the police any idea where she was. Tanzy knew the only hope that the Joneses had was that she hadn't been found dead yet. If she was still missing, there was always a possibility she could be alive.

'Thanks, man,' Tanzy said to Byrd when he placed the steaming coffee next to his keyboard.

Byrd sat down on his chair and pulled himself in.

There was an air of sadness hanging in the office from the news about PC Kim Harrison. It was always the same when something tragic happened to their own. Some of the newer faces hadn't experienced this kind of loss and didn't quite know how to handle it. Instead, they mirrored the sadness of the other team members around them and rode out the storm until it got better. All they could do now was wait for more information from forensics.

Earlier that morning, Byrd and Tanzy had been to see the forensic team about an update on Harrison. Had any pieces of evidence been found to give them anything to go on?

So far, all they knew was that Harrison had received a major head injury — something hard had hit her head, causing a protrusion through the skin and damage to the rear of her skull. Could this have been done before she went into the river, or had it happened when she was in the water? Was she placed at that exact point, or had she floated downriver? 'Just spoke to Jason in the pathology department at the hospital,' Byrd said, taking a sip of his own coffee. 'James Whittaker confirmed the body found at Greenbank Road was indeed that of Karen Whittaker.'

'Fuck.'

'I know . . .'

'We need to find out what's going on here,' Tanzy stated, then looked down at the photograph of the four men on the table again. Byrd also leaned over to have a look. 'Three of their wives have been murdered in a brutal way that you wouldn't wish on anyone.'

'But not the fourth. Maybe the link isn't between these men?'

Tanzy frowned. 'What do you mean?'

'Well so far —' Byrd turned towards him a little, rotating on his chair — 'all we have is Dr Ching.'

Tanzy nodded, listening intently.

'His DNA has been matched at the three sites. It would make sense to presume that he was involved in all three murders.'

'Go on . . .' Tanzy said.

'Well, maybe this photo has nothing to do with it. We're looking at this photo as the link between the three women, but maybe it really is just a coincidence. Darlington's not a big place; plenty of classmates who are barely more than strangers have a picture taken together like this and never see each other again. Our original thoughts . . . well, *my* original thoughts were that these men had done something, and someone is exacting revenge on their loved ones. But perhaps that's just a coincidence that life wants us to believe?'

'I'm . . . I'm not following you here.' Tanzy frowned at him. There were times — many times — when Byrd and Tanzy were singing off the same hymn sheet, but this wasn't one of them. 'There are loads of secondaries in Darlington, and these men were all in the same year, the same *class*. That's more than a coincidence.'

'But maybe the three women are linked in their own way — if not together, then linked individually.'

'Will you just spell it out for me, please?'

Byrd smiled. 'Maybe Dr Ching has treated them in the past?'

Tanzy pondered the idea for a moment. 'Let's check with the hospital to see if Mary Richards, Julia Porter and Karen Whittaker have ever been patients of his.'

Byrd leaned forward, picked up the pen and wrote it down. 'And we need to find out if Dr Ching has ever treated Samantha Timms.'

76

Wednesday afternoon
Police station

After several meetings and a meal deal from the local Sainsburys for his dinner, Byrd returned to his desk. He found the number for the forensics department and put the phone to his ear.

'This is Paul Beech, Forensics department. How can I help?'

'Hi, Paul. It's Max.'

'Hi, Max. How are you doing?'

'I'm good. I was wondering have you looked over Karen Whittaker yet?'

'We have a little, but there's further work to do. You'll have to bear with me, Detective, if that's okay?'

'Yeah, sure, that's no problem. Just let me or Orion know.'

'Okay, will do.'

'Have you had the chance to look over Kim Harrison yet?'

'We have done some work on that. Would you like to speak to Tallow or Hope on this one?'

'No, it's okay,' Byrd said. 'If you can tell me, that's fine.'

'We have identified that her death has nothing to do with the other three. The way the body was intact — unlike the other three — and the way it was presented.'

'Elaborate, please,' Byrd said.

'You're the detective here and I'm still training, so tell me if I'm talking rubbish. It's merely a thought.'

'Go on, Paul.'

'You see . . . Julia, Mary and Karen,' Beech went on, 'were in positions where someone would see them. The body found in Porter's dining room was meant for her husband. The woman hanging from a tree was bound to be seen by the next person who walked down that lane. The woman's head in the bin would be noticed by the bin men. These are all situations where they'd be found.' He stopped for a moment. 'Harrison was found by luck. Her body wasn't on display in my opinion. There was no obvious "hey, look at me" aspect to hers. We found a substantial amount of water in her lungs, which tells us she could have drowned.'

'What about the damage to her head?'

'From the severity of the blow, in my opinion — and it's something I've discussed with Tallow and Hope — the odds that the damage was done while she was underwater are very slim. Underwater, the body moves slower even under the power of a strong current. I think this blow happened before she went into the water. Whatever had caused it had travelled fast through the air, not through water.'

'Okay, so she was attacked?'

'It seems likely.'

Byrd said, 'What did you guys find at Dr Ching's house?'

'Now this is where we nail him. In one of the cupboards in the kitchen, there was a toolset containing an impressive display of surgical tools. After running analyses on the tools, we found three different types of blood on them. I'll give you a guess as to whose blood it is.'

'Julia Porter, Mary Richards and Karen Whittaker?'

'Correct. All evidence so far points to Dr Ching.'

'What I don't understand is why the third kill was so sloppy,' Byrd said.

'What do you mean?'

'Why at his own home? Why were the other two so well thought out, so methodical and clean? And why was the third one so obvious? Blood trails on the floor. Blood spatter all over. His surgical tools were hidden in a cupboard, where they would easily be found if someone were to search the house.' Byrd went quiet, thinking hard. 'I don't know, it just seems weird to me.'

'You know, Max, I'll be honest, I thought exactly the same. The third one is different. But there are undeniable similarities that can't be overlooked. The cut was as clean as the others. It was the layout that was messy. Either way, we have his DNA at three crime scenes and surgical tools hidden in his kitchen that contain the blood of the three victims.'

77

Wednesday night
Darlington

Gregory Timms dragged himself into his living room and sat down on the sofa. He'd had a rough day. Every hour that passed felt like two. But the day was nearly over and all he wanted to do was sit down and do nothing, apart from letting his eyes crawl across the screen of his new Kindle until they were so heavy he'd fall asleep.

Before he settled down to read, he checked his phone and social media updates. He didn't have any notifications of interest, but a post that someone had uploaded really caught his attention. He clicked on the article and scanned it, then scrolled back up to the top of the page and read it again, this time much slower, absorbing the information like a sponge.

'Fuck,' he whispered.

He pulled his phone from the large pocket of his dressing gown, unlocked it and searched through his Facebook connections. He clicked on James Whittaker's name and briefly looked at his profile. In the top-right corner of the screen, he noticed an option to call him so, with his finger hovering over the phone icon, he decided to press it. The screen turned temporarily grey, and the call connected.

He didn't have to wait long before it was answered.

'Gregory? What do you want?' Whittaker replied. His name and Facebook picture must have come up on Whittaker's phone, he realised.

'James, I've just heard about what happened to your wife. I'm so sorry.'

'I don't want to talk to you. Don't know why I—'

'Wait, just hear me out, mate. I need—'

'We are not mates. I haven't seen you since—'

'I know, I know,' Gregory said. 'Since *that night*. But now your wife, Ian's wife, Stuart's wife . . .'

Whittaker said nothing.

'Do you think it has something to do with that night?'

'I don't know. What happened that night is something I don't want to think about ever again, let alone talk about. What we did to that girl was indescribable. We deserve punishment.'

'We do,' Gregory said. 'But not the people we love. They didn't even know us then. Do you think something will happen to my wife?'

'I don't have a crystal ball, do I?'

'But you must have thought the same as me. Someone's found out what we did. After all these years. But why now? It was fifteen years ago, I can't believe that—'

'I need to go. Good luck to you. Don't call me again.' The call ended.

Gregory sat still on the sofa, stunned. He lowered his phone and heard footsteps out in the hallway, growing louder.

Samantha ambled into the living room, dressed in a comfortable gown, wearing a smile on her tanned, thin face. She'd just got out of the bath and lathered herself in moisturiser, her skin glowing against the soft light from the lamp in the corner.

'Hey,' she said. 'There's a car outside with someone in it.'

'A car?'

'Yeah.' She went over, peered out the window. 'A police car. I noticed it from upstairs. I wonder what's going on.'

He smiled, knowing it would be an ideal time to tell her about the protection detail that he'd agreed with Tanzy, but he knew he'd then have to mention why. And that was something he couldn't do.

78

Darlington
Fifteen years ago

Sarah frowned up at Shez.

'Who was it?'

The drug was starting to wear off, but the feeling of grogginess still had a hold on her. 'Shez! Who was it?'

'The boys who did this are in my garage,' Shez explained, frightened.

Sarah got up as quickly as she could. She glanced around the room frantically searching for her top, dress and under-wear, which had been thrown across the room like they were rubbish.

'I'm going to fucking kill them!' she shouted.

'Sarah, Sarah, please calm down. Please. We should call the police. We'll call the police and tell them what's happened.'

'I'm not ringing the police — I'm going to kill them.' She pulled her top over her head quickly, then bent down to grab her underwear. Her hands shook with rage, and her body vibrated with an anger she'd never felt before. How dare they do this to her.

'Is your brother here, Sarah?' she asked.

'No, he isn't. Fuck my brother. I don't need my brother for this. I'll deal with them.'

Once Sarah had got her skirt on, she turned for the door.

Shez grabbed her wrist. 'Wait, Sarah, please—'

'Get the fuck off me!' Sarah screamed, swivelling quickly and pushing Shez hard. Shez staggered across the room until she tripped over a plastic box and hit the back of her head against the wardrobe.

Shez fell to the floor and didn't move.

Sarah charged down the stairs and headed for the garage.

79

Neil McMahon woke thirty minutes early this morning. He had some papers to mark and did so with a strong cup of coffee in front of the television in the dining room.

He was feeling sad; he was missing Evelyn, but he knew life cracked on. The children in the class needed his guidance and support to get over her loss. It would be hard to move on and forget about Evelyn. Then he reminded himself that there was still hope yet.

After he marked the last paper, he placed it on top of the others and finished his coffee. Along the hallway, he heard footsteps approaching and frowned down at his watch. A moment later, Judith came into the room, rubbing her tired eyes.

'Morning. You're up early,' he said. 'Did I wake you?'

'No, I couldn't sleep. I haven't slept most of the night, to be honest.'

'How come? What was wrong?'

'I couldn't stop thinking about the little girl next door, how upset she was the other day.' She gave a sad smile, padded across the fluffy carpet and pulled a seat out at the table. 'Why was she so upset?'

'When I knocked, Alex told me she'd done something wrong and that he'd told her off. Just being a parent, I suppose. It's hard to judge these things through a wall.'

She raised a silencing palm. 'I know it is, Neil, but I'm just wondering if there's something more, something a little sinister.'

Neil shrugged. 'You think?'

'Do you not?' she asked.

'I don't know. I do know, however, that it isn't our business how parents bring up their children in the confines of their own home.'

'But if it's something more?' she said. 'If there's abuse involved?'

'We don't know that . . . we can't assume.'

She glanced away in the direction of next door, almost as if she could see through the brick, to see for herself if the little girl was okay.

'What time are you going to the dentist?' Judith asked.

'Soon. I also need to pop into town before I go to work. One of the other teachers is covering until I get back. Is there anything you need in town?' he asked, standing up.

'No,' Judith said.

'Right, I need to get ready, won't be long.'

Upstairs, Neil took out his phone and stared at it for a while before making a call. After he hung up, he thought hard, wondering if he'd done the right thing.

Time would tell.

Minutes later, Neil came back downstairs. Judith was sitting on the sofa in silence.

'I won't be going just yet,' he told her.

'Why?'

'I've . . . I've called the police.'

She frowned. 'The police — why?'

'I think something is going on next door,' he explained. 'I think you're right. They're coming over now. I'll hang around, I have time to spare before the dentist.'

Judith glanced at her watch. 'How long will they be?'

'The operator said ten minutes.'

'Alex won't be happy.'

* * *

Just over ten minutes later, there was a knock at the door. Neil opened it slowly, the cold morning air creeping in uninvited.

'Mr McMahon?' said the PC.

'Yes. Come on in,' he said.

The PCs stepped inside into the narrow hallway. 'I'm PC Cornty. This —' he pointed to his left — 'is PC Weaver.'

'Can I get you a coffee?' Neil asked.

'We're good, thank you,' replied Cornty gratefully. 'We're following up on your phone call. Could you fill us in with the details?'

The sound of footsteps was heard on the stairs. Judith smiled at the PCs, who glanced up at her for a brief moment.

Neil said, 'We heard crying, sounded like it was coming from upstairs. It wasn't, we don't have children. Then I went next door. They have a young daughter, you see. She sounded upset. I knocked and spoke with her father. He told me that she'd done something wrong and he'd told her off for it. I know when I was younger if I did something wrong I got a good telling off. But . . .'

'But what, sir?'

'We had a daughter,' Neil said. 'Sadly, she went missing at seven, years ago. I may have lost touch with being a parent, but I'm a teacher. I know what's right and what isn't. And I know I certainly wouldn't treat my children that way.'

'Very sorry to hear that,' PC Weaver said, taking over. 'Okay, we'll give next door a knock and speak to her—'

They suddenly heard a cry from somewhere in the house.

'What was that?' Weaver said, tipping her head back, looking upstairs.

Neil sighed lightly. 'We heard it yesterday, and the day before.'

The PCs absorbed his words but listened to the cry.

'It sounds like it's in this house.' Cornty said, also glancing up the stairs.

'We thought the same. The girl's room is against the wall,' Judith explained.

The cry became louder, almost like an animal in pain. Weaver and Cornty exchanged worried gazes. 'We need to check it out,' Weaver told him.

He nodded firmly.

Neil stepped around them and opened his front door for them to leave but turned to see the PCs going up the stairs. 'Where . . . where are you going?'

'It's not this house,' Judith said, watching them dash up the stairs.

'Where the hell are you going?' Neil asked, frowning. 'You need to go next door.' He closed the front door, turned and followed them up the stairs quickly.

Weaver and Cornty reached the top of the stairs and took a right onto the landing.

'In there,' Weaver said, pointing to the back bedroom. She followed Cornty into the medium-sized room, where the curtains were closed, but dull morning light crept around the edges, giving them enough light to see. The crying was louder now.

'Where is that coming from?' Weaver whispered.

Neil stepped into the room behind them. 'What are you doing?'

'Shhhh!' demanded Cornty, turning his head to listen. 'There . . .' He pointed at the large cupboard. 'It's coming from there.'

'No, it's not. It sounds like it's in there, but it's next door,' said Neil, shrugging hopelessly.

'We'd like to see for ourselves,' Cornty told him matter-of-factly, stepping towards the cupboard in the corner.

80

Darlington
Fifteen years ago

Sarah barged into the garage, the door almost coming off its hinges. Stuart, James, Ian and Gregory were huddled closely in the middle of the space. They suddenly stopped talking, split up and glared at her.

'You fucking bastards!' she screamed at them.

'What are you talking about, Sarah — what's wrong?' Stuart raised his hands in mock confusion.

'I know what you did to me!' she bellowed, inches away from Stuart's face. 'I know what all of you did to me . . .' She glared at all of them, one at a time. They stood in a semi-circle around her. 'You fucking sick, sick, little boys.'

'Hold on a second, Sarah. What do you mean?' Ian asked her.

She edged towards him, pointing, the tip of her finger close to his red face. 'You fucking know what. You put something in that drink, didn't you?' Her eyes narrowed at him.

'I . . . I . . .'

'You put something in the drink to knock me out!'

He said nothing, just stared, absorbing her words.

'You couldn't fuck me for real, so you spiked my drink and raped me.'

The garage was as quiet as an empty church — Ian was speechless. He knew what she was saying was true, and he could feel his skin growing warm in embarrassment, his face reddening with each passing second.

'You're pathetic,' she told Ian, then she turned to Stuart. 'You got on top next, didn't you?' She leaned close to him. He backed off, not knowing what she was going to do until she sniffed the air around him. 'I can smell your cheap after-shave. Yeah, it was you. You dirty fucking bastard.'

She glared at Gregory and James with fire in her eyes for a long moment, then turned back to Ian. 'Whatever you gave me didn't knock me out, Ian. I couldn't move, but I heard it all. I remember everything.'

James and Gregory sighed heavily, glancing nervously at each other, their bodies physically deflating. They could see the worry in each other's eyes and what this could mean.

'Listen, Sarah,' Stuart said, his palms in the air, 'I think you have made a mistake. We haven't touched you. We've been down here the whole time. I think you've had a little too much to drink and you're imagining this.' He looked around for support. 'Ian, is she imagining this?'

A sudden sliver of hope appeared on Ian's face. 'Yes, she is. As you said, we've been out here in the garden the whole time.' He turned towards Sarah, meeting the burning rage in her eyes. 'Sarah, you've made a mistake.'

Sarah thought about that for a moment and smiled. 'Okay . . .'

'Okay?' Ian asked.

'If that's how you want to play this,' she said.

'What do you mean?' Stuart asked.

'None of you used a condom, did you? You're not only disgusting but fucking stupid too.'

Ian shook his head. 'I never came in you. There's nothing to go on.'

313

She laughed hysterically, pointing to her skirt. 'The evidence is right fucking here! I wonder what the police will say about this — hell, I'm more concerned about what my family will do to you. Just imagine my brother, just think what he'll do when he finds out . . .' She trailed off, smiling, tilting her head side to side slowly. 'So fucking stupid.'

She laughed then turned, took a step towards the door and—

'The fuck are you going?' Stuart grabbed her wrist.

'I'm going to tell the whole world what pathetic little boys you are. Everyone's going to know. Your lives are ruined,' she told them. She tried to pull away but Stuart didn't let go.

'Get the fuck off me!' she screamed at him, struggling. Stuart was too strong for her and held on tight. Their bodies were against each other as she tried to wriggle free, but he wouldn't let her go, wouldn't let her leave. If she left, that would be the moment everyone would know what they'd done.

She'd been unconscious. She wasn't meant to remember.

'Stuart, let her go,' begged Ian.

'No, she'll tell people. We can't let her leave here.'

Ian frowned at him. 'What? What do you mean?'

'She isn't leaving this garage!' he shouted at them.

She pulled her arm down, and yet again, his grip was too much for her. 'Fucking let me go, Stuart!' she screamed.

He pulled her closer and swung her around, then shoved his free hand over her mouth, the ball of his palm bouncing off her lip in an attempt to mute her anger.

'Shit, shit!' James gasped, his eyes flitting from Gregory to Ian then back to Sarah.

'Heeeeeeeemmmmm!' Sarah shouted through his rough palm. 'Heeeeeeeemmmmm!'

'Stuart, let her fucking go!' Ian said. 'You're making it worse.' He tried to grab Stuart's forearm but he was too strong for him and shrugged him off with ease. Sarah started to shout through his hand, her volume rising with the desperation to be free.

314

'Stuart!' Gregory begged. 'Come on, man!'

Stuart adjusted his hand over her mouth and covered her nose too, blocking the oxygen, and squeezed as tight as he could. Thirty seconds later, he let go and she collapsed to the floor, unconscious.

'Stu, what the fuck have you done?' Ian gasped.

Stuart panted heavily, staring down at her, watching her still body all bent and distorted. He switched his focus to the wall to the left, which was full of tools and other gardening accessories. He rushed over, grabbed something, and came back to Sarah.

'What the fuck is that for?' Ian said. 'Stuart?'

'Pick her up, boys . . .'

81

Thursday, late morning
Darlington

PC Cornty leaned forward, grabbed the handle of the cupboard and pulled it open quickly. He stared inside with wide eyes.

It was a large cupboard, built into the corner of the room by the side of the chimney breast. To the right of the space inside, there were shelves with a gap of around ten inches between each one. Every shelf had something different on it. Underwear. T-shirts. Jeans. Jogging bottoms. To the left, about head height, a pole was fixed across the top of it with a selection of hanging garments: dresses and shirts. It was a mix between his and her clothes and most likely the clothes they seldom wore.

The sound of the cry remained the same but there was no crying child in there.

'It sounds like it's coming from here,' Cornty said, confused. He glanced at Weaver. 'But there's nothing.'

'That's what I was telling you,' Neil said. 'The walls are paper-thin. We've heard her many times.'

Cornty and Weaver didn't reply, instead, they stood at the base of the wardrobe staring into it, side by side, their shoulders almost touching.

'We need to go next door,' Weaver told him. 'That kid sounds in real distress.'

Cornty nodded, but his attention was on the back wall of the cupboard. He saw something unusual. 'Wait. What's that?'

'What's what? I can't see anything but clothes.'

Cornty moved forward a little, ducking down as he climbed into the cupboard.

'What are you doing?' Judith asked. 'What is it?'

'What is . . . that?' he whispered to himself, peering into the dim space. He raised his hand and touched the surface of the side wall, then moved it across to the back. Different textures. The crying was so loud now, almost in his ear, as he turned his head side on to listen.

'What have you found?' Weaver asked, only inches behind.

'Something's not right here . . .'

'What do you mean?' Weaver asked.

'The wall . . . there's something behind it. It isn't a part of the cupboard. Is that a screw sticking out?' He leaned closer. By this point, he was fully inside. Weaver had one foot in there, the other back in the bedroom where Neil McMahon and his wife stood behind them.

'Can you see this wall here?' Cornty asked her.

There was a sudden thud. Cornty felt Weaver collide hard into the back of him, her weight crushing him against the wall.

'Jesus, Amy — what are you—'

The cupboard suddenly became pitch black and the door slammed closed. A chain rattled outside. Weaver was pinning him up against the back wall, his face hard up against the sheet of wood.

'Amy, I can't breathe. Get off me,' he begged, gasping for breath. It didn't take long for him to feel hot, claustrophobic,

317

his breathing now struggling to the point of panic. His body was twisted, his weight — and his partner's weight — caused a horrendous throbbing pain on his twisted leg, worsening by the second.

'Mr McMahon . . . what is going on?' he shouted, but it came out barely audible. 'Mr McMahon . . . please.'

No one answered his plea.

The weight of Weaver's body was unbearable, her face digging hard into his neck, squeezing him into the wall at the back of the cupboard.

'Amy,' he said again, but she didn't reply. He tried to work out if she was still breathing, but the sound of his own heartbeat drowned out everything else.

His right hand was trapped between his thigh and the body of his partner, but he shifted his weight to the left, allowing him enough room to pull it free. His phone was tucked tightly into his chest. After a minute of frustration and his body overheating, he somehow managed to grab it.

'Mr McMahon?' he shouted, this time as loud as he could, the desperate sound of his voice showing his chest was under pressure. The crying near him had stopped now. Did that mean the girl was okay, or did it mean something worse?

Why had Neil McMahon done this to them?

He didn't know and neither did Weaver, unless she'd seen something.

All he could concentrate on was his breathing and trying not to panic. When he was fourteen, he'd been poking about in his parents' garage when he'd managed to knock several boxes down on top of him, which kept him on the floor until his dad came in and freed him. His chest had felt the same then.

The air inside was hot, each breath beyond difficult. The feeling of claustrophobia was taking over him. And there was an unpleasant smell in there, he realised, which was getting stronger.

From his position, he could barely see his phone screen, but he used his thumbprint to unlock and hit the speed button to call the last number he'd rung — Tanzy's number, he hoped.

82

'Who's this now?' Tanzy sighed as his phone rang in his pocket. He'd been in meetings and answering calls most of the morning, much of the work heavily involving the forensics, going over the details about various pieces of evidence recorded.

He plucked it out.

It was Cornty.

'Phil?' Tanzy answered.

Nothing from Cornty.

'Hello . . . Phil?'

'. . . herrmm.'

'Phil, I can't hear you,' Tanzy said, 'can you speak up a little?'

'He's got us.'

'Who has?'

'He's got us,' Cornty repeated.

'Yeah, I heard that part. Who has got you?' Tanzy straightened in his chair. Byrd was sitting next to him looking at some document or other, but stopped and looked Tanzy's way with a sudden interest in the phone call.

319

'Neil McMahon,' Cornty said quietly.

'Evelyn Jones's teacher?' Tanzy frowned.

'Cupboard — back bedroom.' Cornty's voice was strained, as if he had to eke out every word. 'Weaver — hurt — bad.'

Tanzy frowned. 'I can't hear you well, Cornty. Are you saying that Evelyn Jones's Teacher, Neil McMahon, has locked you inside a cupboard in his house?'

'Yeeeaa.'

'Why are you talking like that?'

'Can't move. Can't breathe.'

'We're on our way. We know the address. Hold tight.' Tanzy hung up and called an ambulance as he waved at Byrd to follow him to the car.

'The hell was that?' Byrd asked, once he'd hung up.

'Cornty and Weaver are locked inside a cupboard in a bedroom at Neil McMahon's house. Weaver's hurt somehow. Cornty doesn't sound too good either.'

'Neil McMahon the primary school teacher? This town never ceases to amaze me,' said Byrd.

He called DCI Thornton from the car and told her what was happening. She told him she'd send some PCs after them for support.

It took them three minutes to turn off Woodlands Road into West Crescent. The house they were looking for was up on the right. Tanzy slammed on the brakes outside the white semi-detached house. Parked in front of them was Cornty and Weaver's patrol car. Tanzy pulled the handbrake on, unclipped his seat belt, jumped out of the car and dashed to the white door. Byrd was merely seconds behind as Tanzy tried the handle, but it was locked. Tanzy banged on the door several times.

'Open the door! Police!' His voice echoed in the quiet street.

Byrd stopped just near him, panting hard. Behind them, the marked Astra pulled up, stopping over the driveway. PC Leonard and PC Grearer opened their doors and took a few steps towards the house. They were new faces at the station, unused to this sort of scene.

Tanzy banged another three times. 'Police, open up!'

'There's no car on the drive,' Byrd noted.

'They're in there! We need to get inside.'

'Can I help you?'

They both turned to see an elderly woman standing on the opposite driveway, her face showing concern.

'Have you seen Neil McMahon?' Tanzy asked quickly.

She frowned, then shook her head. 'No, not today. Is he in trouble?'

Tanzy ignored her question. 'We need to see him right now. Do you know if there's anyone in?'

She pointed at a dark blue Mondeo parked on the road. 'That's their car, so I assume they are.' Tanzy recalled seeing it when he met with Evelyn's parents for the media conference.

'We need to get in now!' Tanzy told Byrd.

'I'll go around the back,' Byrd said. 'Leonard, with me.'

The PC eagerly followed him round the side, through a gap between the garage and the house. At the end of the very short alley, a black gate stood firm and straight. Byrd tried the handle and—

'It's open!' Byrd glanced back at Leonard. 'Come on.'

The PC followed him through the gate towards the rear of the house.

* * *

Tanzy hammered at the door before PC Grearer appeared by his side.

'I think I could kick it in,' Grearer said, sounding excited. 'Here, watch out.'

Tanzy moved aside. 'Do your thing.'

PC Grearer wasn't tall or small, but he was stocky, an obvious gym-goer who had legs as thick as tree trunks. He lifted his right leg and lunged forward, the bottom of his shoe colliding with the door below the handle. The door cracked and swung open with a loud bang. Parts of the lock sheared off, falling onto the carpet inside the hallway.

Tanzy held his palm up, holding the PC back, and went inside first. As he crossed over the step, he cocked his head back. 'Stay close,' he told Grearer, who nodded eagerly, following him inside. 'Hello! Police here! Make yourself known wherever you are,' he shouted, projecting his voice throughout the house.

Silence came from all directions.

Tanzy angled to the left towards the base of the stairs.

'Stay behind me,' Tanzy told Grearer, who nodded at his instruction, his hand gripping the baton attached to his belt.

Step by step, they climbed up, listening. Once they reached the top, they took a right up onto the landing, then came to a halt. 'Weaver? Cornty?' Tanzy shouted.

Nothing.

* * *

Byrd and Leonard rounded the corner at the rear of the house and stepped onto the decking. The back door was a few feet along the wall to their right. Byrd tried the handle, which was locked, so he peered through the window into the kitchen. A table was resting against the far wall, with a calendar hanging from a nail above it. Various squiggles of writing lined the dates of the month. There was no one there. Methodically, his eyes ran across the rest of it, the fridge, the freezer, the worktop. A set of knives sat near the sink.

One of the knives was missing.

'See anyone?' PC Leonard asked, a step behind him.

'No. But there's a knife missing from the rack.' He pulled away from the window, lowered his arms and glanced along the back of the house, noticing a window further down. He peered in again through the dirty glass, making a visor with his hands to fight against the low winter sun.

There was a circular wooden table in the centre of the room with four chairs neatly tucked under it. The far wall was filled with old drawings. Child's drawings. The plethora of colours ruined the décor but at the same time made it look beautiful. The left side of the room sported a wide chimney breast and an alcove on either side. In the furthest alcove, sitting on the floor, with her knees up to her chest, was a woman.

Byrd gasped.

'What is it?' asked PC Leonard.

'There . . .' he whispered. 'There's a woman in the room. In the corner. Come on, let's go back around, through the front door.'

As Byrd pulled himself from the glass and moved, he saw the woman's head shoot towards him. Byrd froze as they made eye contact. The woman's eyes widened for a second before she pushed herself up off the floor and darted for the door.

Byrd pushed PC Leonard towards the side gate. 'Go, go now!'

83

Thursday, midday
West Crescent, Darlington

DI Tanzy and PC Grearer stood on the narrow, silent landing.

'Cornty?' Tanzy looked into the back bedroom, took a step—

'Wait!' Grearer said, pulling him back, his hand cupped around his forearm.

'What?' Tanzy turned back. 'What is it?'

'Look.'

Tanzy followed Grearer's pointed finger down at the floor. Blood. Several drops of blood. A small trail, leading towards the front bedroom.

Tanzy took a slow, measured step. 'This is the police, make yourself known!' He cautiously padded into the room first, his baton clenched tightly in his right hand. It felt familiar but strange, as if he hadn't handled it in a while. 'Police, make yourself known,' he repeated.

The room was bright. Tanzy edged around the door, feeling something in the room, something that altered the air molecules. The drops of blood on the floor appeared thicker. His eyes carefully followed a trail that angled around to the right, out of sight.

'Stay close,' he told Grearer, who was inches behind him.

The room was square and had a high ceiling, with enough light coming through the window to see everything. The trail of blood swept around the foot of the bed to a closed wardrobe in the far corner. There was nothing else in the room apart from a bed, bedside units on either side of it, and an ottoman at the window supporting a brown, soft blanket, folded and placed on top.

Tanzy reached out, grabbed the handle of the wardrobe and pulled it open. Inside the small space was a man. His body curled up awkwardly.

Neil McMahon.

Curled up, lying on his side and still. His face was motionless as he stared out at Tanzy. His stomach was smothered in blood with deep cuts through a white shirt. The aged carpet below was soaked in crimson liquid. Under different circumstances, Tanzy would have thrown himself down and checked his pulse, but it was obvious Neil was dead.

'Jesus!' Grearer gasped, standing just behind Tanzy, seeing inside the wardrobe.

Tanzy edged back and took out his phone, pressed a couple of buttons and put it to his ear.

'Yeah,' Tanzy said, 'ID DN522. We need backup and forensics here. There's been a stabbing. We're at West Crescent.'

He moved away from the wardrobe, leaving the door open, and went over to the bay window. He needed a second to compose himself before finding Byrd. But there was something else that he needed to do.

Find Cornty and Weaver.

It was then he heard a rush of footsteps downstairs somewhere. Then outside on the hard concrete. He turned and looked out the window, where he saw a woman dash towards a car then climb in. Within seconds, she pulled away quickly, smoke whirring from the spinning tyres.

'Fuck!'

Then his phone rang.

84

Thursday
West Crescent, Darlington

Byrd and Leonard rounded the corner and passed through the open gate.

The sound of screeching tyres exploded in the air as they galloped down the driveway. When they reached the road, the dark blue Mondeo was off into the distance in a flash. He pulled out his phone and called Tanzy.

'Max!'

'Ori, she's gone, I've—'

'I know, Max, I can see. I'm . . . I'm upstairs in the window.'

Byrd turned and looked up, seeing Tanzy in the bay window. 'We're going after her!' Byrd told him, then darted towards the marked Astra that Leonard and Grearer had arrived in. Leonard jumped into the car with him.

'Go!' he told Leonard, who threw the gear in first and turned on the blues and twos, the wail of the siren bombarding the usually silent street, then slammed his foot down.

'We'll wait here for forensics,' Tanzy said.

'Forensics?' Byrd shouted over the sound of the siren.

'We found Neil McMahon in the wardrobe — dead.'

'Jesus.' Byrd watched the road as PC Leonard guided the car around the bend, shooting after the speeding car, somehow keeping her in sight.

'Keep me updated, Ori!' Byrd yelled.

'I will. I need to find Weaver and Cornty!' Tanzy hung up the phone.

Byrd held on to the phone, lowered it to his lap. As they weaved in and out of traffic towards the traffic lights, he saw the Mondeo drive on the wrong side of the road, narrowly missing an oncoming red Corsa, which blasted its horn. Byrd steadied himself for the next turn, which was left onto Greenbank Road.

Leonard skilfully guided the car around the bend, careful not to lose control on the wet road surface from the earlier drizzle.

The Mondeo was just ahead.

'Stay with her, I'm ringing dispatch,' Byrd told him, focusing down on his phone and finding the number.

'Officer DN443 in pursuit of a dark blue Mondeo on Greenbank Road, heading north, towards the Denes area of Darlington.' He gave the Mondeo's number plate.

'Who's the driver?'

'Female. Blonde hair. Around the age of forty to fifty. Murder suspect, fled the scene.'

'Do you need additional units at the scene?'

'No, Detective Inspector Orion Tanzy — ID DN522 — has called it in. We need support vehicles for now.'

'Okay, additional units are on their way. I'll contact the CCTV control room to track the vehicle down. Do you need NPAS?'

'Hold off on the helicopter for now, we're not far behind. We'll catch up.'

'Call me ASAP if you do, it'll take—'

'I know. Will do, thanks.' Byrd knew the nearest NPAS base was Newcastle, so it would be at least twenty minutes until they had any help from the air.

The Mondeo flew down Greenbank Road, heading towards the Denes park.

'Steady driving. Good.'

PC Leonard nodded. 'We've had good training.'

Byrd liked PC Leonard.

At the bottom of Greenbank Road, the Mondeo took a right onto Widdowfield Street. Seconds later, the Astra did the same, the wheels sliding a little on the wet tarmac, and for a moment Byrd thought Leonard was going to lose it, but his control was exceptional, quickly taking the corner. Up ahead, just as the Mondeo was angling around to the left, a black Civic pulled out of the Salisbury Terrace junction, colliding into the side of it, forcing it up onto the kerb and into the metal railing, causing a horrendous crunch.

The Mondeo came to an abrupt halt. The side of it was smashed in.

'She's stopped, she's stopped!' PC Leonard shouted, slamming the brakes on, forcing the Astra to come to a halt behind the Mondeo.

Byrd climbed out of the passenger seat, closed the door and grabbed his radio from his hip. The Civic was a metre away from it, diagonally across the road.

'This is DI Max Byrd in pursuit of the Mondeo,' he said into the radio. 'Suspect has stopped at the bottom of Salisbury Terrace due to an RTC. Approaching suspect with caution. Send backup to this location. Proceed with attention, members of the public present.' Byrd placed the radio back to his hip, watching the car closely. Through the rear windscreen, he could see the woman in the driver's seat with her hands resting on the top of her head, most likely nursing a blow from the collision.

PC Leonard came to Byrd's side but slowed, allowing him to lead; he had more experience, and more know-how. As Byrd approached the door, he heard the woman shouting from inside the car, followed by a series of bangs as she frantically attempted to open it, but the door was crushed and bent, stuck in the frame of the vehicle. The other side of the Mondeo was crushed into the metal railings, covered in a sea of glass. She began to climb out of the broken driver's window.

Just as she dropped down onto the ground, Byrd took her arm. PC Leonard grabbed the handcuffs from his belt and arrested her.

85

Thursday
West Crescent, Darlington

'Are you going to be sick?' Tanzy asked PC Grearer, who'd gone white, crouched by the bed near the bay window, doing his best not to look at the dead body of Neil McMahon.

Grearer moved his hand from his mouth, shook his head a few times. 'I'll be fine, boss.'

'Come on. We need to find Cornty and Weaver. They're in here somewhere.'

Tanzy returned to the landing and entered the rear bedroom. A set of closed curtains blocked the daylight, making it seem dark and depressing. In the corner of the room was a built-in cupboard.

He adjusted his grip on the baton and padded across the soft carpet towards it while Grearer steadied himself behind him near the door. Tanzy reached forward, pulled the handle, but the door wouldn't open. He tried again, harder this time. Again, nothing.

It was locked. Under the handle, he noticed a small keyhole.

'Fuck,' he muttered. He looked around for a key but had no joy. Grearer tried pulling the door open but also failed. Then they both tried together, but it still wouldn't budge.

'I don't think I should kick this one in, sir, if this is where Cornty and Weaver are,' said Grearer. 'We need to prise it open.'

Tanzy nodded, then frowned. 'Or . . .'

'Where are you going?' Grearer asked Tanzy as he headed for the door and left the room. 'Sir?'

Tanzy went back into the front bedroom to the body of Neil McMahon. He leaned down and carefully padded his left pocket first. Nothing.

'What . . . what are you doing?'

Tanzy ignored the PC and continued his search. Bending down to get himself in a better position, he ducked and managed to get his hand under Neil's right side. He didn't want to move the body, knowing he could mess things up for the forensics who were on their way. He found nothing.

'Try the garage. Anything that will get that door open.'

Two minutes later, PC Grearer returned with a crowbar. 'Here, sir. The ambulance has arrived. I've told them to wait outside until I call them up.'

'That should do,' Tanzy said, taking it and wedging it into the door. He pulled on the bar and the cupboard cracked open.

'Jesus!' Grearer gasped as PC Weaver fell back into the room, landing headfirst on the carpet with a thud. There was a quiet, raspy groan from inside the cupboard. Tanzy saw PC Cornty awkwardly bent, his face and chest against the back wall.

'Call those paramedics up now!' Tanzy ordered. He dropped the crowbar down onto the floor and reached inside.

Grearer disappeared long enough to wave the ambulance crew from the front window and then returned.

'Cornty,' Tanzy panted. Cornty groaned again but didn't move, as if his body had frozen in stone in that position. Very carefully, Tanzy pulled the PC out of the cupboard and lowered him onto the carpet near Weaver.

'Doesn't look like she's breathing,' Grearer said.

'Check her pulse,' Tanzy told him. He lowered himself to her and placed two fingers on her throat.

'It's there, but only slightly. What's this?' There was a cut to the back of her head, her blonde hair matted with blood where it appeared she had been hit. 'Hang on in there,' Grearer said quietly to her.

The paramedics came in, wearing overshoes. They went to Weaver first.

Tanzy's phone rang in his pocket. He sighed, plucked it out and answered it.

'Ori, we fucking got her!' Byrd shouted.

'Good.' Tanzy was concentrating on Cornty beneath him and said nothing more.

'What's happening there? Have you found Cornty and Weaver?'

'We found them. Amy has a cut to the back of her head — she's in a bad way but breathing. Phil is a little more with it but isn't much better. Paramedics have just arrived. Is backup taking the suspect down to the station?'

'Yeah, she's in one of our cars. She's not talking — I'm assuming she's McMahon's wife?'

'It would make sense,' Tanzy replied.

'We need a recovery truck to move this old banger — it's blocking the road.'

Tanzy didn't respond.

'Ori?'

'What is it, Max?'

'How are they?' Byrd asked.

'Amy and Phil? Too soon to tell.' His voice was grim as he watched the paramedics stretcher Weaver away. 'You heading back over here?'

'Yeah, need to see the crime scene. Be with you in two minutes.'

332

Tanzy put the phone back into his pocket. Ever since he'd opened the cupboard in the back bedroom, there was an unpleasant smell. It had grown stronger as the minutes ticked on. He looked away from Cornty, tipped his head back and peered into the cupboard, wondering what it was.

Then he heard a little girl crying from somewhere very close.

86

Thursday
West Crescent, Darlington

'That was my first chase,' Leonard said as they pulled up at the McMahons' house.

'You did good,' Byrd said, giving the PC an encouraging smile. 'Come on, let's go inside.'

They both got out and headed through the open door, Leonard a little apprehensive about what he was about to see.

'Tanzy?' Byrd shouted, projecting his voice through the house.

'Up here, Max.' Tanzy's tone was flat.

Byrd and Leonard climbed the stairs. When they reached the top, they could see Tanzy and Grearer in the rear bedroom. Tanzy was kneeling in the cupboard, inspecting something.

'Hey,' Byrd said, entering the room. 'Cornty and Weaver?'

Tanzy didn't look up. 'On their way to hospital.'

Byrd sniffed the air. 'What's that smell?'

'It's coming from in here.'

They all froze at the sound of crying.

'Where's that coming from?' PC Leonard asked, frowning.

'It's coming . . . I think it's coming from in here?' They all went silent, watching Tanzy. 'I've been all over the upstairs since you called me and it's definitely coming from here. I don't understand.'

'Understand what?' Byrd asked him, frowning.

'There's nothing in here apart from clothes. I can't see . . . hang on a minute.' Tanzy leaned into the cupboard.

'What?' Byrd edged forward, stopped just behind him and bent down to have a look.

'What's this?' Tanzy asked, pointing to a screw hanging out the wood a couple of millimetres on the left-hand side, about halfway up. Tanzy tugged on it but it was solid. Above and below where the screw was, there were empty holes where a screw had been fixed, then removed time and time again.

'What the . . . ?'

'Hello!' Byrd shouted, nearly penetrating Tanzy's eardrum. 'Hello — is anyone there?'

The crying stopped suddenly.

'Help me,' they heard a quiet struggling voice. 'Help.'

'We need a screwdriver, Max.'

Byrd was already searching through the nearby chest of drawers. He found a Phillips screwdriver in the third drawer down. 'Got one, here, try this!' Byrd handed it to Tanzy, who took it and turned back into the tight space.

'Shine a light on it, please, Max. I can barely see.'

Byrd pulled out his phone, turned on the torch function and leaned in, so Tanzy could see the screw to turn it. After a few turns, it popped out and dropped to the floor.

The wooden panel at the back came away an inch from where it was originally seated.

'Help me . . .'

The voice was crystal clear.

'Move back, mate,' Tanzy told Byrd, who got up out of the way. Tanzy found his feet and dragged the rail of clothing to one side. He then dug his fingers down the side of the panel and pulled it towards the room. It opened a few inches.

335

A horrific smell seeped out — human excrement. Tanzy cupped his nose. 'Jesus!'

'What is it, Ori?'

'Call another ambulance, Grearer. We've found Evelyn Jones.'

87

Thursday afternoon
West Crescent, Darlington

'Help me,' Evelyn said. Her voice was so weak it was almost inaudible.

'Evelyn, I'm Detective Inspector Tanzy. You're safe now.'

Tanzy looked around the space. It went about two feet back and was the width of the wardrobe, which was roughly four feet. Evelyn lay on her side on a dirty blanket. Her little body rose and fell with her shallow breathing. To the left back corner, there was a pile of faeces on the floor and it absolutely reeked. To the right, there was a handful of empty bottles and a wooden box, which was maybe a little bigger than a shoebox.

'Can you sit up, Evelyn?'

Evelyn moved so slowly it hurt Tanzy to watch. If she'd been in here for the whole time she'd been missing, it was a level of cruelty he'd never seen before. Ever. She was wearing her school uniform, the same one she had on the day she'd disappeared. Her cheekbones were prominent, her eyes sunken deep into her face — the complete opposite of the photograph that her parents, Ray and Tricia, had given him ten days ago.

Tanzy helped her up. Her body was floppy, her spine almost folding in two. Severe dehydration, he thought. Evelyn could barely sit up properly, as if her spine and muscles had lost the memory of how to. He probably shouldn't move her before the ambulance arrived, but he couldn't bear to make her stay in this fetid cell any longer.

He cautiously lifted her up, then very carefully backed out of the space.

'You're safe now, Evelyn,' Tanzy whispered again. She didn't have the energy to respond. Tanzy told Grearer to grab a blanket or something to lie her down on. He came back with a blanket he'd found in the front bedroom.

'Here.' Grearer laid the blanket out neatly and helped lower Evelyn onto it, a few paces away from PC Weaver, who they'd carefully put in the recovery position 'The ambulance is on its way.'

Byrd looked away from them, went to the cupboard and peered inside the small space. He gagged at the smell, thinking about the pain, the isolation and the emptiness the girl must have felt being inside. He noticed the wooden box in the corner, bent down and picked it up, then carried it out.

'What's that?' PC Leonard asked, curiously.

'I have no idea.'

There was a lock on the front of it. But no key.

'Pass me the screwdriver, please,' Byrd said to Leonard, who'd taken it off Tanzy moments earlier and placed it on the windowsill. He grabbed it. 'Here.'

Byrd prised the lock off and it fell onto the floor. He opened the lid and peered inside.

'Oh my God. Look at this.'

88

Thursday afternoon
Interrogation room, police station

Byrd and Tanzy sat at the desk in silence draining their coffees, readying themselves. The door to their right opened and in came DS Stockdale, who nodded at them before moving aside to make way for PC Cornty and PC Weaver, who escorted Judith McMahon into the room, each holding one of her arms. 'Sit,' Cornty told her, pushing her shoulder down until she hit the chair.

'Thank you,' Byrd said to the PCs, 'you can go.' They bobbed their heads, turned and left the room. Byrd watched Judith McMahon closely. She didn't say a word and kept her focus on the table between them. Sweating from the heat under the interrogation room lights, her skin appeared almost wax-like in the sheen. Her slim body rocked back and forth very slightly. She hadn't said a word since she was arrested, except to refuse a solicitor. Byrd and McMahon interviewed her for ten minutes without getting a sound out of her.

'Judith?' Tanzy said again. 'This is your chance to tell your side of the story. Don't you want to take it?'

She glared at Tanzy, then glanced away.

The detectives had played this game before. They would stay silent until it became too awkward for her. Byrd, in his head, counted forty-seven seconds until she finally spoke.

'Yeah . . .'

'We'd like some answers, Judith,' Tanzy said, then turned to Byrd. 'Should we ask her a couple of questions? You never know, depending on her answers, it might be worth something. It could determine the sentence the judge will give her.'

That got her attention.

She glanced up, finding the confidence to switch her focus between both of the detectives for a few seconds then settling on Byrd.

'We'll start with Evelyn Jones, shall we?' Tanzy said. 'Why her?'

Judith looked at Tanzy, offered a little shrug.

'Why not another seven-year-old? Why not a boy? Or a ten-year-old girl?' asked Tanzy. 'Why lock her up in a cupboard for over ten days? You know —' Tanzy leaned forward a little, his eyes narrowing — 'what you've done is one of the worst things I've ever seen. And believe me, I've seen some terrible things. So, Judith . . . the question is: why?'

'I was protective of her,' she said quietly.

'Protective?'

She nodded.

'Why?'

'She reminded me of my own daughter, Casey.'

'But Evelyn isn't your daughter, Judith. She is Ray and Tricia Jones's child. Not yours.'

'Everything she did, she reminded me of Casey. Neil used to come in after school and tell me about her. About how she would write and draw these amazing pictures. He actually said Evelyn reminded him of Casey.' She paused a second. 'I wanted her. I wanted to keep her safe.'

'By locking her in a cupboard, feeding her scraps of food and not enough water? Not even letting her out to go to the bathroom? Is that what you mean by safe?'

Her eyes got teary. 'I missed Casey so much. I couldn't stand the thought of some other parents having the pleasure of bringing up a daughter who always had a smile on her face. My God, the stories about her were infectious.'

The detectives absorbed her outrageous reasoning for a few moments.

'How did you do it?' Byrd asked.

'I knew I was going to do it for a while . . . I just didn't know when. I'd built the cupboard as a personal project some years ago.' She paused for breath. 'Anyway, I knew exactly which way Evelyn went and grabbed her before she reached home.'

'And Evelyn just happily went along with you?'

She nodded. 'I told her I was her teacher's wife and that he'd bought her a present for doing so well at art. She followed me straight home.'

'Easy as that?' Byrd replied.

'Yup. Pretty simple.'

'Then what?'

'I grabbed her and put her in the cupboard, then locked it. I fed her sandwiches and water. Kept the door to that room closed most of the time and Neil never really went in there. When she used to cry, I used to say it was the girl next door. Neil never suspected a thing.'

'And just how long did you expect to do this for?' Tanzy this time.

She shrugged. 'I don't know. I was going to move her. The smell was getting horrendous in there.'

'I'm not surprised after ten days.'

'Why did you kill your husband?' asked Byrd.

'He called the police about the girl crying — he thought he was reporting our neighbour, but the constables came into our house and got suspicious when they heard Evelyn crying. They were looking inside the cupboard. I pushed the woman in and locked it. Neil asked me what the hell I was doing. I grabbed a screwdriver and I stabbed him with it.'

Tanzy and Byrd didn't move as she spoke. They watched and listened, feeling deeply disturbed by how calm she appeared to be. Tanzy leaned back a little, raised his palms, and placed them on top of his head, while Byrd remained still, his eyes on Judith McMahon.

'Then what happened?' Byrd asked.

'Neil didn't die straight away. He staggered into our bedroom and collapsed near the bed. I suppose he was trying to get away from me. I pulled him across the carpet and put him in the wardrobe.'

Judith McMahon seemed to have a thing for wardrobes, thought Byrd.

'But there's something else, isn't there?' he said. 'Something important I'd like to know more about.'

'I'm listening,' she said.

'We found a box inside the cupboard you hid Evelyn in. Can you confirm, for the recording, what the contents of that box are?'

'I think you know what's in the box, Detectives,' she whispered, glancing down at the table for a moment, then back up at them, switching her focus between Tanzy and Byrd.

The air inside the room suddenly felt cold. Byrd angled his head and took a glance towards Tanzy, who met his stare for a brief moment.

Tanzy said, 'I have an idea. But can you confirm it for the recording?'

'The contents of the box you found were bones,' she said, matter-of-factly.

'Who do they belong to?'

'They belong to my daughter, Casey McMahon.'

89

'Close the door, gents,' DCI June Thornton told them as they entered her office. Byrd and Tanzy sat down. Her office was warm; the scent of lavender emanated from the diffuser behind her, underneath the framed certificates on the wall.

'It's been a rough fucking week,' she said tiredly. She looked pale, her complexion a little deflated. The detectives couldn't argue with that.

'I've heard what's happened with Judith McMahon,' she told them. 'Is Evelyn safe with her parents now?'

'Yes, they're all at Memorial Hospital,' Tanzy replied. 'Evelyn's severely dehydrated and needs to be on IV fluids for a while until she's back to normal.'

'Do the parents know exactly what happened to her?' she asked.

Tanzy nodded. 'Yeah, I told them earlier. They didn't take it very well — as expected. They asked what was going to happen to Judith McMahon.'

She glanced down at her desk. 'I hope she gets put away for a long time. It's awful what she did, unbelievable. Did she say much about the bones?'

'She admitted they were Casey's.'

'Why did she do that to her daughter?' She furrowed her brows.

'She told us she wanted to be in control, that she wanted to keep her safe from the world. She said she'd locked her in the cupboard, the same way she did with Evelyn, but Casey had eventually died after seven days. Neil didn't have a clue, and now that he's dead, he'll never know what his wife did to their daughter.'

'I just don't understand why,' replied Thornton, shaking her head. 'What was she hiding her from specifically?'

'She claimed the world was unsafe, filled with bad people that wanted to hurt others.'

Thornton frowned. 'Did she expand on that?'

'She said her own father mistreated her when she was young.'

'So, instead of making sure that didn't happen to her own, she did exactly that?'

Byrd shrugged. 'I just don't get some people.'

'She'll rot inside — I'm sure the inmates will have a few things to say to her,' she said.

Tanzy gave a sad smile. 'No doubt. The world has gone mad.'

'The world has always been mad. The difference now is we are more aware of it.' She slumped down in the middle of her leather high-topped chair and sighed heavily. 'Any update on the other cases? I've had an update from the new forensic guys, Paul and Amanda — said it was clear Kim Harrison had been hit over the back of the head before she entered the water. They assume the blow likely killed her. Tallow and Hope were examining the scene at Dr Ching's house.'

'Anything back from the pathologist about Karen Whittaker?'

'I'm told her head was removed with surgical precision, similar to the removal of Julia Porter's eyes and Mary Richards' hand.'

The DCI absorbed his words and bobbed her head. 'How confident are you both that Dr Ching is our man?' Her words lingered in the office for a moment.

'His DNA was found at all the crime scenes,' Byrd said. 'The third crime scene was his own house. It places him at all locations where either the murder was committed or the body was present. The issue we have — I wouldn't say an issue — is that he's denying it.' He paused a beat. 'He's denying all of it. The next step is to run it by the CPS. We can hit them with the evidence we have, and they can make the decision. Personally, I'm confident there's enough for a prosecution.'

'Talk me through the progress on Kim Harrison's case,' DCI Thornton said with sad eyes. It was a given she cared for the general public; it was her job. But when it concerned one of her own, there was something more. They were like family, and it was clear to the detectives she wasn't finished discussing it.

'The pathologist says she was attacked with a rock before she hit the water.'

'How do they know for sure?'

'Because she wouldn't have obtained an injury so severe under the water. To put it simply, water slows things down — the injury would be quite different.'

'So it's definitely a homicide,' she said. 'Of a police officer, no less.' She looked less tired, more determined. 'The last couple of weeks haven't been the best for Darlington. But you've done the impossible and found that little girl. Let's see if we can't wrap up the rest of these cases too.'

90

Thursday evening
Darlington

The man sitting at the desk smiled. Everything so far had gone to plan. It had played out to perfection.

All the evidence had pointed to the doctor, and he'd been arrested.

The printer underneath the desk near his right leg whirred and out came a sheet of A4 paper. He leaned over, picked it up and placed it down on the wooden desk in front of him. His smile widened, and his eyes sparkled.

There she was.

The headless body of Karen Whittaker inside the shed. His eyes slowly trailed the blood across the bottom of the shed and up her body to where her head once was.

'Wow,' he whispered, excitement tingling through him.

To his right, the door to the room opened. He watched his wife cautiously step in, staring down at him.

'Did he send it?' she asked.

The man nodded. 'Yeah. Come see.'

The woman stopped behind him, wrapped her arms around his shoulders and studied the image on the desk. 'We're nearly there, aren't we?'

He nodded. 'Just one more.'

'When?'

'Tonight.'

She gasped with excitement. 'Really?'

'Yes,' he said coldly, raising a hand and gripping hers for a moment.

She bent down, kissed his cheek and squeezed him tightly. 'Are you in the clear? Do they think it was the doctor?'

'I haven't been arrested yet,' the man replied, 'and he has, so I think so.'

Another kiss, this time, longer.

'When are you going?' she asked.

'Right now, I need to make a couple of calls. If anyone rings, just say I'm busy.'

The man stood up from the chair and headed for the wardrobe. He grabbed a set of different clothes — darker clothes — and got changed. The curtains behind him were drawn, blocking out the dark world outside. His wife waited in the room, watching him nervously.

'What time will you be in?' she asked.

'Soon. This will all be over tonight.'

He approached her, held her close and kissed her passionately. He went towards the door, turning, and said, 'I'll see you soon.'

There was something in his tone that she felt was different, something not quite right in his words. As if he knew it would be the last time he'd ever see her.

91

Byrd pulled up on his driveway, turned off the engine and sat for a moment. He unclipped his seat belt and opened the door. A wall of cold air hit him. It had been a hectic day, a day he'd never forget.

He needed a drink. Badly.

On his way to his front door, his stomach rumbled, reminding him he hadn't eaten for most of the day. It had been several days since he'd seen Claire, but after speaking on the phone earlier, she told him to give her a text when he got home if he fancied some company and a takeaway. He hadn't indulged in one of those in a while. A night on the sofa, eating shit and watching whatever film they — she — decided to watch sounded good to him.

If he was honest, he wasn't sure it was going well with Claire. The last eighteen months had been good, sometimes great, sometimes even amazing, but over the past few weeks, it hadn't felt the same. The spark that was usually there just wasn't. Was it because of what had happened to his parents in the car crash, the extra demand at work, the higher stress levels?

He didn't know. Maybe.

Either way, Claire wasn't going to hang around for ever if it continued this way. She wouldn't just sit on the sidelines and come on as a substitute when Byrd needed her or craved her attention. He'd either have to change and make more of an effort or decide to let her go.

He stopped thinking about it, stepped into the house and closed the front door. After he locked it, he put the keys on the hooks on the wall on the right. The house was cold and felt emptier than usual, but he didn't know why. He turned the lamp on to his right, the space at the bottom of the stairs coming alive with a warm glow, then he strutted down the hall towards the kitchen, the rhythmic sound of his shoes bringing the house to life.

His mind was doing overtime.

He couldn't stop thinking about things. About what had happened over the past few days and weeks. PC Harrison. Evelyn Jones. Judith McMahon and her gruesome secret. Julia Porter. Mary Richards. Karen Whittaker. And, lastly, Dr Ching. The person responsible for caring for his parents, the person whose job it was to give them the best fighting chance they'd have to wake up.

Something didn't feel right about Dr Ching.

He called Tanzy but got voicemail.

He tried again. Same result. Voicemail.

He'd never needed to, but he tried Tanzy's house phone instead. After four rings, someone picked up: 'Hello?'

'Hi, Pip,' Byrd said. 'Is Orion there?'

'He . . . he was but he's gone out.'

'Where's he gone?'

'Like I give a shit!' she snapped.

Byrd tried to hide his surprise. He liked Pip, thought she liked him. Perhaps she was back to drinking again; she was so different under the influence. 'It's really important. If you see him, can you ask him to call me?'

'Whatever.' The line went dead.

Byrd placed the phone down on the worktop and frowned, then he reached up for a glass and the bottle of Amaretto. He filled the glass to the halfway point, lifted it to his mouth and swallowed it in one.

He stood still in the kitchen, thinking, wondering. He checked his call list and rang his voicemail. There were no new messages. Standing at the worktop, leaning forward with his palms down on the surface to steady his weight, he thought about his parents, thought about how he'd do anything to be able to pop to their house for a cup of coffee. Just to sit with them, even in silence, to watch them absorbed in the programmes they loved to watch. He turned away, wondering if he'd ever get to do that again.

You never know when you'll see someone for the last time. By the time you realise, it could be too late.

He clicked on Tanzy's number again. It went straight to voicemail.

'Ori, where the fuck are you?' he said.

92

Thursday evening
Leafield Road, Darlington

Samantha Timms picked up the phone and called her husband.

'Hey,' said Gregory.

'Hey, where are you? Are you close yet?'

'I'm just leaving. I'll be home in five minutes. It wasn't busy at all. Straight through the tills.'

'Okay.' She folded the towels that had just been washed and dried, and neatly placed them into the airing cupboard at the top of the stairs. 'Hurry up, I'm starving!'

'How have the boys been?'

'Ahh, you know, like boys. Reece was fighting with Jack, but that's nothing new.'

'They in bed?'

'Yeah, just put them down. Why?'

'I have a special treat for you,' he whispered.

'I hope it's flowers. It's been ages since I've had flowers.'

'It isn't flowers, but you'll love it,' he told her. 'Do you want me to tell you?'

'Erm . . . go on,' she said, folding a couple of the boy's T-shirts into an immaculate pile.

She heard the front door open, then close.

She smiled. 'You were quick . . .'

'I don't mess around, you know,' he replied.

She walked to the bedroom and took off her bathrobe, allowing it to drop to the floor, and stepped into the en suite. She leaned through the open shower door and switched on the water.

'Can you make me a coffee please and bring it up?'

'Yeah, I will,' he said.

'Don't worry about before, by the way. They don't mean it. They're just growing up and finding things hard. It's a difficult age for them.'

'Yeah, I know,' he said. 'I just feel distant from them sometimes. It's hard, working long hours. I miss my boys.'

'They miss you too,' she replied. 'What's that sound?'

'The radio. Can you not hear me?'

Frowning, she leaned over and turned the shower off. The en suite dropped to a deafening silence for a few seconds.

'You there?' Gregory asked through the phone.

'The radio? What radio?'

'The car radio,' he said.

'But . . . you're already home?'

'I'm just turning onto Victoria Road now. Be two minutes. I'll bring your coffee up when I get in.'

Samantha glanced towards the bedroom door. She could hear slow footsteps on the stairs.

'Greg — you're not home?'

'I'm on Victoria Road, I'll be—'

'There's someone in the house,' she gasped. 'They're walking up the stairs.'

93

Shez opened her eyes slowly. It took a few seconds for them to adjust to the lighting in her dark bedroom. She lay on her front, her left leg bent awkwardly, facing the bedroom door. Out on the landing, she could see flashing disco lights coming from the party downstairs.

Her head throbbed.

Why was she on the floor? She touched the back of her head and felt something wet. Blood. It was where she'd collided with the wardrobe when Sarah had pushed her over.

'Fuck!' she shouted, trying to find her feet, but she was dazed, almost toppling back onto the floor. She used a nearby set of drawers to aid her.

Dizzy, she staggered across the room, pulled her bedroom door open and stepped out onto the landing. The music downstairs was still loud. Carefully, she descended the stairs one by one, holding on to the handrail, her balance not quite right. The house was less busy. She had no clue about the time. It could be midnight, or it could be three in the morning. She pulled out her phone, which told her it was half one.

She staggered through the kitchen. It was a mess. Pizza crusts were everywhere, empty bottles, squashed cans, fag butts — the kitchen stank of cigarette smoke. The lad who'd tried to kiss her earlier was balanced precariously on a stool at the breakfast bar, snoring heavily.

'Go home,' she said, shoving him, but he didn't move.

She coughed as she went through the kitchen and reached the conservatory, stepping over a girl who'd passed out in the doorway. She veered onto the decking outside.

It was much colder now.

'Sarah?' she shouted. There was no one out there — everyone had retreated inside to enjoy the latter dregs of the night.

She reached the garage and tried the handle; the door was locked.

'Shit,' she whispered.

She went down the narrow, dark alley to the side of the garage, between the brickwork and the external fence. There was a small square window, the light inside the garage weakly illuminating the narrow alley. She peered in.

'Oh my fucking God!' she shouted, throwing a hand up to her mouth. Her whole body started to shake.

Ian Porter, who was still inside with the other three, glanced towards the glass, noticing her peeping in, and pointed in her direction. As quickly as she could, Shez ducked down to the concrete, could feel the cold brick against her back and her heart beating through her chest so hard and fast it seemed to penetrate her rib cage.

She needed to get help. She needed the police. Pushing herself up off the ground, she felt dizzy and disorientated, using her palm against the wall to steady herself. She stopped herself from gagging and throwing up. She needed to get away.

When she reached the end of the wall, she stumbled down the driveway and—

The garage door opened fast. Ian Porter and Stuart Richards ran out, grabbed her quickly, hauled her up and carried her back into the garage. She kicked and scratched like a vicious cat, violently enough for them to drop her just before the garage door.

'Get her in here now!' Stuart shouted to Ian.

She screamed. Before she had the chance to scream again, Ian Porter forced his hand over her mouth. She bit it.

'Ahh, you little bitch!' he yelled, giving her a backhand to the face.

She cowered to the cold concrete, yelping in pain.

'Lads, we need to go now, come on, let's fuck off . . .' Stuart told them. 'Come on, go, go!'

James Whittaker and Gregory Timms stepped out of the garage through the door and ran down the driveway. Stuart dashed after them onto the dark, quiet street.

Ian Porter stood over Shez, who was whimpering on the ground, holding her swollen face. He bent down and whispered in her ear: 'If you tell anyone this was us, we'll come back and do the same to you.' He grabbed her tightly, nipping the outside of her arms. 'She didn't see it coming, and neither will you. Do you understand?'

She nodded at him, tears streaming down her face.

'Not a fucking word,' he told her, leaving her to cry down on the cold, damp ground.

Shez turned onto her back and threw a weak hand out towards the silent garage. 'Sarah . . .'

94

Tanzy was sitting in his Mercedes, parked up in the town, near a bar called the Grange. The town itself wasn't that busy — it was only a Thursday. A few college kids were out in groups, some in twos, and some older couples, who'd probably been out for a meal and wanted to enjoy a few drinks before heading for their taxi home.

The time on the Mercedes dashboard was 11.10 p.m.

He hadn't spoken to Pip all day. He couldn't be bothered with her at the moment. There was too much going on at work and all she did was drain him. He missed the kids like crazy, but they were in safe hands with Pip's mother. She'd been an absolute rock over the past few months.

He turned his phone back on in case he'd missed any important calls. He'd turned it off to shut himself away from the world. Peace and quiet. The screen lit up and the loading icon spun on the display. Looking to the right, out of the window, he saw the entrance sign of Joe's bar down the road, was tempted to go in and have a few pints, feel some music and escape from reality for half an hour. God, he needed—

356

Tanzy jumped a little when his phone rang on the seat. He picked it up and checked the screen. It was a number he hadn't saved or recognised, ending in 406. He pressed answer and raised it slowly to his ear.

'Hello?'

'Detective Tanzy?' the voice was fast, hurried.

'Speaking. Who is—'

'You need to help me — my wife. There's someone at our house. You were right.' The man was out of breath.

'Who is this?' Tanzy asked, confused.

'It's Gregory Timms. You were right. She's in danger. My wife is in danger right now — there's someone in the house.'

'Slow down, Gregory. Please, just take a breath,' Tanzy said calmly. 'Isn't there a unit watching your house? Last I heard someone was there.'

'I don't know. She's in trouble.'

'Where are you?'

'I'm heading home now. There's someone there. I'm a minute away. Please help me.'

'What's your address?'

As Timms gave him the address, Tanzy recalled the location of Leafield Road. 'Okay, okay, I'm heading there now.' Tanzy hung up the phone and called dispatch, asking for units to be sent to Timms' address immediately. He ended the call and phoned Byrd and set it in the hands-free holder.

He planted his foot and the tyres spun on the cold tarmac as he pulled away.

'Pick up, pick up!' he shouted. Then there was a click.

'Orion, I've been trying to—'

'Max, listen, there's no time,' Tanzy said, 'get in your car and get to Leafield Road now!'

'Leafield Road? Why? What's—'

'Just fucking listen, Max, someone's at Gregory Timms' house about to kill his wife.'

'We have a unit there, don't we?'

'I thought we did. I'm on my way over there. Get moving.'

'On my way.'

95

Darlington
Fifteen years ago

The car pulled up outside the house just after two in the morning. Through the large bay window, the young man could see flashing lights and people dancing. Others were flaked out on sofas and others lay on the floor.

He applied the handbrake and got out. The sound of the music seeped through the frosted windows out into the cold, frosty air. He ambled up the driveway, looking through the window. He took his phone out, searched for his sister's number, then pressed CALL.

It rang and rang until it went to voicemail.

He edged the front door open and went inside. The warm hallway smelled of perfume and stale smoke. Some dance anthem from the early nineties was blaring from somewhere.

Down the hall, through the kitchen, he saw a lad sitting awkwardly on a stool bent over a breakfast bar, looking worse for wear.

He looked in the living room. 'Has anyone seen my sister?'

The ones who weren't completely out of it gazed up at him with glassy eyes. 'Hey, you're here—'

'Have you seen my sister?'

Three of them shook their heads.

He then heard another conversation nearby.

'Where?' a girl said behind him, to one of her friends. 'The garage?'

'Come see,' the other person said to her. The two of them went through the kitchen towards the back of the house.

'Hey, what's in the garage?' he shouted. But nobody seemed to know.

He checked the rest of the living room and dining room, then went into the kitchen. Crisps, pizza crusts and empty bottles cluttered the floor. He shook his head. 'Kids.' At the end of the kitchen, he took a right into the conservatory.

And that's when he heard the screams.

They were coming from outside.

He dashed out and, through the back gate, he saw several people standing at the door of the garage, the light inside illuminating their terrified faces. They seemed frozen, unable to move. One of the girls was standing with her hands clamped over her mouth, and another girl started to cry.

He stepped off the decking, went through the open gate. 'What is it?' he asked, approaching the commotion.

One of the lads stopped him, holding his palm onto his chest. 'Mate, don't . . .'

Despite the lad's plea, he frowned and veered around him, then moving the two girls out of the way, he peered inside the garage.

He froze and his whole world was held in suspension for what seemed like a long time. There she was. His sister. Sarah.

Hanging from one of the roof support beams by a rope around her neck.

Her face was purple and drained. Her eyes were open and bulging. He dashed in, grabbed her legs in an attempt to lift her, desperate to free her.

'Help me! Fucking help me!' he begged the girls at the door, who'd decided they weren't going inside and started to cry instead. After realising he couldn't lift her high enough to loosen the rope around her neck, he frantically searched the garage, noticing a chair kicked over on its side a few feet away from where Sarah was hanging.

It took him several seconds to find a pair of gardening shears in a drawer to his left and, using them, he snapped at the rope violently, screaming her name, until it gave way after the fourth attempt. Sarah's body fell to the floor with a sickening thud.

He leaned over her, crying, and held her close.

There was nothing he could do.

She was already dead.

96

Thursday night
Leafield Road, Darlington

DI Orion Tanzy pulled up outside the house and slammed on the brakes, causing the car to skid before it jerked to a halt in front of an unoccupied white van.

'Son of a bitch — the stolen van!'

He dashed over the damp road towards the house, sliding down the gap between two parked cars, and stepped up onto the path towards the front door. At the door, he pushed down hard on the handle, barging into it with his shoulder, causing it to fly open. He almost lost his balance, falling through into the hallway, but somehow managed to stay on his feet.

'Samantha!' he shouted, his voice tearing through the house and rebounding back at him. 'Gregory!'

No response. He must have beaten Gregory here but knew he wouldn't be far behind. He checked all the rooms downstairs, starting with the living room then the dining room and through to a narrow, low-ceilinged kitchen. He galloped to the end of it, finding a small toilet when he barged the door open but found it was empty.

No sign of anyone.

'Fuck!'

He went back through the house and took a cautious right, glaring up the stairs, which were in total darkness. He saw a switch, turned it on quickly, then started to climb them. At this point, he didn't care about being quiet. From what Timms had told him about the phone call with his wife, there was no time to enter without being noticed; he had to enter making as much noise as possible, hopefully deterring whoever was there from harming Samantha Timms.

The door at the top of the stairs was shut. He pushed down on the handle and threw it open.

'Samantha?'

It was the bathroom. He pulled on the cord to his left, and the bathroom filled with light.

No one in there.

He left the bathroom, jumped up a couple of steps onto a higher landing, and could feel his body starting to sweat under his long coat. Ahead of him, there were three doors.

One to the left. One further down on the left. And one straight ahead at the end of the landing.

'Gregory? Samantha?' he bellowed.

Pushing the first door open, he stepped into the darkness, instantly smelling the scent of blood and perfume. His eyes adjusted but not enough to get the full picture, the room filled with shadows. Frantically, he turned to the wall and hit the switch. As the room lit up, he swivelled his focus back to something in the corner.

Then he froze.

Samantha Timms was slumped in the corner, naked and lifeless. Her eyes stared up at the white ceiling, her head against the wall, her body twisted. Above her, written in black marker pen, were the words *She didn't see it coming*.

Very slowly, he padded in, keeping his eyes on her, then looked around the room for anyone else. After a few seconds, his eyes fell to the floor around her. There was more blood than he'd ever seen — the carpet was crimson with it. No wonder the smell of metal consumed the air. It was clear to see she'd been stabbed over and over again in the stomach, chest, arms, legs and feet.

Tanzy stopped, feeling sick at the sight of her torn figure. His heart pounded in his chest, and his skin was damp with sweat under his clothes.

Then he heard it.

Footsteps on the landing behind him. A figure in black shot past.

'Hey!' Tanzy screamed, glaring at the doorway. The figure reached the top of the stairs and started drumming down them, the desperate thuds shaking every beam in the house. Tanzy dashed towards the door. If the wire from the hoover hadn't been trailing across the doorway, he'd have caught up with the killer before they reached the front door. Instead, he went flying, his head colliding with a wooden spindle.

As he fell to the floor, the sound of the pounding footsteps faded. Then the world went black.

97

Thursday night
Leafield Road, Darlington

Tanzy's eyes fluttered open.

The front of his forehead pinged with a throbbing pain that made him wince for a few seconds. The house around him was silent. What the fuck had happened?

He found his feet slowly, using the banister handrail to steady himself.

Then he remembered the figure running along the landing. He darted down the stairs, two at a time, knowing one wrong step would send him tumbling, but there was no time to waste. He ran out into the dark, cold night. The van that was parked in front of the house had gone.

'Fuck!' he roared into the air, first looking left, then looking right. He could see the van at the end of the street, the brake lights illuminating the road below before it turned onto Park Lane, narrowly missing an oncoming car that had to brake suddenly, the tyres screeching in the darkness.

Then the sound of an engine roared to Tanzy's left. It was Byrd in his X5. He stopped the car and Tanzy ran around the bonnet and climbed in.

'Go, go! The van's turned left. Go, Max!' Tanzy shouted.

'Ori, what happened? Why are you—'

'Max, fucking go! There's no time.' Tanzy shouted, pointing, stabbing the air in front of him.

'Okay, okay . . .'

Byrd put his foot down. The wheels of the X5 took a second to grip the damp road, then suddenly the car surged forward. Behind them they heard the sirens of a nearby police car. Byrd noticed the flashing lights in his rear-view mirror but they had no time to stop and explain what was happening.

Tanzy phoned dispatch, explaining what he'd found at the house. They'd pass on the information to the PCs at the scene.

Byrd hit the quiet crossroads and went straight over. At the T-junction, they veered to the left onto Park Lane.

The van was just up ahead.

It took a left at the corner where Hogan's pub used to be, then disappeared out of sight. Byrd was maybe fifty or sixty metres behind but gaining. A few seconds later, he slowed the car and made the same turn.

'Come on, Max!'

'I am!'

He threw the car into third, planted his foot as he chased the van down Victoria Road, approaching the roundabout near the Vue cinema. The van took a right, going all the way around and pulling off onto St Cuthbert's Way.

Byrd pulled off three seconds later, gaining comfortably. His training over the years had come in useful but it'd been a while since he'd driven like this.

Up ahead, standing by the pelican crossing, were two teenagers dressed in tracksuits. Byrd noticed them standing on the edge of the path, waiting to cross the road. The van approached them fast, but for some reason, they stepped down onto the tarmac, assuming they had more time, mis-judging the van's speed.

'No, no, wait!' Byrd shouted at them.

The van hit one of them with the corner of the bumper, catapulting the lad into the air. The other teenager threw his hands on his head and screamed.

The van didn't even slow down and continued on its path.

Tanzy grabbed the radio. 'Dispatch. This is DN522, requesting immediate ambulance support on St Cuthbert's Way at the bottom of Yarm Road. A teenager has been knocked down by the runaway suspect in the white van. Send medical assistance immediately!'

'Roger that, DN522, emergency response being sent now.'

The van took a right at the roundabout onto Haughton Road, finding speed up the slight incline, passing Halfords on the left. Byrd hit the roundabout seconds after, barely braking, the heavy coiled suspension keeping the X5 balanced and guiding it on the same path.

'Ori . . . this isn't going to end well.'

98

It was a sad day for the family. She'd been feeling unwell. It was only a matter of time before it happened because life didn't go on for ever.

He picked up the envelope with his name on it, turned it over and opened it.

It was a letter from his mother, who'd passed away a week earlier. He'd heard the news, but he didn't believe it.

I want you to know that I love you with all my heart. What you're about to read is something I should have told you a long, long time ago, but I didn't have the courage. I didn't know what you would do. If you had found out what really happened to your sister, God rest her soul, you'd no doubt be in prison now, so I didn't want to tell you. I didn't want you to waste your life behind bars, although whoever did it truly deserves it.

Now I'm about to leave this world, it's time for you to know what happened. I won't be here to see the consequences. Maybe that's selfish, but at the same time, these men can't

get away with it for ever, and I know you'll do everything you
can to put things right.

You will give these men what they deserve. They took
Sarah from us. What these men did to her made her hang
herself. They humiliated her so much. She had no choice but
to end her life.

I love you for ever and always,
Your Mum
X

He re-read the words over and over until he was ready
to read the other piece of paper. It was a pathology report,
dated 16 June, from Darlington Memorial Hospital. He read
the following paragraph several times. Tears of anger filled
his eyes.

Death report Paragraph four:
Sarah died due to hanging herself in the garage of a
property in Darlington. This was the main cause of death
due to the bruising of her trachea and indentations on her
skin. Due to further analysis of her deceased body, we can
see bruising on the inside of her thighs and bruising on her
wrists, indicating she'd been held down in some form. From
my experience, it's possible that Sarah had been raped.

The man slammed his clenched fist onto the table and
screamed.

His wife entered the room quickly. 'What's wrong? God,
what's wrong?'

'Look!'

She took hold of the letter while the man dropped his
face into his hands and cried hysterically. She read over the
same paragraph several times. Then she took hold of him and
said, 'We'll get them back. We'll get them back!'

99

Byrd, with his foot flat on the floor, reached fifty-five miles an hour. The van was just ahead, going up over the brow of the hill, crossing the railway line. On the right, Darlington College stood in darkness.

Tanzy's phone rang in his pocket. Quickly, he pulled it out and put it to his ear. 'Hello?'

'Orion, it's Jennifer Lucas from Darlington control room.'

'Hey, Jennifer — kind of a bad time — Jesus!' A car pulled out, not looking, and veered over the white line onto their side of the road, but Byrd swerved it.

'Look where you're going!' Byrd snapped, shaking his head.

'It isn't a good time, Jennifer, sorry, I'll—'

'You might want to hear this, Orion.'

'Go on . . .' Tanzy said quickly.

'I found your man. Remember the footage on High Row in town? The man in the black fleece?'

'Yeah?'

Byrd approached the temporary road works at the round-about and angled round to the left, following the semi-circle then joined the road, heading towards McMullen Road.

'I found a different angle from a shop. The EE shop next to Burger King. It picked him up walking across the road. It had a good shot of him. I ran facial recognition.'

'What came back?'

'It's one of the trainee forensics. Paul Beech.'

Tanzy's eyes widened. 'You sure?'

'Yes. I'm sure. I've met him a few times in the last couple of months — he's usually the one they send over to go through the footage because he's got the IT background.'

Tanzy was speechless for a moment, then he said, 'We're chasing him now, he's on the run. I need to go, thank you for letting me know.'

Tanzy hung up before Jennifer replied and grabbed the radio.

'What's happening?' Byrd asked.

Tanzy held a silencing palm, and Byrd concentrated back on the road.

'Dispatch, this is DN522.'

'Go ahead, DN522,' crackled the voice.

'Just had word on the possible identity of the suspect in the van we're trailing. The name is Paul Beech. He's one of our own. A trainee forensics officer.'

The operator didn't reply straight away.

'Did you get that?' Tanzy asked.

'Received loud and clear, DN522. What's the current situation?'

'Following the suspect at high speed passing through the intersection at McMullen Road, heading straight for the A66 bypass.'

'Roger that.' The line cut off.

Tanzy lowered the radio, glanced at Byrd.

'Paul fucking Beech?' Byrd shouted.

'Yeah. We need to bring this fucker down now!' Tanzy screamed.

Byrd dropped it a gear and planted his foot, the sound of the engine screamed at him, and the surge propelled them forward until they were just behind the van. The digital speed on the dash was eighty-nine miles an hour. The lane split into two up ahead.

'What you gonna do?' Tanzy shouted, loud enough for Byrd to hear over the roaring engine.

'Wait till he slows at the bend up here and take him out.'

There was always a risk when doing anything like that, especially at high speeds. Byrd had been trained well in high-speed driving. It was always different when it happened in real time in a real situation. The adrenaline was there, the chances of an accident with fatal consequences were always present, sometimes inevitable.

The van surged on, closing the distance to the rounda-bout. He'd either take a right, heading towards McDonald's, or a left, heading for the A66. The van's brake lights flashed briefly for a split second and veered into the right-hand lane.

'He's going right!' Tanzy said.

'Just wait . . . wait.' Byrd knew better than that.

As the van slowed in the right-hand lane, suddenly it shot off to the left, timing the gradual bend to perfection. Byrd had seen this in his mind and knew this was coming, so waited in the left lane. When the van angled over, Byrd purposefully clipped the back quarter on the left side, send-ing the van sideways.

The airbags exploded and cushioned the detective's faces as they both screamed.

The rocking van, under its high-speed momentum, tipped onto its side, crashing into the island, then, after a screech of metal against tarmac, crunched to a halt.

'Fucking hell!' Byrd shouted. His nose felt broken. The airbag had hit him harder than he'd thought it would. He glanced left at Tanzy, who seemed a little out of it, blood running from his forehead.

'Ori?'

Tanzy grunted.

'He's down, he's down. The van tipped,' Byrd gasped into the radio, unclipping his seatbelt. Ignoring the responding crackle, he reached over and opened the door. His nose was bloody, so he cupped it with his hand, feeling it fill with warm crimson liquid.

He stepped out carefully, feeling light-headed and unbalanced. The smell of burnt metal filled the cold air. He lowered his hand and let the blood seep onto his jacket. The van was on its side, motionless. Byrd limped painfully to the rear of it, then around to the front.

Through the smashed front windscreen, he bent down a little and peered in.

The seat was empty.

'Where the fuck is—'

Then he felt something hot on his leg, a burning sensation only growing hotter by the second. The pain suddenly became excruciating. He glared down to see a surgical knife sticking out the side of his thigh. He gasped loudly when it was removed and watched the blood gushing from the wound. Turning around, through foggy vision, he noticed Paul Beech on his knees just behind him, struggling up to his feet.

'Paul?' Byrd muttered, but it was almost inaudible. 'Pau—'

Byrd fell back onto the ground, landing on his back.

Paul Beech climbed to his feet, holding his forehead with his right hand, stopping the blood coming from one of his temples. The knife rested in his other hand. After a few seconds, he composed himself and wandered over to Byrd, who was almost to the point of passing out.

'I'm sorry things had to end this way,' Paul whispered, leaning over him. He raised the knife in the air and brought it—

An incredible force collided with the side of Beech, throwing him to the left. Tanzy landed hard on top of him, the knife flying up into the air, landing across the empty road. Tanzy mounted him and punched him in the face.

Relentless blows, over and over and over again until his knuckles became numb.

Paul Beech lost consciousness and passed out.

Then, in the distance, the sound of police sirens filled the air.

Tanzy looked along the road they had driven down, seeing dozens of flashing blue lights heading their way.

100

Darlington
Almost a year ago

Paul Beech thought long and hard about that night. About what he'd seen in the garage, something he'd never forget. His sister, Sarah, hanging from the roof beam with a blue rope wrapped around her neck. Her face was blue and puffy, her eyes were red, bulging and lost.

The feeling she'd hanged herself for no apparent reason had crushed him. Now, he knew the reason — she'd been raped. He needed to find out more. On the night, he remembered seeing Shez Barker . . . God, she was so upset. Sarah's best friend. She told Paul she'd found her in there.

Needing answers, he came back to Darlington, asked around and found out where Shez lived.

Her house was set back a little from the road neatly paved driveway. A brand-new, dark green Vauxhall Corsa covered most of it, the paintwork glistening in the afternoon sun. He'd been watching her movements for a couple of days now. She worked the late shift, usually leaving the house at four in the afternoon.

The time on the dash inside Paul's Jaguar was 3.58 p.m.

He waited and watched.

The black door opened, and out stepped Shez Barker. It had been fifteen years since he'd seen her, but he recognised her features, the way she moved. Shez closed the door, locked it and climbed into the Corsa.

Paul stepped out of the Jaguar. He checked the quiet road and crossed it, keeping his eyes fixed on her. She hadn't noticed him; she was playing around with the radio. He stopped right in front of the car and stared at her through the windscreen.

She glanced up, shuddered, then a second later, raised her hands to her mouth and screamed, the sound of her wail creeping through the seals in the doors. She watched him with wide eyes. She knew exactly who it was.

Paul slowly walked around the side of the car and climbed in the passenger seat. She tried to lock the door but fumbled in terror then froze. Paul stared at her for a while before he said, 'Hi, Shez. It's been a while.'

She was speechless. The silence became deafening.

'Lost your voice?' he asked her.

She stared at him with wide, terrified eyes. 'What—'

'What am I doing here? I need to know the truth. I need to know what happened, Shez. That night.'

'What do you mean?'

'Here, look at this.' He handed her the pathology report that his mother had left him.

Taking it with trembling hands, she unfolded the paper and started reading.

'Read that part . . .' He pointed at the bit about the bruising on her thighs and wrists.

A tear fell from her eye, and she started to shake. When she finished reading, she placed it down on her lap.

'What happened, Shez? You need to be honest with me.'

She took a very long breath. 'She was raped, Paul.'

'I know she was fucking raped!' he shouted, causing her to jump. 'By who?'

She sighed again, staying silent.

'Shez, you need to tell me. I can't settle until I find out. You were there, you were with her that night. You know what happened.'

'I can't say, they told me—'

'Shez, fucking tell me now!'

She threw her hands up. 'Ian Porter, Stuart Richards, James Whittaker and Gregory Timms.'

Paul's skin grew hot. With the anger he felt, he could have put his elbow through her passenger window. Instead, he simply asked, 'Why didn't you tell me? Or the police when they got there?'

'That wasn't everything . . .' she confessed.

'Go on . . .'

'She never hanged herself. She didn't do that to herself.'

Her words ran down his back like a shiver. He knew what was coming next, but he wanted her to say it.

'They said they would kill me if I said anything. I was petrified of them.'

'Say it . . . tell me . . .'

'They killed her, Paul. They did it.'

He clenched his fists so hard, that the whole of his hands turned white.

'Who said they'd kill you if you said anything?'

'Ian said it to me just before he left. He said she didn't see it coming and neither would I. I haven't seen any of them since. The police knew I was at the party and asked me what had happened, mentioning what the pathologist had said. I was so scared they'd kill me if I said anything.'

Paul sighed heavily and sat for a moment. 'You should have told me . . .'

'I'm . . . I'm sorry.'

He nodded and opened the door.

'Where are you going?'

'They think after all these years that they've got away with this,' he said. 'I'm going to prove they haven't.'

He got out of the car, closed the door and walked over to his Jaguar.

101

Byrd and Tanzy watched Paul Beech as he was taken back to his cell from the interrogation room. It was fair to say that he'd be going away for life. He told them he would do it all again in a heartbeat and regretted nothing.

'Beggars belief,' Tanzy said. 'He murdered four women to get back at their husbands.'

'That's what he's telling himself.'

'What do you mean?'

'You don't hurt a rapist by attacking a woman, do you? The person who kidnapped and murdered these women? He got off on it. And so did his accomplice.'

As if on cue, the door opened and PC Leonard guided a woman through it. Nervously, she took a seat and kept her focus on the table.

Tanzy nodded at Leonard, who turned and left, closing the door on his way out.

Byrd leaned forward, pressed the button on the recording device.

'This is Detective Inspector Max Byrd with Detective Inspector Orion Tanzy. We are interviewing Grace Beech in connection with her husband, Paul Beech, concerning her involvement in the murders of Julia Porter, Mary Richards, Karen Whittaker and Samantha Timms. The time is 10.34 a.m. on Friday 22 November.'

From the interview, the detectives were told that after Paul found out what had happened to his sister, he'd applied for a job as a trainee forensic at Darlington. He'd spent four years prior doing a degree in forensic science because he was obsessed with crime scenes.

'Obsessed?' Tanzy asked, frowning.

Grace nodded. 'When he found out what happened to his sister, he started researching crime scenes. What to look for, how to analyse it. He decided to do a degree in that subject and hoped to get a job in the field.' She paused for a second. 'When he got the degree, he received a letter from his mother telling him what happened to his sister. That she was raped. Then he spoke to one of her old friends and found out what really happened that night.'

'Which friend?' Byrd asked.

'I'd rather not say. When he'd been with you guys for a while, he found the confidence to get revenge. He learned how you guys do things and did everything to make sure he wasn't found out.'

'That didn't work out too well for him though, did it?' Tanzy mused.

She raised her eyebrows for a moment. 'No. But he certainly got them back, didn't he? Now they will feel pain for ever, knowing their wives were tortured and murdered, just like his sister was.'

Byrd and Tanzy exchanged a glance.

'And you helped him, didn't you, Grace? Tell us about that. How did you help him kill Julia Porter?'

'When we grabbed Julia Porter last Wednesday night, our guys took her away in the van. Paul and I waited out of sight. When Porter went back to his car, Paul attacked him from behind, knocking him out.'

'So,' Tanzy said, 'if you and Paul didn't kill Julia Porter, then who did?'

'Oh, we certainly played our parts. Julia Porter was the first. We needed it done right. Paul knew a little about crime scenes and how to dismember bodies, but we needed some professional help.'

'Dr Ching?' Byrd asked.

Grace Beech wailed in laughter, rocking her head forward into her hands. Byrd and Tanzy sighed, watching closely, waiting for an explanation.

'Aww, you guys are funny,' she said. Then she lost her smile. 'No, Dr Ching played no part in this. If Paul was never caught, I'd have certainly gone along with the story that Dr Ching was involved. But, seeing as Paul will be going to prison for a long time, there's no need to punish a man for something he never did.'

Byrd frowned. 'The evidence we found placed Dr Ching at the scenes.'

'It did, I have to agree,' she said with a nod.

'What are you not telling us?'

'I took a job as a cleaner at his house and took some of his hair from a brush in his bedroom. Once I got what we needed, I never went back. We then placed the hairs in Julia Porter's car and under the Mary Richards' fingernails. Then, obviously, we put Karen Whittaker's body in his shed and her head in the bin.'

Her words were so casual, so distant from any human feelings.

Byrd nodded.

'All of that for nothing. Paul is under arrest. He's going to prison for life. You too, probably for just as long.'

She nodded in understanding. 'Our mission is complete. If he goes down, I'll go down with him. And I'd do the same again, over and over. The people who raped and killed Paul's sister will suffer for ever. As long as that's done, I'm not both-ered about what happens to us now.'

'It isn't done, though, is it?' said Byrd. 'Do you really believe the type of man who participates in a gang rape has any feeling for the women in his life? All you've done is inconvenience these men.'

A look of uncertainty flitted across her face.

'So . . . who helped you?' Tanzy said, seeing her defences were down. 'Paul can't have done this alone. You didn't just get help from anyone, you got help from someone who knew what they were doing, someone skilled, someone much more skilled than Paul is at his level. He was only training. I don't care how many books on forensics he'd read over the years. That level of skill takes years to develop.'

She smiled at them.

'Who helped you?'

'Now that, my detective friends, is something you'll just have to figure out for yourselves. Now take me away, I'm tired of this. I could do with some sleep.'

102

Friday afternoon
Darlington Memorial Hospital

'You going on your dinner?' the young assistant asked him.

He nodded. 'Yeah. I need some air.'

He left the room with his jacket on. Some of the patients were talking about what they'd heard on the news, about the man responsible for the four murders, that he'd been caught.

He dashed along the corridor, weaving in and out of visitors and patients, and made it outside. The air was cool. The ground was covered with a fine layer of frost.

He pulled out his phone, noticed he had a missed call and a text message.

They were from Grace Beech's spare phone.

The message read:

Paul has been caught and arrested. They're no doubt coming to take me in. I'll tell them everything about what Paul and I did, but I won't mention you and your involvement. You've been a massive help to us and your family is proud of you. You've been more of a brother to Paul than a cousin and we'll always remember that. We won't ever see you again, but we want you

*to know we'll be forever grateful for what you did. Look after
your family. Lots of love, Grace and Paul xx*

He put the phone back inside his coat pocket, took a
deep breath. He didn't reply because he knew she would
destroy the phone so it couldn't be traced back to him. He
stayed in the car park for another ten minutes before he went
back inside.

'That was quick,' the young assistant said behind him.

He jumped. 'Jesus, you scared me . . .'

'Sorry,' she said, smiling.

'Yeah, I wasn't that hungry. I just needed some air, that's
all. Gets a bit too much in here sometimes.' He took his coat
off, placed it on the back of the door inside the office.

'What's on this afternoon?' she asked him.

'We have a body coming in. A woman in her fifties. A
suspicious death.'

'Okay, I need some pictures for my portfolio . . . if that's
okay, Doctor?'

'That's fine,' he replied.

His phone rang in his pocket. 'Excuse me a second,' he
said, stepping out of the office into the corridor. 'Hello, Dr
Jason Lannark speaking?'

103

Friday afternoon
Police station

Tanzy brought a coffee over, placed it on Byrd's desk and sat down in his chair.

'What a fucking day!' Tanzy sighed.

'Tell me about it.' Byrd took his coffee and sipped it.

'How's your mam and dad doing?'

'I don't know . . . I'm going to see them this afternoon. If anything had happened, they'd have phoned, so I assume things are as they were. But I need to decide.'

'What do you mean?'

'If there are no signs of improvement, then I have to decide whether to turn off Dad's life support.'

'That's tough. I'm sorry.'

'It's just life.' Byrd glanced out of the window. 'How are the kids? How's Pip?'

'Kids are fine. At school. I spoke with Pip's mother half an hour ago. They're doing okay.'

'Good. Pip?'

'We need to sit down and talk about things. I haven't had the chance over the past week with what's been going on. I've left her to her own devices. She's probably at home drunk.'

'Yeah. It's been a week from hell, that's for sure. Why don't you go home, Ori? Things are okay here. There are reports to file. I can do that until I go to the hospital. Go home, sort your marriage out.'

'You know, I just might. I need to get out of here.'

'Good man.'

Tanzy stood up, grabbed his coat and went to DCI Thornton's office. He knocked before opening, then stepped inside.

'Hey, is it okay if I take the afternoon off? I know we're busy with what's happened this morning, but the interviews are done, and Max said he'll make a start on the reports. There's a couple of personal things I need to take care of.'

'That's fine, Ori. You take care of your business,' Thornton said, peering over her glasses at him.

'See you tomorrow,' he said.

'You certainly will. Hang in there, okay?'

Tanzy nodded and closed the door. He took a few steps toward Byrd and patted him on the shoulder. 'Catch you tomorrow, chief.'

'Yeah man, take it easy.'

Tanzy left the office and went to his car, turned the engine on and headed for home.

104

PC Kim Harrison walked into the forensic lab, then paused. She could hear Paul Beech on the phone to someone. Not wanting to interrupt, she stayed out of sight, but it was inevitable she would overhear the conversation.

'Listen to me, Grace, they won't find out. Jason has done a fine job with the bodies . . . They won't have a clue it was us . . . Honestly, you're being paranoid. I know how these things work . . . Trust me, Grace . . . Yeah, yeah . . . Did you get the evidence from the doctor? . . . Good. Everything is going to plan. They'll regret what they did.'

The conversation ended. 'Hello?' Paul called into the lab, as if he'd heard her. 'Is someone there?'

Harrison edged back slightly, staying out of sight until she reached the door. As quietly as she could, she opened it and disappeared down the hall, looking for DI Tanzy. When she asked around, someone said he was in a meeting. She didn't want to disturb him, although she was very concerned about what Paul had said on the phone. She tried to find DI

Byrd, but he wasn't at his desk. Instead, she knocked on DCI June Thornton's door.

'Come in.'

Harrison opened the door gently. 'Hi, sorry to bother you.'

'It's no problem. To what do I owe the pleasure, Kim?'

She edged in nervously. 'I know I should go through the right paths. I've tried to find DI Tanzy but he's in a meeting. Can I express my concerns with you, or should I wait to speak with Orion?'

'It's fine — what's on your mind?' Thornton lowered the paperwork in her hand and placed it on her desk.

Harrison told Thornton about Paul's phone call and how she felt he was speaking inappropriately about disturbing matters. Thornton listened to what she had to say, then said, 'He mentioned evidence and people not finding out?'

Harrison nodded confidently.

'Well,' Thornton said, standing to her feet, 'let's go speak with Paul and ask him what this is all about.'

DCI Thornton and PC Harrison headed towards the forensics lab. When they opened the door, Jacob Tallow was sitting on a stool, looking intently at his computer screen.

'Jacob,' DCI Thornton said, 'have you seen Paul?'

'He left a minute ago. He said he needed to go out for a little while.'

Thornton and Harrison left the lab, dashed down the corridor, went through the main door outside and scanned the car park. They saw Paul climb into his car and pull away.

'Have you got car keys?' DCI Thornton asked.

PC Harrison felt her pockets. 'Yeah, I've got them.'

'Pass them here, I'll drive. Come on, let's follow him,' she said, heading towards the marked Astra. They got in, buckled their seat belts and off they went, following Paul Beech cautiously.

'We'll keep well back, so he doesn't see us,' Thornton said.

They hit the roundabout at the top of Victoria Road and followed Beech onto Coniscliffe Road. 'Where's he going?' Harrison asked.

Thornton shrugged. 'As long as we stay on him, it doesn't matter.'

A few minutes later, Paul Beech slowed and took a left into Broken Scar picnic area. Ten seconds later, DCI Thornton slowed, indicated and did the same.

Very slowly, she crawled up the ramp and stopped the car. 'He's gone down there . . .'

Thornton sat for a moment, thinking hard.

'What should we do?' Harrison asked.

'Why is he here? We'll go down, see what he's up to.' Thornton put the gear in first and slowly controlled the car down the steep descent. Paul's car was parked up on the right, but he wasn't inside.

'Where's he gone?' Harrison said, confused.

'We'll find him — he can't have gone far.'

She stopped the car, applied the handbrake and turned off the engine. She unclipped her belt and opened the door. PC Harrison did the same. They looked around.

'Over here,' Thornton said, heading towards a path.

'There!' Harrison said, pointing to the footpath on the right, seeing Paul's back for a brief moment before he disappeared behind a tree. They angled in that direction and kept vigilant, stepping carefully over the wet, muddy trail. At the end, they could either go left or straight on.

A branch snapped to their left. They both froze.

'Down there,' Harrison said. She went first, careful not to slip down the steady decline. They ducked under the awkward hanging branches and stepped down onto a muddy area just before the water.

It was quiet.

No one was there.

'Where did he—?' and then Harrison knew no more.

* * *

DCI Thornton lowered the rock. PC Harrison floated away on the water, blood spreading from the wound to her head.

'You can come out now,' she said, turning around.

Paul stepped out from behind a tree and stood with her, watching PC Kim Harrison's still body on the surface. The underwater currents were tugging on her, easing her over the centre of the river. Soon, she'd be washed away, no doubt found in a couple of days.

'I'd better head back, Paul. People will be wondering where I've got to. I need to take her car back, make it look like she left the station on foot.'

'Okay, I'll come back later. I told Tallow I was popping out for a little while.'

'You take care. Be careful. I'll sort everything out,' she told him.

'Thanks, Auntie June,' he said.

They walked back to the cars without saying anything. Paul climbed in his and DCI Thornton opened the door of the marked Astra. She watched her nephew drive away, then set off in the direction of the station.

105

Byrd glared at the computer, aiming to finish the reports so he could get out of there. What a crazy couple of weeks it had been. He wanted to set his work aside, concentrate on his parents.

Tanzy's work phone was ringing. He picked it up. 'Hello, DI Tanzy's phone.'

'Orion?'

'Eh, no, this is Detective Inspector Max Byrd. Can I take a message?'

'It's Jennifer Lucas from the Town Hall control room,' she said.

'Hi, Jennifer,' Byrd said. 'How can I help?'

'I was hoping to speak to Orion, but maybe you can help me?'

'Yeah, go on, I'm listening.'

'When one of your colleagues, a PC Kim Harrison, went missing, Orion asked me to check the CCTV around the town, starting with the cameras closest to the station — you know, because of what happened.'

'What do you mean because of what happened?' Byrd said, frowning.

'On Friday when your colleague PC Harrison went missing, I checked the cameras at the station. Unfortunately, for some unknown reason, from 3 p.m. till 6 p.m., the cameras were down. I chased it up with the maintenance team, but they weren't aware of any planned work. I was hoping to see Kim Harrison on there — Orion had given me the registration of the Astra she normally uses. Maybe it was a system error. Sometimes, camera systems fail and reboot after a certain length of time.'

'Okay,' Byrd said, deflated.

'But just before half past four, I spotted the car from a camera on Coniscliffe Road, heading west. But she wasn't driving. From the still shot I have of it, she was sitting in the passenger seat.'

'Did you see the driver?' Byrd asked, edging forward.

'It appears to be your DCI, June Thornton.'

Her words ran over Byrd like a shiver. 'Thornton?'

'Yeah. I'll email the still shot over asap so you can see for yourself.'

'If it is her,' Byrd said, 'then she was the last person to see Kim Harrison alive.'

'I'll send it over now.'

'Thanks.' He hung up and waited nervously.

The email pinged through shortly after.

Byrd clicked it open. He gasped when he saw the image. It was indeed DCI June Thornton driving the marked Astra.

'It can't be, it . . .'

He pulled his phone from his pocket and unlocked it, then found the number, and pressed CALL.

'Come on, pick up, pick up.'

'Hello?'

'Ori, listen to me. I've just had a call from Jennifer Lucas at the Town Hall control room.'

'Yeah?' Tanzy said.

'You need to come in. You won't believe it over the phone. You need to see it with your own eyes, Orion.'

'Okay, I'll be there in fifteen minutes, Max.'

Byrd hung up and placed the phone down on the desk. Then he remembered something. The office was empty, but he hadn't seen DCI Thornton leave yet. She was still in her office. He stood up and went over to her closed door. Instead of knocking, he pushed down the handle and went inside.

'June?' he said, cautiously stepping inside. She wasn't at her desk. Before he could check the office, he felt the heavy blow to the temple. He staggered for a moment until his legs collapsed from underneath him, and he crashed to the floor with a loud thud, his head hitting the hard ground.

Then the world went black for DI Max Byrd.

106

Tanzy pulled up in his Golf, turned off the engine and stepped out of the car. Byrd's words played over and over in his mind. What could be so important?

There were only three cars in the car park.

Byrd's X5.

Thornton's Range Rover.

And his Golf.

He stepped through the sliding double doors and walked briskly down the corridor towards the office. When Byrd had phoned, he'd been talking to Pip, trying to have a serious conversation about their marriage. He told her that whatever it was Byrd wanted to show him, he'd be an hour at the most, and they'd continue with it when he returned.

The office was empty.

There wasn't a sound from anywhere.

He glanced along the rows of computers and frowned when he couldn't see Byrd, assuming he'd be at his desk, ready to show him whatever was so important.

Byrd's desk was empty, but his chair was pulled out. His coat was hanging on the back of it.

'Max?' he called, glancing around.

He plucked out his phone and called him.

Somewhere very quiet, he heard his ringtone. He turned around, staring at DCI Thornton's closed door. He recalled seeing her car in the car park, and figured whatever Byrd wanted to show him, he was discussing the matter with Thornton.

'Max?' he called out.

No answer.

He remembered Byrd's words on the phone: *You need to see it with your own eyes, Orion.*

See what? he wondered. He stopped still and thought hard, his mind doing overtime. Then he turned, went over to Byrd's computer screen and leaned over. The screen was in sleep mode. He moved the mouse, causing the log-in screen to appear. Byrd's username was already in; all he needed was the password.

Knowing it, he typed it in, pressed ENTER.

The screen came alive with an email from Jennifer Lucas from the Town Hall. The image was a still shot of the CCTV taken from Coniscliffe Road. The marked Astra. PC Kim Harrison was in the passenger seat. DCI Thornton was in the driver's seat.

His eyes widened when he noticed the time stamp in the top right corner. Calculating the last time anyone had ever seen Kim Harrison, he made the same assumption that Byrd had: Thornton was the last person to see Kim Harrison alive.

'Shit,' he whispered, then glanced around. 'Max?'

His heartbeat increased suddenly as he faced Thornton's door. Very quietly, he padded over and stopped just outside it. He took a couple of deep breaths.

'DCI Thornton?' he said.

There was no answer.

'If anyone can hear me, I'm opening the door now.'

393

He grabbed the handle, pushed it down and, in a sudden movement, he threw the door open and very quickly jumped back, just avoiding DCI Thornton's swinging arm as it brushed past his face. She was holding a knife. After she missed the swing, she fell forward, losing her balance and colliding with the open door. Tanzy took a few steps back, staying light on his feet.

Thornton found her balance and turned towards Tanzy, then charged out of her office towards him holding the knife high above her head. When she was close enough, Tanzy decided to charge at her, an attempt to take her by surprise.

It did.

He went in hard and low with his right shoulder, crashing into her stomach, and lifted her, driving her back until they both clattered into the stud wall of her office. The plaster dented under the huge impact, causing her to wail out in pain and drop the knife, which landed on the hard floor several paces from them. Tanzy let her go and she crumpled to the floor.

'Max?' he shouted, stepping away from her and darting into her office.

In the corner near the window, Byrd was unconscious, lying on his front with his eyes closed. Blood had pooled around Byrd's head from the blow to the left side of his temple. Tanzy bent down and shook him a few times.

'Max? Fucking wake up!' He shook him again, this time harder. Finally, Byrd grunted something but didn't move. 'Wake up, come on!' He let out another inaudible grunt, telling Tanzy he was alive at least. 'Wait here, I'll be back,' Tanzy told him.

He dashed out of the office and looked to his right, glaring down at DCI June Thornton, who had been severely winded from the blow.

He grabbed his radio and called dispatch.

'DN522, DI Orion Tanzy, requesting emergency assistance.'

'DI Tanzy, what assistance do you require?'

'Ambulance and police.' He stepped back and stared at Byrd, who was still on the floor of DCI Thornton's office. 'We have an officer down — repeat, an officer down requiring emergency medical attention. Send immediately.'

'Location?'

'DCI Thornton's office at the station,' Tanzy told the operator.

'Can you . . . can you repeat that?'

He did.

'Copy that, DI Tanzy, requesting immediate assistance.'

Tanzy sighed heavily. Thornton was still trying to catch her breath. She squinted up at him.

Tanzy lifted the radio back to his mouth. 'Better make that two ambulances. The suspect will also require medical attention.'

'Copy that, DI Tanzy. They'll be with you shortly.'

Tanzy lowered the radio from his mouth and leaned over Thornton. 'June Thornton, I'm arresting you on suspicion of murder. You do not have to say anything, but it may harm your defence if you do not mention when questioned something you may later rely on in court. Anything you do say may be given in evidence.'

It wasn't long until he heard the sirens outside.

He went back into DCI Thornton's office and lowered himself to the floor next to Byrd. 'You okay, Max?' he asked, placing a palm on his back.

Byrd, finally conscious, opened his eyes and stared up at him.

'Hey,' Byrd said, his voice flat.

'How are you doing, Max?' Tanzy asked. 'How's the head?'

'Feels like I've been hit with a hammer.' Byrd sighed. 'What a day it's been, Orion!'

'Never a dull day in Darlington, Max, you know that.' He helped him to his feet and placed Byrd's arm over his shoulder, then slowly left DCI June Thornton's office, stepping around her.

The main entrance door opened and a handful of officers came storming in. Tanzy briefly told PC Leonard what had happened and pointed to Thornton. They didn't stay to see the arrest.

'Thanks for coming, Orion,' Byrd said, struggling along.

Tanzy smiled, holding him up. 'Come on, Max, let's get you fixed up.'

THE END

ACKNOWLEDGEMENTS

I hope you enjoyed this book as much as I did writing it. Creating Max Byrd and Orion Tanzy and letting them loose around my home town of Darlington was great fun.

A big thank you goes to my family and friends. Their support in my passion is an eternal blessing, and I really appreciate it. From my experience, and as many writers will know, it's very hard finding the time to write (and read) when you work full-time and have a family, not to mention day-to-day living, so a big thanks go to them for their patience.

Huge thanks goes to my publisher, Joffe Books, for giving me this opportunity to become a member of their writing family; to be a part of this team is a dream I'd never thought would be a reality. Massive thanks to my commissioning editor, Steph Carey, for her support and expertise, right from that very first email to the publication of this complete novel. You've been a star. A very special mention to Sam Matthews, who made some excellent changes to this book, ready for the world to see, Nebošja Zorić for the amazing cover design, and Matthew Grundy Haigh for the final touches, along with the rest of the magical team at Joffe.

My last thank you is to you, the reader. You make all of this possible.

THE JOFFE BOOKS STORY

We began in 2014 when Jasper agreed to publish his mum's much-rejected romance novel and it became a bestseller.

Since then we've grown into the largest independent publisher in the UK. We're extremely proud to publish some of the very best writers in the world, including Joy Ellis, Faith Martin, Caro Ramsay, Helen Forrester, Simon Brett and Robert Goddard. Everyone at Joffe Books loves reading and we never forget that it all begins with the magic of an author telling a story.

We are proud to publish talented first-time authors, as well as established writers whose books we love introducing to a new generation of readers.

We have been shortlisted for Independent Publisher of the Year at the British Book Awards three times, in 2020, 2021 and 2022, and for the Diversity and Inclusivity Award at the Independent Publishing Awards in 2022.

We built this company with your help, and we love to hear from you, so please email us about absolutely anything bookish at feedback@joffebooks.com

If you want to receive free books every Friday and hear about all our new releases, join our mailing list: www.joffebooks.com/contact

And when you tell your friends about us, just remember: it's pronounced Joffe as in coffee or toffee!

Made in United States
Orlando, FL
23 July 2023

35403827R00243